LOST SOURCE

LOST SOURCE

John Martin

iUniverse, Inc.
Bloomington

Lost Source

This is a work of fiction. All of the characters, names, incidents, organizations, and dialogue in this novel are either the products of the author's imagination or are used fictitiously.

iUniverse books may be ordered through booksellers or by contacting:

iUniverse
1663 Liberty Drive
Bloomington, IN 47403
www.iuniverse.com
1-800-Authors (1-800-288-4677)

ISBN: 978-1-4759-5175-2 (sc)
ISBN: 978-1-4759-5176-9 (e)
ISBN: 978-1-4759-5177-6 (dj)

Printed in the United States of America

iUniverse rev. date: 12/5/2012

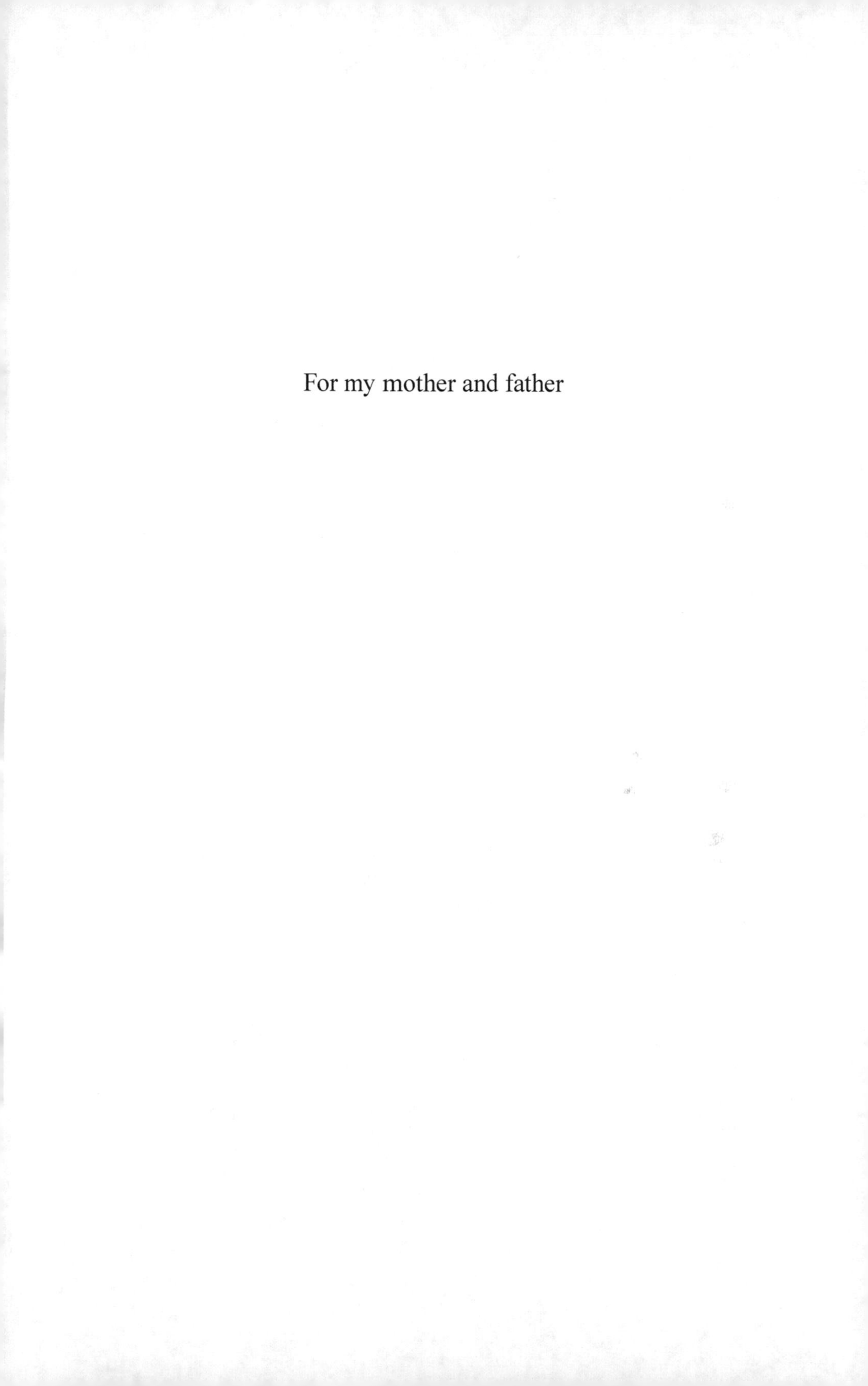

For my mother and father

one

Shenzhen, Guangdong Province, People's Republic of China

A bum rummaged through a Dumpster in the lot. As he picked over the trash, he glanced at the tractor trailers lined up outside a loading dock, their idling engines filling the air with fumes. Several men were sitting on the edge of the dock, smoking and talking. A man came out of the factory and kicked one of them. The men jumped off the dock and put out their butts. They returned to their rigs and climbed into the cabs.

As the bum pulled something from the garbage, he caught a glimpse of a forklift, with LAMBAL INTERIOR stenciled on the side, driving out of the plant and into the open back of a truck. The driver lowered the forks and withdrew them, leaving the pallet in the vehicle; he backed up beeping as another forklift driver passed him with a load.

The truck filled quickly. The workmen shut the doors and secured them with a lock. The truck pulled away from the bay. The next truck backed up slowly to the loading zone, until it pressed against the concrete wall.

The bum was now sitting at the base of the Dumpster, a lunch bag of discarded food on his lap. He was chewing, holding a fragment of sandwich in his left hand—which was shaking. Lin Xueqin was a long way from the lecture halls of Tsinghua University in Beijing, where he taught differential equations to undergraduates as a teaching assistant. The skinny thirty-year-old had a scruffy beard from a month's growth and matted hair from not bathing for weeks, to make him look older and smell awful.

He tried to steady his trembling hand by reaffirming his unshakable purpose—the Chinese worker deserves a better life. That failing, he took a more practical tack, pressing his left elbow against his body. Then, as the first vehicle pulled past him and turned onto the road, he began to text with his right thumb on the mobile concealed beneath the bag.

A mile up the road, a man dozing in a car in the parking lot of a strip mall woke with a start to the ringtone from "My City," by Hong Kong rapper DopeBoy8Five2. He found himself singing the song's hook unconsciously as he sat up straight and read the text message on the screen. As he turned the key in the ignition and started the car, he looked left and spotted the semi he was supposed to follow.

two

New York City

John Shay sat next to Jack Cafferty, the head of the United Machinists; the other members of the union bargaining team were on either side of them. Peter Lambal, owner and chief executive of Lambal Interior—the auto supplier they were striking—sat across the table. He was flanked likewise by lieutenants.

Cafferty leaned in to Shay. The union chief was heavyset, but thick white hair and a rough face offset the otherwise weakened look of extra flesh.

"Should I give them the keys to the house, John?"

Shay shook his head.

Cafferty turned back to Lambal. "My partner says no. That means it must be too good a deal for you."

Lambal had a patrician look—tall, thin, groomed. He had dressed less elegantly than usual, at his chief negotiator's request. This was the first time he had attended a session.

"How long did you rehearse that exchange?"

"You should smile when you make jokes," Cafferty said. "Otherwise I'll think you're just a son of a bitch and have no intention whatsoever of coming to an agreement with us. And if I think that, I'll get up and leave this table and not come back. And everything you ever worked for—excuse me, your daddy ever worked for, and put under your Christmas tree—will go to hell."

"Jack, Jack," said George Lyons. He was Lambal's chief negotiator, seated to his right. "Don't make this personal."

Cafferty raised his thick eyebrows. "Don't make this personal?" He turned to Shay. "Did you hear that, John? Don't make this personal?"

Here it comes, Shay thought.

Cafferty glared at Lambal. "You want my members—the ones who are left—to work overtime and be too dog-tired to spend time with their families so you won't have to hire anybody new and shell out for more benefits. Then you want them to double their contribution to your health insurance plan. Switch to a 401(k) defined-contribution pension plan—where the only thing defined is the *contribution*, not the *benefit*."

He slammed his hand on the table. "You want my men"—he looked down the table at the lone woman on his team—"excuse me, my men and women to give up the seniority they sweated for, year in and year out, working over a lifetime in your plants, so one day you can dump them and get a temp or low-wage replacement to take their place. On top of that, you threaten to send more work to China. We're not supposed to take that personally? That's not personal?"

Cafferty looked at Shay and then across to Lambal. "What the hell is personal if that's not personal? The kind of French aftershave—excuse me, cologne, you moneyed bastard—you put on your silky, smooth skin this morning?"

Lambal popped up like a jack-in-the-box. "That's it—I'm out of here."

He was at the door before the rest of his management team could react and follow. They caught up with him in the hallway.

When they had left, Cafferty turned to Shay, and they both began laughing.

three

Shay left the negotiating room at the New York Marriott Eastside and went downstairs to the 525LEX lounge. The bartender flicked his head when he saw him take a seat at the bar and reached into the cooler for his usual.

Shay leaned forward and put his arms on the bar. His wrists and forearms showed past the sleeves of his navy sport coat; he was wearing a tan T-shirt underneath. He was thirty-eight, fair Irish. Blue eyes, brown hair cut short. Two-day stubble.

He pulled out his cell and tapped the touch screen. Got her machine.

"Hi, it's me," he said after the beep; he nodded to the barkeep as he plopped down the bottle. "I love you. I'm sorry it happened. We'll do better next time."

Shay hung up. He had argued with his wife that morning. At breakfast he reached into the pantry for cereal—and pulled out an empty box. His wife and son did it all the time—finished something and put back the container, even into the refrigerator. Mostly he made it a family joke—as in, why are we paying for electricity to cool a carton?

This time he'd snapped, spewed out a string of curses. She'd countered with how hard she worked—at her job, with their son, around the house—and said she didn't have time to worry about some damn box. He had thrown back his own list of drudgery.

He took a swig of beer. If he'd let her vent, she would have been fine. Then he realized he'd broken the cardinal rule—don't talk first thing in the morning. In the self-help department, he knew that if he hadn't overreacted, it wouldn't have started.

Truth was, they'd been at it for months, he thought. They had been together eleven years—ten married, one off the books. Gotten into the rut most people do, especially after a child. You get swamped by things you have to take care of, start snapping at each other. You go to kiss her good-bye; she turns her head. You have a question but don't ask, because you don't feel like getting into a discussion.

"Lost in thought?"

Shay turned and smiled at Hannah Stein, the woman negotiator on the team. "Buy you a drink?"

She flicked her head at his bottle. "Same. I could use one after Jack's performance upstairs."

Shay ordered another. "He needed to show them something, and he did."

"What's that?"

"That he's so crazy, he might do something not in the interest of his members."

Hannah nodded to Shay as the bartender brought another bottle of Stella. When she smiled in thanks, he looked like he had gotten a fifty-dollar tip.

The bartender walked toward the other end of the bar, glancing back at Hannah as she clenched a green elastic band between her teeth. She was twenty-seven and looked taller than her five foot eight as she sat erect, pulling her hair back in a ponytail, which she choked with the band. She had dark brown eyes and thin lips she clamped tightly at the center point; a few freckles were splashed about her cheekbones. She was wearing a tight apple-green tee with high-cut sleeves, jeans, and sneakers.

"Taking the train home?" she asked.

"Driving. How about you? Big date tonight?"

She smiled. "No." She took a slug of beer.

"Why not?"

Hannah shrugged; she wondered if he knew. She took another drink.

Shay glanced at the caption on the TV; he asked the bartender to turn it up.

"The United States and China are on the verge of a trade war," the news anchor said. "China's government announced today that it will retaliate for trade sanctions imposed by the president. President Rodgers ratcheted up the pressure on the Chinese by levying a whopping 100 percent tariff on China's solar cell exports to the United States, citing both unfair government assistance and dumping below cost. With unemployment rising across the country, Rodgers also pinned a 25 percent tariff on Chinese clothing exports, after a major garment manufacturer closed up shop in North Carolina."

Hannah and Shay watched as the screen flashed a shot of the shuttered plant. The anchor handed off the story to a reporter. She was walking alongside the chain-link fence on the sidewalk in front of the factory; weeds had already reclaimed the cracks between the sections. Shay saw "Textile" on the building sign before the camera cut away.

It might as well be Steel, Electronics … Machinery, Paper … Furniture, Shoes, Toys … he thought, ticking off industries where companies had folded against the onslaught of cheap goods—or rushed for the exits themselves to produce offshore.

"The president cited the World Trade Organization's 'safeguard action' provision as justification for his latest measures," the reporter said. "WTO safeguard actions provide temporary assistance, and an opportunity to adjust, to any industry found to suffer serious injury as a direct result of increased imports. A high-ranking commerce official put it this way: 'We're through sparring. It's time to deliver some real body blows.'"

The Chinese reacted furiously, even as the administration tried to walk back the comment. The newscast ran a clip of a Shanghai politician who called a press conference at a construction site, where he promptly leapt into a US-made construction vehicle, drove it off rough ground onto a paved lot, and began smashing it with a sledgehammer. Onlookers joined in, taking turns swinging the heavy hammer.

"This is getting serious," Hannah said.

Shay smiled at the antics on the screen. "The Chinese remind me of Jack."

"One big difference," she said.

"What's that?"

"They'll really do something that's not in their interest."

"Let them," Shay said. "This has to come to a head. Every freakin' thing in the stores is made in China. Most of the people who were making that stuff here don't know how to do anything else. We've got to buy them time while they—maybe it'll be their kids—figure out what to do next."

"That's the first explanation I've heard that makes sense," Hannah said. "A lot of the guys just want to roll back the clock, as if we can take back all that work."

"Maybe we can," the voice boomed as Cafferty inserted himself between them. "Bobby, bring me a beer, and another for my buddy. Hannah?"

"I'll have to pick up my pace." She lifted the bottle, took a swallow.

Cafferty watched her and smiled. "Bobby, you know Hannah?" he asked.

The bartender shook his head. He was tall, built square and strong—manufactured quality. Cafferty introduced them and added a postscript. "Bobby was a defensive tackle in high school, switched to linebacker by his coach at Cortland State. Four-year starter. He just joined the marines, heading to Parris Island … when?"

"Six weeks," the bartender said.

"We salute you," Cafferty said. Shay and Hannah raised their bottles.

"Thank you, Mr. Cafferty," Bobby said, and then he moved away to a customer holding his hand in the air.

"Where've you been?" Shay asked. "Chasing Lambal to hell and back?"

"I'm not going after him. He's coming back to me."

"When?" Hannah asked.

"Don't know," Cafferty said. "They said they didn't feel it would be 'productive' to schedule more talks right now."

He grabbed the bar menu. "Who wants plantains? The cook here is half–Puerto Rican, fries up a mean pan. You'll swear you're back on the island." The Machinists had held several annual conventions in Ponce, on Puerto Rico's southern coast.

Hannah and Shay went along. Cafferty ordered the sweet bananas.

"How's the line holding?" Shay asked.

"Strong," Cafferty said. "They pushed one button too many when they threatened to close more operations and build a second plant in China."

The bartender clanged down three beers. Cafferty tapped his bottle against Shay's and clinked Hannah's, brushing against her as he took a swig.

"One button too many," he repeated.

four

Shay was awakened in the middle of the night; he knocked a bottle of water off the night table, fumbling for the cell. The sleep passed from his face as he listened.

"I'll come right away."

He sat up on the edge of the bed.

"What is it?" his wife, Anne, asked.

He told her.

"Oh my God."

Shay drove into the city to Roosevelt Hospital. He exited the elevator on Hannah's floor and walked down the hall to the nursing station. He was directed to a waiting room crammed with people. He embraced her mother and father. "How is she?"

Her father nodded. "She's good. Doc says she'll be fine. Couple of days here." He looked down the hall. "She's sleeping now. You can see her later."

Shay put his hands on her father's shoulders and squeezed; he kissed her mother on the cheek. He moved away as relatives came over, and joined a group of union people—a mix of officers, board members, and admins. He shook hands with some and hugged others.

Bill Lewis, second-in-command to Cafferty in the United Machinists, came up to him. They embraced. Lewis pulled him away from the group.

"I can't believe it," he said when they were alone in a corner.

"Where's Doris?" Shay asked.

"She's home. I'm going over there in a few minutes."

Shay realized how tough it was going to be—Cafferty's wife had just beaten back cancer. "What happened on the road?"

Lewis was a couple of inches taller than Shay, six foot two. He was a little overweight, beginner's level, with a salt-and-mostly-pepper goatee, hair not quite short, hint of Afro. He was sixty-four. "We don't know much. They left the hotel together after the talks. A few hours later they were driving southbound on the West Side Highway. Someone hit them. They smashed through a section of temporary barrier, hit a tree. The air bags engaged, saved them. But he had a heart attack."

Lewis leaned in. "Did you know those two ...?"

Shay nodded.

Lewis took a breath, the exhale audible. "Listen, leadership's been talking. We want you to take over negotiations."

"That's yours, Bill. You're next in line."

"That's the point. I'll be going in every direction, getting things straightened out. I need you to bring this one home."

"What about my other work?" Shay had run negotiations, but his main job was training organizers. He also evaluated IT and production technology and their effect on contracts, work rules, and member skills and training.

"I'll parcel it out. We can get by."

Shay nodded. "Sure, I'll do it. One condition."

"What's that?"

"Hannah's my number two."

"If you think she's ready."

Hannah had been with the union three years, plucked by Shay from a pool of candidates coming out of Cornell University's School of Industrial and Labor Relations.

"She is," Shay said, as he eyed a policeman walking toward them.

"Hey, Tony," Lewis said.

The cop stuck out his hand. "I'm really sorry about Jack," he said as they shook.

"Thanks, Tony. John, this is Tony Palazzo. Tony, John Shay."

They shook hands.

"Tony's a good friend of the union," Lewis said.

The cop looked around the room. "Can we talk somewhere?"

"You can say it right here. John's in our circle."

"I spoke with the lead investigator at the scene," Palazzo said. "They think someone ran Jack off the road."

The funeral Mass was held at St. Patrick's Cathedral. Machinists' members and local labor leaders were joined by labor leaders from around the country. The crowd that assembled to pay their respects included New York's governor and the city's mayor. The president sent the secretary of labor.

"Let us pray for the soul of Jack Cafferty," the archbishop said during the remembrance, speaking from the main altar of the sanctuary. "Let us not say our final good-byes, because we know he lives in God, in our hearts, and in the union he loved. But let us pray for him and for his family."

Shay gazed upward at the curved ribs that formed the vaulted ceiling; for an instant they seemed lifelike. He had been raised Catholic and still felt a reverence for the mystery and grandeur—especially in death. He had clowned around with the faith like most kids. He and his friends had taken the money their parents gave them for the collection and spent it on breakfast at a diner across the street from the church—then sat squirming in the pew as the box was passed in front of them and they had nothing to put in. Breaking fast also freed him from the self-conscious shuffle to the front of the church to receive Holy Communion—and not having confessed his impure thoughts, he didn't think he was eligible for the sacrament anyway.

He had gotten jacked up for his confirmation, though—when Catholics receive the Holy Spirit. He'd belted an inside-the-park home run at a Little League game the morning of the ceremony. His first semester in college, he'd gone on a two-day retreat at a monastery near the school outside Rochester, New York. He'd walked amid the autumn colors of the secluded grounds, vowed to get more … something. It wasn't clear to him what that something was.

He came back and never went to Mass again.

The archbishop placed his prayer book on the podium and looked up at the gathering with his ample, reddened face.

"Jack was a friend of mine," he said. "As many of you know, I am of Irish extraction myself—and *extraction* is the word, if you know your Irish history."

The crowd laughed.

The clergyman continued. "I knew Jack's family from Inwood, where a lot of Irish lived. His great-grandfather dug tunnels for the city's subway. His family has worked and worshipped in New York since they came from Dingle, in their native Kerry, in the late 1800s.

"Jack followed a long Irish tradition of standing up for the workingman. In the early 1900s, the presidents of half the major unions were Irish. He spoke to me many times of his favorite Irish leaders: Terence Powderly, whose parents emigrated out of County Meath and became head of the Knights of Labor—and who, like Jack, began his working career as a machinist. Mary Harris of Cork, who married a man named Jones and became known as Mother Jones, a hard-luck seamstress who organized mine workers. And Jack's favorite—Peter McGuire, who grew up in a Lower East Side tenement—took the lead in making Labor Day a national holiday.

"Jack used to say that the Irish and unions were a natural fit. They were working class, their emigration coincided with the birth of organized labor, they had a history of fighting oppression at home, and the Church supported their right to organize." He smiled. "Jack chided me, as a member of that church, for not doing enough. He said I should follow in the tradition of the 'labor priests'—Edward McGlynn of New York, Thomas Malone of Denver, Peter Yorke of San Francisco—who stood up for unions and worked side by side with them for better wages and working conditions."

The archbishop smiled again. "'Plus, we're just contrary,' he used to say, in explaining why the Irish were born labor agitators." The people laughed again.

"Jack had that same oversized personality, and bluster, as the leaders who came before him," the archbishop continued. "He sought to improve this city and the lot of its working people. He rose to the position he had as president of the United Machinists because of his love of the workingman and workingwoman and his dedication to their well-being."

The archbishop paused. "In these hard times in America, for all working people, let us pray that his works go on."

"Amen," the crowd intoned.

The prelate picked up his book and continued with prayers. Shay took Hannah's hand as she began to sob. She had been released from the hospital after two nights. Shay's wife, Anne, was sitting on the other side of him. The three of them were sitting in the second row of pews, behind Cafferty's wife and two grown sons.

Doris Cafferty turned around and touched Hannah's arm.

Hannah managed a nod.

The pallbearers carried the casket through the open bronze doors and down the steps of St. Patrick's to the sound of bagpipes. The hearse drove down Fifth Avenue, throngs of people standing on either side; the city had closed the motorcade route to traffic. New York City cops, firefighters, construction workers, ironworkers, longshoremen, teachers, hospital workers, and others—including Machinists' members from locals across the country—had turned out in the thousands.

Shay was sitting in the back of a Town Car, between Hannah and Anne. He held their hands as the sedan drove in the procession. He choked up as he saw the bystanders. Felt how removed he had become as he rose through the ranks over fourteen years—from factory organizer to vice president—and as the money got better and the workload was more managerial. You think it's never going to happen to you, he thought. Your passion's different; it can't dim like the others.

Anne squeezed his arm. He leaned in, kissed her on the lips. He realized he hadn't done it in a while; he had been pecking her on the cheek, on her hair. He looked at her. She had green eyes specked with bursts of brown. Her brown hair was cut short, high on her neck, something between perky page and styled woman. She was thirty-six, had put on a little weight. But she was still nicely figured—plus breasts, curvy hips, solid butt.

The car turned left onto Forty-Second Street and headed crosstown to the FDR Drive to leave the city. There was a smaller group at the cemetery. Lewis pulled Shay aside after the service.

"We've got something. I want you to meet me in the city tonight."

five

Shay drove down the narrow center of Prince Street, between twin walls of parked cars sardined facing westbound on either side of the one-way road. He turned left onto Thompson, smiling as what Cafferty called "urban colonizers" swarmed the sidewalks and spilled into the streets.

Cafferty often talked about what the neighborhood was like years ago, when it was industrial. He would hang around for drinks after visiting workers in the local shops. He said there were just a couple of bars then, the Broome Street Bar and the Spring Street Bar—named after the streets, he claimed, because that was the only way you could find them; he called them lanterns, the way they shone in the dark. Shay remembered him saying that walking those silent cobblestone streets at night—blackened by rain, in the shadow of the quieted factories—was one of the most pleasurable things you could do in New York. There were no taxis or cars—just peace and quiet, a reverie in old New York. Cafferty called it his downtown Cloisters—after the uptown retreat, built from disassembled French abbeys, that overlooks the Hudson in Fort Tryon Park.

Cafferty had some poet in him, Shay thought. He recalled how they battled at first, Cafferty old school, Shay with a foot in the old and new. The first few years Shay worked with the Machinists, Cafferty barely spoke to him. But the union chief eventually warmed to Shay's take on the changing times—and he always liked Cafferty's throwback style.

He thought about Cafferty and Hannah. He hadn't thought much of it before. Meaning just that—he didn't think about it. The cons were easy to see, but people did what they did. He wondered if that was where he was headed. Life gets routine, you look for a spark, start to diddle around. He had already caught himself getting extra flirty around the office, on trips, in bars. He even took someone's number when she offered.

He forced himself to throw it away.

As he crawled through traffic, Shay thought back to how he became a machinist. He had just gotten out of college and was fed up with intellectuals. He remembered the feeling he had at the time—too mental, from all the thinking and talking.

Plato to potholes, he thought—remembering a job he took shoveling asphalt on a road crew. After that he shaped up for day labor at a temp company, waiting in a room at six in the morning with a brown-bag lunch as the dispatcher fielded calls—like the one that sent him to a factory to vacuum thick white dust off ceiling pipes; probably asbestos, he worried later. He lugged eighty-pound bundles of shingles on his shoulder up ladders onto roofs, sliding back and forth across the hot roof in the baking sun nailing them down. He worked the midnight shift at a trucking company, unloading long-haul trailers and reloading short-hauls for local deliveries; after work he would fall asleep in a hot bath and wake up twenty minutes later in cold water with a warm beer in his hand and shriveled skin. He sanded the tops of concrete wall sections for modular homes in another cloud of dust—when he asked for a mask, the guy said, "You're not American, are you?"

He eventually bluffed his way into a machine shop, fumbled around until he got skilled. The union approached him while he was working at a South Boston electrical components company. They needed someone to organize the tool-and-die department, where he and other machinists built master tooling for the downstairs production area, where four hundred workers—mostly women of Portuguese ancestry—assembled the final goods.

He remembered the factory, old brick, set on a triangular plot. The tip of the building jutted out to the sidewalk at the edge of the street; you saw it as soon as you got off the subway car on the elevated line. He walked down the subway stairs each morning, with workers headed there or to other plants in the neighborhood. At the bottom of the steps were a bar and a luncheonette. The men fanned left or right, for a shot or a buttered roll and coffee. He stuck to the roll—mostly.

Shay thought about how he saw the world then—workers good, bosses evil. He read Emile Zola, with his brutal portraits of working-class life. He would stand at the lathe and read during long cuts while the autofeed was engaged. He still had the paperbacks—*L'Assommoir, Germinal*—their pages blackened from his dirty hands.

As he tap-tapped the brake through the stop-and-go, he remembered how, after work, he would dig an abrasive paste from a tub, rub the rough grit between his hands to loosen the dirt, and rinse in big gray industrial sinks.

The name of the hand cleaner popped into his head—Goop.

Shay spotted a garage at the corner of Broome and left his car with the attendant. Outside a bum was sprawled on the sidewalk, his head propped against a wall. Shay handed him a twenty, said good luck—skipping his usual snap eligibility read to decide if the guy was a forgotten man or just someone who forgot to do what he was supposed to do.

"God bless," the man called as Shay crossed the street.

Be a day-maker, not a day-breaker, he thought, remembering his wife's saying as he passed through a courtyard and into the hotel. Inside, the concierge pointed to stairs that led to the mezzanine. He climbed the steps and entered the bar area through an open glass door. He saw Lewis and Hannah sitting in the corner with a man in his early thirties, average height, rail thin. He was wearing black cargo pants, a black T-shirt, and thick horn-rimmed glasses. As Shay approached, he stood.

"Dieter, this is John Shay," Lewis said. "John, Dieter Stempel."

Shay shook his hand. "Hallo," the man said in a German accent.

"Drink?" Lewis asked.

Stempel nodded as he and Shay sat down.

Shay smiled at Hannah; she nodded back. She had a black eye, and bruising around her face. For some reason he remembered the slam she invited him to when he was courting her to join the union. She had been a member of Wail Away, a group of slam poets. The performance was at a club in Williamsburg, in Brooklyn. She tore into the über-philanthropists, went on about how they amassed fortunes bullying everybody and never sharing the profit with the people who worked for them, and then later got all Goody Two–shoes about helping the world—after a lifetime of fucking over each and every individual in it. She came across bonkers, hothead; the crowd loved it. He had second thoughts about whether to hire her.

Lewis motioned to a waitress, ordered. To Shay, he said, "Dieter is from Frankfurt. He's with the German metalworkers."

Shay had wondered why Lewis picked the place; now he figured the guy did, was a guest in the upstairs hotel.

The waitress came back and set four Harps—Cafferty's favorite—on the low blackwood table between them. They raised the bottles and clinked.

"To your dear friend," Stempel said.

Hannah had to turn away; she looked around the room. It was lit by recessed lighting, set in cutout panels on the walls and ceiling. There was a white votive candle in a glass on each small table. The seating was club chairs and ottomans. Underneath her feet was a brown-and-white cowhide rug, one of several thrown on the dark-stain hardwood floor. Fort Worth meets Kyoto, popped into her head. The thought came flat, her mind on Jack. She felt him, inside her. Comforting her, telling her not to blame herself. She looked at Lewis and Shay. Wondered if they—if anyone—knew. If they blamed her.

Her hand began to tremble; she put it under the table. It can't be PD, she thought. Not this early. It must be stress, or from the accident.

She suddenly felt the urge to slam. She hadn't stopped by choice; it just didn't pay the bills. She had seen a tweet about an upcoming slam on the endless financial crisis. She wondered if she could put something together.

"Dieter has an interesting story," Lewis said.

Stempel nodded. "Do you know Lambal Interior, the company you are striking, wants to take a financial interest in a German company?"

Shay looked at Lewis, back at Stempel. "He's doing more business in Europe. Wants to team with a local."

Stempel nodded. "Mr. Lambal made a presentation to the board of one of our largest automotive suppliers. He made an offer to purchase a stake in the company."

"What did they say?" Shay asked.

"They were interested," Stempel said. "They saw this as an opportunity to sell in North America and gain access to new capital."

"But they want a stable partner," Hannah said.

Stempel nodded. "We have reached a long-term agreement with this company to ensure labor peace. It was expensive for them, but that is understood in Germany—at least, until recently. It is starting to get more like here, where companies are more aggressive in reducing costs. German auto suppliers have sent tens of thousands of jobs to Eastern Europe and Turkey."

"What does this have to do with Jack's death?" Shay asked.

"During Mr. Lambal's presentation to the board, he was asked about the strike and the long-term stability of labor relations at Lambal Interior. Mr. Lambal said they should not be worried. He said the strike was being led by a militant leader who would not be in charge much longer."

"That was just wishful thinking. A line he was feeding them," Shay said.

"Tell him the rest," Lewis said.

Stempel took a gulp of beer. "The company …"

"What's their name?" Hannah asked.

"Meinrich Aktiengesellschaft—Meinrich AG, in Munich. The company sponsors a Formula One team. One of the drivers has a gambling problem." Stempel paused. "This driver took a trip to the United States last week. To New York."

"How do you know all this?" Shay asked.

"Dirt is everyone's business, Mr. Shay. When our union realized what Meinrich's driver was like, we started keeping an eye on him. We have documented a number of compromising incidents. This behavior would be very embarrassing to the company and its management if it came out."

"Why would they care?" Hannah asked. "The driver's that good?"

"He is Wolfgang Meinrich," Stempel said. "Mr. Meinrich's son."

The waitress came by, asked if anyone wanted another. Lewis waved her off, adding a quick smile when he realized his abruptness.

"So he's in New York," Shay said. "It's a hangout for the rich."

"He made a pit stop," Lewis said. "In Cleveland."

Shay eased back in his chair.

"He arrived in New York, went to Cleveland—Lambal's headquarters city," Lewis said. "Then he comes back to New York. Tony Palazzo, our cop friend, says eyewitnesses and tire marks indicate someone may have hit the car deliberately. That's at high speed—the investigator says Jack was doing 80 miles an hour. He goes into the barrier, and the other car speeds away, without getting caught up in the accident."

"Professional," Hannah said.

Everyone looked at her. The moment flashed through her mind. The car swerving and hitting them. Jack turning hard. The crash.

"It happened so fast," she said. "There's no way I could tell. It was a blur." *I was half-asleep. We just had sex.*

"They wanted Jack out of the way that much?" Shay asked.

"The day after Mr. Jack Cafferty had been killed, all of Wolfgang Meinrich's debt disappeared," Stempel said. "Monte Carlo, Las Vegas, Macao. Three million US dollars. Cleared up overnight."

"Maybe the father took care of it," Hannah said.

Stempel shook his head. "The father is not your man. The drafts came from an offshore account. The money was—how do you say it?—'washed.' We are working with a contact at FATF to determine its origin."

"Laundered," Hannah said.

"Ya," Stempel said, nodding.

"FATF?" Shay asked.

"The Financial Action Task Force," Hannah said. "Set up by the G7 to combat money laundering and terrorist financing. It's a policy and advisory organization."

She clasped her hands together so she could squeeze the one that began to shake again. Please don't make it young-onset, she thought. She remembered the odds—diagnosed in one family member, 10 to 15 percent chance it would show up in another.

"That's correct," Stempel said. "But some of the people who work there track dirty money. Our contact believes the funds came from the United States."

six

Shay sat down in the negotiation room at the Marriott Eastside—a union hotel, a must for the talks. He cupped his hands on the table, and turned as Hannah sat to his right. Negotiators from the Machinists and Lambal Interior filled the seats, a half dozen to each side.

Peter Lambal took his seat across from Shay.

"We want to begin by expressing our deepest condolences for Jack Cafferty," Lambal said. "As difficult as these negotiations have been, we all respected him, and we understood that everything he did was in the service of his union and its members."

Shay nodded, couldn't bring himself to say thanks. You son of a bitch, he thought.

"We called you back today, so we'll take the initiative," Lambal said.

He nodded to a woman dressed in a crisp pin-striped suit at the end of the table.

She got up and placed a booklet on the table in front of each person on the Machinists' side. She smiled at Hannah, who ignored her.

"We've put together a new proposal," Lambal said. "We want to end this strike and get your people back to work."

He turned to George Lyons, his number two. Lyons was cookie-cutter management but had a warm face; he went up to the whiteboard.

"I'm going to highlight some key points," Lyons said.

Shay looked at Lambal. The Machinists had hired a private investigator with close ties to the NYPD to look into the accident. They sent another one to Cleveland, to see if Meinrich and Lambal had met. So far nothing had turned up.

Shay tuned to Lyons's voice midsentence. "... so that extra contribution to the health plan won't be an unreasonable burden to your members. Second point—while we can't make any promises on the issue of outsourcing and opening another plant in China, we will commit to continuous investment in our US facilities, and work as hard as we can with your members to improve productivity so neither of us will have to face that choice."

"That won't cut it," Shay said.

"It's the best we can do," Lyons said. "Detroit's got its moxie back, but order volumes are a shadow of the past. Look at all the auto suppliers who filed Chapter 11. If they're not bankrupt, they're like us—stock price in the toilet, debt junk-grade, no financing. Do you think we would send this work outside if we didn't have to? If we can't compete, your members will lose their jobs. Why not work with us to make the plants more efficient?"

"Why not guarantee that if we make them more efficient, you'll keep the work inside?" Hannah said.

Shay looked at her, all clenched up. He figured she could barely contain herself with Lambal in the room, knowing he might have been involved in Jack's death. He felt the same way.

"And oh, by the way," she said, "we already have. We played ball—relaxed work rules, let you regroup your production equipment into flexible cells. Our members retrained, went from single-task operators to cross-skilled caretakers of complex processes. They practically run your business for you—communicate with the automakers over the web from ruggedized PC kiosks on the shop floor, rove around the plant with 4G LTE tablets, adjusting output to match the change orders that pour in hourly from Detroit assembly lines." She was in a rhythm; it felt like slamming. Then worried—excitement can make the tremors worse. "Our people put their pride and problem-solving abilities to work, and productivity skyrocketed in your plants, anywhere from 4 to 9 percent a year, just like it has across the board in manufacturing the past decade—letting you live large and us live less. But that still hasn't kept you—and everyone else—from moving production to China. Six damn million jobs in ten years."

"Who can guarantee anything?" Lyons asked. "The world is completely different than it was twenty-five years ago. Lambal Interior has to compete with workers making a buck or two an hour. We're matched up against companies that don't pay health benefits, have no legal or regulatory costs, don't support an army of retirees. Do you really think we're just out to stiff you?"

He shook his head. "We just cancelled work with a company in Green Bay. It's a nonprofit, employs people with disabilities—men and women with cerebral palsy, seizures, autism. They did light assembly for us, best damn workers we ever saw; fast as the dickens, quality top-notch. The jobs gave them purpose, helped them pay for apartments, live on their own. They bawled like babies when we pulled the plug."

He put down the marker. "Christ, we live in the same towns as your members do, worship at the same churches. Our kids play on the same ball fields. Do you think we like this any more than you?"

Shay knew the Machinists were fighting a battle unlike any other. It wasn't about how to divvy up the pie anymore—it was about just trying to bake it, with a mob in the kitchen and everyone's mitts on the pots and pans. There were a billion people in Asia—whatever the math was—working for peanuts, making things they never made before, things that had been made in the West. The result was the "China price," and everyone had to meet it.

Lambal wasn't alone. Everyone was digging in their heels—refusing increases, reopening contracts, demanding givebacks. The feeling going around was, why not bite the bullet once and for all—wring out the labor costs they'd been trying to get at for years. They had nothing to lose they wouldn't lose anyway—to lowball competitors taking away their customers—if they didn't get their costs down.

All the union got was a double cross. Shay had gone over it a thousand times, but it always came out the same. Workers feared job loss because a company wasn't competitive. But their jobs were also in danger—made redundant by efficiency—if they pitched in to help it compete.

"Look, we know there's a world out there, and you have to succeed in it," he said. "But you have to bring us with you. We have to know—upfront, in writing—that if we help you improve your operations, we'll still have our hands on the machines at the end of the day. That we'll still have a plant, still have a job. Because it isn't going to get any easier. And if each time you hit a roadblock you demand more concessions, pretty soon there won't be any more to give. So if you want to reopen your plants, and build the interiors for the cars of the twenty-first century, you have to tell us this: 'we will bring you along.'"

He got up and walked out of the room, Hannah and the other team members in lockstep behind. They left Lambal's booklets on the table.

seven

The moonlight shone flat and still on the Hudson as Shay drove up the West Side Highway. He glanced across the median at the spot where Cafferty lost his life, and offered a silent prayer. He remembered what Cafferty always said about strikes—it was like pulling on elastic. You yanked and yanked, and when you let go, there was more than before.

Unless you pulled too far, and it frayed, Shay thought, looking ahead at the necklaced lights of the George Washington Bridge. The strike had gone on for forty-seven days. The fund was low, the union almost broke, the workers hurting. Lambal's newest offer wasn't that bad. Especially today, when you were lucky to have a job.

He was outside the city now, in the Westchester suburbs. He pulled off the parkway and navigated the streets to his development. He looked at his house as he turned into the driveway. It was a colonial, white with green shutters, set back a hundred feet from the street on a treed lot—cedar, elm, black walnut, green apple, a Japanese maple. Everything but the evergreens was starting to turn in the late September chill; in a few weeks the colors would be in full riot. Their first fall in the house, Anne said it felt like they were living in a pot of gold.

They moved there from Manhattan four years ago, when their son was about to start school. His remembered his parents did the same thing when he was five, left the Bronx for the suburbs. With a lot less fussing over location and schools—his father went down to

Penn Station one day and asked the agent at the window for a ticket to a town that was a one-hour train ride from the city.

Shay didn't miss the city—not apartment living, anyway. It drove him crazy, people clanging above and below and on the sides—it was like living on a shelf. He seemed snake-bit every time he rented one. He had a six-floor walkup on East Fourth Street between Bowery and Second—a rooster in the airshaft crowed his brains out at dawn. Switched to Park Slope in Brooklyn, a fourth-floor railroad flat on Union—woke up every night from the noise coming from a social club across the street that opened at two in the morning. He moved a few blocks down to President—was driven out by the smell coming through the bathroom vents from a couple below, who had a menagerie of cats and dirty clothes and empty pizza boxes strewn on the floor like dense underbrush.

Zany, fun years, he thought; but he didn't want to go back. He liked to lie down at night and hear his thoughts. He didn't get all the negativity about suburbs; it was the best tradeoff he could figure. A mix of country peace and quiet—he woke up to birdsong—and some city perks and people. Less than a full helping of each, but no OD on either. It was great for his son too. He ran wild in the ravine behind the house, snagging crayfish in the runoff stream. He caught frogs in the pond at the end of the block. In late fall, Shay and his neighbors cut away the pond's tall reeds, so the kids could play hockey when the water froze.

Shay turned into the garage, staying far enough to the right to leave room to open his car door without hitting the center post yet not so close that he ran over the crap that jutted out two feet from the wall—an old bike frame, rusted toolboxes, half-empty oil and windshield wiper containers, sleds, fishing gear. He inched up to another pile of junk extending from the back wall of the garage until the bumper grazed the broken wet vac.

He got out of the car, thinking as he always did about cleaning out the mess. He hit the wall pad to shut the garage door, wincing at the racket as he always did, as the rollers dragged their angry, sorry-ass, never-lubed metal in fits and starts down the tracks.

He opened the door to the mudroom.

His nine-year-old attacked him in the doorway.

"Hey, watch it, you don't know who you're messin' with," Shay said.

Michael's eyes lit up. "Oh yeah? Well, you don't know who *you're* messin' with." He cocked a roundhouse right and punched his father in the stomach.

"Oh!" Shay gasped. He crumpled onto the floor.

Michael was on him in an instant.

"Now we'll see who's got the power," he said, pounding him over and over.

"Hey you two, that floor's filthy," Anne said, approaching the combatants.

"How was your day?" she asked when Shay got up.

"Couldn't have been as tough as yours," he said—needling her about her earlier blowup, about being overworked.

She shoved him.

After dinner Shay played chess and then cards with his son. Shay pushed for Texas Hold 'Em, but Michael wanted "baseball"—five-card draw, threes and nines wild. Kids go for the deus ex machina, he thought as he dealt, remembering his high-school Latin—someone galloping in out of nowhere to save the day.

He opened a beer and flicked on the TV when Anne took Michael up to bed. He raised his foot onto the ottoman—it was killing him—and leaned forward, pulling on the toes to give it a stretch. He had aggravated it horsing around with Michael. He had damaged the soft tissue in his heel from too much running and biking. Stuff that used to heal fast was starting to linger. When he was twenty it was a tweak; at thirty it was a pull; at forty—he added two for sympathy—it was a tear. The only consolation was that each new injury distracted from the previous one—the pain got distributed, and therefore more bearable.

He clicked on cable business news. A newscaster sitting on a stool wearing a hiked skirt and spiked heels with floss straps—hooker in an Amsterdam storefront came to mind—kicked off the hour with breaking news on the United States and China.

"China's government has hit back against the US trade sanctions," she said.

Nice knees, Shay thought—superior patellar bone structure was a must-have in cable hiring.

Knees continued. "In a tit for tat, China canceled an order for fifteen wide-body aircraft and demanded that the World Trade Organization block the new US tariffs. Congress countered by calling for even tighter restrictions on Chinese imports and more punitive tariffs to protect US industry. Many members are calling for an across-the-board tariff on all Chinese goods coming into the country."

Anne came down after tucking Michael in; she sat down as the news went to a drug commercial. She shook her head as she watched the ad.

"You can't tell the pharmaceutical ads, with their lists of possible side effects, from the lawyer ads, saying if you have any of these symptoms call us."

Shay laughed.

"How did the talks go?" she asked.

"They made a pretty good offer."

"And?"

"I didn't take it."

"Why not?"

"I want to hold out a little longer. See if there's a connection between the race car driver and Jack's death."

He took a slug of beer and put the bottle on the table. She picked it up and took a sip.

"I spoke to Jack's wife," Anne said. "The kids will hold her together."

He nodded.

A few-second lull.

"You seem run down," she said.

"There's a lot going on."

She put her arm around him. “Anything I can do?”

Shay smiled. “You’re doing fine already.”

He kissed her. When their lips parted, she pulled down his head to rest against her breast. He looked out sideways at the family room. On the floor were a baseball, swim goggles and flippers, stacks of collectible cards, a Frisbee, and a Lego chopper.

“You get to the oral surgeon?”

Shay nodded. “The thirty tooth is shot. I let the dentist play endodontist, and he botched the root canal; the endo re-treat failed as well. Now it’s two grand to extract.”

“Ouch.”

“That includes five hundred for gas, so I won’t wriggle around and distract him. And for the bone graft material. It’s another five thousand if I go for the implant and follow-on cosmetics. And no time plan. ‘Payment is expected at the time of surgery.’”

“What did you say?”

“I said it’s a miracle. The tooth suddenly feels fine.”

Anne laughed. After a pause she said, “You should see your son’s music evaluation.”

“How’s Paganini doing?”

“He’s doing great.”

“I’ll look at it later.” Shay flashed a memory of piano lessons as a child; he drove the teacher to distraction and she quit. Michael was doing better. Anne kept on him, forced him to practice. He was complaining about having to play with little kids; the others started earlier, some as young as two. The instructors gave them cardboard violins and bows. At group lessons they pretended to play while they shit in their diapers and glanced nervously at the phalanx of eager parents on the other side of the room.

Shay didn’t mind. Where he grew up, he had to hide his brains, steer clear of the arts, to fit in. The kids at the music school were focused on achievement, even if some of the parents overdid it. He wanted his son to have the same success they were planning for their kids.

“We have to sign it, return it tomorrow,” Anne said.

Shay nodded. “You’re doing a great job with him.”

“Thanks.” She ran her fingers through his hair. “He’s got a great dad too.”

“You think?”

“Oh yeah.”

Shay smiled. “Let’s see that music report.”

eight

Hannah was walking down Lexington Avenue on the way to the Machinists' building. She passed two guys wearing T-shirts with the Croatian flag on their backs arguing in thick accents with a three-card monte dealer, who was trying to scoop up the cards and collapse his portable table and get away. She could swear she heard the man next to her say into his cell phone, "Take me to your leader." She saw a man standing in front of a clothing store, doffing his hat over and over again, each time saying "Hel-lo, ladies" to the female mannequins in the window, laughing wildly with every utterance.

Hannah waited on the curb at the corner for the light. She got green and stepped off the curb with the other walkers. The lead car on the crosstown street barely acknowledged the red light, rolling past the crosswalk and almost into the southbound avenue. The walkers had to circle around its hood, putting them on the edge of the heavy Lexington traffic. One guy, passing around the car, banged on the hood in anger. The driver got out, cursed, and started toward him. The other pedestrians screamed at the driver to get back in his car—which he did, combining his retreat with a scowl to salvage some manhood.

Hannah was smiling at the everyday New York mayhem as she crossed and headed down the side street to the Machinists' headquarters. For a moment it took her mind off the pain of what had happened, and the guilt that Jack's death was her fault.

She thought about how things had changed at work since Jack's death. Before, it was research, talks, hours around the table. Now she was working with Shay, setting strategy. She would be out on the lines with the strikers; she loved that.

But at what a price …

As she entered the HQ building, she thought about her last job, a summer internship at an NGO that pushed developing-world causes like debt reduction, free medicine, and microlending for village startups. The activist group did a lot of demonstrating and street theater.

She remembered the night they ambushed a banker at an upscale restaurant—he wouldn't fund an irrigation project in Cambodia. They dumped kitty litter on his table—they didn't want to waste real rice.

Hannah was thinking about what Lambal's guy said about people with seizures—would that be her in five years?—when Shay greeted her outside Lewis's office.

Shay held open the door for Hannah. He followed her in and scanned the room, which Lewis said he was keeping even after being elevated to president. Shay always got a kick out of Lewis's furnishings, especially now that he was head of the union.

Lewis was sitting behind an old steel desk on a fifty-nine-dollar chair. There was a sofa off to the side with chairs and a low table; both the couch and chairs had duct-tape repairs on their worn arms. His view was that union money collected from members goes to basics, nothing else.

His only splurge was on the walls. On the one behind his desk were framed and signed photos of himself with previous union presidents, national labor leaders, and US presidents. On the opposite wall hung autographed photos of basketball players—Oscar Robertson, Connie Hawkins, Lenny Wilkens, and his all-time favorite, Elgin Baylor. Lewis was old school, barely watched the modern NBA. He liked to tell anybody who would listen—there were fewer and fewer of them—that he ran a more sophisticated offense as a sixth-grade point guard fifty years ago in the city Police Athletic League than professional players ran today.

He motioned for them to sit. "How'd it go at the table?"

"Lambal wants to rip up the playing field," Shay said. "Install a new turf."

"You got that right; the son of a bitch," Lewis said. He picked up a water bottle. "They're all watching too. All his buddies—in rubber, steel, aluminum, mining, chemical, paper, aerospace …" He shook his head. "It feels like the 1930s all over again."

"Maybe we have to act that way too," Shay said.

"I don't remember you being so tough."

"I don't remember things being so tough."

Lewis nodded.

"Any news from the investigation?" Shay asked.

"Nothing much. But the German guy said he'll have something tomorrow. He wants someone to travel over there to Germany."

Shay noted Lewis's customary attire: dark suit, white shirt, and red tie. He wore suits at work; he wore them at social events. He wore them when he coached the boys' basketball team at the Harlem PAL on Manhattan Avenue—even at practice. He had told Shay he wanted to show the kids how to look, how to present themselves.

Lewis took a slug from the bottle. "I want you to go. I've got too much going on here."

Lewis had been sworn in as president two nights ago. The union was still buzzing about the ceremony. The council speaker who would shortly induct him ended his remarks by referring to him as the first person of color to serve in this role.

Lewis took center stage. Looking into the audience, a sly grin came over his face. "I didn't realize white wasn't a color," he said.

Machinists' members, black and white, broke into laughter, stood, and clapped.

Shay thought Lewis's joke had done as much for race relations in the union as the last ten years of diversity training. Although, he also figured, it took all that stuff to soften the ground for his end run around the PC phrase.

Lewis got up and walked to the window; it overlooked Third Avenue. Cars and taxis were streaming up the rainy street. The vehicles were bunched tight, lurching forward inches at a time, guarding their spacing so no one could cut in. He had just gotten a lecture from his doctor about a cholesterol reading through the roof and a buildup of plaque—the traffic reminded him of a diagram the doc showed him. You see what your heart looks like, he wanted to tell the MD. You be the first black president of the union, take over when it's broke, on strike against forces you can't control.

Lewis had been a machinist in the navy, could make or fix anything—you had to out at sea. He joined the union after discharge, worked his way up over twenty-five years. Yet some guys thought he was a rainbow appointment and were watching to see if he measured up or messed up. He was overeating for comfort, and he had cut back exercising—there was no time.

No wonder African-American health numbers suck, he thought. There was too much tension being black.

He turned to Shay. "It's good business. We don't do as much with the global unions as we should."

"What do you want me to come back with?"

"They want to give us some information about Jack. In person."

"Didn't they just win a strike?" Hannah asked.

Lewis nodded. "Industry-wide. Got a pay raise twice the rate of inflation." He laughed. "Probably put them all out of business." He shook his head. "This is a screwy line of work. They try to take it from you; you try to grab it from them."

"'Tug-of-war,'" Shay said. "My son and his friends play it."

"Only they get ice cream afterward," Lewis said. "Not what happened to Jack."

Shay and Anne watched TV after Michael went to bed.

"You have everything you need?" she asked.

"I'm all set. Thanks for helping me pack."

Anne nodded.

"Everything all right?" Shay asked.

"Sure." She took his hand; he squeezed hers. They sat silently for a moment.

"I'm proud of you," she said.

"I'm proud too," Shay said.

She hit him. "You're defective. What's your return policy?"

Shay laughed. "I mean, I'm proud of you. Proud of your work outside, and proud of what you do here. With this home. With our son."

No one could raise a child like she could, he thought. The way she took care of him, stayed on him. The way she loved him—he had never ever seen, nor did he think he ever would see, a love like the love between them. She made him feel like home was a paradise. It was what every childhood should be: a time in life where you know you belong, where you have a place in the world. It was a feeling you carried with you for life.

"You never said that before," Anne said. She wiped away a tear.

"It doesn't mean I never thought it."

"Say it again sometime. It means a lot."

"I will. I promise."

Shay held her when they got into bed. He kissed her gently and then opened his mouth and found her tongue. He caressed her hair, held her head lightly in his hands as they kissed. He climbed onto her, kissed her harder.

"Say you want me," she said.

"I want you."

She pulled him closer, digging her fingers into the small of his back.

"Say it again. Say I want you."

Shay thought it was a game, to turn them on. But then he heard the need in her voice. In her tone, he heard her questioning his love, his desire. Maybe doubting herself.

"I want you. I want you," he said, more loudly the second time. He kissed her, put his hand between her legs, clasped tightly. "I want you. So much, sweetheart."

"Oh John."

She took him in her hand and put him inside. They both moaned.

That was hot, he thought, lying there afterward and stroking her hair.

Jack's death had brought them closer. Restored context, focused on what's important.

He thought, death brings you to life.

nine

Shay cleared customs at Frankfurt Airport and was met by Dieter Stempel, the guy from the SoHo bar. "Mr. Shay, good to see you again. Did you have a good flight?"

"The plane went up, the plane came down," Shay said. "I had a good flight."

They walked through the glistening terminal.

"What have you got on Jack?" Shay asked.

"Please, come with me."

They exited the airport and got into a dark blue Mercedes. Stempel roared the Benz into traffic. "It is a short ride. I would like to wait until we have arrived to say more."

Shay looked out the window. He didn't remember the drive from seventeen years ago. He knocked around Europe the summer after finishing college, killed a few weeks in London and Paris before going to Frankfurt. He crashed with an expat friend until he found an apartment share on the south side of the Main River, in an old building with twelve-foot ceilings and huge wooden shutters on the windows.

As the car sped toward the city center, he called up snapshots of that time. The kiosk across the street from his apartment on the Gartenstrasse—Die Gartenstrasse Vier, for 4; he remembered the address—where he bought beer so strong that one bottle did the trick. The Stadtbad, the huge city pool with an admission price of ninety cents, where he would stretch out on multicolored heated tiles to rest after laps. The American bookstore where he bought books. The people at an outdoor market, breaking into laughter when he held out a small shopping bag and ordered "zwei hundert kilogram carrotten"—440 pounds of carrots; he should have said grams.

The memories sweetened when he recalled the rail trips along the Rhine to Aachen, a university town near the Dutch and Belgian borders, where he was seeing a German student. Her name was Ute—tall, blonde, a great big smile. He met her in line for the bus that took them from a London train station to Dover for the night ferry to Calais. They talked all night during the rocking passage across the Channel. On the train leg from the French coast to Germany, she taught him his first German word, "spion," told him to say it to the guards at the border. Mercifully called it off when the Dutch border police came down the aisle for the passport check—it meant spy.

"Do you like European football?" Stempel asked as the car sped along the highway. "What you call soccer?"

Shay exited sweet memory. "We like our games with an opposable thumb."

Stempel screwed up his face. "I don't understand."

Shay pressed his thumb against his fingers. "You know, opposable thumb? It crosses over, touches the other fingers? Let's you grip a ball in your hands … throw it, catch it. As in … stand upright, walk. We left the trees, and we use our hands now."

Stempel laughed. "You are saying our game is primitive?"

Shay smiled. "But still a great game. I watch the English league; we get it in the States. Who's your favorite player?"

"Bastian Schweinsteiger. Midfield, Bayern München. Do you know him?"

"I saw him in a Euro tournament. Made some great runs. Scored twice, I think."

Stempel nodded. "That's right, very good. Do you have a favorite?"

"Berbatov."

"Ya, he is fantastic," Stempel said. "He used to play in Germany, for Bayer Leverkusen. Incredible feet."

"He could still live in the trees," Shay said.

Stempel laughed as he pulled back into the right lane after passing.

"In Europe, we wonder why more Americans do not like soccer," he said. "We think it is the low scoring. In America, you like to see a lot of success. But in Europe, we believe life is hard. That if you are successful once in a lifetime, if you score once in a game, in the face of all the obstacles … this is a great achievement. This is why soccer is our game. It is the game of life."

"Baseball is our failure game," Shay said. "If you are successful three hundred times out of a thousand over a career, trying to hit a ball less than three inches in diameter, thrown at you off a raised mound from a distance of sixty feet six inches at speeds approaching 100 miles per hour, with seventy-five milliseconds to recognize the type of pitch, speed, where it's headed, and what you're going to do … you are remembered forever, in our Hall of Fame."

He paused. "We understand how tough life can be too."

The union headquarters was a towering brick building fronted by a perfectly maintained plaza with fountains, greenery, and two slanted rows of flags fluttering in the cool fall breeze. They took the elevator to the ninth floor and entered a reception area. Stempel opened a closet for Shay's carry-on. He nodded to a woman behind a desk as he led Shay past her and down the hall. At the corner office, he knocked once and opened the door. Inside, Shay saw a man standing at the window, looking out at the cityscape. The guy turned around. He was five foot eight, with a big belly that looked hard as stone. He had thick brown hair combed straight back. His eyes were heavily lined but still playful.

"Mr. Shay," Stempel said, "this is Klaus Henders, our union president."

Henders strode over to him. "Mr. Shay, it is good of you to come."

Shay greeted him and shook his hand. The three men sat down in modern, Scandinavian-look chairs around a low slate table ringed with wood, a manila folder placed conspicuously at the center. The door opened and a woman came in with a tray of coffee and cookies. She placed it on the table, careful not to disturb the folder.

"Danke, Iris," Henders said. She smiled and left.

Henders expressed his condolences about Jack Cafferty as Stempel poured the coffee. After some pleasantries, Shay put down his cup.

"What have you found out about Jack?"

Stempel looked at Henders, who nodded.

"Wolfgang Meinrich, the race car driver, did it," Stempel said.

"How do you know?" Shay asked.

"His girlfriend told us. She traveled with him to New York. The day Mr. Cafferty was killed, a man came to their hotel room and gave Meinrich keys to a car. Meinrich left the room, came back later. She said he was a mess, told her he had to do an awful thing."

"I have to be certain," Shay said.

"Meinrich's girlfriend described the man who gave him the keys," Stempel said. "He sounded familiar. We showed her some pictures. She identified him."

"Who is he?"

"He works for Peter Lambal," Henders said. "He came with him on the trip to Germany, when Mr. Lambal made the presentation about buying a stake in the company. There were photos taken that day. The man could be seen in the background."

"You have the picture?"

Henders reached for the folder and handed it to Shay. Shay opened it and looked at the man. He had seen him before, hanging around Lambal; he had figured he was a bodyguard. He closed the folder.

"Thanks for this," he said, slapping it with the back of his hand.

"No problem, Mr. Shay," Henders said. He placed his hand on Shay's shoulder. "Our two unions should work together more often."

The union had scheduled a program—video, factory tour, meet and greet with the executive council. Henders and Stempel accompanied Shay to a small auditorium for the film. The storyline traced the history of the organization from its roots in the late nineteenth century. The depression that hammered Germany in the late 1920s forced the union to give back much of what it had won in those earlier years. Many members paid with their lives in the fight against Hitler.

German trade unions became active again after World War II; the metalworkers rebooted in the 1950s. It was a strong outfit, winning a thirty-five-hour workweek and thirty days paid vacation a year. But the union had lost one-third its membership in the past twenty-five years. German unemployment was inching toward double digits.

After the video, Henders led Shay on a tour of a factory that made off-road equipment, a mini-Caterpillar or Deere. It was an industrial cathedral—spick-and-span, workers dressed in white coats or pressed overalls, the air fresh. Germany was heads to our tails, Shay thought. Its companies invested in health and safety and training, paid well, gave you time off to have a life. But it was a highly structured system, channeling people into trade apprenticeships early, cutting off choices and slotting them for life.

As he looked around the plant, as much as he knew American workers would envy the pay, perks, and working conditions, Shay thought we were too rowdy to accept the straitjacket that came with the tradeoff. Life in the United States for a blue-collar worker was anxious and insecure. But as tough as things might get, as long as you could accept the consequences, one thing was still true—you could do what you please.

Until the financial nuke, he corrected himself. Now we were scared, moving toward a European view. It was demographics too. We were skewing older, thinking about security, benefits. Getting pessimistic, as we watched the way the world was turning out.

The Europeans knew all about the world going bad—they majored in it. That's why they tried to preserve and protect—their workers, companies, markets. The good side was obvious. So was the bad—like one twenty-five-year stretch when they didn't create a single net new job within their formaldehyde economy.

It struck Shay that America was great when you were young; the European model was the ticket as you got older. Or when times got tough.

Until times got *real* tough—like now, with the mess in Europe. Then, everybody was up shit creek.

Henders chaired a meeting of the executive council after the tour.

"I am pleased to introduce all of you to Mr. John Shay, from the United Machinists Union. Mr. Shay, as you know, is leading the Machinists' strike against Lambal Interior, the US automotive supplier that has been looking for a partner in Germany. Mr. Shay has come over to meet with us at our request." Henders looked around the table. "As we have all agreed, our two unions should not let geography separate their mutual interests."

The council members nodded. A woman spoke first. "Mr. Shay, why do you think Mr. Lambal is taking such a hard line in your strike? We are anxious to know more about this man and his intentions."

"He wants to break us," Shay said. "We had his factories sewn up for years. We wouldn't do the simplest things to make the plants more efficient, because we had a work rule or job classification that prohibited it. These rules were well-intentioned—we fought for them over the years to keep management from working us to death. But as times changed, we should have bent. Especially as the competition became global, and so fierce."

He clasped his hands on the table. "Now both sides have hardened. We eventually made concessions, increased productivity, but management said it wasn't enough. They just wanted more and more."

He paused. "Executives are different today. Years ago, most everyone came from the working class. They started at the bottom, in production, and worked their way up. They were steeped in the company—in its traditions, its values, the surrounding community. Today, most bosses come from finance or sales. It's all about money. And price—the price of goods and the share price. Keep the first low to be competitive. The second high—to lure investors, reduce the cost of capital, make stock an incentive for recruiting executives. It all boils down to slashing costs. It's a poisoned atmosphere on the shop floor. It's a wonder product gets out the door."

"What is your forecast for the length of the strike?" someone asked.

Shay shrugged. "We'll go back eventually. But it will never end, really."

"The workers' struggle is eternal," someone said.

It wasn't how he would put it, but … yeah.

Shay talked with the group for a hour. The bulk of the discussion was around how the two unions could cooperate more. Both had organized plants in multinational companies that did business in both Germany and the United States. They discussed how they could use that as leverage—when a local was trying to resolve an issue in one country, another could exert pressure in the other.

At the end, Henders walked Shay to the door. "We are very pleased you could come, Mr. Shay."

Shay shook his hand. "Thanks for your help."

Henders nodded. "Is there anything else we can do?"

"No. We'll take it from here."

ten

Shay slept through most of the red-eye to JFK. He walked out of the terminal and took a shuttle to his car. He exited the airport lot and got onto the Van Wyck. Just north of Rockaway Boulevard in South Ozone Park, a Civic roared alongside in the left lane. Shay glanced over as the front-seat passenger in a ski mask leveled a shotgun at his head.

Shay ducked and floored his Impala SS; the blast shattered his rear window. He downshifted into second for a redline boost and pulled ahead of the Honda, cutting it off hard. The Civic veered into the right lane and then pulled back up alongside. Shay buried the gas pedal as a shooter fired from the backseat, shattering his passenger-side rear window.

Shay upshifted and wound out the small-block V8 in third, weaving in and out of traffic. Two shots were fired from behind, obliterating his rear windshield. He reached for the glove compartment as his left hand steered the twitching car; it was locked. "Shit!"

When he reached down to the center console, his car glanced into the divider and bounced off; he bumped the car next to him, sending it skidding onto the shoulder. He got control, reached down again, and grabbed the second key. He leaned over again, unlocked the glove box, and pulled out a gun.

The Honda was closing on the right. Shay eased off the throttle. As the car pulled even, he lowered his window, raised the Ruger, and fired, emptying the ten-round magazine into the vehicle. He watched the driver go down and then the shooter in back.

When the driver slumped forward, the shooter in the front passenger seat had a clear shot. But the Civic pulled to the right from the weight of the driver's body on the steering wheel before he could get it off. The car jumped the guardrail and crashed into a ditch. It burst into flames.

Shay pulled over and fumbled for the cell, rattled. He dialed Lewis, told him what happened. Told him to get a couple of guys to his wife and son's school right away, take them home and stay with them. Then he called his wife and told her. He tried to settle her nerves; that helped him settle his.

Shay got out of the car, picking glass from his clothes as he walked back toward the vehicle. He figured the car was chipped—no way a Civic could keep up without a board swap; he remembered it was the car of choice for gangbangers and hoods.

He was glad he spent those hours practicing at the gun range. The Machinists made it mandatory for officers after some kook threatened the union two years ago.

A cop car arrived. "You okay, buddy?" one of the cops asked.

Shay nodded as he watched the car burn.

The other cop was trying to get closer with a fire extinguisher. "You know them?" the first cop asked.

Shay shook his head. "Masks." He paused. "There's a gun on my front seat; it's been fired. I've got a permit in the glove compartment."

He and the policeman stepped back; the heat was intense.

"Let me see your license and registration," the cop said.

Shay pulled the cards out of his wallet as two more patrol cars converged on the site. The first cop sent one of the new arrivals to Shay's car to retrieve the Ruger. Traffic on the expressway slowed as drivers rubbernecked the destruction alongside the road. A fourth Crown Vic made its way through the jam and pulled over.

Tony Palazzo got out of the vehicle and walked to the scene.

"You okay, John?" he asked.

"Yeah, Tony."

"You know this guy?" the other cop asked Palazzo.

"Yeah."

The cop returned Shay's DMV paper.

"What happened?" Palazzo asked.

"Probably tailed me from the airport." Shay told him how it went down. He wondered how the shooters knew about his flight. Maybe they had been following him all along—tagged behind to the airport, staked out the car until he returned. He figured he should get the car swept; might be a bug, they could have been keeping tabs remotely.

Palazzo shook his head. "Broad daylight on the Van Wyck? This is some low-rent crew."

Shay nodded and then looked at him. "How'd you get here so fast?"

"I'm on a case in Brooklyn. I heard it on the radio; they called in your plates."

"Thanks for coming by." After a pause, "Tony, do me a favor?" Shay asked him to call the police in his town and have them send a car to the elementary school where his wife taught and his son attended, in case someone from the Machinists hadn't gotten there yet. "If they're not there, someone from the union already took them home," he said. He paused. "Maybe the cops could stop by the house." He didn't know if Anne and Michael were in danger. He had zero interest in finding out after the fact.

"Sure," Palazzo said. He went back to the car and made the call.

"All set," he said when he came back.

"Thanks," Shay said.

The car was still smoldering. Palazzo shook his head. "Same as Jack."

Shay nodded. "But now they're batting .500."

eleven

Shay walked into Lewis's office; Hannah was already there. He handed Lewis the photo he brought back from Germany of the guy who worked for Lambal.

Lewis smashed his fist on the desk. "Those bastards. Those fucking bastards."

He looked at Shay. "Lambal's going to jail. Unless I kill him myself."

Hannah was looking at the picture. She shook her head.

"What?" Lewis asked.

"It's too obvious," she said. "Meinrich flying to Cleveland? Then Lambal's bodyguard handing him the keys in New York, with a girlfriend watching?"

"Lambal's a race buff," Lewis said. "Meinrich sponsors Formula One; his son is a driver. These guys are stars, they do a lot of glad-handing. Lambal says he wants to meet him. The father sends the kid on a personal visit, to move the business transaction along. Lambal knows about his gambling problem, makes a deal with him to run Jack off the road, clear his markers. The girlfriend … that's a slipup. The bodyguard didn't expect anyone else to be in the room when he brought the keys."

"Maybe," she said.

"Let's play the card facedown," Shay said.

"We've got him dead to rights," Lewis said. "We have to turn him in." He paused. "They'll settle like lambs. On our terms."

"It'll look bad, for sure," Shay said. "But it's not open-and-shut. Lambal could say the keys were for an exotic car, he wanted the race pro to take it for a spin."

"It's enough to start an investigation."

"Lambal's no dummy. He must have covered his tracks."

Lewis got up and walked to the window. It was a windy day, traffic lights swinging wildly on the wires. "What do we do then? While he figures out another way to kill you."

It was the why Shay couldn't figure. Cafferty had been a tough bargainer; Lambal wanted him out of the picture. But he couldn't keep killing everybody who took over until he got a compliant negotiator.

"Tail Lambal's bodyguard," Shay said. "Call what's-his-name—have him shake the guy a little, see what falls out."

The labor movement had come a long way from the 1930s, when it hired professional boxers, wrestlers, and street thugs to defend itself against corporate hires like the Pinkerton Detective Agency. But it could still work the back alleys when it had to.

Lewis sat on the corner of his desk. "All right. We'll hold off a few days. See what the cops come up with. What's your next move?"

"Hannah has an idea," Shay said; they had hashed it out before the meeting.

Lewis turned to her.

"We move out the perimeter of the line," she said. "Downstream, we picket his suppliers—the companies that send him raw materials, the subcontractors that make his components and subassemblies. Upstream, we go after sales—the car dealerships, where customers buy cars fitted with Lambal interiors."

"Ever hear of the Taft-Hartley Act?" Lewis asked.

Hannah smiled—she knew it backward and forward from labor relations school. The federal law was enacted in 1947 following an upsurge in labor actions—more than five million workers had gone on strike the first year alone after the defeat of Japan. Taft-Hartley restricted the power of unions. A later amendment and related statute prohibited secondary boycotts and "common situs" picketing—

meaning interfering with any businesses associated with the target of a strike.

That ruled out taking action against the dealerships and suppliers.

"They won't use it," she said. "The economy's too rough, too many people are hurting. They'll hesitate to push back—it could lead to more job actions, bigger unrest. They'll give us room to let off steam."

"The autoworkers won't like it," Lewis said. "The Big Three are just getting back on their feet. The strike already has their plants low on inventory, cutting back shifts."

"I put in a call to them," Shay said. "We're flying to Detroit this afternoon."

"Oh yeah?" Lewis said. "Who the hell is running this union, anyway?"

"Shouldn't pickoff throws count toward pitch count?" Shay asked.

"What?"

"You know, pickoffs. The runner's on first, he's fast. The pitcher's in the stretch, he throws to the base, over and over. On some tosses he's whipping the ball, it adds up. Shouldn't the pitching coach record the throws on the clicker? Part of the pitch count?"

"What the hell are you talking about?"

"Maybe one click every three or four throws," Shay said.

He moved to the door. "You are," he said as he opened the door. "Running the union. But I'm running this strike."

Lewis looked at Hannah after Shay walked out the door.

She gave him her best smile.

twelve

Shay answered his cell; blocked number, not promising. "Yeah?"

"Is this John Shay? Executive Vice President, United Machinists?"

"That's me. Who's this?"

"My name is Tom Moss. I'm an agent with the Bureau of Immigration and Customs Enforcement, Department of Homeland Security."

"What can I do for you, Agent Moss?"

Shay's first thought was that the feds were taking off the gloves, looking to squeeze the union to settle. But ICE—and DHS—didn't fit. He wondered if he should ask him for a callback number, make sure he's legit.

"Mr. Shay, I have in custody a man named Luis Calderon. Do you know him?"

"Never heard of him. What's this have to do with me?"

"Mr. Calderon is a Mexican citizen. He works across the border, in a factory in Ciudad Juarez. At a company called Lambal Interior."

"I know the company," Shay said. "We're striking them in the United States."

"But not in Mexico," Moss said.

"That's why the company's there. To get away from us."

Moss didn't react to that. "Mr. Calderon walked into a US Customs and Border Protection office. He said he was afraid for his life. He won't tell us anything, wants to speak with you. You don't know him at all?"

"Not a clue."

"I'd like you to come to El Paso, Mr. Shay," Moss said. "This may be nothing, but we're pretty skittish about border issues these days."

"Sure. Whatever you need."

thirteen

Hannah and Shay were met at Detroit Metro by a driver from the Machinists' local. Outside the terminal, the guy opened the door of a double-parked car. They got in.

There was a gun in the seatback netting. Shay picked it up. "How's it going here?" he asked, checking the weapon.

"Good, Mr. Shay," the driver said, looking in the rearview mirror. "You two gonna have time to stop at the local?"

"It's John. Sure, if your guys give it the thumbs up."

The driver craned his neck, glanced back. "Guys would like that."

"What's your name?" Hannah asked.

"Paul Dorsay."

"Drive full-time?"

He shrugged. "Driver, gofer … whatever the local needs." He looked over his shoulder. "I was a tool-and-die maker. Got hurt lifting something."

Hannah nodded. Twenty minutes later, they pulled in front of the auto union headquarters. The low, squat concrete building was stretched wide, with long slits etched across each story for windows. It looked like a fortress primed for siege. The driver turned around.

"Better leave that piece with me," he said to Shay.

Inside they sat across from Jerry Bogdanich, who headed up interunion relations. Bogdanich was in his seventies and had a chiseled, weather-beaten face, thin lips, rock-breaker eyes. They had met him at the funeral service for Jack Cafferty. "You guys need money?" he asked.

"Always," Shay said.

"Support on the line?"

"Never hurts." He paused. "That's not why we're here."

"What is it then?"

Hannah took over. "We want to take the strike outside the plant," she said. "To Lambal's suppliers." She paused. "To the public. The showrooms."

"You think they give a shit about you?" Bogdanich asked.

"Maybe not," Hannah said. "But the dealers will. They'll push it back to the automakers, pressure Lambal to settle."

"You don't think Detroit hasn't picked sides? They *want* Lambal to break you. They want *us* to see it can be done. Once they repay the government the money they borrowed, they'll be back to their old tricks. They'll try to tear apart the whole show—spin off every operation to outside, nonunion companies. Keep control, but get rid of us. That's what they really want, to become a *shell*—brand name, marketing, financing. The body inside the shell? Making the fucking cars? That's too messy. They want the money without the sweat and tears. Let somebody overseas do the work."

He shook his head. "They'll go to any dirt-water country to make vehicles. They want to build cars offshore for a song and then export them back here to sell to us. Except they laid us off, so we don't have the money to buy the car."

He laughed. "Somebody put two and two together and came up with five."

The phone rang. Bogdanich picked up, listened. He held up a finger.

Hannah liked him; he reminded her of Jack. She wondered why she was drawn to older men. They had seen more—she liked their blend of scarred and healthy emotional tissue. And they appreciated her; they had made enough wrong turns, and mistakes, to savor the time together. She liked the way they desired her, thought about the games during sex. She had the upper hand, liked to dominate. With Jack it was lighthearted, fun and games. With another guy, it got away from them. She straddled him, slapped him; he loved it, begged for more. Showed her how to recoil when she hit, not follow through, to minimize the effects.

The upper hand is the open hand; sick, she thought. But we all have a touch of something. Somebody always has the power. And someone is always ready to give it up.

She glanced at Shay, gave him a mechanical smile as she wondered if it was safety—with older guys she didn't have to get involved. Then her thoughts turned to her father. She thought about how he overwhelmed, suffocated her. The thing you try to escape is the thing you cling to …

Then she thought, with sadness, she feared losing him to the illness—functionally or forever; maybe I'm seeking a replacement. It struck her, it was a way to show her love for him. The way we twist and mask a thing, not to face it directly.

Then she realized, not everything was about her. When you act out your stuff, it's in a world with others. Look what it got Jack.

"Then we got the Japanese," Bogdanich said, putting down the phone. "Ever hear of 'karoshi'? It means working yourself to death. It's a legal, recognized condition over there. Some guy died; put in eighty hours of overtime a month, six straight months. Keeled over. He was thirty-three, had a couple of kids. The family won the court case."

He shook his head. "He was a quality engineer at one of the automakers. I wanna tell everybody, put that in your pipe and smoke it next time you buy a foreign car; maybe that poor guy inspected it. Or how about those factory workers jumping off the roof at Chinese plants. Jesus, what kind of world is this?"

"You left out the part about Asian carp taking over the Great Lakes," Shay said.

Bogdanich laughed. "All right, I'll stop ranting and raving. But that's what we're up against. So I'm not sure your boycott is such a good idea."

"When we hit the showrooms, the carmakers will force Lambal back to the table," Hannah said.

"That's a hard sell around here right now. The economy is on skip, jumping from one bad thing to another. Members are just glad to be working. Now you got our plants on the verge of closing, 'cause we're running out of Lambal seats and interiors. And you want to pressure the showrooms? I'd have a riot on my hands."

"We've always stood up for each other," Hannah said.

"We always picked our spots too."

"Sometimes spots get picked for us," said Shay.

Bogdanich smiled. "You're younger than me, Shay." He looked at Hannah. "And you're a *lot* younger. Maybe you two got more fire in your belly." He looked back at Shay. "You must be pissed off too—someone tried to kill you. I know I would be. But you haven't seen what I've seen. And what I see now is that this isn't the right spot."

"You won't stand behind us if we go after the showrooms?" Hannah asked.

Bogdanich shrugged. "Let me talk to some people."

"We can't wait long," Hannah said.

"Oh, you can't wait long? You come out here, to the heart of the auto industry, to tell us *you* can't wait long? Who the hell …"

Bogdanich took a sharp breath. He opened a drawer and pulled out a prescription bottle. He twisted off the cap and popped a pill, chased it with a gulp of water.

"Listen, this is a business," he said. "It's a passion too. We all—most of us—started the same way, came up a hard ladder. But it's a business. Lambal, the automakers—they're in business. We have to make businesslike decisions. Not go off half-cocked."

"This isn't half-cocked," Hannah said. "Lambal wants to cut our throats. He's already got blood on his hands."

"What the hell does that mean?" Bogdanich asked.

Hannah felt Shay's eyes on her. "I mean, he's just sucking it from us."

"Look, both of you, go back to Bill Lewis, tell him we had a good talk," Bogdanich said. He stood up and walked them to the door. "Let me speak to my people."

They waited outside the elevator down the hall. Hannah was mad at herself; she pushed G when they got inside. She couldn't believe she spilled Lambal's possible role in Jack's death. Then she had to backtrack—say something that made her seem like a ditz.

The elevator opened on the ground floor. Shay put his arm on her shoulder as they walked to the outside doors.

"Forget it," he said.

fourteen

Shay and Hannah visited the Machinists' local in Detroit before flying to Cleveland. They were met at Hopkins Airport by local leaders who drove them to the line. The strikers roared when Shay got out of the car. He waded through a group that broke off the picket line to greet him, shaking hands with each striker.

"You're doing great," he said, "you're doing great." He picked up a sign from a barrel—"No American Workers: No America"—and marched with the strikers alongside the chain-link fence. Others carried placards that said "Save American Jobs," "Stop the War on Workers," "Stay Union Strong," and "Invest in the American Workforce."

"Jobs here, not China," Shay chanted with the men.

A news crew was setting up nearby for an interview. An assistant came over, told Shay they could be ready in five if he'd talk with them.

"Grab a coffee," a picketer said, pointing to a card table with pots and cups.

Shay swapped sports talk and bad jokes with the strikers as he poured a cup. He stood next to a burn barrel; the crackle and warmth of the scrap wood in the steel drum felt good in the fall air. The other strikers returned to the line. One was an older man. As Shay watched him, he thought about his father. Shay was the first kid in the family, even in the neighborhood, to go to college. He pulled away from his parents then, especially his father. He went to a private university, was hanging out with an intellectual, more privileged crowd. He was self-conscious his parents weren't educated and polished.

I wasn't, and I blamed them. He felt like he had never set it right.

He had stopped by yesterday, to settle them down after the attack on his life. His father was legally blind from diabetes and glaucoma and had had a stroke. His mother had congestive heart failure; she was hooked to an oxygen tank. They barely left the house, except to get food and go to the doctor. He had straightened up the countertop, wiped up a week's worth of crumbs, and put away the food. He felt badly he wasn't helping more—stopping by to look in, shopping, taking them to appointments. He and his sister were paying for aides to come by and help, trying to convince them to move to an apartment, give up the house.

Shay remembered the story his father told him last night. He was an FDNY captain, retired before 9/11. During his first posting in Harlem, the guys had put out a fire in an apartment where a woman lived with her children. When they looked around, they saw there was no food in the house. They went down to the corner store, emptied their pockets on the counter. The shoppers asked them what was going on; when they told them, some customers added their own money.

The clerk bagged the food and the firefighters brought it back to the apartment. As they walked down the street, word got out, and people in the neighborhood began clapping.

Shay choked up at the thought his father and mother would one day pass.

That was privilege, he thought. To be brought up by them.

Shay looked beyond the line to the Lambal factory complex. He liked industrial sites. They were raw, accomplished—defiant, lance in the ground. This one was huge, building after building, stretching for acres, echoing the great "works" of American industry—Ford River Rouge, GM Buick City, Bethlehem Steel Sparrows Point.

All shot to hell, he thought. From casting metal, to casting shadows.

Lambal founded the company to provide automotive seating to the Big Three. Soon he began making other interior parts—armrests, vanity mirrors, window motors, glove compartments. He moved on to gauges—speedometers, odometers, tachometers—then to dashboard assemblies. Today, he could supply an entire car interior—everything from seating systems through flooring, door panels and trim, instrument panels and cockpit systems, and the electrical and electronics to integrate the package.

Lambal had stepped on a lot of toes building his empire, Shay thought. Some of the small suppliers he muscled out had accused him of intimidation; he was investigated for making threats. Would he go as far as murder?

"Mr. Shay, we're all set," a TV crew member said.

Shay nodded as the reporter then approached.

"Mr. Shay, I'm Joan Summers, of WWNW," she said. "Thanks for taking a moment this morning."

"You're welcome. Happy to do it."

She flicked her head to the cameraman to start shooting.

"Good morning, Cleveland, this is Joan Summers for WWNW. I'm live on-site at Lambal Interior, Cleveland's largest manufacturing employer, where striking workers have halted production at the plant, a key supplier to car companies, and threatened to bring the auto industry to its knees. I'm here with John Shay, a vice president in the United Machinists Union. Mr. Shay, any progress in the talks?"

"No further meetings are scheduled."

"How would you summarize the impasse?"

"The usual suspects. Job security. Money. Benefits."

"Have any issues been resolved?"

"A few minor things."

"Mr. Shay, do you have any comment at all on the recent statement by the president, urging all parties to come to an agreement before more damage is done to the automotive industry and the economy? The president is concerned about the ripple effect of the shutdown, as auto plants are beginning to slow down due to a shortage of parts."

"We share the president's interest in resolving the matter."

"What about people who say you should be grateful just to have a job in times like these? When nearly 20 percent of America is either out of work, working less hours than they want, or too discouraged to look."

"I would say we're your last line of defense. Stand with us, as we fight to keep the few good jobs in manufacturing still here, and the wages and benefits they offer."

"What about those who say you are just one more special interest group?"

"We *are* a special interest group—we have a special interest in working people, who don't have enough protection on the job. At our heart, we're the *organized* version of every anxious man and woman—whether they're having problems at work, sitting around their kitchen table at night worrying about job security, thinking about how they can pay for their child's sports team or music lesson, going over the bills. How we *are* different is we're united. Instead of you fighting alone, we're here to show you we can battle together. And that this is your—our—only chance to prevail."

Shay and the reporter turned at the sound of a commotion behind them. A truck was inching toward the gate; the workers blocking it were yelling at the driver. The security guards opened the gate. The strikers were under strict orders not to trespass. They stepped back, but banged on the truck as it parted them.

Shay ran to the scene and jumped on the truck's front bumper. He hopped up on the hood and laid down across the windshield. The driver lowered his window, stuck out his head to see. The strikers pelted him with coffee cups and McMuffins.

The driver closed the window and the truck stopped. The strikers let out a cheer, broke open the back door, and emptied the vehicle. They trashed the boxes they pulled out.

Shay snapped off a windshield wiper and tossed it to the ground.

He climbed down and was mobbed by the men.

Local officials drove Shay and Hannah to an older development of small homes in Cleveland's inner-ring suburbs. Foreclosure signs and raggedy lawns broke the tidy look of the modest neighborhood. They pulled into the driveway of a well-kept home and parked behind a black, lifted Ford F-250 with Moto Metal wheels. They got out of the car and rang the bell. The door was opened by a big guy in his forties with thinning hair, extra belly, and a harsh yet hospitable face. The head of the local introduced them.

"This is Tom Locanto, a worker at the Lambal plant. Tom, meet John Shay, Hannah Stein, from national."

They shook hands; Locanto invited them into the house. Shay and Hannah heard a vehicle pull up as they crossed the threshold. They turned to see a news van.

Inside, they were shown into the living room. A woman and child were sitting on the couch. Locanto introduced his wife and daughter, Christine and Amanda.

"Sit down, Mr. Shay, Ms. Stein," Locanto said. "Make yourselves at home."

"Call me John."

"Hannah," Hannah said.

There was a setting of coffee and buns on the table between them. Shay leaned forward and poured a cup, pushed it to Locanto's wife. She smiled and thanked him.

"I want to thank you for opening your home to us," Shay said. "I especially want to thank you for sticking it out on the line. I know it's tough."

Locanto nodded. He looked at his wife and then back at Shay.

"We wanted to tell you how sorry we are about Jack," he said. His wife nodded.

"Thanks. We appreciate that."

Locanto held his hands over his daughter's ears. "And we really liked that stunt you pulled with the windshield wiper at the plant."

Shay smiled as he watched the little girl wrestle with her dad's hands.

"Anything yet from Lambal?" Locanto asked.

"He hasn't come back to the table. But we think he will."

Shay looked at the local officials; some were seated, others stood against the wall.

"We've got a little surprise for him," Shay said in their direction.

He turned back to Locanto. "They clear this news thing with you?"

"Ever see a house so clean?"

His wife jabbed an elbow in his ribs. Everyone laughed.

"Why don't we bring them in," Shay said to the head of the local.

Shay turned to Locanto. "What do you do at Lambal?"

"Machinist."

"Mills? Lathes?"

"Both. Mostly mills. Machining centers, really. You know them?"

"I've run them. Automatic tool changers?"

Locanto nodded. "Thirty slots."

"Vertical? Horizontal?"

"Vertical."

"Work envelope?"

"Sixty-five in X, thirty-five in Y and Z. Extended Z-axis travel for the headstock."

"Bed traverse?" Shay asked. He looked at the others. "Brings back memories."

Shay had done a lot of machining in the five years he worked at the trade—milling parts in a job shop off Boston's Route 128 high-tech corridor; knurling control knobs for motion-picture equipment in a West Side Midtown shop; cutting parts and building gadgets for the chemistry and physics departments at NYU; remachining sewing machine parts for a West Twenty-Third Street repair shop that served what was left of New York City's garment manufacturers.

"The thing moves," Locanto said. "The bed rapid-travels at 900 ipm in X and Y, 700 ipm in Z, accurate to plus-or-minus two ten-thousandths. Thirty horses power the spindle; it revs to 15,000 rpm. You can cut up to 400 ipm. Rotary table for four-axis work, probes for in-process inspection, software links to a manufacturing execution system—to feed throughput and operational effectiveness metrics to the honchos."

Shay nodded. "Whose CNC?"

CNC stands for Computerized Numerical Control. It started as a punched-tape computer system developed by an air force–sponsored project at MIT in the late forties, to automate the machining of complex shapes for jet-engine turbine blades. Today CNCs were hooked to virtually every machine tool. Their microprocessor brains spooled software commands that directed the lightning-fast movements of the machine and cutting tool to transform raw stock to finished specs. CNC was a big reason why productivity had surged in manufacturing. And why fewer and fewer people were needed to produce more and more goods.

"Fanuc." Locanto looked around the room. "Guy knows his stuff."

"Let's hope so," Shay said.

Hannah had been watching Locanto; he looked anxious. Manufacturing workers live check-to-check. Turn off the spigot, bills pile up quickly, especially with a bad economy. Strike pay was $150 a week. She remembered a story she read, about three guys laid off from a steel plant outside Buffalo; within a few weeks, they all died of heart attacks.

"Things tough now?" she asked.

Locanto nodded. "Payin' bills, no frills." He looked at his wife. "We haven't gone to Code Spaghetti yet."

Christine wrapped her arms inside his. "We'll be fine. But maybe you can tell my husband that the mortgage comes before the truck payment."

Locanto grinned. "You can sleep in the truck. You can't drive the house."

Everyone laughed.

Hannah remembered a World Bank report that documented economic growth in the developing nations, citing big declines in poverty and inequality. The global labor force had doubled as China,

India, and others barged into world production and trade. China alone had lifted hundreds of millions out of poverty.

That should be good news, she thought. But it wasn't the beatific uplift of the world's masses she used to imagine. These people were out to get their own, take it from us if need be. Leading a strike against the outsourcing of jobs to that developing world, her sympathies weren't so clear-cut anymore. At least not in the short term.

The term we live in, she thought. What was pulling one family out of poverty overseas was dragging down another's livelihood here. Workers were getting bounced from job to job—if they could even find one. Each job paid less than the last, with weaker pensions and health care. Retirees were losing benefits altogether as companies declared bankruptcy to void their obligations.

She thought about all the old people she had seen go back to work. She remembered Lillian, the elderly woman at the checkout line in the market near her apartment, leaning on the counter between customers.

Union or no, there were no promises anymore.

The news crew was setting up. Hannah turned to Locanto's daughter; she looked seven or eight. "Your friends going to watch you on TV?" she asked.

The girl nodded quickly and then burrowed into her mother.

"Do you work, Christine?" Shay asked.

"I'm at home."

"My wife stayed home five years," Shay said. "Our son loved it."

"Got a picture?"

Shay pulled out his wallet. He flipped it open and passed it across the table. The photo showed he, Anne, and Michael sitting around a table on their deck.

Locanto's wife smiled when she saw Michael's beaming face. "He's really handsome. He lights up everything around him," she said. Then she added, "He has your wife's smile." She showed the photo to her daughter and then her husband.

"What's your wife's name?"

"Anne."

"She's beautiful," Christine said. "You've got a lovely family."

Shay took the wallet back. "Thanks, so do you."

"How about you, Hannah?" Christine asked. "Married?"

Hannah shook her head.

"Still looking?" Christine asked.

"I guess," thinking it was a little late now, with Parkinson's creeping up on her. Her new calling card; not much of a deal for a guy. She thought about the things her mother had to do to care for her father; remembered watching her tie his shoelaces while he barked at her in frustration. She thought about the extra effort it had been taking her lately to do her own stuff. She felt fatigue, muscle aches; it was hard to concentrate.

Bunch of plain-vanilla complaints; could be anything, she thought. Maybe a touch of depression, or anxiety; she always seemed to sense a dark canvas lurking nearby. Dark made her think of the substantia nigra, so-called because its nerve cells contain black pigment. She wondered if it was beginning to happen inside her—degeneration and death of the nerve cells that send signals to the striatum in the cerebral cortex to control motor function. The striatum then can't handle the muscle control computations required for normal movement.

At least she knew the science cold.

The local official tapped Shay on the shoulder; the news crew was set. Shay swung around to face a different reporter. The camera started rolling. The newshound recapped the strike situation, its effect on Cleveland and the national economy, the toll on workers and their families. He introduced the Locantos and then Shay and Hannah.

"What's the next step?" he asked Shay. "Any plans to return to the table?"

Shay nodded. "We're announcing it here, tonight." He looked at Hannah.

Hannah turned to the reporter. Christine and her daughter were watching her intently.

"We're returning to the table, only the table has moved," Hannah said. "It's no longer just a conference room in a New York hotel. It's not only the picket lines outside the Lambal Interior plants. It's all over the country. At the car dealerships, that sell cars with Lambal seats and interiors. At the suppliers, who send materials and parts to Lambal. Anything that goes into Lambal product, anything that goes out with Lambal product in it, that's our negotiating table."

The local officials beamed. One began to clap. The others followed.

The camera panned the room, taking in the scene, as Christine Locanto reached across the table and shook Hannah's hand.

fifteen

Lewis slammed his fist on the desk. "Let me get this straight. Because I want to wrap it up in a neat package, so I can bring it before the executive council and get the two of you censured and removed from the leadership of the strike." He glared at Shay. "First, you broke the law on the picket line, almost started a riot." He smiled. "I kind of liked that."

The smile lasted as long as an electron in a particle smasher.

"But before you did that, you sashayed over to the autoworkers, didn't get their blessing to extend the line to the dealerships, and then went to Cleveland to announce the new action at the home of a striker."

"That's what we did," Shay said. "And that's what we're going to do."

"Now wait a minute, you upstart son of a … That's what *we're* going to do? Who the hell do you think you are?" Lewis pointed his finger at him. "I should have never promoted you so fast to fill Jack's shoes."

"Take it away, then."

Lewis shook his head. "You son of a bitch. Everyone on the shop floor at Lambal is behind you. I cut off your legs, they scream for my head."

There was a knock on the door. Hannah opened it and came in.

"Listen, Bill," Shay said as she took a seat, "you put me in charge of the strike because you knew the workers would listen to me. Well, now we're listening to them. You should have seen that family we met. Sitting in their living room, worried as hell. There are people just like them, in homes all over Cleveland. In Michigan, Indiana, Illinois, Wisconsin, where Lambal has his other plants. What's he employ, fifteen thousand?"

"And there are people like them all over the country, working for other companies," Hannah said. "Who've lost jobs, or are about to get axed. Fighting to hold on to wages and benefits they built their lives around."

"That's where you two went wrong," Lewis said. "We're not trying to save America. We're trying to get our members a good deal at an automotive supply company headquartered in Cleveland."

"We're not trying to save the country," Hannah said. "We're trying to *enlist* it. We think people will get behind us."

"What, not buy a car they need for work because of some guy in a living room in Cleveland?"

Shay glared at Lewis. "What happened to the guy who ran cash to the ANC?"

"Rebelling takes one way of thinking," Lewis said. "Governing, another."

The images from thirty years ago came to Lewis's mind. Disguised in Ovambo tribal dress in the backseat of a beater 4Runner. Accompanied by guerrilla fighters from the military wing of the South West Africa People's Organization, pretending to be migrant workmen. Driving from Walvis Bay down the Namibian coast. Traversing the Namib Desert. The gravel roads, the three-hundred-yard-high red sand dunes at Sossusvlei—the soldiers, who spoke a little English when they weren't chattering in their native Oshiwambo language, arguing whether they were the tallest dunes in the world. Skeletal shipwrecks, a hundred and fifty yards inland, as the desert crept westward and reclaimed the sea. Heading toward the South African border and the rendezvous with Umkhonto we Sizwe—Spear of the Nation, the African National Congress military wing. A duffel bag full of cash, another with guns, under the floorboards. Crossing the Orange River into South Africa. Hard looks from Afrikaner guards as they thumbed through their papers.

Lewis suddenly thought of his high school team's nickname: Warriors.

Shay stood up. "You're one jaded son of a bitch."

"I'm a …" Lewis walked around the table, got in his face. "I'm a jaded son of a bitch? You're telling me that?"

"Calm down," Shay said.

"Calm down? I've got auto union brass chewing off my ear for taking an action that could slow down their plants and affect their members without consulting them. I've got the federal government cautioning me about disrupting the economy and threatening me with a Taft-Hartley injunction. I've got my own executive council asking me who the hell are John Shay and Hannah Stein and why are they running my union. The strike assistance fund is shot. A rival union is raiding our Wichita local, trying to peel it off. A New Jersey lodge is under indictment for a kickback scheme with the plant manager. An LA local has been charged with operating a prostitution ring—inside the plant! And you're telling me to calm down?"

Shay grinned. "It's not like everybody's watching to see how you do."

Hannah whirled and glared at Shay. She felt unsteady from the quick movement.

Lewis managed a halting laugh before he shoved Shay—hard—toward the door.

At home, Shay put Michael to bed. "Did you send Joe an e-mail thanking him?"

Michael nodded. Shay's cousin Joe O'Malley, his mom's sister's son, was an Army Ranger. He had sent Michael a *pakol*, the soft, round-top wool hat worn by Afghan men, and a sniper patch from a French unit working with his NATO battalion in Afghanistan.

"Did you say a prayer for him tonight? For all our soldiers, sailors, and airmen?"

"Guardsmen and marines."

Shay looked at him.

"They say that too, now," Michael said. He was tossing a baseball up and down.

"I took cookies to the police," Michael said. The local cops were still sending a car around.

"That's good," Shay said.

"Dad, are we doing dopey drills tomorrow?"

Shay smiled. "You guys like them?"

Michael nodded. Shay helped coach his son's soccer team. He devised drills to teach the kids what to do, by showing them what not to do. He called them dopey drills, because the kids looked stupid when they did them. In one, he had a defender run directly at an attacker. When the kid got there, the offensive player was long gone, there was nothing but grass. Everyone would laugh. The point was to teach them to run where the play was going, not where it was.

"Dad?"

"Yes, son."

"Why don't they make loaves of bread just ends?"

Shay laughed. His son, unlike most kids, liked the end pieces.

"Dad, can I get a knife for Scouts? Mom said ask you."

"Sure."

Michael smiled. He pulled the blanket to his neck. "A kid at school said a man shot at you and you killed him."

Shay took an audible breath. "Mom and I spoke to you about that."

"You shot him, how?" Michael asked. He cocked his fingers like a gun, pointed it at his father. "Pow? Pow?"

Shay smiled—against his better nature. "It's not a game, son."

"I know, Dad." He fired his imaginary gun another time, silently into the air. "But it's still better if you win, right?"

Shay smiled. "Right."

"Tell me a story, Dad."

"What book should I read?"

"No. *Tell* me a story."

"Make up?"

Michael nodded.

Shay took a breath. "Okay. Once upon a time there was this bicycle. It was blue. Like your eyes." He leaned in, brought their eyes socket-to-socket. Michael laughed.

"The bicycle was riding down the street by itself one day. The kids were yelling, 'Hey, where's your rider? Can I be your rider?' The bicycle acted like it couldn't hear them, it just kept riding. So the kids began chasing it. They were running behind it, yelling, but the bicycle just kept going. Soon it got to the end of the neighborhood and crossed a street. The kids stopped there—they weren't allowed to go any farther. The bicycle went through another neighborhood, and then another, with kids from each neighborhood chasing it. Then it came to the end of the neighborhoods and saw a field. It started to ride over the bumpy land, over small hills, and then through a forest. Animals were chasing it now, squirrels, rabbits, deer, crows overhead.

"Then the bicycle came to a stream. It tried to cross, but the water was moving so swiftly it couldn't make it. It was carried down the stream, not too fast at first and then more quickly, fish swimming all around it. Soon it was in the rapids, bouncing off the rocks, shouting, 'Ouch, ouch.' Then it looked ahead and saw a waterfall. It tried to get to the bank, but it couldn't. Suddenly it was at the edge of the waterfall. It closed its eyes."

"Where were its eyes?" Michael asked.

"On the handlebars. It closed its eyes, and suddenly it was in the air. It opened its eyes and looked down, and there were the kids from all the neighborhoods. They were standing in a pool at the bottom of the waterfall in their swimming trunks. The bicycle was falling toward them, and then it started to fall slower, like it was on a parachute. It landed in the middle of the kids. They rolled it out of the water onto the land and climbed on, taking turns, and rode around until their parents called them home for dinner. The end."

Shay looked at his son.

He was lying on his back, his fingers linked behind his head, smiling.

Shay joined Anne downstairs. The phone rang. She got up. "Probably my mom."

She picked it up and exchanged a few words. "Just a moment." She held her hand over the receiver. "You want to take this?"

"Who is it?"

"Somebody from Texas. About an accident, at a chemical plant."

Shay nodded; he had seen the story on the web. Anne handed him the phone.

"Yes?"

"Mr. Shay?"

"Yeah."

"This is Tom Hardin, from the chemical workers."

"Yes, Tom. How are you?"

"I'm okay, thanks. I'm sorry to bother you at home; I know we don't know each other. Is this a bad time?"

"No, it's fine. What's up?"

"First up, I'm sorry about Jack Cafferty. I got to meet him a few times. He was a good man."

"Thanks."

"Cops finger the clowns who came at you?"

"Not yet."

Hardin paused. "You saw the story on the news, what happened in Houston?"

"I did. Those were your people?"

"That was us," Hardin said. "An explosion blew out twenty-five-foot-high concrete walls, left a crater five feet deep."

"How many inside?"

"Eight. Five dead, two pulled out in bad shape, one still missing."

"Jeez. I'm so sorry. Anything we can do?"

Hardin paused again. "Maybe. Think you might consider coming down here?"

"Sure. Be happy to."

"I don't want to throw off your negotiations back East."

"Already did that myself."

Hardin laughed. "Been there. We can leave you a ticket at the airport. Which airline do you fly?"

"Don't worry about it," Shay said. "You just take care of your people."

"Thanks, Mr. Shay. You'll be most welcome out here."

"It's John. I'll fly in tomorrow." He paused. "I'm going to bring someone, if that's all right."

"Whatever you want. Call our office with the particulars; we'll pick you up."

"Will do. See you tomorrow."

"I'm looking forward to it."

Shay turned to Anne after he hung up the phone.

She smiled. "They'll appreciate that. It will mean a lot."

sixteen

Hardin drove Hannah and Shay from the airport to the accident site. The plant had been leveled, a mass of twisted steel and concrete rubble.

"It's amazing anyone survived," Hannah said.

"The ones who did, didn't by much," Hardin said.

He was five foot ten, broad build, jowly face. He wore a black tee with his union's emblem, jeans, and cowboy boots. "Here, I want you to meet someone," he said.

He flashed his union ID to a cop outside a cordoned area; the cop touched Hardin on the arm and let them in. They walked over to a man who was picking through the site.

"This is Ted Salkey," Hardin said, introducing Hannah and Shay. "Ted's our environmental safety officer."

They shook hands. Salkey gave Hannah a second look.

"Turn up anything?" Hardin asked.

Salkey nodded quickly. He was thin, with an overflow beard and jittery manner. He led them to a spot off by themselves, where no one was combing through the wreckage.

"Those sons of bitches," he said.

"What'd you find?"

"They were using it," Salkey said. "Or at least, it was still in the facility."

Hardin shook his head as he looked over the devastation. "I ought to kill those bastards myself."

"What is it?" Shay asked.

Salkey looked at Hardin, who nodded.

"We caught them with a solvent in the plant that shouldn't be there," Salkey said. "It was a fluke we found out—one of the men broke out in a rash and had to go to the hospital."

Shay remembered when the same thing happened to him in a machine shop.

"When he was tested, they discovered traces of the chemical," Salkey said. "It's legal but volatile, especially in combination with some other agents in the processing operation."

"It's legal, though?" Hannah asked.

Salkey nodded. "So far. We filed a brief with the EPA. They issued some temporary handling regulations, pending further tests, to keep the stuff out of contact with chemicals that might cause a reaction. But we've been unable to get it banned. We threatened a job action if the company didn't get rid of it voluntarily. They said they did."

"Thanks, Ted," Hardin said, "appreciate your work here. Call that in to the union right away, will you?"

They drove to the hospital where the survivors were being treated. Hardin led Shay and Hannah to the burn unit. People were clustered in the waiting room, having quiet conversations. Several nodded to Hardin as they entered the room. A man broke off from one group and stuck out his hand to the union official.

"Tom," he said.

"Hello, Jim, how are you?" Hardin asked.

"Holding up. Trying to hold up the others." He flicked his head across the room.

"Any word?"

"They're just doing their job in there. All they really tell us is to pray and keep our hopes up."

Hardin nodded. "Jim, this is John Shay and Hannah Stein, from the Machinists. John, Hannah, Jim Geiger. Jim's boy Ron is here. He's an operator in the plant."

Shay shook hands with the man. "I'll pray for your son," he said.

Geiger nodded. "That's kind of you."

"I'm very sorry," Hannah said, clasping her other hand around his as they shook.

"Thank you," Geiger said. He looked over to the group he had left. "I'm going back to my wife and daughter." Hardin touched his shoulder as Geiger turned to leave.

Hardin spoke to family members of the injured, along with workers who had come to the waiting room, before he drove Shay and Hannah to the local. The lobby was filled with men and women, some kids. A news crew was interviewing two of the men.

"What the hell you going to do about this, Tom?" a man called out.

"You mean what the hell are *we* going to do about this?" a woman said.

Others murmured in agreement. The camerawoman turned her lens on Hardin.

"We're going to do plenty," Hardin said. "Brothers and sisters, this is John Shay, from the United Machinists. He's come out from back East to lend us his support. You might remember him from the TV the other night. He's the son of a bitch who climbed on that truck outside the auto supplier plant in Cleveland and stopped it cold in its tracks."

The workers let out a cheer.

"John is here with Hannah Stein, another Machinists' official," Hardin said. "John, did you want to say a few words to your union brothers and sisters?"

"It'd be an honor."

Shay looked at the group. The men were rough cut, with full faces and stocky builds. Several women mingled with them; another group of women stood off to the side. The kids stood beside their parents.

"First of all, I want to tell you how sorry we are for your loss," Shay said. "I want to convey to you, on behalf of all our members, our deepest sympathy."

He looked around the room. Parents were quieting the littlest kids.

"I toured the plant site this morning; I'm sure you've seen it yourself. This is dangerous work, you all know that. I bet you take pride in that as well." He thought about his father, running into burning buildings. "But there are lots of dangerous things in the world. That's why we have laws, and rules and regulations. That's why we have unions."

"You bet your ass," a man said.

"Well, I've been told that some of those laws, some of those regulations, didn't keep up with the situation. So you took over. You told management what it had to do to make a safe workplace. I'm also told the union uncovered evidence that management didn't listen. Now, I don't know if that's true."

"I sure as hell do," a man said, stepping forward. "Those SOBs kept it in the building. It's cheap as crap, one more damn shortcut. Now look what happened."

"If they did," Hannah said, "there'll be hell to pay."

The workers clapped.

"And this time the explosion will level the boardroom, not the plant."

The workers cheered as Hardin led Hannah and Shay to the elevator.

"You two did good," Hardin said after the doors closed.

Hannah smiled. Shay watched the numbers light up as the car ascended.

That's because this stuff is getting to me, he thought.

All over again.

Shay thought about Anne and Michael on the flight back to New York. Seeing the families at the hospital, he was feeling how much his meant to him. He didn't always act that way, but it didn't change the way he felt. Men never get that straight.

"You're a wild card," he said, turning to Hannah.

“I was thinking that,” she said. “Maybe I spoke too soon. Suppose the explosion was caused by worker negligence?”

Shay shrugged. “Those people liked seeing you get riled up. It let them know someone cared. That someone was as pissed off as they were.”

seventeen

New York

As the elevator clanged down to the lobby of her prewar building on Manhattan's Upper West Side, Hannah wondered if her father was taking his medication. As his responsiveness to the levodopa lessened, he had to adjust the dosage upward, to offset his brain's diminishing production of the neurotransmitter dopamine. More medicine meant dyskinesia—repeated wild, involuntary bodily movements. Cutting back sucked too—bradykynesia, slowness of movement.

She thought about his psychological swings—despondent bitterness, alternating with inspired resolve. He would curse his fate—how can the most simple pleasures be taken from me? A minute later it would be, how can anything that grabbed hold of Muhammad Ali and Michael J. Fox be all bad? And why should I worry? With the pace of science today, in a few years nanobots will escort molecules to each errant alpha synuclein protein and fix them to the receptors to reverse their malfunction.

Years ago she wanted to become a doctor, to take care of him.

Lately, when she visited, he was regaling her with sports memories. The Pirates Series win in '79, where fans at home games stood and sang, "We Are Family." A 1974 World Cup semifinal he watched on a big screen in Madison Square Garden, with twenty-five thousand Brazilians chanting "Brazil! Brazil!" the entire game. Moses Malone, the Sixers' center, when asked his prediction for a three-round, best-of-seven playoffs: "Fo', Fo', Fo'."

He's recreating triumphs, she thought—trying to rouse himself for his own challenge. She felt decked again at the thought it might be happening to her.

Maybe it wasn't Parkinson's.

I can't tell him. It would break his heart.

Hannah stepped outside her apartment building, looking up and down West End Avenue for a cab. She lived in a four-story runt of a building wedged between taller apartment structures. The building was owned by a Jewish agency that rented at below-market rates to Holocaust survivors or their descendants. Neither Hannah nor her family qualified; she was there on a sublet.

As she waited for a taxi, she looked up at the building. The old man in the apartment above had been murdered. She came home a month ago and saw a kid with a hard stare bounding down the stairs. She figured he was a delivery boy, but realized later it was probably the killer. It gave her a chill again, imagining the calculation that might have taken place in his mind when he saw her. The police interviewed everyone in the building and brought her to the precinct. She gave a description; they called her back a few times to leaf through suspect photos. The case was still open.

She felt like death was all around her as she hailed a cab.

As the taxi sped uptown, she worried she wouldn't be able to take care of herself if it was Parkinson's; she would have to give up her apartment, life on her own. She wondered how long she would be able to hike. She and her girlfriends went to the Adirondacks every summer to climb; they snow-camped in winter.

She took a breath—it was a long way off before she had to face that. She remembered a book she read by a Mayo Clinic surgeon who had Parkinson's. He coined the acronym PARK, what you needed to face it: P for patience, A for analysis, R for resourcefulness, K for keep trying. She wondered if she had the right temperament. No one does, she thought—the thing tempers you. Or not.

I need a drink.

The cabbie dropped her off at a bar on Broadway called the Lower Depths. She walked down the steps to the basement dive. Inside, she sat at the bar, looking around at the familiar sights: professors, grad students, off-duty cops, beats who looked beat. Her parents had brought her here since she was a little girl. She remembered lining up on the old buffet line on Sundays, for meat loaf and mashed potatoes. Steam rising from the rectangular metal containers. Returning to the booth, listening to them and their friends talk politics, as she slid to the edge of the plumped bench to reach the table and food. They were professors, he sociology, she women's studies. Schooled in the sixties, marched on a dime, you name the cause. She drank in their lectures as she grew up, especially her father's. Railing against injustice, urging her to fight for a better world.

She killed the Bass pint and snapped down a Midleton chaser to clinch the deal. Jack had introduced her to the whiskey. She remembered his story. He was in a Galway pub, had a load on. He said he pointed to the row of bottles against the wall and asked the bartender which one he would drink if price was no object. Shame to rush good whiskey, she thought, licking the sleek gloss from her lips as she paid the tab. She was no stranger to the routine. She downed the same pairing before going onstage to slam.

Hannah left the bar and walked to her parents' building on 116th Street. As she pressed the button for 4C on the outside panel and waited, she saw a teen walking a dog. She remembered her own when she was a child. A border collie, splotched in black and white, big grin on his face; a wagger, a happy camper. She named him Bail, for all the times he bailed her out of her bad feelings and sad moods. It never struck her as much of anything before. Suddenly, it seemed a strange thing for a child to do.

Her mother buzzed her in. Hannah took a deep breath on the elevator, another as she unlocked the apartment door; thought she felt her heart speed up. She never knew what she was going to walk into. She hadn't been by for a while; she didn't have the patience for the cycle of abuse and apology her mother had to endure.

Her mother was standing in the foyer when she opened the door. Hannah's eyes lit up during an up-and-down scan. Her mother was wearing a buttoned reddish-orange blouse, straw flax pants, and ballet-style flats in a sequined fabric, with three flower embellishments on the toe. She had teased out her hair; jelled it, to body-up the thinning strands. She had on gold circle earrings set with tiny rubies and a matching bracelet.

"You look so sharp."

Her mother gave her a kiss. "I'm listening to my baby girl." She looked down at her shoes. "Tory Burch. Lilac Flat. I saw them in *People StyleWatch*."

Hannah laughed. She had been taking her mother shopping, trying to get her mind off things—and wean her from the burlap of her fellow professors. She kissed her on the cheek. "You look great." She looked into the apartment. "How's he doing tonight?"

"You've just crossed over into the Twilight Zone," her mother said, in passable Rod Serling. "But thank God for little miracles. He stopped saying, 'Fo', Fo', Fo'.'"

Hannah smiled. "You've got that down good."

"It's burned into my brain."

Music started up in the other room, and just as suddenly stopped. Her mother shook her head. "Just like his oldies. That's his latest thing. The 'girl' groups."

Hannah walked into the living room. Her father was leaning forward in his chair, trying to put the needle at the end of the arm onto a forty-five spinning on the turntable. His hand was shaking, and he kept dropping it onto the record or platen. She took the arm out of his hands and placed the needle on the edge of the disk. She kissed him on the cheek as the scratched disc hissed and popped. "Hi, Daddy."

He smiled. "Hi, baby." He looked behind her. "Where's the TV crew?"

She laughed. She had been on the news, interviewed about the strike.

"We thought they followed you everywhere," he said.

"That's Jessica Simpson."

The song started up. "Speaking of young girls." He looked at his wife; she shook her head. "Take a listen to Rosie Hamlin. Rosie and the Originals," he said. "'Angel Baby.' What a voice. A real looker too."

Hannah listened to the first few bars. Her father sat back in his chair, his six-foot-one frame stooped and rounded. She wondered if he was doing his exercises to counter the muscle deterioration. She glanced at his walker as he sang along, imitating the high voice. He made her play two more for him: "Be My Baby" by the Ronettes, and Kathy Young belting out "A Thousand Stars."

She rejoined her mother in the kitchen while he sang with Kathy.

"How are you holding up?" she asked her.

"Oh, I'm fine." She smiled. "For better or for worse."

"You getting out at all?"

"I see the girls. And we have visiting nurses and aides come by; they help with bathing, and other things." She shook her head. "A different one each week. If they last that long. He wears them out quick."

Her father called out for her, in that towering voice stamped on her psyche. She came back and sat down next to him. He took her hand; she worried hers would shake and he would notice. Unless we shake in tandem, she thought, almost laughing.

"The oldies remind me of today's best songs," her father said. "They come right at you. They're direct, fresh."

"What about the sixties?" Hannah asked, wondering why he picked the fifties over what she always thought were his defining years.

"The sixties don't count," he said. "A self-induced fog, to get to the other side."

"What side was that?"

He squeezed her hand. "You had to live in the fifties to understand. Everything was a certain way." He spoke in a slow, monotone voice. His face was frozen—Parkinson's "masked face," a loss of animation caused by slowing and rigidity of the muscles. At first she had trouble getting used to it. Before Parkinson's, before it progressed so far, he was wildly expressive, like a crazed orchestra conductor.

What could you do? she thought. You remember what was; you deal with what is.

"You couldn't think, or do, anything off the beaten path," he said. "I know we went too far. But your generation corrected that, found a middle path. A way to be your individual, eccentric self, yet still take part in work and society. Back then we couldn't. There were two choices: in or out. Now you can be in, and out at the same time."

Oh, Daddy, she thought. He could still get to the point like no one else.

He squeezed her hand again. He's so weak, she thought. All the power he exerted over me, gone. The big bad wolf is …

"That's why you don't need drugs," he said. "Like we did, to break the spell."

"You know I never do that."

"Forgive me. You never stop bringing up your children. No matter how old you—or they—get." He smiled. "You're looking at me like I'm stupid. That's good; it means we did our job. You're supposed to turn out smarter than us and think we're stupid. If you don't think we're stupid, we failed."

She smiled. He seemed unusually tender.

"Did I ever tell you about the night in 1968, when my car broke down on the New York State Thruway?"

She shook her head no. She had heard it a hundred times.

"I had a '58 Chevy Bel Air; it was cherry. My father bought it for me from an old lady; she kept it garaged, barely drove it. Dumbbell that I was, I never checked the oil. It threw a connecting rod on the Thruway. I got towed to a garage; it was totaled, so I sold it to the mechanic for a couple hundred dollars. I had to take the Greyhound to New York City the next morning. I stayed in a rat hotel in Herkimer, New York. It was the night Elvin Hayes—'The Big E'—and Houston beat Lew Alcindor and UCLA, ending a forty-seven-game win streak. I was watching the game on a small TV at the end of the bar. Suddenly, a coaster flew right by me. I didn't pay much attention. Then, another one. I looked down at the end of the bar, saw some rednecks smiling. I turned back to the game. They started throwing quarters at me. Those things are hard; I had to keep my eyes peeled. Then they called me a marijuana monkey." He laughed. "Which I was."

He paused. "I'd like to fire a Winchester rifle before I die."

Hannah laughed. "I love you, Daddy." She choked up, couldn't imagine life without him. After years of wanting nothing but. She said, "Let's play Rosie again. 'Angel Baby.'"

An hour later, she said good night to her father, thinking he was having a good day. Or maybe she just wasn't staying long enough.

In the hallway, she said, "I'm sorry I don't come more, Mom."

"It's fine, dear," her mother said. "You've got enough to do with the strike; we're very proud of you. What's your TV schedule this week? When are you on?"

eighteen

Hannah and Shay entered Lewis's office as the phone was ringing.

Lewis picked it up, listened, and then said, "Send him in."

The guy who opened the door was Shay's height, in his twenties; fair complexion, reddish-brown hair. He was wearing jeans, work boots, and an unzipped black-nylon Machinists jacket over a white tee.

"This is Sean Hamill," Lewis said.

Hamill shook hands with Shay and Hannah; then he moved away and leaned against the wall.

"Sean's your twin," Lewis said to Shay. "He stays with you."

"Where you from, kid?" Shay asked.

"West Side. Hell's Kitchen."

Shay turned to Lewis. "He's a pro?"

"He's a machinist. He worked in a shop by the river. Don't ask questions."

"What did you want to see me about?" Shay asked.

"We got a call from Lambal's people. They want to come back to the table."

"I'll bet they do."

Lewis came around the desk and looked at Hamill; the bodyguard stepped outside, closing the door behind him.

Lewis turned to Shay after Hamill left the room. "I want you to make a deal. They're going to come with concessions. Take them, add a little, and settle. When it's done, we turn over what we have on Lambal to the police. Let them handle it."

"They won't nail him," Shay said.

"Maybe, maybe not. But it's not up to our members to pay the price. We can't hold this negotiation hostage to getting Lambal for Jack's death."

"We're not," Hannah said. "We're taking a hard line because we have to. They're trying to take away too much."

"Well, they're going to stop," Lewis said. "They're coming back to the table."

"How do you know that?" Shay asked. "This deal's done, isn't it?"

Lewis shook his head. "No, it's your deal. You make it."

"You made it, didn't you?"

"Close it out," Lewis said. "You're going to get a lot. You're going to look good."

"So the boycott's off?" Hannah said.

"The boycott never got started. You announced it, and they caved in."

"*Who* caved in, that's what I want to know," Shay said.

"You took us out too far. The autoworkers are hot. The feds are calling. Everybody wants this to stop. You can't commit more than you can deliver. How are we supposed to run this boycott? Where do we get the people?"

Shay got up and walked to the door.

"You with me on this, John?" Lewis asked.

Shay walked out the door without looking back. Hannah stormed out behind him.

Hamill came to the doorway. Lewis nodded; he followed Shay down the hall.

Shay sat up late in front of the TV. Anne came down in her robe. Plush job, silly crest—an impulse buy at a luxury hotel they stayed at a couple of years ago. He had insisted.

"Anything interesting?" she asked, glancing at the television.

"Bald eagles can fly at ten thousand feet, lift a four-pound salmon. Condors have a ten-foot wingspan. Elk are deer. Old Faithful erupts at intervals of forty-five minutes to two hours. Badgers are hyperaggressive." After a pause, he added, "Just can't sleep."

"What's up?"

He clicked off the set. "They think I'm pushing this too far."

"Don't you always?"

He smiled. "Do I?"

"I would say so. But I like that about you." After a few seconds, she said, "Speaking of overdoing it, how's the foot? You see the physical therapist?"

"He told me to lay off running and biking for two weeks. He said I really should be on the DL six weeks, but I'm such a knucklehead he knew that's as long as I'd wait."

She smiled. "Tell me about the strike."

He took a breath. "There are a lot of people involved. A lot of lives."

He looked at her. "Including yours, and Michael's."

The attempt on his life had shaken her. But she didn't skip a beat, just ran her fingers through his hair. "You'll do the right thing." After a pause, she asked, "How's Hannah doing?"

"Good. I'm glad I bumped her up."

She nodded. "What's on the agenda tomorrow?"

"Back to the table."

"Your call?"

"Lewis. He says Lambal wants a deal. But I think Lewis made it already."

"It's got to be your deal," Anne said.

"How'd you get so tough?" Shay asked, squeezing her biceps. "Must have been the factory work."

Anne's father had been team lead in fuselage assembly at an aircraft plant outside Omaha before his early death from a heart attack; he got all the mechanical training he needed as a kid, fixing equipment and building contraptions on the family farm, where they grew corn. She worked at the factory summers during high school and college, filling bins with small parts and tools from the warehouse stores and delivering them to assembly stations on a full-size three-wheeler bicycle she used to get around the cavernous plant, with the totes attached to the handlebars or in a wagon pulled behind.

She went to Nebraska, got her MEd in special education. She came East fifteen years ago looking for sophisticated people. Now she wanted to move back, to get away from them.

"I've always been tough. Farm girl."

"Tougher than us New Yorkers?"

"That's no trick. That's why people from the Midwest and New York mate. It's a DNA correction—for the New Yorker."

Shay laughed.

She stood up. "You want to talk? I have to get up early."

"Meeting?"

She nodded. "A parent. And her lawyer."

"Just you?"

"You kidding? We're going in full battle-rattle—special-ed staff, the kid's teacher. We're bringing the union rep and district lawyer."

She shook her head. "The kid's got real problems. We're trying so hard, pulling out all the stops to help him. He got frustrated the other day, threw himself on the ground, and scraped a knee. The mom took him to the hospital. The docs called the cops, standard procedure. Now she wants a meeting." She pushed out a breath. "Nothing we do is good enough. Administration told us to pull our files, black out names. I said, 'say redacted.'"

"That'll show 'em who they're dealing with."

"Damn tootin'."

nineteen

El Paso

Shay flew to El Paso and was escorted to the third floor of the ICE field office and processing center on Montana Avenue. A man came into the reception area. He was Shay's height, dark blue suit, nondescript tie. He had a buzz cut, linebacker face, military bearing. He stuck out his hand.

"Mr. Shay, I'm Agent Tom Moss. Bureau of Immigration and Customs Enforcement, Department of Homeland Security—ICE, DHS. I'm the AFOD—assistant field office director. Thanks for coming, sir."

ICE enforces federal immigration, customs, and air security laws. It's the long arm of DHS, with a mandate to deter, interdict, and investigate threats arising from the movement of people and goods into and out of the country.

"No problem," Shay said. "Sounds like you've got an odd duck on your hands."

"Tough to line them up in a row," Moss said, smiling over his shoulder as he led Shay down the corridor. He opened the door to a room and nodded for Shay to go in first.

Two men were sitting at the conference table. One of them stood up, came around the table, and offered his hand. "Agent Donell Ramsey," he said, "supervisory detention and deportation officer."

He was a thin black guy with a Deep South marker in his voice.

"You're the SDDO," Shay said, shaking his hand.

Both agents grinned. "Now you've got the hang of it, sir," Ramsey said.

"Please sit down, Mr. Shay," Moss said.

Shay glanced at the man at the end of the table as he took a seat. Calderon returned the look and then turned to the ICE agents.

"I would like to speak with Mr. Shay in private," he said.

Ramsey looked at Moss, who nodded. They both got up.

"No problem," Moss said. "Mr. Calderon has committed no crime, nor is he a suspect in any investigation."

After the ICE agents left the room, Calderon stood and approached Shay. He was five foot eight, thin, medium-to-dark complected. He had a well-groomed short beard and dark brown eyes. He lifted the pitcher of water and flicked his eyes at Shay's glass.

"Thanks," Shay said.

Calderon poured the water. He brought the pitcher back to his seat and poured himself a glass. He sat down.

"What can I do for you, Mr. Calderon?" Shay asked.

"Do you work at Lambal Interior?"

"I work directly for the United Machinists."

Calderon nodded as he took a sip of water. He got up again, walked to the window. Outside, he could see the bridge to Juarez; between the bridge and the Federal Building were a bunch of rundown industrial buildings. As he looked at the Franklin mountains, the southernmost tip of the Rockies and the Continental Divide, he thought about his wife and daughters. He had sent them to her sister's house in Salina Cruz, a seaport on the Pacific coast of the Mexican state of Oaxaca, for safety.

He turned back to Shay.

"I am a line supervisor at the Lambal plant in Ciudad Juarez. You are familiar with our operation there?"

Shay nodded. Lambal had opened the plant in 1990 to take advantage of the maquiladora initiative, Mexico's plan to lower unemployment in the border towns. The program allowed non-Mexican companies to import raw materials, parts, and machinery duty-free. The companies processed and assembled their products with low-cost Mexican labor and sent them to the United States; duty was only charged on the value added in Mexico. In colonial Mexico, *maquila* was the charge millers collected for processing grain.

"I can imagine what you think of us," Calderon said. "We work for a small portion of your wages. But it is good for us. We are able to have families, homes. We send our children to school, buy them clothing."

Shay knew the plant was very well regarded within the company. He had spoken to a Lambal manager who spent a couple of years there. He told Shay the workers were eager, came in with a clean slate. They took to industrial equipment—had no resistance to it; it wasn't something they had been doing for twenty years and were sick of. He said they were like sponges, absorbed everything you threw at them. That they were hardworking, wanted to get ahead. He told Shay he got four to five times more requests for schooling assistance there than from the workforce in the States.

Calderon asked, "Do you know Oaxaca, Mr. Shay?"

Shay shook his head.

"I come from there. I am Mixtec. We are Indian, the poorest of the poor. I crossed the border to work the farms. I got into the factories; then this job at Lambal, in Juarez."

He smiled. "But I understand, as we move up, it is at your expense."

Shay remembered his exchange with Lewis about tug-of-war—children's game, adult blood sport. "We're fighting to keep what we have; you're struggling to get what you need," he said. "I don't blame you. If I were in your position I would do the same. But you must understand—I will try to take this job back from you."

Calderon smiled. "Don't worry about that. The job is no longer mine. Not after what I have seen." He paused. "And who is after me."

Calderon sat down. Above him on the wall was a sepia-toned photograph of Constable John Selman, the outlaw turned peace officer who shot John Wesley Hardin in 1895 at the Acme Saloon, just down the block from the Federal Building. Back when El Paso was a stop on the Butterfield Stage, and the Six-Shooter Capital of the World.

"Have you seen the factory in China?" Calderon asked.

Shay shook his head.

"China is a crazy country," Calderon said. "Crazier than Mexico. Did you ever see workers wearing flip-flops operating press brakes?"

Press brakes are heavy-tonnage machines that shear, punch, or form sheets of metal. It didn't surprise Shay—people making next to nothing don't buy steel-toe boots.

"I know my job very well, Mr. Shay," Calderon said. "The company sent me to Shenzhen when they built the plant, to train the workers. I spent six months in China. I was sent back two months ago, to upgrade the production processes. One day, I left some papers at work that I needed to review. I returned at night to get them; I was friendly with a janitor, he would let me in. The production line was in full operation."

"So?" Shay said.

Calderon glanced at the door and then back at Shay. "There is no night shift."

"What do you mean?"

"We operate one shift. We don't have enough work to run a second."

"What was going on?"

"I rang the buzzer at the factory. One of the managers came to the door. I could see a lot of workers, the machines running. He told me they were doing maintenance."

"Sounds right."

Calderon shook his head. "No. As part of my job, I would have known this. I would not have been refused entry into the plant."

He reached for the glass, took another sip of water. "And that would not explain why two Chinese men are following me in Juarez."

Standing behind a one-way mirror in an adjacent room, Moss and Ramsey looked at one another at the mention of the Chinese tails.

They listened as Shay offered the Mexican a plane ticket on the spot, to come to New York.

The ICE agents decided to cut Calderon loose; it was a private sector matter. But they caught a whiff of something, and agreed to push it up the chain.

twenty

Back in New York, Shay deposited Calderon at the New York Marriott Eastside. Shay told him someone from the union would call the next morning. He gave Calderon a voucher for meals at the hotel. He recommended the plantains, Cafferty's favorite.

The next morning, Hamill was waiting outside Shay's house. As Shay approached the car, he waved to a neighbor walking his dog. Every kid on the block wanted a dog. But Shay never saw a kid walking a dog, only their parents.

"It's nice around here," Hamill said, leaning back against the driver's side door. "We had to write a poem about fall once in high school. Got me sent to the office."

Shay had his hand on the door handle to the backseat; Hamill wasn't getting into the car. He bit. "What did it say?"

"Leaves change color. Then drop dead."

Shay laughed. "That's good."

"They thought I was messin' with them," Hamill said, getting into the car.

Hamill took a different route than Shay normally drove. It didn't take long to get him going, with his black Dodge Challenger idling in traffic—not the thing a 6.4-liter Hemi V8 with 470 neighing horses wants to do. The dual-pipe exhaust made the point loud and clear.

"What the hell are these people doing? They're red-light hunters. They go slow on purpose, just to catch one."

Shay was going through some paperwork in the back. He smiled.

"Oh look, two buddies," Hamill said, waving his hand in disgust. "One in the left lane, one in the right, both going the same speed. Isn't that sweet?" He flashed the headlights, honked. "What's next? One of those goofs who plunks himself in the left lane ten miles before the turn? Every time I get in the car, this shit happens."

Shay tried to concentrate.

"That's what's great about NASCAR," Hamill said, looking in the mirror. "Open wheel, F1 … sure, they got the technology, they go faster. Their drivers and fans say, NASCAR? It's just a car, it's what you drive every day. But that's the point—it's what you drive every day, only you drive the shit out of it."

He grinned. "Like you on the Van Wyck. Number 14 would be proud. You know Tony Stewart drives a Super Sport?"

Shay smiled as Hamill stomped on the pedal and broke free in a burst of torque. The car exploded forward: quick veer left, correction right. Shay slid on the seat until the belt tensioner kicked in. Hamill shook his head when the car settled in the lane.

"Fuckin' climate change. Gonna ruin cars."

Shay laughed. "How old are you?" he asked, putting the papers in his briefcase.

"Twenty-five."

"How'd you get to be a machinist?"

"Trade classes in high school."

"How'd you get into shooting?"

Hamill glanced in the rearview mirror. "You mean security?"

"Whatever."

"There was some trouble on the job. A fight between the foreman and union rep. I stepped in. End of problem with the foreman."

"You watching me *for me*, or for Lewis?" Shay asked.

Hamill looked in the mirror and didn't reply.

Shay remembered the kid came from Hell's Kitchen. He thought about the apartment his father gave him, a rent-stabilized studio on

West Forty-Fourth Street at the northeast corner of Tenth Avenue. His father had it while he was a firefighter; he crashed there after long shifts, handed Shay the keys when he wanted to move to Manhattan. Told him how he used to see Broderick Crawford in the neighborhood, from the old show *Highway Patrol*. Took him around, introduced him to the hookers and bookies. Made a point of telling him he knew the women as neighborhood people, not professionals. The girls backed him up, swore his father was the best people they knew.

He suddenly remembered how ticked his father got when he called him a fireman. "Firemen stoke boilers," he told him—"I'm a fire*fighter*." He recalled how, after a few shots of rye one night with his firehouse buddies in the den at their home, one of the guys described what they did—"we put the wet stuff on the red stuff."

Shay laughed. Hamill looked up in the mirror.

They were on the West Side Highway now, speeding alongside the Hudson. Shay loved the look of the river in the city—broad, flat, eye level. It was one of the legendary waterways of the world, flowing from headwaters in the Adirondacks, becoming a tidal estuary south of Troy as it started to feel the pulse of the ocean, the fresh and salty water comingling as it got closer to New York harbor and the Atlantic. The Indians called it Mahicantuck—great waters in constant motion, or river that flows two ways; the current ran north and south below Troy, changing with the tide. He remembered being struck by its history as a kid—an ancient travel route for Native Americans; Henry Hudson sailing upriver on the *Half Moon*, opening the fur trade as he searched for the Northwest Passage. Hudson Valley wheat and timber, shipped downriver to New York for export to the world. The Erie Canal, opening the river to the Great Lakes and the West.

Shay reconnected to the city's history after 9/11. He read a couple of books that traced its origins, the early years. New York was at the heart of America's push into the modern world. And it had been attacked because of that modernity.

They got off the highway at Fifty-Sixth Street. Shay saw a huge ship docked as they made the left turn. He wondered if it was the *Queen Mary 2*.

"Probably not big enough," Hamill said, when Shay asked. Hamill laughed. "How the hell would I know?"

Shay smiled. "Turn that thing up."

Hamill turned the dial on the car stereo. It was the Dalom Kids and Splash. The band played Mqanga—Soweto township music—mixed with pop and electronics. Lewis had given Shay the CD; he gave it to Hamill to play on the ride in to the city.

Shay bobbed his head as they edged through Midtown traffic. Stopped in a jam, he watched a crane lift huge iron girders toward the upper floors of a building under construction. The beams swayed back and forth, dangled out over the street, directly above them. As he glanced ahead to see if traffic was starting to move, he thought about what hung over the city now, always, after 9/11. The whole country, really. Between terrorism, war, and the economy, there was a bit of dread every day.

Then he thought about how, after 9/11—even after the 2008 financial meltdown—he didn't dwell on working-class authenticity like he used to, or on the differences between New Yorkers. After the World Trade Center, he chose to see them as more alike than not. It had claimed them all together—the Wall Street hotshot, the Port Authority electrician, the Windows on the World waiter—in its indiscriminate slaughter.

"They should have put them back up the way they were," Shay said out loud.

Hamill looked in the rearview mirror.

"The Twin Towers," Shay said. "Have a memorial for the families and the nation, sure. But build them identical on the outside, with a hardened interior. Forget the architectural dress-up; make New York the way it was. *That* would be a fitting tribute."

Shay paused. "What drives you crazy if you're trying to get at someone?"

Hamill grinned in the mirror. "When they just keep going about their business like nothing's happened. No matter what you do."

They couldn't make a dent in the crosstown traffic. Hamill tapped his fingers on the steering wheel, glanced over his shoulder. "Best hardwood flooring ad."

Shay thought for a second. "Don't have one."

"Just say no to rugs."

Shay laughed. Kept his head down, working again.

"Jets fan?" Hamill asked.

"Packers."

Hamill paused. "Don't you hate Belichick?" Sticking with the AFC East.

Shay had done a 360 on that one. "Imagine him superintendent of your kid's school, or heading up a drive to cure cancer. His obsession with detail. The way he attacks weakness. The way he always seems … to find a way."

Hamill nodded. "He thinks so much it hurts. That's the look on his face."

"Best Ken Singleton joke," Shay said. The ex-Oriole was a Yankee broadcaster.

"When a leftfielder lost the ball in the sun, he said, 'How can a thing that's ninety-three million miles away be causing a problem down here in the Bronx?'"

Shay laughed. "When a squirrel spent the ballgame on the foul pole netting," he said. "After the cameraman showed it about ten times, Singleton said, 'You better stop showing that; it's going to encourage the other squirrels to do it.'"

Hamill's turn to laugh. Shay got a kick out of him. He felt like he was back in the shops, wisecracking the world into submission.

"Best thing you'd like to see in baseball," Shay said.

"Besides the varsity coach not cutting me in high school?"

Shay kept to himself that he did better. He played second base on a high-school team that went to States twice. They won on their second try. It always happens that way.

"The people sitting behind home plate, on cell phones, waving? Cover their faces with those blur circles, like they do for perp walks or wardrobe malfunctions."

Hamill turned his head to the side. "And less replays. Use the time to show us good-looking women in the stands."

Shay smiled. "You know how they play the first few bars of a guy's favorite song when he comes to the plate? On Memorial Day, July 4, 9/11? The players pick the national anthem or 'God Bless America.'"

Hamill pulled up in front of the Marriott on Lexington Avenue at Forty-Ninth Street. He gave the valet a twenty, told him to take good care of the car. Inside, they took the elevator upstairs. Hamill leaned against the wall in the hallway as Shay entered the room.

Lambal was standing at the coffee trolley. He nodded when he saw Shay.

"Everybody ready?" Shay asked, ignoring him and moving to his seat.

Negotiators on both sides rustled, took their seats. Hannah sat next to Shay.

Shay looked across the table. "It's your meeting," he said.

Lambal turned to Lyons, who handed him a folder. Lambal leafed through it. He looked up at Shay.

"This has gone on long enough," he said. "It's hurt both of us. We want to get back to business—our business, your business."

Lambal nodded to the young woman at the end of the table. She stood up, placed new folders in front of each member of the Machinists' team. She didn't smile at Hannah this time, after the cold shoulder she got at the previous session.

"This is what we propose," Lambal said, after giving everyone a moment to scan the document. "First of all, a 2-percent increase in pay for the life of the contract."

"We boosted productivity more than that—it's a take back, not an increase," Shay said. "Not to mention cost of living—you check food prices lately? Or would that be your personal chef?" Channeling Cafferty—something he would say.

"That brings me to item two," Lambal said, unruffled. "In addition to the cross-the-board raise, we will apply merit increases for all section teams, based on increases in productivity. We will pay these as a one-shot bonus of twenty-five hundred dollars per person, to reflect past efforts. We will apply them annually after that, based on a calculation that reflects the previous year's work. The details are in your packet."

The offer was up from last session. But not as much as Shay thought it would be after Lewis went behind his back and told him he was going to get a sweeter deal.

"Next is job security," Lambal said. "We will pledge to keep our plants open in the United States, if you work with us to make them more efficient. As a gesture of goodwill, we will consult with the union about siting the second plant in China."

"How about, instead, shutting the one you've already got there?" Hannah said.

Lambal looked at her. "I cannot dismantle my company as it is presently constituted. I can only look forward."

"And keep that hanging over our heads," Hannah said.

"What do you want me to do?" Lambal asked. "Roll back the clock to the fifties? When the Japanese were making plastic flowers and transistor radios? When the Chinese were cheering every time a rice shoot popped out of the ground, instead of churning out everything I can in factories that operate at a fraction of my costs?"

He looked back and forth at the line of union negotiators. "Do you think we like this? Don't you think we would give anything to get back what we both once had? Well, it can't be done. It's not going to happen. The gravy train is gone. The only thing we can do is roll up our sleeves and find another way. That means more initiative, more inventiveness … and, yes, more productivity."

"Or you take your business elsewhere," Hannah said.

"You know this isn't only about costs," Lambal said. "You have to be in China to sell in China. All the major automakers are there, demanding their suppliers follow. We have to deliver just-in-time to their joint-venture plants, match Chinese supplier prices. The country has 1.3 billion people, and they're going to need a lot of cars. If I—if we—are successful there, those profits will drive R&D and tooling work in the States. That's more jobs, more money for your members."

"Sounds like you already have extra money," Hannah said. "Why pay executive bonuses at a time like this? You're shoving it in our faces."

"Because we have to keep our management talent. Otherwise, when they see a company sinking, they're going to leave."

"Keep the 'talent' that got you into this? What are you paying for? Pulse?"

That's got to be in a slam, she thought—even though she had stolen it from another union leader. I'm going to do it. She felt like she had to make clear decisions on what to commit her energy to, in case it was not going to be there later.

Later, now, maybe coming sooner than later.

"The rest of the offer is in the packet," Lambal said. "I would urge you to examine it carefully, and then decide if this is something you can take to your membership."

"We'll bring it to a vote," Shay said, "if everything you produce in Mexico or China gets sold only in Latin America and Asia."

"You know I can't promise that," Lambal said. "We serve a world market, operate a global supply chain. I have to ship product where needed, when needed. If demand surges in one market and I can't meet it, I have to ship from somewhere else."

Shay knew that was true. But Lambal also used it as a smokescreen. He shipped goods from low-wage Mexican and Chinese plants to North American and European markets to sidestep the higher-paid production workers there.

"That's not good enough," Shay said.

"I'm sorry to hear that," Lambal said. He nodded to Lyons.

"Is there anything else we can clarify today?" Lyons asked.

"I had a little traffic accident the other day," Shay said. He paused. "What I want to know is, when are you going to stop trying to run us off the road?"

"You must be kidding," Lyons said.

"Am I? Like you're kidding with this offer?"

"This is a sound offer, the only way we can keep operating without government help," Lambal said. He heaved a breath. "Unless you want me to end up in a hearing room on Capitol Hill like the automakers a few years back. Dressed down by a bunch of numbskull congressmen who wouldn't know a chassis line from an aquarium."

Shay almost laughed; Lambal hit that nail on the head. "It's not enough," he said.

"Do you have some other things you would like us to consider?"

"No more layoffs. No spike in insurance premiums. No 'second tier' for new hires, where guys making thirteen dollars an hour work side by side with guys making twenty-six dollars. A 4 percent raise. Switch back the pensions to defined payout, from defined contribution."

Shay paused. "And the China plant gets shut."

"That's impossible, and you know it," Lambal said.

"I guess I'll have to drive extra careful then, won't I?"

twenty-one

The jet backed away from the gate. Shay watched the ground worker wave two fluorescent wands, directing the cockpit crew. He thought about what the archbishop said—how Jack claimed the Irish were natural labor leaders because they were so contrary. He wondered again if he was taking too hard a line.

He remembered Jack had showed him his family tree. Shay didn't know much about his own ancestry, just a story his father told him—how his grandfather, Shay's great-grandfather, was once mercilessly teasing his sister, until she said, "If you don't stop, I'll tell everybody why you really had to leave Ireland." He shut up like a clam, didn't say a word the rest of the day, Shay's father said.

Jack had asked him about his family history. Shay made a joke, which he kind of believed: "The only thing Americans care about family history is that they're happy they got out of all those places where all families think about is their history."

After the plane reached altitude, he turned to Hannah. "Are we making the right move, or taking it too far?"

"You know me. Push it."

"I wonder if you know how badly things can turn out."

She was looking out the window. They were above the clouds. It was all-white tuft below, inviting but fall-through, as far as the eye could see.

"I saw Jack die. He tried to push me out. I screamed no, but he kept pushing. He had no strength; I could barely feel his hands. He wanted me out, before something worse happened. Then his hands dropped to his side, and he died."

"Oh jeez," Shay said. He put his hand on hers; it was shaking. "I'm so sorry."

The plane touched down in Cleveland. Shay and Hannah were whisked to the union hall. Hundreds of people milled in front of the building as the car pulled around back.

"The room is packed," the driver said. "The crowd overflowed into the hallways, out into the lot. We're stringing wire to connect outside speakers to the PA system."

They entered the local through the back door. People greeted them warmly. They entered a small room, where the local leadership had assembled.

"Thanks for the crowd," Shay said.

"It was easy," the local's president said. "You two are a big draw."

"We've got people from all the unions, not just Machinists," another official said. "Steel, construction, truckers … you name it, they came out."

"Let's not keep them waiting," Shay said.

He stood in the wings as he was being introduced by the local's president. As he rehearsed what he was going to say, he remembered his confirmation again. There was a big row in the house when he wouldn't take his father's middle name, Joseph. He wanted Michael, after the archangel who strode forth with his sword to right all wrongs.

Thinking that was over the top—another Irish Catholic trait.

Then thinking … maybe not. Maybe it was just what was needed today.

"Brothers and sisters, I'd like you to give a warm welcome to John Shay," the speaker concluded.

Shay walked onto the stage. Everyone was standing, clapping, hooting. People held up placards identifying their union, zinging it to Lambal. Shay raised his hands several times to quell the noise. "Thank you for the welcome," he began.

"You ain't seen nothin'," someone yelled. The crowd got louder.

Shay held up his hands. "If you shout any more, you won't have anything left for the line."

"Hell we won't," someone called out. Everyone laughed.

"Hell you won't is right," Shay said. "Because I'm going to ask you to go back to the line. I'm going to ask you to go back to the line and then make a new one—at the dealerships, where Lambal interiors fill those new cars. And then I want you to make another one—at the supplier plants, where Lambal gets his materials, subcomponents."

The crowd cheered.

"I just flew in from New York," Shay said. "Lambal came back, made another offer. He's moving in the right direction. Some will tell you he's come as far as he can, and we should take it."

"We're with you, John," someone yelled. "You tell us when."

The trade unionists whistled and cheered.

Shay raised his hands. "Look, this is how I see it," he said. "They've been rolling us back for decades in manufacturing. First they went to the South, where there were no unions. Then they packed their bags for Mexico, with the maquiladoras and NAFTA. Now they've stamped their passports for China. We all know why they did it. Competition is stiff, and that crap overseas doesn't cost a dime to make. So we bent a little, helped them get their house in order—hoping they'd keep the jobs here. But it's gone on long enough. We lost millions of jobs in the process."

He paused. "Used to be, you could always go to a factory and get a job. Grimy, ordinary work, maybe … but it was a job, and it was a start."

"Damn straight!" a woman shouted from the audience.

"Now those jobs aren't here, just when we need them," Shay said. "Every one of those jobs now is precious. And I'll be damned if I'm going to stand here and tell you I cut a deal that sent more jobs to those metal shacks they call factories in China, while you have to pack up and move, pull your kids out of school, away from their friends. While you have to leave your own friends, your parents behind, shuffle off like some packhorse to the next town that hasn't yet shut its plants."

The crowd erupted in applause. "Shay! Shay! Shay!" they chanted.

He raised his hands. "And let me tell you one more thing, before they give me the hook. Everyone is talking about the 'new' economy. We're all going to be service workers, information workers, knowledge workers. I know there's some decent jobs there—good-paying, clean, ways to move up. If you want to, study for those jobs, train for them. Let your kids know that's the way to go. But I'm here tonight to tell Lambal Interior, and all American companies, that wherever you're going with this economy, you will bring us along. We're not some old plant or piece of equipment you leave out back to rust. We built this place. We will continue to build this place. America will always need manufacturing to be strong. All those people who say manufacturing isn't important anymore—then how come it made China so strong?"

Someone yelled, "Hell yeah!"

"So when you build fabrication equipment for your high-tech chip plants … When you need high-quality machining for advanced medical products …" He looked around the room. "When push comes to shove in that crazy world out there, and you have to arm, and supply, the finest fighting force in the world …"

The crowd stood and roared.

"You will bring us with you."

Shay held up his hands as the crowd kept cheering. He had grown up around firefighters, cops, aircraft mechanics, factory workers. Like Anne, with her feelings about the Midwest, he wanted to get away. When he did, and saw the other side, he felt the pull back. Part of him had left this place; part of him felt out of place without it. It felt good to be back. Especially now when they needed him, when they needed each other. These were the good guys, the way the country was going.

"Because we are the workforce," Shay said over the din. "And you will reckon with this force."

As Shay walked off the stage, people applauded, smiled, smacked high fives. Offstage, union officials clapped, patted him on the shoulder as he moved past.

He was nabbed outside by a news crew. The reporter asked him for a comment.

"Just keeping everyone's spirits up," he said.

"Do you think America will respond to your plight?" the reporter asked.

Shay was opening the door to the car. He stopped and turned to her. She was in her early twenties. "What does your father do for a living?" he asked her.

The crewman lowered his lens. The reporter twirled her finger to keep rolling.

She looked at Shay. "He's in sales."

"His father?"

"A carpenter."

"Before him?"

"He worked on the Erie Canal locks."

"I can hear the pride in your voice when you say that," Shay said.

Hannah leaned across the car seat to listen.

"Not that you can't be proud of sales, what your father does," he said. "I'm only asking America this—as we move forward into a new economy, don't forget your past. Your fathers and mothers, grandfathers and grandmothers, great-grandfathers and great-grandmothers—the men and women who built this country, with their hands and tools. And don't forget that past is still present. As you sit at a computer workstation, talk around a conference table, do research in a lab … don't forget we're still here, still working with our hands, with tools, making the things you need. Don't forget that behind the canned food on the shelves, there are people working at food-processing plants. That behind the coffeemaker, the microwave, the lawnmower, there's a toolmaker crafting master tooling for the production runs, operators at molding machines churning out parts, assemblers putting them together. Don't forget, in our case, every time you sit in your car, someone built the seat, assembled and fitted the dash, attached the turn-signal stalk to the steering column. As you go about your busy lives, don't forget us. Help us get what we all need—a secure living, the thing we all want for our families."

He got in the car and turned to Hannah. He thought she was looking at him differently.

The driver dropped them at the Intercontinental Hotel and Conference Center on Carnegie Avenue, another union spot. They stepped out of the elevator on their floor.

Shay checked the numbers and arrows on the brass plate on the wall.

"I'm left; you're right."

Hannah nodded. "That was a great speech you gave. You really touched people."

Shay had an urge to pull her close. He remembered her poetry slam; at the party afterward, they drank and talked, kissed a little. It took everything he had that night to pull away. He wondered what she was thinking right now.

"The more I get back into this, the more I remember what drew me in in the first place," he said. "It seems like everyone we're pulling for has disappeared from view in American life, at least in the media and culture. The only time you see them is truck ads, or on *Dirty Jobs* or *Undercover Boss*."

Hannah laughed. "We're small potatoes. Nobody makes stuff anymore, they just 'arrange' things—make deals, push paper. Stride around like world-beaters, those stupid little phones against their ears. Figure out angles, ways to separate us from our money—without doing anything themselves but the figuring. That's 'hardworking' today."

Shay almost laughed at her dig about mobile phones—she was wedded to her smartphone. And you could hardly call a software developer plumbing the depths of search, or a biomedical researcher decoding the genome of the AIDS virus, paper pushers. But she was right: more and more people didn't do manual work; a lot of them didn't even know what it was. Labor had become the country's autonomic system, toiling behind the scenes, in a country that was splitting in two, an ever-widening gulf separating the have-lots and have-nots.

He looked at her. She smiled, pressed her trembling fingers against her jeans, thought about what the next stage would be. More tremors on the same side—arm, leg, even the chin. She ran her mind up and down her side, trying to sense anything. There would be slowing movement too. Changes in posture and gait. Feeling clumsy, unsteady balance. She had already felt that once.

She wanted him to hold her.

“It’s late,” she said, kissing him on the cheek.

They headed in opposite directions down the hallway to their rooms.

twenty-two

Bill Lewis sat at the head of the conference table in the boardroom at headquarters. Above him on the wall was a commemorative painting of the seven machinists who met during lunch break in a stapler factory in Queens in 1923 to found the union.

Lewis looked up as Shay came in. Thinking, I have to do it—it doesn't have to feel good. He swept his gaze around the council members—including two who were spreading the word he was a preferential promotion. Nothing KKK, just a racial tinge; he didn't go overboard, graded this stuff on a curve. Still …

"I think we're set to go," Lewis said, cupping his hands on the table. "I called this meeting of the executive council to motion that John Shay be removed as chief negotiator on the Lambal strike. Furthermore, I move that he be suspended from his position with the Machinists, with pay, until such time as we can fully investigate his actions during the strike, and overall performance as an executive in the union."

He looked around the room. "Discussion?"

"Second," said one of the officials.

Shay looked at Lewis. He couldn't blame him. It might even be the right call.

"Hold it, for Chrissakes," someone said.

Everyone turned to the elderly man.

"What are you railroading this man for?" he asked. "For beating the stuffing out of Lambal?"

"Ted, we all know what you've done for this union, and we hold you in the highest regard," Lewis said. "But John ignored a specific directive to accept the current offer on the table. He bypassed the council and went to the autoworkers and asked for their support in a nationwide boycott. Then, when they said they didn't like the idea, he went ahead and announced it anyway, on national television, without consulting us."

"So what?" the man said. His name was Ted Sparks. He held an honorific position on the council, a holdover from his earlier days of union activism.

"What the heck did he do, anyway?" Sparks asked. "Not stop doing what he believed was best for the strikers? Not take an offer when he thought he could get a better one? Since when is that a crime in this union?"

"Ted, this is a *union*. It's not a one-man show," Lewis said.

"Well, maybe it takes one man to show us the way sometimes," Sparks said.

One woman too, Shay thought. Lewis had pulled him aside before the meeting to tell him what was going down; he told him the board wanted to dump Hannah too. Shay convinced him to let her off with a reprimand.

Sparks opened a folder. He slid it across the table to Shay.

"Now, I know you've all seen these," he said, looking around the room. "But you sure as hell haven't talked about them at this meeting."

Shay leafed through a stack of letters, faxes, e-mail printouts.

"Let me read one," Sparks said.

He motioned to Shay to push back the folder. Sparks picked up the top sheet.

"Dear Machinists Union," he read. "This letter is to support you in your effort to gain a fair deal for your members in your strike against Lambal Interior. We are a small group of workers in the South, trying to unionize a health-care facility down here. We take care of old people but only get paid the minimum wage. We have to lift them, bathe them, assist them around the home all day long. It is very hard and tiring work. Thank you for inspiring us to work that much harder to get a union."

Sparks put it down and picked up another.

"Dear Union. I am a maintenance man at a software company in Seattle. I see these kids strutting around all day, barking back and forth at each other like teenagers, drinking Coke and clicking away at their keyboards. These people think computers can do everything. They don't know a thing about manual labor. You are a reminder of how hard some of us have to work to get by. Keep up the good work."

Sparks shuffled through the stack. Shay watched his arthritic hands struggle with the paper. He remembered Sparks was closing in on ninety; he was born between the First World War and the Depression. As a teen, he marched for the Fair Labor Standards Act of 1938, which created the forty-hour workweek. The old-timer had a bumper sticker on his car: "Unions—the folks who brought you the weekend."

"Here's one more," Sparks said. "Dear Mr. Shay and Ms. Stein. I lost my father in an industrial accident many years ago. I thought of him when I saw the two of you on TV the other day. He had a factory job too. You reminded me of how good a man my father was. How hard he worked to build the everyday things we take for granted. I know most of this stuff isn't built in America anymore, and a lot of Americans don't even want the work. But I will always respect the people who do it, who work hard to make the things we need and a living for themselves. Good luck to you. You have my support."

Sparks put down the letter. "Now you tell me John Shay is doing a bad thing. You tell me that just because he did an end-run around you guys, you should crucify him."

He shook his head. "I'll tell you what. I know I'm an old codger, and most of you would rather I not even be here. But I know this much. It's guys like this"—he jabbed his finger across the table at Shay—"who built this union. And maybe it's another guy like this who's just what we need, to get us off our duffs and back into action."

Sparks grabbed a water bottle and unscrewed the cap. He looked at Shay as he brought the drink to his mouth.

The council tabled the motion after Sparks's speech, leaving Shay in charge.

twenty-three

"See today's paper?" Lewis asked, handing a story cutout to Shay.

Shay took it; he had already read it. He smiled.

"I'm glad someone thinks it's funny," Lewis said.

The *New York Times* had reported that a wide swath of groups had mobilized to support the labor action. Some were welcome, like fair labor and sweatshop-watch organizations, which monitored abuses in emerging-world factories. Others weren't—like a band of sustainiacs who said we shouldn't drive cars anyway and they were happy to picket dealerships.

As prelude to a forced march from the suburbs into the cities in the name of "density," Shay figured. If ever a word described something …

He had nosed around some left-wingers in college—for more time than he cared to admit. He finally got it though his thick skull that they were a bunch of well-off types who—their screeching certainty notwithstanding—knew as much about what the working class wanted as he did about the Queen of England's preference in china.

"You can't stop this stuff; it's part of life today," he said. "We have to focus on the people and organizations that matter, who can help us win the strike."

"I don't want this turning into a circus," Lewis said. "'Occupy Terre Haute' protesters flashing their titties."

"They do that in Terre Haute?" Like maybe he should visit.

“Just tell Hannah to keep the organic farming, ‘Crap on Crops: To Do or Not to Doo-Doo’ crowd away from the lines.”

Shay laughed. “That nasty.”

“Oh, you a brother now?”

Shay smiled.

“I got a call from the president’s office,” Lewis said. “They told me he’s following the situation closely, has a strong interest in resolving the conflict. He’s concerned about lower car sales, the multiplier effect on the economy. The business climate has him spooked.”

“I guess everybody’s happy I’m no longer leading the strike.”

“That’s cute,” Lewis said. “One more thing. He requested a meeting with someone from the union.”

“That would be you,” Shay said.

“I don’t think so, buddy. You stuck your neck out this far. Why not stick it out all the way?”

twenty-four

Washington

Shay and Hannah had been briefed by researchers and think tankers in preparation for the meeting. Shay looked at Hannah as they went over their materials one last time. Her idea to stretch the line from Lambal's plants to the supplier factories and auto dealers was taking off. A number of unions—mostly older, industrial organizations, whose members worked in steel plants, mines, trucking—were putting bodies on the ground.

He had put her in charge of the boycott. She was a whirlwind, talking, texting, traveling the country, making the case to other unions and the public. She appeared on the news in cities and towns across the United States. She was on national news—the major networks, FOX, CNN. Her Facebook page, blogs, and tweets roped in a ton of followers.

The Machinists' action had reinvigorated the national debate about the loss of manufacturing jobs. News stories rehashed the loss of agricultural jobs as we developed into an industrial society—now repeated with factory work as we moved to a service economy. The benefits to consumers, who were paying cheaper prices for goods from low-wage countries. The danger to the infrastructure of our economy and defense establishment, as we lost manufacturing capacity and capability. The benefits to our export industries, as development in the emerging world generated wages, purchasing power, and demand for products and services from America.

Shay put down the papers. We're too good at it, he thought—making things. We're losing jobs not only with outsourcing, but because information technology, better equipment, and smarter practices enabled workers to produce a lot more in a lot less time. Manufacturing had been picked apart, streamlined, automated; much of it now operated on cruise control. One generation's rocket science had become another's toy blocks.

Technology was unstoppable. It kept marching forward, breaking down what it replaced. You had to keep pace. You couldn't get by on just energy and hustle anymore. You had to upgrade your skills, get new ones, look out for yourself.

Knowledge was the new trade union, Shay thought. The best way to protect your job.

Just when America seemed to be getting dumbed down, and least capable of dealing with this.

"Know what I think?"

Hannah looked up from her notes.

"That the union can only do so much. We're leading a collective job action. But I'm telling myself, it's the individual who has to deal with these changes."

"You know, Jack taught me one thing," she said.

She choked up as she put down the papers.

"What's that?"

"That even when you lose the starry-eyed view, unions are still important. You *have* to have them. Whatever the downside … less flexibility for a company, getting paid the same as a coworker no matter how hard you work … it's unions that keep wages and benefits high. Or at least, the floor from collapsing. Without them, there's no protection at all. It'd be a free fall."

She wiped an eye. "Unions keep people in the game."

At the White House, Hannah and Shay were ushered into the room by an aide.

"The president has fifteen minutes," he said.

Shay nodded to the aide. "It's kind of him to make time to see us."

The aide smirked. "You've kind of forced his hand. This is not the kind of stress on the economy we're happy about."

"No one's happy on our side either," Hannah said. *Twerp.*

The aide nodded quickly as the door opened and the president came in. Shay and Hannah stood up as he strode toward them. "Mr. Shay," he said. "Ms. Stein."

"Mr. President," Shay said. "Mr. President," said Hannah.

After they shook hands, the president extended his arm toward their chairs and sat down across from them. Ron Rodgers was in his sixties, requisite height and hair, a warm look to his face. The Democratic moderate from Indiana was a welcome respite from both parties' extreme candidates, and had been elected on that platform—as a person who could find a sensible, middle way, which was how you resolved most things in real life.

He had been in office two years, but little had changed. Congress was as deadlocked as ever; Shay wondered why we keep electing such hardheaded people. But you had to be crazy to endure a campaign for political office—so it stood to reason that anyone elected was out of their mind. Even the president had begun to weaken, had begun to worry more about reelection than about forging consensus between the warring parties. Shay thought he looked fatigued, although a determined—or possibly insane—energy kept his eyes animated.

The job washed out everyone, Shay thought. His numbers were way down. He had worn out his welcome. They all do.

The aide placed an open folder on the table in front of the president, along with a notebook and pen. He poured everyone a glass of water and left the room.

"I wanted to begin by expressing my deepest condolences for Jack Cafferty," the president said.

"Thank you," Shay said.

"I'm also very upset about the attempt on your life. No one wants to see this kind of violence. Are the police making any progress?"

"They'll come up with something."

"Good," Rodgers said. Paused. "Do you have a family, Mr. Shay?"

"Wife and son."

"How old is your boy?"

"He's nine."

The president nodded. He looked at Hannah.

"How about you, Ms. Stein? Married? Family?"

Hannah shook her head.

The president took a drink of water and put down the glass. "Mr. Shay, Ms. Stein, I believe the working people of this country deserve the best we can give them, and I have fought for legislation to increase jobs. I also know we need healthy, profitable businesses—which are the source of jobs and opportunities for your union members."

"We get that," Shay said. "Some people push themselves hard to start or run businesses. They work long hours, and they deserve the lion's share—although we don't think they should make by noon on January 1 what the average worker makes the whole year. Others just want to show up each day, put in a shift, and go home to their lives. Both ways are fine. Both need each other."

"So why can't you cut a deal?"

Shay was caught off-guard by the aggressive tone. "The difficulty is not the usual compromises," he said, muffling a heated response out of respect for the office. "The problem is outsourcing. If it wasn't for that, we'd split our differences and settle."

"Sounds like running the country," the president said; all folksy again, the practiced everyman at a diner campaign stop. "I'd sleep better if all I had to deal with were domestic issues. It's the outside world that keeps fouling me up."

"Helluva place out there," Shay said.

"You don't know the half of it," the president said.

Then, after pausing, he said, "I understand how difficult this is. Your members work hard, often for many years, only to find themselves without jobs when their company feels it can only compete by moving overseas. The strength of this country has always been its working class. The majority of the immigrants who came here, who continue to come here, are working people. It troubles me to lead a country that can't provide well-paying jobs for unskilled, semiskilled, even skilled workers, and through those jobs passage to the middle class. It also costs a ton of money we no longer have—for unemployment benefits, Medicaid, lost revenue to local, state, and federal governments. If there were more manufacturing jobs, people drawing benefits would be paying taxes instead. And others would have jobs in the industries and services that support manufacturing.

"But at the same time, I am reluctant to interfere in the natural path of history—the emergence of the developing world, and its industrialization. I believe there are many benefits to be derived from bringing these millions of people into the global economic community. And although I have taken a strong stand against Chinese trading practices, I also believe I can do more harm than good by intervening too heavily, and maybe throwing one god-awful monkey wrench into the global economy."

After another pause he said, "But I also understand that people need assistance during this time. Is there something more we can do to help you deal with this?"

"Short of raising the wages of Chinese workers by a factor of twenty, and upping the valuation of the yuan by 30 percent?" Hannah asked.

Rodgers smiled. "Yes, short of that."

"We need federally financed retraining centers," Hannah said. "We need incentives for companies in growth sectors—renewable energy, information technology, nanotechnology, biotech, digital media, health care—to launch apprenticeship programs. We need tuition assistance for displaced workers, to attend community colleges in specific skills programs. Nationwide mapping of help-wanted ads and skills shortages, to match needs against regions suffering from layoffs. SWAT-like local, state, and federal help, rapid-response teams that swoop in to assist laid-off workers—you gotta treat this stuff like life or death." She caught her breath. "Extend the Trade Adjustment Assistance program to all workers who lose their jobs because of trade. Wage insurance—pay for workers who lose a job and take a lower paid one, to make up the difference while they look or study for something else. Give tax breaks to companies that produce here.

And go after the counterfeiters—they've destroyed 750,000 jobs in the United States."

"That's quite a laundry list."

"There's a lot of dirty wash."

The president smiled and jotted down a note. "These are all good ideas. Some programs are already operating, although perhaps not as well as they should."

Hannah leaned forward. "And you can make it easier for people to join unions—card check, more rights during organizing. Unions are the only stimulus package you'll ever need. Union wages mean more disposable income, more spending, demand flowing through the economy. Companies expanding and hiring to meet that demand and then those new hires buying things, creating even more demand."

Rodgers smiled.

There's a response, she thought.

"Mr. President, we appreciate your dropping the hammer on the Chinese for their trade shenanigans," Shay said. "But a number of unions have filed petitions with the Office of the US Trade Representative, seeking economic sanctions against China for repressing worker rights. We're not getting any action. We also want companies to disclose wages and working conditions of contractors in China. There's a lot of awful stuff going on to keep wages low and attract investment. Businesses gaining advantage by trampling workers' rights."

"We have urged countries to enforce their labor laws," the president said. "Where these countries lack appropriate legislation, we have urged them to adopt it."

Urged them? Hannah thought.

"It's too much pressure on wages," Shay said. "That's as bad as the job losses."

"And the losses are getting worse," Hannah said. "Everyone's only talking about it now because it finally hit the white collars. One study said ten million service jobs could be sent offshore near-term. Banking, insurance, pharmaceutical, engineering, accounting … you name it. A prominent economist who believes in free trade says thirty to forty million jobs could go in the next couple of decades.

Outsourcing has decimated the working class—fifty thousand manufacturing plants closed, millions of jobs lost. Now it's going to carve up the middle class. Income inequality is already off the charts. Soon there'll be nothing left but high rollers and no rollers."

She leaned forward. "Manufacturing workers were the canaries in the mine. If you can move something electronically—a billing statement, a chemical formula, legal documents, architectural drawings, a doctor's tape-recorded patient notes … or in our business, a product's design and manufacturing instructions … you can do it offshore."

She shook her head. "They're even cyberstealing entire companies' operating plans. Hacking the design and product manufacturing instructions and then reerecting the entire business in China, right down to the same plant floor and cubicle layout, even the placement of the"—she almost said *fucking*—"bathrooms."

"Something's got to give," Shay said. "At some point, someone's not going to take it anymore. Either us with the lost jobs, or them with the low wages. Nobody sits on their hands forever. The pain will become too great on one side. Something will blow."

"One more damn thing to worry about," the president said.

Shay and Hannah laughed.

Rodgers glanced at his folder. "You spoke about rewarding companies for producing in the United States. But companies overseas outsource to us too. The US arms of foreign corporations employ more than five million Americans, two million of them in manufacturing. You can read about it every day: a Japanese automaker puts an assembly plant in Indiana; a Korean concern sites a chip plant in Texas; a European pharmaceutical company moves R&D to Massachusetts. If we pass laws that keep our companies from going elsewhere, what's to stop other countries from doing the same?"

"The genie's out of the bottle—we don't want you to shut down trade with the world," Shay said. "But you have to balance things, take care of your own. And think strategically—in terms of sectors, assets, skills. Entire industries, and the manufacturing skills that support them, are going the way of cursive—nobody knows how to do it anymore. Look at the shape we're in because of the countries that dominate oil. Imagine if another group of nasty players controlled manufacturing."

He paused. "If it's free competition, we'll win plenty of face-offs. It's just going to take time. And federal help, during the transition."

"And fair rules," Hannah said.

"You're not going to get those. Not out there in that world," the president said.

"That's where you come in," Hannah said.

The president laughed. Then he showed them a harder look. "About this strike. This is a more fragile economy than at any time in recent history. I have refrained so far from invoking the Taft-Hartley Act—even though I'm being urged to do so by the automakers, dealerships, other business organizations, and my own officials."

The aide knocked and came into the room. Rodgers stood up; Shay and Hannah did the same. The president extended his hand to Hannah and then Shay.

"I'm not going to sit on my federal injunction powers forever," he said as they shook.

Then you can kiss the union vote good-bye. Shay left the thought unsaid—it was up to bigger fish than him to make that point to the president.

Rodgers walked them to the door.

He said to Shay, "I understand you have a family member serving."

Shay nodded. "My cousin. He vets local translators assigned to our forward op bases on the AfPak border. The translators go out with the soldiers as the patrols uncoil into the outlying districts and villages to work with local leaders."

Hannah looked at Shay and wondered why she didn't know that. A lot of Machinists' members, men and women, had deployed. She and some girlfriends adopted a platoon in Afghanistan. They sent boxes with chocolate, travel-size toiletries, DVDs. One night, drunk, they talked about taking photos of their tattoos and sending them; thought better of it.

Rodgers put his hand on Shay's shoulder. "You tell him that I personally—as president, and as an American—am very proud of him, and very thankful for his service."

"I will, Mr. President."

twenty-five

Shay and Hannah briefed the executive council after the meeting with the president.

"We need to settle," Lewis said. The rest of the members nodded in agreement.

"I want to go to China, see what Calderon is talking about," Shay said.

"What's the point?" Lewis asked. "The workers are Chinese, they make less money. What else do we need to find out? That the Chinese counterfeit and steal? That they're making a few parts after hours? That's your news flash? That's why you flew a Mexican foreman from Lambal's Juarez plant here on an all-expenses-paid junket?"

Lewis had spoken with Calderon. He didn't think his story would help negotiations. Everyone knew what they were getting into with China.

"We've opened a channel to the White House," Hannah said. "This kind of follow-up and on-site expertise will get us called us back to Washington. For hearings, committee sessions. To advise on legislation."

Lewis and the council bought Hannah's argument. Lewis called Lyons, Lambal's lead negotiator. The company had resisted giving them access to the plant in the past, but went along when Lewis said it was key to settling the strike. Lewis's admin Dolores booked Shay a flight to the Far East for the next day.

At home, Anne helped him pack.

"Just eat at the hotel," she said, pulling a shirt from the dresser.

"No charbroiled civet cat from a sidewalk pushcart?"

"Funny. I mean it, there's some nasty stuff over there."

Shay was flying to Hong Kong and then would head up the Pearl River Delta to Lambal's plant in Shenzhen, in Guangdong Province.

He watched her place the shirt in the suitcase, remembering the day they were standing on the Alexandra Bridge, between Ottawa and Hull. There was a dull sky above, gray and beautiful in that European way. They were leaning on the railing. She looked stunning, a scarf around her neck, a content smile. He asked her to marry him.

Michael came into the room pressing the tip of a pool cue against his cheek. Which is what he did when he wasn't bouncing a ball on the floorboards or making a clucking sound with his mouth or training with a plastic sword.

"You want something from China?"

Michael shrugged.

"Dude, you must want something," Shay said.

Anne screwed up her eyes. "After a signed baseball from the president? I don't think we need anything else, Michael." Shay had brought the ball to Washington.

"How about a watch with Chinese letters?" Michael asked.

"Done."

"So am I," Anne said. "That should be enough clothes for a few days."

"I'll bring it downstairs," Michael said.

He grabbed the handle, let the suitcase crash onto the floor, and then dragged and bounced it down the stairs. Shay and Anne looked at each other and smiled.

"Kwazy wabbit," Shay yelled after him. He put his arm around Anne. "He's the best thing that ever happened to me. How about you?"

She nodded, smiling.

"Even if it took you to get him," he said.

Hard punch to the arm.

Halfway down the stairs, the best thing that ever happened to them uttered the dreaded words, "Mom, what's for dinner?"

Anne threw up her hands. "I give up."

She sat down on the bed and shook her head. "I never get a minute to myself."

Uh-oh, trouble in paradise. He noticed a few gray strands in her hair. She had been having migraines. "Beat?"

She ignored him. He thought about how anxious she had been over problems at school. At home, she was always talking about all the things she had to do, everything she had to leave unfinished.

He remembered she had been taking care of others for most of her life. She was the second of seven children and had rolled up her sleeves early, helped with the younger ones—cooked, cleaned, organized play, got them ready for school and bed. She talked wistfully about becoming an interior designer. Whenever he brought her cut flowers, she arranged them beautifully. He figured it was the French in her; she was descended from one of the "voyageurs" who left the settlements of New France—today's Quebec—and headed westward into the woods to hunt and trap, eventually coming down from Canada and plying the Missouri and Mississippi, trading his furs. Her favorite place was Île d'Orléans, the island in the St. Lawrence just east of Quebec City. They would rent bikes and pedal its roads, passing old stone churches and farms. She would point at the picturesque cottages, with their colorful flowers set neatly in planters on the sills.

He looked at her. She had grown up modestly, could make something out of anything. They had joked about a name for the business: *Something from Nada.*

"You talking to yourself?" he asked, breaking the silence.

"It's the only way I get the answers I want." She paused. "It's the work. I love the kids … the looks on their faces when they make progress, the thanks from the parents as they see them get confident, start to fit in. But the other stuff … the paperwork, meetings, legal hearings … it's exhausting."

She brought home thick folders every night for the reports she was always preparing, on top of days spent with students. He remembered her dead-to-the-world posture the other night, slumped in the chair over the keyboard.

He wasn't doing enough to help, he thought. He shopped for food, took out the garbage, mowed, cleaned a bit—mainly his own spaces. But she didn't make it easy to pitch in; she was a perfectionist, scoffed at much of his effort. Like every guy, he probably took a little advantage too, he admitted to himself.

He felt badly she had to go back to work; she liked staying home with Michael. But however they did the math, they were coming up short. He had had a chance to make big money, but was never able to pull the trigger during the run-up in stocks. Which was especially dumb in his case—he had early knowledge of future winners from his dealings with the software industry, checking out the information technology that companies like Lambal wanted to install in their plants.

He was a cash-in-hand guy, he couldn't shake it. He would think nothing of dropping a fifty-dollar bill on the bar, buying a round for everyone; but he shied away from plunking down that same money for shares. He missed the boat big-time. He was down to Lotto and Publishers Clearing House.

He told himself at the time that he only liked to bet on himself, but it sounded now like a grandstand statement to mask failure. It was probably for the best, he thought—if he'd gotten rich, he'd be a shit like everybody else with big bucks.

Dead certain he'd take the money in a second.

Then he thought, it was their own fault. They got sucked in during the boom years, like everybody else. Went a little luxe; bought bigger, and more, than they needed. Fancy-ass appliances—remembering the repair guy hadn't called; a stovetop burner was shot. The crap cost three times standard-issue Sears and broke down ten times as often. He should have followed his grandfather's lead. His father told him his grandfather was so cheap, you could shake him with a machine and a nickel wouldn't come out.

"Maybe we should rethink it," he said. "You working. We could manage."

"I'm fine," she said. "I just need some sleep."

She paused. "You know, I like it too. The first year back, I was rusty. But I've gotten good again."

Shay felt a load lift—he thought the job was killing her.

Anne smiled. "There was this kid today, he knows everything about dinosaurs. He said, 'My dad and I saw a meat-eater in the sky.' I said, what? He said, 'We went outside last night, and there was a meat-eater in the sky. You know … a meat-eater shower."

Shay laughed. "Remember Michael in Ottawa? What he said on the street corner when he saw that guy with the spiky Mohawk?"

She smiled. "'Look, a stegosaurus.' Everybody turned and looked at the guy … How about when the teacher had to speak to him in kindergarten?"

Shay shook his head; he didn't remember.

"She said he wouldn't stop talking in class. I sent him to school in a pair of pants with dinosaur prints on the legs. He told me he was talking to them."

"I love you," Shay said. He leaned in and kissed her.

"I love you too."

"Mom, what's for dinner?" Michael yelled again, sounding desperate.

Anne looked at Shay. "You know how we cut up the retaining rings that hold six packs of soda, so the birds won't strangle themselves in the landfill? Suppose it isn't accidental? They wake up each day in the nest to those screaming, upraised mouths and throats, shrieking for worms and bugs from sunrise to sunset. Maybe they just can't take it anymore; they wriggle their necks into one of the openings. Suicide by plastic ring."

twenty-six

Shay flew to San Francisco to catch a flight over the Pacific. It let him schedule a layover to speak with the dockworkers; if they agreed to a stoppage, it would put more pressure on Lambal. But the leadership wouldn't commit to direct support. They had just come off a job action themselves, staring down a lockout by the port operators to win work guarantees in the face of automation.

Shay shook hands with everyone after the meeting. He called Hannah en route to the airport and gave her the names of the guys he talked with, telling her to keep on them.

He watched the earth rise hilly and then mountainous as the jet moved up the coastal route from San Francisco to Vancouver on the first leg of the trip. Even in September, the mountaintops were cold, a mass of rock and snow. One peak stood high among the rest, a monarch, the snow a white-streaked robe flowing down its sides.

His eye turned to a father and young son seated nearby. The kid offered his father some candy, pushed it on him really. The father took it and made a motion toward his mouth with the sweets. As his hand reached his mouth, the child looked away. The man brought his hand down to his sport coat side pocket and stuck the candy inside. He resumed reading.

Shay smiled. On the plane, relaxed, he realized that he had been dwelling too much on the hard parts of marriage and family life, being a baby about the responsibility. He recognized that things had changed at home too; they'd eased up a little. As Michael grew into boyhood, the full-time maintenance surrounding a baby and young child had lessened. He had become more of a companion. They were always running around together: fishing, science shows, the archery range, soccer and baseball practice.

He got a kick out of Michael's new attitude. One day he didn't get home from school when he was supposed to; Shay called around to find him. Turned out he was at the neighborhood pond; some boys detoured there after getting off the bus, to catch frogs. A week later, they were watching television when Michael said, "If I'm not home on time tomorrow, why don't you wait a few hours before you send out a search party?"

Shay laughed out loud. His seatmate looked up from his book.

As Shay took a sip of beer, he wondered, as Michael grew, if he would be able to talk with him. And not just about sports, where he and his father got snagged. Then he remembered: his father did try to talk to him. He was a know-it-all, and he wouldn't listen.

Shay sipped the beer thinking, so what if he didn't listen to his father, or his son didn't listen to him? It was a great time in life, to be young and stupid—to not listen to anybody, do whatever you want.

Then thinking, talking about sports was fine. Guys don't need to talk much anyway. For men—for himself—the thinking about things was enough.

The plane touched down in Vancouver, and business class filled up. The stewardess went through flight instructions as they taxied from the gate. The big turbines roared as the aircraft sped down the runway and rose into the sky. Looking out the window, Shay saw low-slung industrial buildings and then a river, with logs scattered near one bank. The plane began its long, slow turn left for the flight across the Pacific.

The flight attendant picked up the can and topped off his beer. He thanked her, and flicked on the seatback monitor. He found a BBC special on labor unrest. It kicked off with a profile of German workers marching at the Brandenburg Gate in the center of Berlin, with flowing red banners that said "WARNSTREIK." The newscaster said the unions were conducting warning strikes, protesting the transfer of jobs to Eastern Europe and Asia; Shay saw metalworker union signs in the crowd.

The feature flashed snippets of strikes in France, England, Spain, and Italy. Marchers carried signs that said, "No to Austerity," protesting the wave of budget cuts across Europe. Madrid protesters fought with police, who gassed them and fired rubber bullets. In France, glass workers "bossnapped" a manager and were holding him hostage; workers burned tires in front of a closed plant. At another French plant, workers put the company's products in a parking lot and surrounded them with gas canisters, threatening to blow them up if their demands for layoff pay were not met.

The story turned to Russia, where mill, mine, and factory closings had brought workers into the streets. A cell phone video showed cement workers in Pikalyovo, near St. Petersburg, staging a sit-in on a highway. In Korea, police were battling workers who took over a car plant. The workers, driven from one building to the next, holed up in the paint facility and posted signs on the windows: "Layoffs are murder." In Argentina, workers at a glassmaking factory, a hotel, a caterer—some two hundred companies in all—were squatting at the facilities and keeping them running after the owners shut them down.

Shay remembered the US workers who occupied a factory in Chicago when the company closed down without notice or severance.

Everybody was behind the eight ball at the same time. And fed up.

If the world wasn't going up in flames, there were sure a lot of lit matches.

Shay shut off the monitor and pulled out a folder. He began to familiarize himself with China's economic development, courtesy of a backgrounder from Machinists' research. The numbers were staggering. China accounted for one-third of annual global economic growth. The country was the second-largest importer of oil. It sucked up half of the world's steel, coal, and cement, 40 percent of its copper.

It was the second-largest economy. It would catch the United States by 2020, be twice as large by 2050.

There was no letup in sight. The Chinese were paving the country with roads, building airports, high-speed rail, and ports, lofting skyscrapers and housing blocks in the cities. Businesses were gobbling up farmland and throwing up factories across the country. Millions of farmers had poured into the cities to work; millions were in line behind them. It was a pool of low-wage labor that would take generations to exhaust.

For the US labor movement, it was hard to see a way out. China was developing at an accelerated pace, on an unprecedented scale. It had become an economic powerhouse. No company could ignore it—as consumers of their goods and for access to its labor.

The Chinese were milking it for all it was worth. They dangled the carrot of cheap labor and huge markets and then raised the stick of technology transfer—you want to come here, you give us the know-how to compete and drive you out of business.

Shay flipped through a list of US companies that bit. A telecom giant built a technology center in the country. A software company opened a research complex in Shanghai. A manufacturer moved a major health-care business unit to China. A consumer products firm was investing three billion dollars in new plants.

We're showing them too much of the ball, he thought. From soccer—when you dribble and push the ball too far out in front, give the defender a chance to take it away.

He took a sip of beer, thinking, it's just like Japan after World War II. We helped build a modern economy, and bred some of the toughest competitors in the world. He wondered if there was room for another big nation—with even greater economic prowess and much less democratic inclination—on an increasingly crowded and belligerent world stage.

twenty-seven

The plane landed at Hong Kong's Chek Lap Kok Airport. Shay passed through customs and got his bag. The heat and humidity took his breath away as he exited the terminal. He grabbed an urban red cab and found himself dozing from the flight. He woke in fits and starts, saw peaks in the distance, passed office towers and trade expo signs, saw the tall sails of the Tsing Ma Bridge.

The cab dropped him at the Kowloon Shangri-La on Mody Road. He looked around the gleaming, cavernous lobby while the clerk processed his reservation. Porters and attendants were rushing everywhere. The guests were well-to-do, business-rich.

Except the slob who got into the elevator with him and the bellhop. The guy was five foot five, fat, wearing a tie but no sport coat. His shirttail corner stuck out, and two buttons were open where his belly reached its full arc. His face was covered with stubble. He was grousing at a Chinese man in a blue suit, who listened politely.

"Fuck that shit. I'm not gonna pay that. Who the hell does he think he is? I'll pay half that for shirts somewhere else in Asia, and New York will love them. Fuck him. Where did you find that fuckhead?"

Shay got off on the nineteenth floor. The room was comfortable, with blond sycamore furnishings. The window ran the width of the room. He pressed the button on the night table to open the drapes, revealing the black waters of Hong Kong harbor on a moonless, clouded night.

Across the small stretch of water, he was looking at Hong Kong Central, the financial and business district. Huge corporate signs dominated the skyline, the purples, whites, and blues from their neon reflected as strips of color on the water. He saw yachts, excursion craft, and harbor tour boats moving through the waters. Fishing junks, their backs raised high, bobbed on the waves.

Shay checked out the minibar and grabbed a can of San Miguel. He sat down on the sofa and took a gulp. He was wired from the flight. It was 11:15 p.m. local time, 10:15 a.m. in New York. He figured he'd walk. He finished the beer and left the room.

Outside, he crossed Mody Road and was besieged by neon. Brightly lit signs in Chinese and English stretched out from the storefronts and into the streets, rubbing, overlapping, crowding each other for attention. Merchandise descriptions for luggage, jewelry, cameras, pens, consumer electronics. Shoppers everywhere, even at this hour, walking into and out of shops.

A tailor stepped out from his door and grabbed Shay by the sleeve. "Suit? Shirt? I make good clothes for you. Two day."

Shay pulled his arm away. He looked into the shop windows as he walked through the streets. He had never seen so many watches in his life, eyeing what was displayed behind much of the glass.

He saw something else—the reflection of a man across the street, who seemed to be keeping pace with him. He had figured Jack's death, and the attempted hit on him, had to do with what was going on in the States. Why would anyone here be involved? Could they have sent someone to finish the job in Hong Kong?

Shay eyed a bar and headed for it. He opened the old wooden door and entered an Aussie-themed tavern. It was a creaker, dimly lit, with rotted plank flooring and tables that matched. The bar itself was L-shaped, with a surface of chipped wood. Behind it a young Chinese woman sat sullenly on a stool, picking with one hand from a stack of receipts impaled on a stick, entering the totals on a calculator with the other.

The pub was mobbed. Shay wedged himself in at the bar next to a thick beam that ran from floor to ceiling. He read the sign on the wall above the liquor bottles: "Our credit manager is Helen Waite. If you want credit, go to Helen Waite."

The bartender came down from the other end.

"San Miguel," Shay said.

The man poured a draft and plopped it on the bar.

"Twenty-five, mate."

Shay put down three Hong Kong ten notes and waved off the change. The Hong Kong dollar is pegged to the US dollar, at just under eight Hong Kong to one US.

He took a gulp of beer and sat down at the bar when a stool opened up. He glanced at the window and didn't see the guy. He surveyed the room. A corner table caught his eye. Four men in their mid- to late-twenties—one Asian, three whites who sounded Australian. Scruffy, shirts half-unbuttoned, talking too loud. Two women came over and talked with them. One wore a snug tee; Shay looked at the tattoo on the small of her back. He remembered Hannah had one. He had snuck a look—or two or three—at a union picnic. He couldn't make out the design—the girl's or Hannah's. You never could. That wasn't the point.

The scene reminded him of a night years ago when he was single and lived in the city. He was sitting in Phebe's, at the corner of Bowery and East Fourth Street. When he put down the *New York Times*, the woman next to him asked if she could read his paper. He told her he could tell her the hockey scores, save her the trouble. At two in the morning, the line was good enough.

He lived nomadic those days—New York, Chicago, Boston, St. Louis, San Francisco. He liked plopping himself down in new cities and exploring them. He remembered when he moved to St. Louis how he would get up at dawn, prowl the rundown riverfront sections, breakfast in a beaten diner. He could still see in his mind the faded lettering on the abandoned factories and warehouses, forgotten sentinels, towering more obstinate than proud above the west bank of the Mississippi.

He was with a lot of women during that drifting time. Nothing lasted more than a few months; sometimes they didn't stick, sometimes he didn't. He wondered if he could ever get used to being with one person—thinking about the woman he struck up a conversation with in the Vancouver airport lounge, not so innocently. He wondered if maybe he could blame it on Catholic school. The nuns drilled it into your head for so many years that you shouldn't have sex, that for the rest of your life that's all you ever wanted to do.

He took a sip of beer. You don't, he thought—get used to it. You just live with it, like you live with a lot of things that maybe aren't your fantasy world but are mostly right. How thick could he be that this came across as an insight? And it's not just one person, it's two, adding in Michael. A family …

He remembered Anne's stories about drifting around Europe on Vespas with her sister, their antics and misadventures, staying in hostels in converted jails. When she got back, she worked odd jobs until she began using her special-ed degree. She might have closed as many bars as he did; that's what they did on their first dates. They still hired a sitter to reprise the drill—sit at the bar with wings and beer, take out donuts on the way home, watch a late-night show.

Brains and bumble—or bungle—that's what we were. A couple of strays. We went along, found—or lost—ourselves in one thing after the other. *We* should run dopey drills, he thought—learn where the play was going, not where it was. It was circumstantial life, not directional. We strolled along, saw what life would bring.

Until it brought us each other.

He suddenly pictured the canal at the end of the dead-end street where he grew up; it ran for a mile before opening into a series of Atlantic bays and then the ocean itself. He spent his youth on it—fishing off the dock at the edge of the first bay for snappers, snatching blue claws off the pylons with a dip net on a long pole, playing in the reeds.

It was filled in now, a park and marina. Still nice, but all structured-up. Like my life.

A woman approached the stool to Shay's left when it came free. She was five foot six and wore a white blouse, dark blazer and skirt, stockings, and heels. She had a slim build and was holding a mug of beer.

"This taken?" she asked.

"Sit down," Shay said.

She put out her hand. "Nora Young."

"John Shay." They shook hands.

She sat down and took a sip from her mug. "Visiting? Work here?"

"Visit. How about yourself?"

"Same. Business."

"Where do you work?"

"The Legal Software Consortium." She fished out a card and handed it over.

As Shay glanced at it, she said, "Trying for the impossible—a legal digital world. LSC advocates for the software industry, educates businesses and consumers about copyright protection. All the big software companies are involved."

"Does sound like a losing cause," he said.

"Pretty much like life. You make the best deal you can."

"My line of work."

"What's that?"

"The labor movement. I work for the United Machinists."

"We still have unions?" She smiled. "Just kidding."

Shay wasn't surprised by the dig. Less than 7 percent of private sector workers in the United States were union, only a quarter of them factory hands.

"What's an American union official doing in Hong Kong?" she asked.

"Touring a plant in China. Getting a feel for the competition."

Shay glanced at the windows but didn't see anything. Figured he wouldn't see the guy even if he was still outside. Looked at Nora and wondered if she was a plant, if he had been handed off to her.

She smirked. "What competition? You can't compete with these people. It's like time travel—somebody making modern wages, competing with serf labor from hundreds of years ago." She took a sip of beer. "A doll retails for $9.99—the China factory gets thirty-five cents." She shook her head. "And wait till they move upmarket—from the poison infant formula and pet food, the baby bibs with lead, the antifreeze cough syrup and toothpaste, the drywall and furniture with weird smells. It's happening already, in chips, pharma, telecom, aerospace … The only thing left in the United States will be the corner barbershop—because the plane fare to Asia will cross out the cheap haircut. Just barely."

Shay smiled. "What number beer you working on?"

"Three, actually."

"I'd be afraid to buy you a fourth."

"Take a chance," she said, downing the rest in a steady stream.

Nora placed the empty mug on the table. Shay figured late twenties. Brown eyes, narrow, diet face. Her hair was light brown, cut a couple of inches below her chin; it kept sliding across her face. She kept pushing it back, giving him a better look.

He ordered the round. "Where you from?" he asked.

"Dallas."

"What are you doing on this trip?"

"Liaison work. Our Singapore and Hong Kong offices."

Nora looked around the bar and then back at Shay. "First time in the Far East?"

He nodded. "But not you."

"When 80 percent of the software in China is pirated, it's hard to avoid the place."

"Making any progress?"

"That's down from 97 percent; it took us twenty years to lower it. People think the knockoff programmers are heroes, stiffing it to the big bad Americans. It's tolerated even in the government and military. But we need China's cooperation—in business, politics. We can only push so hard. Then we have to hug the Panda."

Shay smiled. "They've got some scam. Business wants their labor and markets, consumers are hooked on their prices, government needs their cash to fund the deficit and to help us with the thug countries they befriend. They get away with murder."

The waitress brought the drinks. Nora stuck hers forward and clinked.

"Welcome to the Chinese miracle," she said.

twenty-eight

Shay walked back to the hotel after leaving the bar; he didn't see anybody on his tail. He went right to bed. The next morning he called home and talked with Anne. She told him Michael had gotten a special commendation in school for math.

"Looks like all your grocery trips paid off," she said.

When Shay took Michael shopping, they played a game in produce, turning the four-digit codes into problems. Shay would grab some bananas, give them to Michael to be weighed and priced on the self-serve scale. The code for bananas was 4001. When Michael asked for it, Shay would say something like, "16,004 divided by 4."

After he hung up, he plugged his laptop into the room port. An e-mail from Hannah contained a link to a website. Shay clicked; it was a snip from a TV interview.

"The catch phrase in business is 'C-level,'" Hannah said to the woman interviewing her. "The CEO, the CFO, the COO—what they do for the company, what they're worth, how you get their attention."

The camera panned to linger on the journalist as she sat expressionless; he couldn't be the only one who hated that.

"Well, it's time for a 'C change,'" Hannah said, the lens mercifully returning to her. "It's time to talk about another C-level—about custodians, carpenters, cafeteria workers. About clerks, call center workers, cooks, cashiers, carpet layers, car washers."

Cool, he thought.

An hour later a man met him in the Shangri-La lobby as scheduled, to take him to Lambal's plant.

"Mr. Shay, how do you do? My name is Ma Yongrui."

Ma was five foot seven and wore a blue suit. Looked like any businessman, except his complexion was rough and pockmarked. They shook hands and exited the hotel.

"I lived in the United States for years," Ma said as they walked past the line of luxury cars the hotel maintained for guests. "Many Chinese have come back, to take advantage of the economic opportunity in our country. They call us 'sea turtles,' because we returned to the shores of our birth. Please, this way."

They got into the car and pulled away from the hotel. "We are taking a boat to Shekou," Ma said. "It's a coastal town in the southern part of China called Shenzhen, in Guangdong Province. Guangdong is perhaps better known to you by its English name, Canton. Canton was also the name of the capital city, until it was renamed Guangzhou."

Shay nodded as the black Mercedes raced through the streets. Cars move quickly in Hong Kong. The drivers tail each other closely, gobbling up chunks of road in fast bursts, punctuated by occasional braking for lights that stay red only a few seconds. Their aim in traffic—as in trade and money—is to keep everything moving.

As Ma's driver navigated the streets of Tsim Sha Tsui, there were signs of building activity everywhere. Razed lots awaited the next apartment complex or office tower. Pieces of rebar stood upright in square patterns in the foundations, waiting for concrete to be poured around them. Bamboo scaffolding—covered with green netting to prevent debris from falling below—surrounded the skeletons of building frames.

They passed through neighborhoods packed tight with people and industry. Workers spilled out of factories into the streets, lugging or pushing carts of merchandise. Trucks were parked on the sidewalks of the narrow streets while they made their pickups and deliveries, making it difficult for people to pass.

"You work at Lambal?" Shay asked.

"The company asked me to assist as a translator and guide," Ma said. "I match US companies with Chinese manufacturing expertise."

"That must keep you busy."

Ma smiled. "But it does not make you happy."

"More work for you is less work for my members."

"Perhaps," Ma said. "But if more work in China means more wages and more purchasing power for our people, perhaps they will want to import something a US company makes. And then another US company benefits, along with its workers."

"I'll believe it when your country is more open," Shay said. "When it doesn't use subsidies to give locals a price edge. When it stops making foreign manufacturers sign coproduction agreements so you can steal technology. Right now, it's a one-way street."

"That is not so, Mr. Shay," Ma said. "Huge container ships queue outside China's harbors every day, delivering imported raw materials and commodities for our production facilities. The United States has sold billions of dollars of aircraft to China."

"You run a 250-billion-a-year trade surplus with us, and it's on the up elevator," Shay said. "The stuff we sell you is a drop in the bucket."

Ma smiled. "You shouldn't be blaming China. More than half of what we export to you is produced by your own companies, operating on our soil. These are goods imported by your own retailers, for sale to you. Everything you do, you do to yourself."

The car emerged from the dense streets onto a road that ran alongside the harbor. They pulled over to the curb at a drop-off zone for passengers disembarking at the pier and entered a building. It was loud inside—people clamoring for places in line, babies crying, men in suits standing assured, while laborers and poorer travelers in work clothes waited with more anxious expressions.

They took a seat on a wooden bench to wait for the boarding call. Ma picked up their discussion again.

"How do you fill a bucket, if not with drops?" he said. "Mr. Shay, China is emerging from years of underdevelopment. Our ability to absorb your high-technology exports is limited. As we prosper, we will buy more goods from you, and from others in the developed world."

Bunch of well-rehearsed BS, Shay thought. He wondered how things would look in twenty-five years. Would we come off the turn still loaded?—the expression from horse racing, when a horse had plenty left after the turn for the straightaway. Would it be a thriving, bustling America, always renewing, creating knowledge-based goods and services for the world? Or a tired, hollowed-out country, at the end of a 250-year run, turning in upon itself—and its people, on each other—as it tried to stem decline while maintaining order in the world?

Shay had the feeling we had stalled, we were losing. It seemed like we couldn't rise to the challenge of this bloody, scheming world anymore. Maybe our time, our leadership, was transient. Why not? Everything was.

We might even end up a strongman country, he thought. Tired of the failings, and flailings, of democracy, clamoring for someone tough to come in and clean up the mess.

Belichick. He almost laughed out loud.

The boarding announcement crackled over the PA system; they rose with the other travelers and exited the back door to the pier. The wind had more zip out back, turning the quiet mist into a raw chill. The hovercraft filled quickly. They couldn't find seats together, so sat in different rows.

Shay looked out the window as the boat sped up the estuary channel toward Shekou. Everything was gray—the hills, the sky, the waves. Water sloshed back and forth across the floorboards inside the cabin. The air was damp, heavy with sleep. There was no conversation between the commuters on the boat.

It reminded him of a subway ride he used to take years ago, to a machine shop on Zerega Avenue in the Bronx. It was an early morning trip, before rush hour, men and women off to work in the factories that opened hours before the offices, sitting quietly on the train as it rocked back and forth, everyone bone-tired. He had an image of himself leaning forward in his seat, forearms on his thighs, one hand holding a Styrofoam cup that he would bring to his mouth to sip the coffee.

Shay sipped today's coffee. He liked manufacturing—got a jolt from the power of the factories, the equipment. He liked working with metal, machining the raw stock into finished shapes. He liked the exactness—at the Bronx shop, he turned down steel bar stock to a diameter that couldn't vary by more than three ten-thousandths of an inch. Three-tenths, he thought, remembering how the machinists said it.

He felt something else was being lost in the passing of these jobs—something more personal, beyond the economic rationale, the fuller employment, a chance to grab hold of the economic engine. We were moving away from what got us here—working with our hands and tools, yanking a living from reluctant nature.

He was glad he worked those years as a machinist. He felt like he had captured something—something hardy, precise, gruff—through the work. The years in the plants had settled him, stretched and strengthened his mind. Put something inside him he liked.

But it was a tough life—early hours, long days, few breaks. His father said it best—the bell rings and you start working, and you keep working until the bell rings again. At the South Boston shop, he got two ten-minute breaks, twenty minutes for lunch. One day he got tangled in the business end of a high-speed grinding wheel, almost lost a pinky. He looked at the scar; kind of liked it, a badge. At another shop, he was machining aluminum. The spot where the cutting tool met the metal was flooded with coolant. The machine guard had been removed; blue-green liquid was getting on him, and he was inhaling the mist. He broke out in a full-body rash, tingling, on fire everywhere. He went to the hospital for tests; they showed nothing. He quit the job, the rash went away. He wondered if a time bomb had been planted inside that would go off one day.

He understood why a lot of people wanted out of factories—the crappy ones, anyway. Still, he wondered if the country missed that kind of job more than it realized. So many people today seemed tinny, almost hysterical, all over the place. Factory work had focused his mind, put his feet on the ground. You worked hard, and the equipment was dangerous. You had to think straight; you were accountable.

Manufacturing was unforgiving, he thought. Everything you made had to be within a dimensional tolerance—plus or minus some exact number for the length, width, thickness, diameter, or whatever measurement. You had to be within that band, or the part was scrapped. He remembered the go/no-go gauges; you inserted the parts into them to validate their size. The part was right or it wasn't—it fit the gauge or it didn't.

An announcement came over the loudspeaker in Chinese and English; they were arriving in Shenzhen. The rain had picked up and was pelting the hovercraft window. Shay watched the moving beads of water, drops landing on one corner of the pane, racing diagonally to the other. Noiseless scratches, leaving momentary lines before dispersing altogether.

The country seemed stronger when it was working class, he thought—thinking of his parents, and the generation formed in the fields and factories of the Depression and World War II. They were passing, along with their blue-collar backbone.

With everything the world was throwing at us now, he wondered if America—himself included—could be as strong, as self-sacrificing, without those kinds of people. Without the kind of work that framed them, made them who they were.

Through outsourcing, we were losing that source, he thought; sending it out, away. We were outsourcing solid, productive work—a source of character. And we were losing our people—our ultimate source of strength—who were becoming demoralized, despairing, defeated, without that work. Work that was a source of self-respect, and the foundation for stable families, decent neighborhoods, and civic pride.

But then he thought, leaving that work behind was the aim all along. To do it so well we could free ourselves from hard labor. Or pass it along to someone else. To the next emerging country and aspiring people, queued in desperate lines to do it for us.

Manufacturing—*manu factum*, made by hand—had become the world's hot potato, tossed in a searing aluminum wrapper to the next set of cupped, outstretched hands.

twenty-nine

The engine roared with a downshift as the hovercraft slowed to a crawl and edged into the Shenzhen dock. The boat nestled into its mooring, and the passengers filed out. After clearing the passport check, they exited into a large plaza, where traffic and pedestrians navigated their way. The rain had slackened to a drizzle. In the distance, the hills were deep green, felt, dotted with spots of rock and dirt. The clouds pressed down on the hills, cutting off the peaks with gray wisps—like the smoke that encircles the tips of the incense sticks called joss that the Chinese burn incessantly to bring good fortune.

They were met in the plaza by a car and driver. "This area was once completely undeveloped," Ma said as they drove past newly completed industrial buildings and housing projects or land torn up at the excavation, foundation, or structural framing stage. "China's experiment with capitalism started here twenty-five years ago. Millions of people are streaming into Shenzhen and Guangzhou still."

He pointed ahead. "I want to show you this first."

Shay looked out the window at a dull collection of buildings made of concrete and corrugated tin. The lot outside was unpaved and had turned to mud. They parked, entered the building, and climbed the staircase. They turned left at the top and walked down a hallway that opened into the main plant. It was huge, stretching three stories high, occupying the entire left side of the building. There were large windows along the three walls that faced the outside, but the factory was dark. The windows were filthy, streaked so badly that what little light there was on the rainy day barely filtered through.

Shay took a quick survey of the production equipment. The machines were old, caked with dust, black, cast-iron lumps that looked straight out of the industrial revolution. Ancient ovens for heat treating lined one wall. It was worse than he imagined, even after Calderon's crack about Chinese workers in flip-flops. Which was what a couple of workers were wearing.

"This was China, twenty-five years ago," Ma said. "Let me show you China's future."

They drove a few miles and turned into an industrial park with well-kept grounds. Shay saw the LAMBAL INTERIOR sign at the entrance to a series of buildings. The car dropped them off at the first building. Ma opened the door to the main plant and ushered Shay in. They breezed past the reception desk and stopped in an administrative office, where Shay was introduced to three executives. The reception was icy.

"They are busy. I will show you the plant myself," Ma said.

They navigated several hallways and entered a room filled with computer workstations. "Here, Mr. Shay, we have our computer-aided design and engineering systems," Ma said. "We simulate designs, analyze kinematics, model structural analysis, examine mold flow prior to production. We simulate sheet-metal manufacturing. We do computational fluid-dynamics analysis, to predict air and heat transference."

Shay moved closer to one of the workstations. The engineer glanced over his shoulder and then went back to manipulating the 3-D model on the screen.

"Our software is linked electronically with an on-site tooling facility to complete prototypes in a fraction of the time customers expect," Ma said. "We manage all tool development on location—from design through manufacture and tryout—to accelerate project completion. Rapid prototyping enables us to go quickly from 'art to part.'"

They left the engineering section and walked into the main plant. As they toured the line, Shay saw equipment that equaled Lambal's best plants in the United States—computer-controlled equipment, pick-and-place robotics, robotic welding, multistage forming presses, special-purpose test systems.

They exited the back and entered an adjacent facility. "We are working on other automotive interior systems as well," Ma said. "In this plant, we produce flooring and acoustics, door panels, instrument panels and cockpit systems, overheads, and electronic and electrical products."

Two workers were walking in the opposite direction. Shay moved to the side but not fast enough. One of the workmen jostled him. Shay shot him a look.

Shay and Ma stopped at an assembly station. "The overhead components of a car's interior used to be just sun visors and a decorative headliner, covering the sheet metal and roof structure. The sun visors and headliners are still there. But our systems now have air distribution ducts, wiring, grab handles, lighting, and other convenience and comfort features." They moved to the instrument panel section as Ma emceed. "Our newest panels integrate everything—air bags, HVAC components, instrument clusters, turn-signal switches, wiring, electrical management system, user interface."

Shay took in the sight as they retraced their steps. The union had guessed Lambal was headed upmarket in China—from simple parts to higher-value subassemblies that went straight to the car plants for final build. Shay had no idea it was happening so fast.

"What do you think, Mr. Shay?" Ma asked.

I think we're fucked, Shay said to himself.

thirty

The driver took them to the hovercraft, and they returned to Hong Kong. As he took the elevator to his floor, Shay thought about what he had seen. He remembered the numbers Nora threw at him: China was building hundreds of research centers and universities, graduating six hundred thousand engineers a year, filing eight hundred thousand patents annually. Not only was the union screwed—America had it coming too. The Chinese had used cheap labor to ante up. Now they had a chip pile and were looking to push all in.

With US business cheering in the gallery. Moving jobs offshore for cheap labor was a "best practice." Outsourcing had decimated the working class; now it was carving up the middle class. US companies were leading a mass exodus—manufacturers, software firms, pharmaceutical corporations, financial institutions. First they made hard goods offshore, then they processed paper, and now they were taking away their knowledge work. They were setting up offshore offices and campuses with thousands, sometimes tens of thousands, of people, rivaling the size and importance of their home locations.

Home? he thought. They didn't know the meaning of the word.

Outside the door, Shay reached into his pocket for the room card. He felt a piece of paper and pulled it out. On it was written an address on Shanghai Street. And a time, five this afternoon.

The guy who bumped me in the plant.

He called Hannah to check on the strike.

"You won't believe what's going on," she said. "A number of unions have stepped up. We've got demonstration lines at dealerships in more than twenty states."

"Not manned by a bunch of crazies, I hope."

Hannah laughed. "Yeah, we're combining vegan diet with industrial action—eat better, drive less."

"Seriously," Shay said.

"I'm not that crazy; not anymore," she said. "This is old-fashioned union action. I'm keeping a lid on who supports us. At least publicly, on the lines."

"Anything from NYPD on Jack?"

"Bill says nothing new." She paused. "Those bastards, if someone did it."

"Someone did it, and tried to do it to me," Shay said. "You have to be careful."

"Sean's keeping an eye on me," she said. She laughed. "He's a fountain of knowledge. Yesterday he asks me, how do you attract women to a bar? I say, hire a good-looking guy to tend bar? He says no, you hire an attractive woman bartender. That brings in the guys, and *that* draws the women. Who knew?"

Huh, Shay thought.

"Oh, he told me to ask you—best band name no one has thought of."

Shay thought for a second. "Carbon Carbon."

She laughed. "His favorite element. How's China, seen the plant?"

"An eye-opener."

"How so?"

"They can do anything we can. Not as well—you can't match the experience our guys have; I doubt their volumes and quality touch ours. But it's all there, at a fraction of the wage. It's only a matter of time."

"That's what you're trying to buy, isn't it?"

"I guess. Just delay it, hold it back."

"Jack used to say, 'roll' it back." Her voice cracked.

"You doing okay?" Shay asked. "I mean, personally?"

She paused. "If you mean can I run this job action, I can do it."

"I know you can. It's just a question, between friends."

"It's nice of you to ask."

"You call me anytime. Okay?"

"I will," she said. "Thanks."

Shay skipped the cab when the concierge told him the address was a twenty-minute walk. He wanted to stretch his legs, and see if he was still being followed. He headed up Nathan Road, turned left onto Jordan Road. To his right, he saw small, densely packed streets. After passing a few, he found the one he wanted.

Shanghai Street runs parallel to Nathan Road. The street offers a riot of shops and small industrial enterprises—fruit and vegetable stands, household goods marts, outdoor machine shops, medicine and herb stores, luncheonettes where the cooking is done in adjacent alleys. Above the shops rose eight-story apartment buildings. The flats facing the street had small terraces enclosed by ornamental grating; corrugated sheet metal or hand-me-down wood was used for flooring; potted vegetables and herbs grew everywhere. Clothing hung from lines that stretched between the railings, and from bamboo poles that extended out over the street.

Shay was beginning to sweat. Moisture was everywhere—the air was laden with tropical humidity, people on the street were spitting, the rattletrap air-conditioners sticking out from the shop windows and hanging over the sidewalk were leaking a steady stream of water onto passersby. As the streets narrowed and became more congested, he became aware of the sounds—generators powering industrial equipment in alleyways, the clacking of mah-jongg tiles on card tables on the sidewalk, chickens squawking as they were pulled from their cages to be hacked up and hung from shop ceilings, the whir of key-duplicating machines in open-air locksmith shops.

Shay stepped aside to avoid a leaking air-conditioner; he used the motion to glance around. It didn't appear anyone was following him. He wondered, surrounded by a sea of Chinese, how would he know? He decided he was going to institute surveillance training when he returned to the States. The Machinists never bothered with it before; there was no need. He knew just the guys—a couple of NYPD Robbery/Homicide detectives from the Midtown North precinct who could use the after-hours cash.

He crossed the street at the corner where the teahouse was located. He heard birds chirping as he entered the restaurant. The patrons were all Chinese; he had long since lost sight of Westerners. They were all men, older, bent, thin. They were wearing white short-sleeve shirts, baggy black trousers, and thong sandals.

He made his way up a winding staircase. At the top was a large room with canteen-style tables in the center. Men sat by the windows at high-back hardwood benches along the walls. Large wooden fans turned slowly overhead.

Shay made his way past the stare of the cashier and entered the room. The birdsong was louder, clear, coming from all directions, chaotic and sweet. He saw the singers—tiny birds, yellow, blue, white, green, chirping in cages that hung on hooks above their owners, seated at the benches eating rice and sipping tea.

He took a seat at a wooden table with a large piece of glass for a top. The tabletop was filthy, covered with food crumbs and flecks of seaweed. A small bowl of toothpicks was set in the corner. A metal spittoon on the floor next to the bench was crammed with folded paper, debris, and discolored mucus.

A bent-over old man walked slowly down the aisle with a tray, repeating a short, rhythmic call. A rope around the back of his neck was attached to both ends of the tray, which held covered pots of food.

Shay asked for tea. The man scribbled the order on a pad and returned with a dirty teapot and cup. Shay picked up the pot and poured tea into the small cup. He was about to take a sip of the transparent yellow liquid when he flinched at the filth and put it down.

He waited half an hour. He had just checked his watch again when a Chinese man sat down. He looked to be in his thirties, black hair cut plainly like an inverted bowl, dark brown eyes. The waiter returned and set down another cup. The man picked up the pot and poured the tea. He took a sip and leaned back against the hardwood bench. He looked out the window. It was large, maybe eight feet high, framed in metal. It was pushed open, looking out over Shanghai Street. He turned to Shay.

"I have a deal for you. Information, in exchange for support."

"And you are?"

"Someone who cannot share his name. Not until we reach agreement."

"What do you have?" Shay asked. "And what do you want?"

"I am in the trade-union movement, like yourself," the man said. "Only in China, it is not the same. We have government unions run by the Communist Party." He smiled. "According to Chinese law, unions must accept economic development as the central task, and 'uphold the socialist road and primacy of the Chinese Communist Party.' The right to strike was removed from China's constitution in 1982, because the political system had 'eradicated problems between the proletariat and enterprise owners.'"

He took a sip of tea. "Mr. Shay, while workers' rights are guaranteed by the constitution, the reality is different. Attempts to establish independent worker organizations are repressed. Workers and labor activists are imprisoned for exercising what are accepted by other nations as everyday rights—the ability to freely associate, organize, bargain collectively. When detained, they are denied access to lawyers. They can be tried as criminals without a lawyer present. When convicted, they can be sentenced to forced labor, and the sentences extended at the discretion of the authorities. Some have been imprisoned in psychiatric wards. Many return from their time in jail with severe physical problems or mental illness."

"So when you say you are in the trade-union movement, you don't mean the government version," Shay said.

"I am part of a network of labor activists operating across the country."

He leaned forward. "Working conditions in China are terrible. Industrial accidents kill and injure tens of thousands each year. Many are forced to work up to eighteen hours a day, living in company dormitories that are little more than prisons. If you think it is bad to find lead in your child's toys, imagine the workers in our plants—poisoned by the lead used to make the toys. The situation has become even more brutal as multinational companies demand even faster delivery and lower prices, and Chinese suppliers respond with production speedup and less safety."

He looked around the room. "In response, an underground union movement has emerged in China. As you can imagine, we are not welcome. The Communist Party, while becoming more open, wishes to control the pace of change in Chinese society. But the industrial exploitation we are suffering requires more dramatic action."

The guy's enthusiasm reminded Shay of himself when he first joined the Machinists. Probably more accurately, it harked back to the early labor leaders the archbishop cited in his eulogy to Jack. The men and women who fought—and died—in the violent strikes and resistance that gave birth to the American labor movement.

"You need money?" Shay asked.

"Of course. But more than that, we require support. Especially from the United States, since many American companies invest in China. Just as your union is targeting consumers and suppliers in the automotive industry to assist your strike, we need to go beyond our immediate environment for support. We can do very little on our own. Our workers are harassed and easily fired."

"You told me what you want. What do you have for me?"

"You will provide this support?"

"We already aid struggling union movements worldwide," Shay said. "It's also in our self-interest—if we help you get better wages and conditions, your country will be more expensive to do business in."

The man sipped the tea and shook his head. "We attract business because we are cheap. Then, when we want more money, the business will go elsewhere."

"Capital is a wanderer, Mr. … ?"

"Lin. Lin Xueqin."

"Capital roams the world for opportunity," Shay said. "It builds countries and breaks them, moves them forward and drags them back. We'd be poorer without it. Yet we must fight it, to hold off poverty."

"You sound like a philosopher, Mr. Shay. You understand the life force as a single entity, consisting of two things locked in eternal battle."

"What's your information?"

Lin smiled. "Ah yes. Not the time for philosophical reflection."

His eyes scanned the room. "The Lambal factory in Shenzhen schedules one shift a day. But it is producing extra—products that are sent somewhere else."

"What kinds of volumes are we talking about?"

"An entire shift."

"The same volume the plant produces legitimately?"

Lin nodded.

"That's a big sideshow. Who's running it?"

"We are not sure."

"Where is the production sent?"

"Somewhere outside Shanghai. Trucks pull up to the shipping dock and load goods. I watched one vehicle load"—the stench from the Dumpster and the half-eaten sandwich he retrieved from the trash came back to his mind; he almost gagged—"then my friend drove behind until it turned off the highway near Shanghai. It would have been too dangerous to follow it to the final destination."

Shay nodded. "This is very useful. You have my word—we will make a strong effort to make sure your union movement gets the recognition—and results—you seek."

"That is all I ask," Lin said.

"Can you get me into the Lambal plant when no one's working?" Shay asked.

"Yes," Lin said. He stood up; Shay did the same. As they shook hands, Lin gave him a small piece of paper. "If you need to reach me."

"I think I've been followed at least once since I arrived in Hong Kong," Shay said, putting it in his pocket. "I didn't see anybody today."

Lin smiled grimly and looked around the room. "Welcome to our world."

thirty-one

Shay spent the next day as a tourist—Star Ferry across the harbor to Central, funicular tram excursion to the Peak, junk ride in the bay. He haggled in the Kowloon jade market for a necklace for Anne and a couple of mythical creatures for Michael. It filled the day, and gave him a chance to spot a tail. He didn't see anyone—he figured he either passed or failed that test with flying colors.

Back in the hotel that evening, his infected tooth was killing him; he had let up on the ibuprofen. He looked at the area in the bathroom mirror as he pulled on his lower lip. He saw reddish/whitish swelling in the gum below the tooth. He pressed hard with his thumb and popped the pus, splattering the mirror.

As he shaved, he wondered what people would think about the low prices of Chinese goods if they could talk to Lin Xueqin. He thought back to the guy in the elevator when he checked into the hotel, cursing out his supplier's rep, a little taste of the ugliness that went on behind the scenes to get those prices. That, and people jumping off sweatshop roofs. It wasn't pretty, and Lin had banged it home even harder.

He slapped on some aftershave from the hotel minibottle, thinking that all the outsourcing, the frenzy around profit margins, stock price … it was debasing life. Not only that—everything you bought today was crap, nothing worked right. And if you had a problem with something, you couldn't reach anybody. Customer service had turned into customer avoidance—at FAQ-you, nobody-home companies. As business drove cost out of every process, it drove out people, quality, and service, too.

Did we really want to become China?

The phone rang. "Yes?"

"Mr. Shay, Mr. Ma. Am I disturbing you?"

"No."

"I was hoping you might have time to visit another facility. It's located in an industrial estate in Tai Po, in Hong Kong's New Territories. The company does design and engineering work for US automotive suppliers, like Lambal Interior."

"Sure," Shay said. He wanted more time to check out the Lambal plant. This would be good cover.

"Good," Ma said. "I will pick you up tomorrow morning. Nine o'clock?"

"I'll be ready."

Fifteen minutes later, Shay left the hotel and retraced his steps from the night before to the bar. He had arranged to see Nora again, to pick her brain about product counterfeiting. Although it sounded like the plant in Shenzhen wasn't turning out fake goods. Someone was using Lambal designs and equipment and stealing the output. It was only counterfeiting in the legal definition—by law, anything produced at a factory making legitimate goods for a manufacturer, beyond the quantity authorized by that manufacturer, was a knockoff.

In the bar Shay sat with a beer, thinking he didn't make the date just to talk shop.

He stood as Nora came to the table. She was wearing a short black dress with thin shoulder straps and high heels. He could feel her body as much as see it.

"You look great," he said. Feeling guilty as sin.

"Thanks. After today, I didn't think I could."

Shay waved to the waitress to bring another beer.

"Tough one?" he asked.

"I was at a meeting with some Chinese officials." She shook her head. "Even in government offices, they use pirated software, right in front of you. It's a stretch to think they're going to crack down on industries, and individuals, doing the same thing."

"But you got something," Shay said.

Nora smiled. She grabbed the San Miguel after the waitress put it down, raised it, clinked mugs. "You're starting to understand my ways." She took a long first sip, like a deep drag on a cigarette. "Now you have to figure out the Chinese."

"Have you?"

"I heard something on my first trip over. I was talking to an anthropologist on the plane. He was coming back to spend a second year in a remote province of China. I asked him what the Chinese were like. He said, 'They're like any people you don't know. After a week you want to write a book, after a month you'll write an article, after three months you don't want to write anything. First they seem so different, and you're excited. Then, when you see how different they really are, you get homesick. Then, after another while, you begin to see yourself in them.'"

The last part rang true for Shay. Capitalism in the West wasn't much more than banditry in its early days. Counterfeiting took place in every developed country, just too long ago to remember; the United States did it big-time in the eighteenth century when we were getting off the ground. There was even a modern variant: "design around." You tore down a competitor's product, examined it, made just enough changes when you built your own version to skirt the patents. Lawyers managed the fallout.

We're not all that different, he thought, dueling China for notoriety with our own mine disasters, lethal baby cribs, defective medical devices … a relentless procession of safety violations and junk products plagued both countries.

"Yuan for your thoughts," Nora said.

"I was just thinking—business is a dirty proposition."

"What else can you expect on a big ball of dirt, rock, and inner molten fire, spinning like a top in space?"

Shay smiled.

Nora caught her hair falling forward, pulled it back. Shay admired her slender fingers. Her nails were black.

"I know your job is software," he said. "Do you know much about industrial counterfeiting, who's doing it?"

"It pretty much works the same, regardless of product. It all depends on scale. If it's small-time, garages and cheesy entrepreneurs. Big-time, army and state."

"Army?"

Nora nodded. "That's why the Communists want capitalism without democracy—capitalism generates the profits, they loot the money. The military's into it in a big way."

She glanced around the room. "Something you're interested in?"

"Maybe."

"Better watch your step. It's one thing to go to a scheduled meeting and sip tea, poke around politely. It's something else altogether to wander off on your own."

Shay didn't react.

"I mean it," she said.

She took another drink and sat back in her chair. "Where you from, anyway?"

"New York."

"You don't have much of an accent. Those people are barely comprehensible."

"Unlike Texans."

Nora laughed. "How about your wife?" She flicked her head at the ring.

"Nebraska."

"Kids?"

"Son. Nine … How about you?" Shay asked. "Entangled?"

Nora laughed. "That's some way to put it. No, I'm not. Have been, will be again. But not right now."

They sat quietly for a moment. Glanced at one another, and around the room.

"Why don't I start?" she said. "That way you can blame me after." She took a drink of beer. "Sitting here talking to you is great. Sitting here with you, not talking, is good too. I'm going home in a few days; you are too. We could try to meet again, but something will come up."

She fingered her beer. "I'd like to spend more time with you tonight. Would you like to come back to my apartment?"

"Yeah, I would," Shay found himself saying. Maybe it was the stress of the strike, or the attempt on his life. He felt like he needed to let go.

The cab took the harbor tunnel from Kowloon to Central. Aboveground they passed through business and shopping districts and then residential streets. It looked like a cross between London and Hawaii, Shay thought, his mind swerving on and off what he was about to do. After I just made peace with married life, he thought—recapping his reflections last night in the bar. The human mind—or was it just his?—was such a loser.

The taxi dropped them off in an upscale neighborhood.

"They treat you good," Shay said, looking around inside the corporate flat.

"Don't tell me union execs don't find a way to live well."

Nora dropped her purse on a table and walked over to the refrigerator. She opened it and grabbed two bottles of Carlsberg. She handed him one. "Have a seat."

They sat down on the couch. Nora thumbed the dimmer, lowering the light.

She smiled. "You're not as comfortable as you should be, sitting in a piece of furniture made so well."

"You picked up on that."

"About as difficult as finding a needle in a … sewing kit."

Shay smiled.

"I've been with a married man before," Nora said. "I didn't invite you back here lightly, because I know the drill—wild passion, gloomy regret." She took a sip of beer. "If you want this and can enjoy it, without looking like hell warmed-over after, that's great. If not, let's spin a few wheels talking and call it a night."

Shay kissed her. Nora opened her mouth, inviting his tongue. He put it in, moved around slowly. He pulled back, looked at her. She leaned forward, kissed him. He slid the dress straps off her shoulders.

As he kissed each shoulder, she pushed them into his mouth, gagging him on soft flesh and hard bone, until he made a sound.

She slid down on the couch, pulled him onto her. He pressed hard against her body. She began moaning. They got down off the couch, onto the floor. Nora undid his belt and then his pants button; Shay rolled onto his back to remove them. When he did, Nora climbed on top. She raised her dress over her head and tossed it to the side. She removed her bra, brought his hands to her breasts. He caressed them, looking at the tattoo between them. It was a red circle on a red rectangular field, a series of white triangular shapes resting on the circumference jutting outward, a mash-up of star, snowflake, and sun.

She got off, rolled onto her back. He got on top, pulled her arms above her head, locked her fingers. He moved slowly on top of her, pressing down hard. She pushed his hand down to her panties; he pulled them down. She raised her head, licked his nipples, and bit one until he cried out. She pulled down his boxers.

"Wait," she said.

She slid him off, kissing him all the time. She stood up, opened her purse, and pulled out a condom. She got back on top, kissed him, put the condom on the rug beside them. She rolled over, pulling him on top. Shay reached for the foil, tore off the corner. When he saw the flesh-tone latex, he stopped; took what seemed to him a long look.

He rolled off her. Feeling good wasn't feeling good.

Nora sat up and looked at him.

"I'm sorry," he said. Could not cross the line.

A few minutes later, they were dressed, sitting on the couch. Nora shook her head.

"I never should have lured you anyway."

Shay smiled. "It's an all-volunteer army."

She laughed and took a drink of beer. "You're better off anyway. Never get mixed up with a woman with father issues."

"That's way too restrictive," Shay said. "Men couldn't mate."

Nora laughed, took another slug of beer. Then, a deep breath.

"Never been lucky in love, anyway."

"What's luck got to do with it?" Shay asked.

"That's a good point. As you go, as your life goes, so goes your love."

"You don't look unlucky in life."

"Don't let this designer dress and fully stamped passport fool you."

Nora stood up and walked over to the smartphone dock, pressed Play. She boosted herself onto the countertop and slipped off her heels. They dropped to the floor as slow drive hip-hop streamed through the speakers. Shay glanced at her stockinged feet.

"Who's that playing?" he asked.

"War Party. It's a native rap group from Canada. The song's called 'Feelin' Reserved.' Like you—feeling reserved."

Shay smiled.

Nora swayed to the beat. "I'm part Indian," she said. "Oglala Sioux." She laughed. "Actually, Russian." She shook her head. "My brother says that. He's a cop on the rez. He says, 'Our ancestors came from Siberia. They crossed the Bering land bridge into Alaska when the sea was frozen. We're fucking Russians!'"

Shay laughed.

She smiled. "My great-great-great-grandfather lived on the Pine Ridge reservation, in South Dakota." She paused. "The tribe was divided into bands. His was the Kiyuksa band. Little Wound's party."

She stopped swaying and took a sip of beer. "I lost my dad when I was a kid. I was eleven. Two years older than your boy."

"I'm sorry."

Nora nodded. "It's funny. Oglala means 'to scatter one's own.' I left home at sixteen. My mom was a wreck; she never got it back together. I went to Texas, bounced around. I hooked up with a software company; I could always think straight."

She paused. "Got that from my dad."

Shay came over to her. "Then he's still with you."

"Oh, jeez," she said.

Tears ran down her cheeks. Shay put his arm around her; she put her head on his chest. She stayed there for a moment and then sat upright and wiped her eyes. She took a deep breath.

"Where were we? Oh yeah." She looked at him. "I can't have you either."

"You've got a piece of me," Shay said. "From these two nights."

She nodded. "Maybe that's the consolation. Whatever doesn't come true, we've got what happens instead. Maybe that's your life—more than the wants, the regrets. It's the pieces you *get*, instead of what you imagined. Tie 'em all together—voila. Got yourself a person and a life, to try and make sense of."

As she opened up to him, Shay felt the connection deepen. He wanted to start up again, where they left off. It felt so natural. But it felt just as natural to stop.

They talked some more. She called a cab. They stood outside in the humid air.

"I meant what I said—watch what you do around here," Nora said. "I'm not sure what you're looking at, but it sounds big-time. And big-time means big trouble."

"I'll be careful," Shay said.

The cab pulled up to the curb. Shay kissed her lightly on the lips.

"Mmm," she said. "Another piece of you."

"For me too," Shay said.

He touched her hair, turned, and walked down the steps.

The taxi sped off and descended the hill on Hollywood Road, where the antique shops congregate side by side. On the sidewalk, Shay saw the life-size plaster gods, wise men and mythological beasts they offer for sale during the day, chained to steel grates at night, keeping watch over the city with expressions that ranged from serene to wildly excited to simply amused.

During the cab ride to the hotel, Shay replayed how far he went before he stopped. It was a sloppy victory, he thought—the only real kind. An inner voice challenged him to vow it would be the last as he slipped the ring back on his finger. Then he thought, the way to resist temptation was to tell yourself there will always be another chance. If you do that, you never give in, but you never give up the possibility.

He thought that was super guy stuff.

thirty-two

Shay rolled over and checked the clock; Ma Yongrui would be by in an hour. He reached over and held the button on the night table, opening the drapes onto the harbor. He got up and walked to the window. As he did shoulder shrugs and looked out onto the water, he felt good and bad. Good because he had left Nora's apartment and returned to the hotel. Bad because he had left Nora's apartment and returned to the hotel. A split decision.

It was always that, he thought, as he did his stretches in front of the window—good and bad. Either you gave in and felt good and then bad, or you held back and felt bad and then good. It was quick good/long bad or quick bad/long good. Take your pick.

He thought, on the way to the bathroom, you need denial in life. It was the realm of youth to let go, to lunge from one thing to another. At his age, in his situation, you need to hold on. It was cool for anything to go through your mind; it wasn't okay to act on everything. Repression had a seat at the table; some things were best kept to yourself.

But as he brushed his teeth and remembered the evening, he was having trouble convincing himself.

Shay met Ma downstairs, and they drove out of the city. As the car sped along the highway for Tai Po, Shay got his first look at the rural expanse of the New Territories, which stretch back from the edge of the Kowloon peninsula to mainland China. When the car banked right around an inclined curve, they passed a large planting of evergreens. Beyond the trees, he saw villas in the recesses between the hills. The hills themselves were thick with grass, bush, and groves of banana trees.

"There is another aspect of US/China relations that is important to your country," Ma said, resuming their discussion.

"What's that?" Shay asked. The guy was becoming a bore.

"All those dollars you send us, to buy our goods? We reinvest them in US Treasury securities, corporate bonds, and mortgage certificates. This money provides your government, businesses, and individuals with capital, at modest interest rates. Money they would be otherwise starved for—since your citizens save so little."

"Let me see if I get this straight," Shay said. "If we saved our money instead of spending it on your stuff, we could accomplish the same thing—have excess savings to fund our economy at low interest rates, while denying you the cash that you turn around and lend back to us, keeping us in hock for centuries."

"Hock?"

"Debt." The I.O.U.S.A., Shay thought.

Ma smiled. "An interesting formulation. But these goods I speak of are necessities—clothing, kitchen utensils, bicycles for your children. You would buy these anyway. Who would supply them, if not China?"

"Our own workers."

"At prices so much higher than ours—because of your higher wages—you would no longer have the difference in your pocket to save."

Prick, Shay thought.

On the outskirts of Tai Po, it looked as if they were heading into a sheer wall of apartment towers. To the right was Tolo Harbor, which narrows into Tolo Channel and flows into Mirs Bay. The car crossed a river bridge and skirted the north side of the city. They passed an automobile junkyard and came to a sign that said "Tai Po Industrial

Estate." The car turned right, made the first left, and then came to a halt three factories up.

They entered the concrete building. A man slouching at the reception desk sat up straight. Ma nodded to him as he led Shay to an open elevator on the right. Ma pushed the button for the second floor. He gave Shay a mechanical smile as the car dragged its way up the shaft in a noisy crawl.

The elevator door opened into a hallway. Ma extended his hand to the right. They walked down the hall, turning into an office that looked like it belonged to an engineer or foreman; blueprints and metal parts were lying on a shelf above the desk.

"Mr. Shay, if you'll be seated, I'll get the plant manager and one of the company principals," Ma said.

Shay stayed on his feet and browsed through a book on the shelf.

A minute later, a man came down the hall and stepped into the office. He had wide shoulders and a bony build. His black hair was slicked back. He held a Glock in his left hand. "Through here," he said, moving behind the desk.

He reached for the doorknob to open a second, interior door. "Through here," he repeated.

Shay weighed options. There was too much distance between him and the gunman; a lunge would be beaten by a gunshot. There was nothing in reach to grab and throw. Of all his choices, none of the above was the best.

Shay moved to the door as directed and entered a small, dimly lit room. He looked to his left when he heard a foot scuff. A man was sitting on the floor. His mouth was gagged, his hands tied behind his back.

Lin Xueqin.

thirty-three

The gunman flicked his head for Shay to move against the wall. A second man came into the room. He grabbed Shay's arms and tied his hands behind his back. He gagged him with duct tape. When he slapped him, Shay kneed him in the crotch. The guy dropped the tape roll and bent forward. Shay kicked him in the chest, knocking him back.

The gunman rushed in from the side. Shay spun to face him and took a leg kick to the face; he stumbled back. The man pointed his gun, motioning Shay to turn around. When he did, the gunman cracked him on the back of the head with the handle of the gun.

When Shay came to, he was on the floor. His hands were tied behind his back, his mouth was gagged, and his feet were bound at the ankles. His head throbbed. The pain in his ribs made him think the man he kicked had exacted his revenge.

He glanced at Lin, who was laying still on the ground. He surveyed the rest of the room. It was small, with bare walls, cracked grayish paint, and no windows. The only light came from a single bulb in the center of the ceiling.

He wondered how much time had passed. He could feel the tightened skin where blood had caked at the back of his head. He listened for sounds; he heard machinery down the hall, a truck on the street outside.

The door opened and three men came in—Ma, the gunman, and a tall Westerner wearing dark slacks and a tan work shirt.

"Ah, Mr. Shay," the man said in a German accent. The gunman pulled off Shay's gag and took a position to the side. Ma stayed by the door.

Shay managed to sit up. He made a sound as his hurt ribs bore the brunt.

"Mr. Shay, first things first," the man said. "You won't be hurt anymore. As long as you cooperate. You are no good to us dead." He paused. "Of course, you are not out of danger. I am going to make a telephone call. Your life will depend upon it."

"Who are you?"

"Call me Karl. Karl Bodewig."

"What is it I've done that my life should depend on anything?" Shay asked.

Lin woke at the sound of the voices. He sat up.

The man smiled. "Come now, Mr. Shay. Don't underestimate anyone here. We're all intelligent, all very informed. We have been watching Mr. Calderon since he began demanding more money for his services. We know you met him. We also know you met with Mr. Lin here,"—he waved his hand behind him—"the trade-union organizer. And we know Mr. Lin and Mr. Calderon know what is going on in the Shenzhen plant."

"I came to China to see what the union was up against," Shay said. "Calderon told me the working conditions in Shenzhen were bad. I figured he thought Lambal Interior was going to close the Juarez factory and send everything to China, so he wanted to make some trouble. The meeting with Lin was a courtesy—we meet with trade unionists all over the world."

"Mr. Calderon, a patriot? Afraid his country would lose out in the battle to attract foreign investment? We should have killed him, not followed him around Juarez to scare him." He looked at Ma. "And not hired someone's Triad wannabe cousins in Chinatown for the other job."

The Van Wyck muck-up, Shay thought.

Bodewig turned to Shay. "I'm afraid you didn't get to know Mr. Calderon very well. You should have; he's a talented individual. A terrific mechanical mind—a specialist in quick-change tooling. We could have never made the production modifications without him. But his greed threatened our business."

"Which is?" Shay asked.

"I suppose there is no harm telling you," Bodewig said. "Our operation has been uncovered; we will have to close up shop anyway."

They're going to kill me.

"It's all about *brands*, Mr. Shay," Bodewig said.

"Brands?"

"The Chinese have succeeded by offering inexpensive labor to become the manufacturing workshop of the world. But Santa's elves are tired of working for a fraction of the reward their master reaps. They know what they are paid, and they know what the final product sells for. There's a lot of money in the middle they never see. They want that money for themselves."

Bodewig lit a cigarette. He was six foot two, with blond hair and blue eyes. He looked indifferent to life, and everything in it.

"It is like an opportunistic machinist working in your America, Mr. Shay," he said, exhaling the smoke. "He sees the value he is producing, but he knows he is not being paid fairly for it. So he starts his own shop, builds his own product. And when he sells something, the entire check—not a small portion—is made out to him."

"The Chinese are going into the automobile business?" Shay said.

Bodewig nodded. "You have no idea." He dragged on his smoke. "Mr. Shay, the Chinese automotive industry is one of the largest business opportunities in the world. Sales of cars made in China, primarily by joint-venture companies, are increasing at fantastic rates. China has overtaken America as the largest market for new cars in the world. One day soon, the Chinese will have as many cars as exist in all of the world today. China wants its own producers to control this market. The government is encouraging local carmakers to do everything they can to gain the upper hand."

He smiled. "As legal disputes between the Chinese carmakers and Western firms over copyright theft so clearly demonstrate."

Bodewig shook his head. "Amazing, when you think about it. More than a billion people in China, and most will one day trade in a bicycle for a car. Do you have any idea how much money there is to be made in a market that big? What economies of scale are available to producers? How much leverage they will have to dictate prices to suppliers? With such a large, diverse country, China's carmakers will build product for every budget and taste. This will develop the capacity to offer multiple car lines, at attractive prices, for export to the rest of the world. China already exports a million cars a year. The first Chinese-made cars have arrived in Europe. The first car built solely by a Chinese company will go on sale in the United States next year. If you think your economy is hurt now by the Chinese, wait until they begin sending you their automobiles."

"But there's a hitch," Shay said. "They don't have the expertise."

Bodewig nodded. "They invited the majors in, to form joint ventures. Promised them the chance to build cars cheaply—first for sale in China and then for export."

"And the agreements come with technology-transfer provisions, so the Chinese can learn the business," Shay said. "In the case of Lambal, they didn't wait. They added a shift and hijacked the goods."

That's why they killed Jack, and tried to kill me. A strike settlement on our terms would have crimped Lambal's operations in China. But now the focus of the crime had shifted to China. He wondered if Lambal was in with them.

"It's a race against time," Bodewig said. "You see, there's a wild card in the plan—the Chinese consumer. Chinese car buyers like Western and Japanese automobiles. These companies are pouring millions into new capacity in China. If it takes China's domestic auto manufacturers too long to get up to speed, they will lose market share and brand loyalty to the foreign firms. State edict or not, this will be tough to regain. As your Big Three in America found out, when they awoke late to the Japanese challenge."

Bodewig crushed the butt on the floor and waved the gunman toward Shay. The goon stood him up and led him to the door. As Shay shuffled his bound feet across the room, he looked down at Lin, who nodded and then lowered his eyes.

thirty-four

Lewis's admin told him there was a call from Hong Kong from a man claiming to have information about Shay. Lewis didn't know what she was talking about. Shay had been checking in regularly. As far as Lewis knew, he was staying another day to poke around.

He told the admin to patch the call in. "Yes?"

"Am I speaking to an executive of the United Machinists?"

"My name is William Lewis; I'm president of the union. Is John Shay all right? Who is this?"

"He's fine," the man said. "My name is Karl Bodewig."

"What is this about?"

"I have a proposal for you," Bodewig said. "I am holding your Mr. Shay. I will release him for $10 million US."

"Put Shay on the line," Lewis said.

"Of course. Why make a deal if we don't have him?"

Bodewig paused. "Or if he's not alive."

"Put him on the phone."

"Just a moment."

Bodewig waved to Ma, who gave the gunman an order. The man left the room and returned with Shay.

Bodewig held the phone to Shay's mouth. "Just a quick word," he said.

Ma barked at the gunman, who pulled the tape off Shay's mouth.

Shay looked at Bodewig and then at Ma.

"Calderon's involved, the Shenzhen plant, they're diverting produc—"

Bodewig knocked Shay to the ground. The gunman shoved the barrel of his gun against his head.

Lewis heard what Shay said and then the struggle.

"Don't hurt him!" he shouted.

"I'll have to call you back, Mr. Lewis."

"Don't get off," Lewis said. "Let's settle this now."

"Very well. Remain on the line."

Bodewig muted the phone. He went over to Ma, and they spoke.

Lewis called Hannah into the room and told her what had happened.

"Bring Calderon here," she said.

He was on the floor below, being grilled by the Machinists' research department; he was a trove of information on how Lambal operated outside the country, without union constraints. Lewis called in Hamill and told him to get Calderon. I should have sent him with Shay, Lewis thought, watching the Hell's Kitchen tough race out of the room. But Hamill had a record; it would have been tough to get him across a border, even with phony papers.

Lewis and Hannah glanced at each other as they waited, Hannah still processing the facts, Lewis trying to figure out how to stall Bodewig when he got back on the phone.

Away from the phone, Bodewig and Ma argued about what to do.

It didn't take Hamill long.

"What's going on in the China plant?" Lewis asked Calderon when Hamill brought him through the door.

"What do you mean?" Calderon said.

Lewis moved closer, looming over the Mexican. He had the build of the three-sport high-school athlete he once was, although his shoulders sloped downward now and his muscles were covered with an extra layer of flesh. "I don't have time for bullshit," he said. "I've got a guy on the phone in Hong Kong who's holding John Shay. He says he won't kill him for a bucketful of money. Shay says you're involved. I'm asking you again—what is going on?"

Calderon shook his head. "I don't know."

Lewis handed the phone to Hannah. Calderon managed to cover his face before Lewis smacked him with an open hand, knocking him onto the couch. Lewis lunged forward, slapped him repeatedly, alternating the palm and the back of his hand.

"Talk, you son of a bitch."

Hannah froze, too stunned to intervene. Hamill stepped forward.

"Hold it, Mr. Lewis," he said, grabbing his arm. "Give him to me."

Lewis released Calderon. He looked at Hannah when he realized what he had done. And was going to keep doing.

He turned to Calderon.

"Not a split second to lose, you bastard." He cocked his fist.

"Mr. Lewis, are you there?" Bodewig asked into the telephone.

"He's here," Hannah said. She handed Lewis the phone.

"Where's Shay?" Lewis asked.

"He is all right."

"I want to hear his voice again."

"That will not be possible," Bodewig said. "And the terms have changed. We now require $20 million. I will call in one hour for your decision. If you agree, you will have forty-eight hours to transfer the money to an account we will specify."

Bodewig hung up.

Lewis put down the phone. He looked at Calderon, who was bleeding from the nose. The Mexican gulped a breath before he got out the words.

"I was afraid to tell you. I think these men are Triad. They forced me to work for them."

"Doing what?" Lewis asked.

Calderon wiped the blood from his nose. "Making seats for another company. Using the Lambal plant."

"What company?" Lewis asked.

"I don't know," Calderon said. "I was told to make new tooling for the line that could be changed over quickly when the regular shift ended, and torn down before regular production started in the morning. The changes were to a number of dimensions and fitting points. It made me think the seats were for another manufacturer's vehicle."

Lewis turned to Hannah. "Triads? Chinese hoods?"

"Secret societies," Hannah said. "They were formed years ago, to resist the tribes that swept down from the north and ruled China. When their dynasty was overthrown and the Chinese republic established, there was no reason for the Triads to exist, except the criminal element. They fled to Hong Kong after the Second World War, when the Communists took over and came down hard on crime."

"We're tangled with them in Hong Kong?" Lewis asked.

"We have to go to the police," Hannah said.

"What about John?" Lewis asked. "What do you think will happen to him if we do that? Even if I give them the money, there's no guarantee they'll let him go."

He paused, thinking. "We can't send someone in there; we don't even know where he is. I doubt we can even stall."

Lewis walked around his desk and sat down. He tapped on the phone a couple of times and then picked it up. "Dolores, get Peter Lambal on the line. Right away."

Hannah stared at him.

"It's his plant," Lewis said. "And he's got money."

"He might be involved," Hannah said.

Lewis nodded. "During the talks, he said he had enough orders for a second plant. Maybe he's doing that business on the sly, while we negotiate the issue at the table." He shook his head. "But grabbing John? I guess if he killed Jack, why not?"

"We could pay them," she said.

Lewis was closer to the finances. "The strike has drawn us down. The pension fund is off 40 percent—investments gone bad. There's no way we could hide it either. The government is fishing around, trying to pressure us. They're auditing us for compliance with disclosure rules about how we spend dues money."

He shook his head. "I'd shift the money in a heartbeat if we had it, government prosecutors or not."

The phone beeped. Lewis picked up.

"Peter Lambal, Bill," Dolores said. She clicked him in.

"Hello, Peter," Lewis said.

"Bill," Lambal said. "what can I do for you?"

"We've got a situation. Maybe you can help us."

"Something that can't be handled by the negotiating team?"

"Someone in Hong Kong is holding John Shay and demanding a $20 million ransom," Lewis said. "They put John on the phone to prove he's alive. He blurted out something about your Shenzhen plant. Something about diverting production. Do you know anything about that?"

Lambal didn't answer right away. "We've had plenty of problems," he said. "Missing materials, stolen tools. Cash disbursements without receipts."

"What did he mean about diverting production? Are any finished goods not accounted for?"

"Not that I'm aware of. We're running one shift, producing a fixed amount that maps to our order rate to fulfill those orders for our customers."

"Who are … ?"

Lambal hesitated.

"John Shay's life is at stake, Peter."

"We supply a number of European and US car manufacturers' joint-venture plants in China," Lambal said. He paused. "What was Shay doing there? Besides visiting the plant? Is there anything else that could have gotten him into this situation?"

"We got a call from a guy who works at your Ciudad Juarez plant," Lewis said. "He spent some time at the Shenzhen facility, told us something funny was going on. He said the plant was running a night shift."

"Who is this man?"

"His name is Luis Calderon. Ring a bell?"

"No," Lambal said. "We only run one shift a day in Shenzhen. We don't have the business to justify two."

"Then why are you telling us you have to build a second plant in China?"

"To do business up north," Lambal said. "The Shenzhen plant serves automotive customers in Guangdong and adjacent provinces. The Chinese are redirecting development to the central and northern regions. The auto companies there want their suppliers close to them. They want inventory delivered every few hours to match the build rate, rather than have the stuff shipped in beforehand and lay around, taking up space and tying up capital."

"Calderon said two Chinese men followed him when he returned to Mexico."

"So you sent Mr. Shay to China to look into it," Lambal said. "After telling us you wanted to tour the facility for information gathering, to help settle the strike."

"That's right," Lewis said. He paused. "It's too much money for us. We can raise two, three … maybe five. Will you help?"

Lambal thought for a second. "You don't know who you're dealing with. What's the guarantee they'll release him?"

"None."

"That's a tough call," Lambal said. "We're not in such great shape ourselves. Especially with your strike shutting down our revenue stream."

Lewis read him loud and clear. "You son of a bitch," he said. "You're not getting a strike settlement for the money, if that's what you're thinking. But you will get us back to the table, that much I can promise. Then you can call your goons off—Jack Cafferty's blood on your hands is already enough to punch your ticket to hell. And hopefully to Supermax, for the rest of your days on earth."

"Are you out of your mind?!" Lambal said. "I had nothing to do with Jack Cafferty's death. I ought to slam this receiver down right now and begin shutting every one of my plants, one by one. I've got all the money in the bank I'll ever need. I don't need to put up with this nonsense any longer."

"That's your father's legacy; you'll do nothing of the kind," Lewis said. "It's also fifteen thousand men and women, working for their families, and each one of them will hound you to hell. We'll march up and down every street and every neighborhood you and your family try to live in, in every corner of the globe, for the rest of your life. The Labor Department will come down on you like a ton of bricks. Don't threaten someone who will stand toe-to-toe with you every step of the way."

Lewis glanced at Hannah during the silence that followed. She looked like she had been flash frozen. He smiled at her. She thawed and smiled back.

"Okay, now we've gotten that off our chests," Lewis said after a pause. He knew he had to take the lead; Shay's life was at stake. "Peter, I meant what I said about coming back to the table. Do this for us. It's been a rocky road between the union and company. Maybe we can pave it more smoothly after this."

Another pause. It was killing Lewis.

"All right," Lambal finally said.

"Thank you," Lewis said, as much with an exhale as words. "We're supposed to get a call about the arrangements. It's a forty-eight-hour timetable."

"I'll set things up on my end."

"He's going to want plenty in return," Hannah said after Lewis hung up.

"I'll be happy to give it to him if it saves John's life."

Lewis thinking, maybe that's what this is—a setup, to settle the strike. And if Lambal's involved, he'll just be paying himself.

"I'm going to Hong Kong," Hannah said.

Lewis nodded. "We need someone there." He picked up the phone. "Dolores, scramble a charter. Arrange for a helicopter to fly Hannah to Kennedy or Newark."

"Where to?"

"Hong Kong."

"I have to stop by John's house first," Hannah said.

"What do we say?"

"The truth. And call that guy who does documents."

Lewis picked up the phone.

thirty-five

Hannah followed the nav commands through the suburbs. She was glad she had to focus as much on the driving and directions as the upcoming task. She had never owned a car, never needed one in the city; she borrowed this one from one of the union guys.

Hannah stopped in front of the house rather than pulling up the driveway; she wanted to walk it, to collect herself. She rang the bell.

Anne answered the door. "Hannah, what a surprise. Come in."

They sat down in the living room.

"Can I get you something?"

Hannah shook her head. "I've come about John."

Anne froze. "Just tell me he's all right."

"He is. But there's a problem. We got a call an hour ago, demanding a ransom."

"Oh God." She wrapped her arms around her sides, as if she was trying to get an embrace or hold something in.

"It has something to do with Lambal's plant in China. I'm leaving in two hours on a charter for Hong Kong."

Anne looked up the stairs to Michael's bedroom. She began to cry.

Hannah put an arm around her. She balled her fingers in a fist when they trembled.

"He'll be all right," she said. "I'll bring him back to you."

Shay was seated against the wall, bound and gagged. A hood came in and stood near him. Shay pretended to be asleep; the guy moved closer. When he got close enough, Shay shot his bound feet forward into the guy's knee. His leg buckled and he fell to the ground.

He got up screaming and kicked Shay in the face, snapping his head to the side. Blood streamed down Shay's nostrils as the hood knelt down, straddled his legs, and slammed his head against the wall. He began to beat him, alternating fists, pounding the punches into Shay's face.

Shay's head snapped back and forth as the tough worked him over. When he realized it wasn't going to stop anytime soon, he tried to disengage from the pain.

He thought of Anne's voice, felt it inside him. It had such a tone, husky, quieting; it always put things right. He thought about Michael, how he would be without him, if he didn't make it through. He would find the strength, with Anne. He tried to tell him something—that we had a full life together, already, no matter how short our time. I am inside you, son, and will be, all your days.

Then he got back to business—fighting for his life. He made himself remember his father's sharp elbows when they played basketball in the driveway, trying to harden his game, in the style of the YMCA leagues where his dad used to play in the city. Toughen up, he thought, but then felt himself slipping away. He felt something emptying, and something filling too. He had the sensation he was being turned inside out. He couldn't tell if he was light approaching dark or dark approaching light; day turning to night, or night becoming day. He was on the doorstep of the mystery.

The man stopped. Shay's face was swollen, and the back of his head seeped blood. He was slumped against the wall, barely conscious. He was losing strength.

Finish with pride, he told himself. Finish strong.

I'm going to kill these fucks.

If I don't, Lewis will kill them.

Every fucking one of them.

He saw a blurred form standing over him. Dad …

The goon kicked him in the ribs. Shay moaned and then went unconscious.

He dreamed he was in a rowboat, sinking into an underground lagoon; his father was with him. As water filled the bottom of the boat, the planks cracked. Suddenly he was flying alone, down a long tunnel with dirt walls. Below him, on either side, were plaster heads, mounted on pedestals. In the next scene, two little boys were standing on the porch of a house to keep from getting wet. They were laughing as they tried to shove each other into the rain. He was back in the tunnel again; the plaster heads had turned to skulls. He flew along rapidly; there was no body orientation because there was no body, just his eyes. He was in a jungle now, running through thick brush, up and down mounds of dirt and through ravines. Men were chasing him with machetes. He climbed a tree, and someone began to hack him terribly. Now he was in a dark box in the sky, a deck of cards spilled out on his belly; they were all hearts, jacks and kings. And then there was sand, nothing but sand, and on a great dune in the distance, the small figures of a caravan. And then the front of the caravan swooped up like the arched neck of a snake and climbed into the sky, its tail whipping across the desert floor; he grabbed it and held on for dear life ...

thirty-six

The Machinists had a guy who forged documents. They used the paper for visits to countries that outlawed unions, sometimes even traveled with them in the United States when organizing drives got nasty. Hannah traveled to Hong Kong under her own passport but brought a fake with Shay's last name. After a brief conversation with a manager at the Shangri-La, she convinced him she was Shay's wife and he gave her a key to the room.

Her hand shook as she slid the card in the slot and opened the door. The lights were on. The bed was turned down but untouched. There was a wood tray with the laundry card and bags at the foot of the bed. She put down her bag and looked into the bathroom and closet. She walked to the window, with the view of Victoria Harbor. She tried to close the drapes, but they wouldn't shut. She turned back to the room and looked around slowly. She went through the dresser and desk drawers, but didn't find anything.

She returned to the closet. Among the hotel hangers were three wooden ones with UNITED MACHINISTS written across the face. Hannah removed the shirts and sport coat they held and laid the hangers on the bed. She unscrewed the hooks, and took a cylindrical tool from her purse. She inserted it into the threaded hole and turned it clockwise, beyond the depth of the hook, and lifted a dowel-like insert out of each hole. She held the first dowel in both hands and twisted it at the center, breaking the thread seal.

She wondered if she imagined the lack of strength in her wrists, or if it was real.

She unscrewed the thread and looked inside. Nothing. She unscrewed the second dowel and separated the parts. There was a small piece of paper. She unrolled it and saw a name and phone number. She dialed the number, remembering how Shay always reminded her to carry the tool to check for messages in an emergency.

A woman answered in Chinese.

"Hello? Do you speak English?" Hannah asked.

"Yes, a little. What can I help?"

"My name is Hannah Stein. I'm from the United Machinists Union in the United States. I'm trying to find my associate, John Shay. Is Lin Xueqin there?" The name Shay had written on the paper.

There was a pause on the other end. "Mr. Lin not here."

"Do you know when he will come back?"

Another delay. "You are from American union? Really?"

"Yes, the United Machinists. If you will meet me, I will show you my identification. Please, this is very important."

"Where did you get phone number?"

"John Shay gave it to me."

"Okay, I come. You are where, please?"

Hannah told her and described herself. She asked the woman to meet her in the lobby—she wanted a public space, didn't know who she was getting involved with.

"I come one hour," the woman said.

Hannah wondered what they had gotten into as she waited. Shay hadn't said anything about anyone named Lin, but maybe that was the point—he didn't feel he could talk safely about him on the phone. Why was there trouble here? The Machinists figured Cafferty's death and the hit on Shay were linked to Lambal. She wondered who Shay had met here and why the China plant was involved.

She went down to the lobby fifteen minutes early to scout it out. Nobody seemed out of the ordinary, no one seemed to pay her any mind; just a bunch of well-dressed business types scurrying back and forth on their oh-so-important matters.

At precisely the one-hour mark, a woman came over and sat down. She was Hannah's age, dressed stylish biz, blending with the upscale scene. The ends of her pin-straight black hair rested on her shoulders. She picked up a magazine and leafed through it. A minute later, she put the periodical on the table that separated their chairs.

"Your identification," she said. "Put in magazine."

Hannah picked up the magazine, stuck her union ID card inside, and then thumbed through some pages. As she put it down and grabbed another, her fingers trembled. She glanced at the woman, who was looking at her hand.

The woman picked up the magazine Hannah had discarded. Hannah watched her turn the pages, stopping at one that piqued her interest. She figured they were about the same age. She had brown eyes, thin lips, a milky complexion. Her cheekbones solved the puzzle of being both prominent and soft. Hannah thought she was beautiful.

The woman placed the magazine back on the table.

"My name is Mei Wang," she said. "I am friend of Lin Xuequin. John Shay met him two days ago. Lin said he happy with meeting. Mr. Shay say he help us form unions in China. Free unions."

"Where is Mr. Lin now?" Hannah asked, as she swapped magazines and retrieved her ID.

"Do not know. He not return last night."

"Are you worried?"

Mei nodded. "China not want unions. China not want democracy too, on mainland or Hong Kong. Lin Xueqin in both movements. He is big problem for China."

"Do you have any idea where they might be? Do you know anyone else I can contact for information?"

Mei shook her head. A man walked by. Mei glanced at him and got up and left.

Hannah went back upstairs. She was trying to figure out what to do when the phone rang.

"Hello?"

No one answered.

"Please, speak to me," Hannah said. "My name is Hannah Stein; I'm a friend of John Shay."

"My name is Nora Young. Is John there?"

"Who are you?" Hannah asked.

"John and I met socially. I was calling to say hello."

"He's not here. We don't know where he is. He hasn't checked back with the office or slept in his room. When did you see him last?"

"Two nights ago," Nora said. "We had a drink, talked a bit."

Hannah got the feeling it was more than drinks.

Nora said, "I called yesterday, but he wasn't in. I thought I'd try again." She paused. "Do you think there might be trouble?"

"Do you?"

Silence on the line.

"What do you do, Ms. Young?" Hannah asked.

"It's Nora."

Hannah listened as Nora told her about her work combating digital piracy.

"Did John tell you why he was here?"

"Yes, a little."

"Did that sound like something that might get him into trouble?"

"Yes, it did."

"Do you have any idea where I might look for him?"

"I might."

"Can you come right over then?"

"Of course."

Hannah called Bill Lewis while Nora was en route to the hotel. She got him up to speed on her end. "Anything new there?" she asked.

"Lambal said he has the money," Lewis said. "The guy from Hong Kong called back, gave us an account number. A bank in the Cook Islands."

"What about the strike? What's going on?"

"The dockworkers are joining us."

"That's incredible." Her tone was flat, focused on Shay.

"They won't unload Asian or European cars on either coast. It'll stop foreign carmakers from taking advantage of parts shortages at US plants to grab market share." He managed a clipped laugh. "Looks like your harassment worked."

"Let's hope it works here as well," she said.

Nora Young arrived within the hour. The women shook hands.

"Tell me how you can help," Hannah said after offering her a chair.

"I need information," Nora said, sitting down. "Where was John going in China?"

"Shenzhen. A plant owned by Lambal Interior. We're striking them in the United States."

"What does the plant make?"

"Automotive seating, primarily. A range of interior car components."

"Who do they sell to in China?"

"Western, Japanese carmakers. Why is this important?"

"I'm trying to map the business relationships, see a way in."

Hannah told her about the after-hours production. And the ransom demand.

Nora pulled a phone out of her soft briefcase and dialed a number. She spoke in Chinese. "Okay," she said after several minutes. She hung up.

"What?" Hannah asked.

"We may have something."

"Tell me."

"I can't," Nora said. "Not immediately. We should hear back in an hour."

"Who were you speaking with?"

"A contact in China."

"You think they're holding John there?"

"Impossible to say. But I spoke to someone who may be able to find out. He has a strong interest in the situation."

"What 'situation'?" Hannah said.

Nora got up, grabbed two waters from the minibar. She held one in Hannah's direction as she returned to the chair. Each unscrewed the caps and took a swig.

Nora put down the bottle and picked up the phone. Hannah stared at it.

"Encrypted," Nora said, noting her eyes. "We even bring different laptops and smartphones when we come to China, toss them after the trip. We're afraid someone will introduce a virus while we're here—something that will spread to our networks when we return and let them surveil our systems."

"Who are you calling?" Hannah asked as Nora walked toward the door.

"The Department of Homeland Security," she said, stepping into the bathroom and closing the door behind her.

Hannah couldn't piece it together as she waited for Nora to return. She tiptoed to the bathroom door, but only heard a muffled voice. The only thing that was obvious was that what had been happening had more to do with the China plant than anyone had imagined.

Nora wasn't long.

"Tell me," Hannah said.

Nora nodded. "I've been with the Legal Software Consortium for five years. After 9/11, the government sought out people with certain specialties to help them in the war against terror. My area is commercial piracy; I handle that for LSC. I liaise for them with a US organization focusing on intellectual property rights. I rep them internationally as well—with Interpol's property crime group and various international anticounterfeiting coalitions.

"I got a call one day, a request to meet with someone from Homeland Security. He explained to me how terrorists raise cash by dealing in counterfeit goods. DHS also coordinates with the Naval Criminal Investigative Service and the Defense Criminal Investigative Services, to keep knockoff goods out of the military supply chain. The DHS guy said he wanted my 'eyes and ears.'"

She took a slug of water. "Of course, I said yes. I'm not a DHS agent or anything, just a loyal citizen. And I know a lot of people in China from my work. Last year I bumped into an officer in one of China's southern armies at an out-of-the-way restaurant in Hong Kong. He was eating with someone who appeared to be of Middle Eastern descent. When he saw me—rather, when he saw that I had seen him—he waved me over to the table and introduced us. His manner was exaggerated; something wasn't right. 'See something, say something'—I reported it to Homeland Security."

"And?" Hannah asked.

"Nothing. I never heard anything more about it. They took the information and my description of the other man, that was it."

"Who did you call before? When you were speaking Chinese?"

"An official in Guangzhou, the Guangdong capital. Someone trying to help us stamp out piracy in the province."

She paused. "Someone I also told about the meeting between the army officer and the guy from the Middle East."

"Why did you think he could help?"

"John was interested in industrial counterfeiting. This guy in Guangzhou knows everything there is to know about it. I thought he might have some information."

"Did he?"

"I think so. He was cagey. But I think so."

"Can you call him again?"

She shook her head. "He told me not to. He said he would call me as soon as he found out anything."

"You've got to call him," Hannah said.

"This man is very powerful," Nora said. "When he says not to call, he means it. He has good reason for it."

Hannah picked up the phone. "Operator? Get me the *South China Morning Post*."

"You New Yorkers are all trouble, aren't you?" She put her hand on Hannah's and pushed down gently, hanging up the receiver.

Nora picked up her mobile and dialed. She began speaking in Chinese.

thirty-seven

Guangzhou, capital, Guangdong Province

Gao Liang tapped a pencil on the desk after the second call from Nora Young. The walls of his office were decorated with portraits of China's leaders, from Mao Zedong to the present. A colorful poster for a performance by the Guangzhou City Orchestra broke the spell of officialdom cast by the Communist rulers; Gao played viola in the group. Another wall sported a signed team photo of the Guangdong Leopards, one of seven teams in the Chinese Baseball League. Gao's nephew played shortstop for the team. There was a separate portrait of him at bat.

Gao was six feet tall and stood out in most gatherings. His hair was cut officialdom-style to not stand out. He was athletically lean, from years of sports. His face and eyes had a glow that had receded in most men his age. He was sixty-three.

Gao picked up the phone and called the army base. He told his secretary to cancel his appointments for the rest of the afternoon and have the driver bring the car out front.

Outside, he told the chauffeur to drive him to Sun Yat-sen Memorial Hall. When they arrived, he got out of the car and told the driver to wait.

The memorial building is at the original site of Sun Yat-sen's presidential office on Dongfeng Xi Lu. Built in 1925, it sits back off the street, prefaced by an expanse of lawn, carefully tended flowers and shrubs, and several paved walkways leading from the gate to the memorial itself.

Gao shook his head when he saw a young salesclerk sleeping with her head on the table at a souvenir postcard stand outside the grounds. He banged on the table as he entered one of the gates, waking her with a start.

Gao strolled down a walk paved with eighteen-inch-square concrete blocks that were partially covered with moss, irrepressible in the dampness. Two lovers sat on a stone bench to the side of the walkway. The woman was laughing and fidgeting like a young fawn. The man was still and intent, but smiling broadly, as he held her tightly with one arm wrapped around her shoulder.

Gao passed a huge tree, whose trunk rose upward as seven or eight large limbs. Hundreds of roots showed themselves aboveground at the base, converging from all sides to begin their ascent as the trunk. The trunk was not a single form, but an assemblage of tangled roots that thickened and hugged one another as they moved upward and split into the limbs that took separate paths to the sky.

Is this what must happen to China? he thought.

Gao approached the hall. It was a traditional structure, several stories high. Each story had partial roofs that curved upward at the edges pagoda-style and were covered with bright, cornflower-blue tiles. Six red cylindrical columns rose from the pavement to support a front overhang. On the lawn directly in front of the building stood a large bronze statue of Sun Yat-sen, walking stick in his right hand, his left hand resting on his side. His head was erect, looking out over the city.

Gao came here when he sought internal counsel. Looking at the memorial, he wondered how he could take advantage of the opportunity that had dropped into his lap.

As part of the economic reforms launched by Deng Xiaoping in 1980, Guangdong Province was allotted four Special Economic Zones, where businesses were allowed to operate more independently than state-owned companies. The SEZs enabled the province to get a head start on the rest of the country as China took baby steps into the global capitalist mix.

Guangdong now had the highest per-capita income in China. Beijing and Shanghai—especially the latter and the rest of the Yangtze River Basin, an area of four hundred million people that stretched from Shanghai on the East China Sea through Sichuan, the country's most populous province—were envious of its success.

The government had been delivering high-flying Guangdong numerous slaps in the face. Lending restrictions were tightened and credit withheld. Materials were not delivered as promised. Companies were refused permission to purchase farmland to build new factories. Minor infractions of policy were pursued as full-blown witch hunts.

Beijing and Shanghai wanted to reassert their dominance over the South. They were going to ghettoize Guangdong, Gao thought. Keep it manufacturing low-value goods, while they established their glamour cities and nurtured the knowledge-based industries and service economy of the future for themselves.

Gao was fed up. His ministry had helped develop Guangdong into a magnet for industrious Chinese. From everywhere in the province and throughout China, laborers had left farms and state-run factories to come to his region, where new factories, apartment buildings, and service establishments had sprouted up without interference.

It was boomtown in a country that had suffered from the idea that spirit and drive in work could come from collective ownership and moral exhortation. Removing those restraints had unleashed the entrepreneurial genius of the people in Guangdong Province and its capital, Guangzhou. And stirred ire in the seat of the middle kingdom, Beijing.

The struggle was grounded in historical roots that never seemed to disappear. Years ago, Guangzhou had been a center for maritime commerce, importing glass, wool, and linens from the Roman Empire and Asia, and exporting silk and handicrafts in turn. In ancient China, it had been the earliest point of entry for foreigners.

The city had also been the center for anti-imperial and revolutionary movements at the beginning of the twentieth century. When the Manchu dynasty collapsed in 1912 and the republic was established, it was in large part thanks to the republic's first leader, Sun Yat-sen, a Guangdong native.

And Triad member, when that organization played a stronger role in the political life of China.

Gao looked around before he made his way back to the gate. He left the memorial gardens and turned right. At the first stoplight, he waited to cross the broad avenue. When the light changed, he crossed the street and headed toward Renmin Park, a small refuge for Guangzhou's citizens a few blocks off Dongfeng Xi Lu. Gao picked up his pace as he cut through side streets toward the park.

He sat down on a stone bench near a gazebo in the center of the park. Behind him in the grass, an elderly woman was stretching in the slow, graceful movements of Tai Chi. Nearby, among the manicured beds of ivy and flowers, he saw a large bust of a woman's head. Her eyes were closed, and her lips were pushed together in a content smile. The statue, cut from pink stone, rested on a polished marble base that contained the single inscription, "Bride."

Gao heard the squeal of children's laughter from a playground at the other end of the park. A few moments later, a man approached the bench. He was young, in his early thirties, plump for that age, with a functionary's soft, bloated face. He sat down on the bench next to Gao's, and the two men talked quietly, looking straight ahead into the park. The old woman continued to exercise behind them as the men spoke for ten minutes. Then the man from the Ministry of State Security got up and walked away.

Gao stayed another ten minutes, admiring the flowers, the sunlight, the blue sky, and the laughter of the children, before getting up himself and leaving. He checked his watch and picked up his gait as he headed back to the Sun Yat-sen memorial. His driver met him there five minutes after Gao had returned.

It had gotten cloudy since his rendezvous in Renmin Park; the sky was now whitish gray, one continuous cloud cover stretching over the entire city and as far as the eye could see in all directions along the horizon. His driver told him he had taken a quick spin and the car wasn't tailed. He told the driver to take him to the White Swan Hotel.

En route they passed sidewalks where vendors plied their trades in open-air "shops"—a person sitting on the ground repairing flat bicycle tires, another replacing zippers on luggage and clothing, someone putting taps on shoes. A man with a scale offered to weigh passersby. Someone was selling metal casters for furniture legs. Others sold small electrical components, towels, anything you might need.

The car stopped at a traffic light. On the corner, Gao saw a man and a woman squatting over a rectangular tablecloth laid out on the pavement stones. They were hunters, dressed coarsely, their faces large and round. The woman wore multiple strings of red and orange beads around her neck. The man was dressed in a khaki shirt, his green work pants rolled above his knees. On the tablecloth were animal bones, a skull that looked like it had come from a panther or some wild cat, dried slices of meat, a molted snake skin, and bear paws. Onlookers were staring at the objects. A boy about four years old stood perfectly still above the display, transfixed, the little fingers of his two hands clasped together and pressed against his waist.

Gao smoked as the car edged through traffic. It had begun to rain. Bicyclists were wearing green vinyl ponchos to keep them dry as they maneuvered the city streets—all theirs twenty years ago, he thought, now jammed with automobiles. Gao chuckled as a woman passed their car. She was wearing a pink poncho that flowed down her waist and stretched forward to cover her arms and the handlebars. She had curlers in her hair.

"Perhaps she requested a loan of the barber's cloth," he joked to his driver, who bobbed his head in delight.

The Buick crossed onto Shamian Island, a small piece of land set in the Pearl River just a stone's throw from Guangzhou's mainland. During the mid–nineteenth century, it was operated as a French and British concession within the city. Still standing are the Victorian buildings and European-style churches of the foreigners who made their way up the Pearl River Delta to establish a trading beachhead in Guangzhou, a thousand miles from Beijing and the introverted heart of the Dragon Throne.

The driver dropped Gao off at the White Swan. Gao walked through the hotel lobby, stopping on a footbridge in the atrium to admire the orange carp that were swimming below in the rocky pool. The water and surrounding foliage gave the lobby a moist, soothing, tropical air.

Gao followed the waitress to a table after indicating with his finger that he wished a seat by the window. He sipped a Tsing Tao beer and looked out at the river. Twenty feet from shore, a man was standing bare-chested in waist-high water, next to a long pole stuck into the river bottom. Attached to the top of the pole was a square net; loose netting saturated with water trailed down the pole, hugging it. The man held a wooden basket that bobbed on the surface of the water. Gao watched his muscular back ripple from the effort to hold the basket still against the current as he scanned the river for fish.

A few minutes later, a man in the officer's dress uniform of the People's Liberation Army took a seat across from Gao. He nodded when the waitress asked if he'd like a beer. His manner was easygoing, but he sat perfectly erect. He was five foot six, square-shouldered, in his early fifties. He had close-cropped black hair, a round face, and thick lips that looked like he could smile or strike with equally powerful effect.

More radical than Gao in his views toward the central government, more conversant with the use of force to achieve advantage, Hu Weimin's dream was to one day see South China—the wealthier and more forward-looking area of the country, located south of the Yangtze River and comprised of some three hundred million people—unite with Hong Kong and Taiwan into a breakaway nation that could lead its people irreversibly into the modern world.

The waitress returned with the beer and poured half a glass. She bowed and withdrew.

"It's the Year of the Snake," Hu toasted. "What better time for a bold move?"

thirty-eight

Thirty hours after the ransom demand, while Shay lay still in a pool of blood, a truck with Hu Weimin behind the wheel and three men in the back made its way slowly through Sha Tau Kok, a small town on the edge of marshlands that open into Starling Inlet on the northeast coast of Hong Kong's New Territories.

Hu looked to his left at the marshes that link the shore to the inlet, long blades of slender grass that rose like antennae from the cross between sand and earth, waving like stick figures in the breeze. He saw well in the darkness—it was a clear night, three-quarters of a moon hanging in the sky.

The marshlands turned to mudflats as the truck descended from the higher elevations of the northern New Territories. It wound its way around Starling Inlet and headed toward the reservoir at Plover Cove. Lacking large rivers, lakes, or underground water supplies, Hong Kong has constructed dams and reservoirs in several large valleys. Plover Cove is one of the largest, and marked the point where the vehicle would bend west along Tolo Harbor and head for the industrial estate where Hu's intel from his army sources indicated Shay was held prisoner.

In the moonlit night, Hu could make out barbecue pits and picnic areas along the side of the road as he approached Bride's Pool, on the northwest side of the reservoir. According to legend, the place got its name from a bride who fell to her death there. She was being transported to her groom by bearers on a raised chair when one of them slipped, sending both the chair and bride crashing over the falls.

A few bicyclists were still on the trails even at night, some riding, most of them standing and talking among themselves at the end of the day's outing, their bikes resting against the trunks of trees. Hu was sorry this wasn't a recreation trip; he wanted to see Bride's Pool. He had heard it was one of the prettiest waterfalls in Hong Kong.

The truck slowed as it passed the sign for the waterfall. A half mile beyond, it pulled over at a roadside stand, a claptrap wooden shack with a Coke machine out front. The yard was strewn with cans and bottles, tires, plastic chairs, car parts, and toys.

Hu shut off the engine and got out of the truck. The shack and a house behind it were dark. A hen and her chicks squawked and scattered as he went around back. He walked over to a pickup truck with a canvas-covered bed and pulled aside the cloth. The truck reeked of fish and contained straw baskets darkened by the stain of saltwater. Hu rummaged around until he found a black plastic bag. He undid the tie and pulled out the guns and ammunition clips. He took a pistol for himself and stuck it in his pants.

Three men were crouching behind a nearby shed; Hu waved them toward him and distributed the guns and ammo. The men reached into the back of the pickup and changed into the fishermen's clothing they found there. They were laughing at the stench of the sea that surrounded them. Hu talked with them as they finished changing. One of the men got in front to drive, and the other two climbed in back. Hu said a few words to the driver before slapping his palm on the door of the cab.

Hu returned to the truck out front and distributed the remaining weapons and ammunition to the men he had arrived with. He started the engine as the smaller pickup moved slowly out of the yard, rising and falling over the uneven ridges of the dirt terrain. The pickup pulled onto the road behind his truck.

The road began to twist and turn as the trucks maneuvered the bend alongside Plover Cove. Hu saw wooden-slat houses set on bamboo stilts on the side of the road as they passed the cove and drove alongside Tolo Harbor. The boat rental signs got harder to read as clouds filled the sky and darkened the moon; he was glad to see the light obscured. The trucks were on the outskirts of town, near the industrial estate. There was little traffic at this hour as they cut inland off the harbor, leaving the water behind. Hu saw a sign for Ting Kok Road. The industrial estate was less than a mile away.

He signaled for a left turn at Dai Kwai Street on the back edge of the estate. He drove slowly past the industrial buildings; several floors were lit where night shifts were working. Some of the companies had low concrete walls out front; others taller, chain-link fences.

Hu signaled right and turned onto Dai Cheong Street. A hundred feet from Dai Wang Street, he pulled to the side of the road. The pickup with the men dressed as fishermen parked behind him and stayed put as Hu pulled the first truck away from the rough shoulder and approached Dai Wang. He turned left onto the street and parked the truck in front of the building where Shay was held.

Hu and his men, dressed like factory workers, got out of the truck. Their information was correct; the gate to the walkway wasn't secured. They swung it open and walked up the path. His intel said that two guards stood watch outside the upstairs office where Shay and Lin were held, a third patrolled the factory, and a fourth was stationed downstairs in the reception area.

Hu and two of his men stood to the side as the fourth, carrying a toolbox, rang the doorbell. Maintenance men often came at night to repair machinery. Seeing the workman with his toolbox, the downstairs guard didn't make an effort to shout through the glass panel in the door to ask what he wanted. He unlatched the locks and cracked the door.

Hu's man pushed it open and threw the toolbox forward, smashing the square metal edge, heavy with tools, against the chest of the surprised guard. The guard flew backward with a loud groan. Hu's man smashed his head with the toolbox until he lay still in a heap.

Hu and the others entered the building. They split into twos, each taking one of the side-by-side elevators. The cars creaked up the shaft to the second floor. When the elevators reached the floor, the left door opened first. Hu saw a man raise his gun, but the man didn't fire, distracted by the second door opening. Guns lunged out of both elevators, cutting him down.

Shay heard the gunfire and raised himself up and leaned against the wall; Lin did the same. The two men looked at each other.

Hu and his men made their way to the corner where the elevator bank met the corridor. He waved two men around the corner; a guard fired on them as they darted into a cubicle. Hu and the other man sprang into the corridor and fired a burst of rounds at the guard; the men who had taken cover in the office jumped to a standing position and added their fire.

Bullets were ricocheting and Plexiglas shattering everywhere. After a few seconds, the guard fell onto the desk. As his legs buckled, the trunk of his body slid slowly across the face of the desk, pulling onto the floor with him the pencils, papers, and framed family picture of the engineer who worked there during the day.

Shay saw the door open; one of the original guards entered the room. Shay watched the gagged Lin plead with his eyes as the guard walked over and put a bullet in his head.

The goon turned to Shay.

thirty-nine

When the guard reached for him, Shay kicked him in the crotch with his bound feet. The man staggered and leaned against the wall. Shay pivoted on his butt, drew his legs back, and kicked up, smashing him in the throat.

The guard gagged and spit a rush of blood. He held his windpipe as he dragged the fingers of his other hand along the wall, sagging to the ground.

Shay straightened himself up against the wall. He could hear people moving through the factory. A second later, they kicked in the door. Shay watched them lower their guns when they saw the two men down and him bound and gagged.

A fourth man came through the doorway and surveyed the scene. One of the men checked Lin and then looked up and shook his head at the man who had just come in. Shay watched as the man, who appeared to be an underling, went over to the guard, checked his pulse, and shot him in the head. Shay flinched at the close-by bang.

Hu sent his men to secure the remaining offices and search the factory area. He stuck his gun in his waistband and walked across the room to Shay. He undid Shay's gag and then reached behind to untie the rope around his hands. He mumbled what sounded like a curse before he reached into his boot and pulled out a knife.

"Who are you?" Shay asked as Hu cut the rope.

Hu didn't reply. Shay rubbed his wrists and then reached for the back of his head to feel the wound. He traced the contour of clotted blood. The skin was spongy where he had been struck.

"Let me see," Hu said, pulling away Shay's hand. "It's not bad. Can you walk?"

"Why should I?" Shay asked.

"Get up."

Hu helped Shay to his feet. When he stood up, his ribs—probably broken, he thought—sheared his side.

He hesitated on the way to the door as he glanced at Lin, a pool of blood by his head. Hu pushed him forward. They made their way up the corridor, stepping over shards of hard plastic and spent shells. Shay saw the body of the dead guard in one of the cubicles, and the other guard lying dead across from the elevator.

The five men crowded into a single elevator car. Two in front readied their weapons as the elevator nestled into position on the ground floor. They bounded out when the door opened and swung their guns around; then they motioned for the others to follow. Shay saw the downstairs guard, whose head had been bashed in with the toolbox.

The men exited the building and walked down the path toward the truck. Hu kept Shay to his right, the barrel of his gun in Shay's side and out of view of the factory workers, who had come from a nearby building at the sound of the gunfire.

They got into the truck, Hu and one man in front, the other two sandwiching Shay in back. Hu pulled the vehicle away from the curb with a roar, winding out first and second gears down Dai Wang Street and into the right turn onto Dai Fai. He barely glanced left to check for oncoming traffic as he turned right onto Ting Kok Road. Stones were scattering as he veered from the shoulder into traffic.

A mile ahead, Hu pulled off the road into a parking lot, where the second truck was waiting. "Get out," he said to Shay.

Hu led him to the back of the pickup and parted the canvas backing. When Shay climbed in, Hu pushed him past two men to the far wall that demarcated the cab and bed. Shay barely avoided slipping on the fish slop on the floor. He took a seat on the bench.

Hu took a seat across from him and rapped twice on the cab wall. The pickup pulled slowly out of the driveway and turned left onto Ting Kok Road, headed west.

A few seconds later, the larger truck screeched back onto the highway heading eastbound and began to retrace the route it had taken from Sha Tau Kok.

forty

Shay was sitting on a plank that ran lengthwise along the inside wall of the pickup. The makeshift bench was eighteen inches above the film of fish guts, scales, and blood that spotted the floor.

Hu reached under the bench and fumbled around until he found a plastic bag. He slid it to the center of the truck bed and undid the tie. He pulled out a set of loose-fitting clothes—the black shirt, trousers, and thong sandals of the Hong Kong fisherman, the same garb the other men in the truck were wearing.

"Put these on," he said.

Shay changed into the clothing. He was going along, didn't see his opening out. Hu changed as well, put their original clothes in the bag, and slid it under the seat.

The pickup drove at normal speeds along the winding road that ringed the outskirts of Tai Po. Originally a market town, where farmers and fishermen gathered to sell their harvest and catch, rows of chalk-white apartment towers with a Mediterranean look now reached up to the sky against a backing of green hills. Where you didn't see buildings, the ground was broken and turned in preparation, the dirt a dark, orange-brown hue. Large pipes lay along the roadside, awaiting burial as the conduits for water-in and sewage-out to support the life that would teem above.

Heading in the opposite direction, the decoy truck raced along the shore of Tolo Harbor on its way to Sha Tau Kok.

One of the workmen who saw the men leave the factory ran back to his plant and called the police. The others made their way slowly up the walkway and looked in through the glass door. Some recoiled in horror, while others continued to look, mesmerized by the sight of the dead guard.

The cops came quickly from a nearby station. The workmen led them up the path to the foyer where the guard lay dead. The men told them the truck had the red-on-black/black-on-yellow plates of vehicles licensed to operate in both Guangdong and Hong Kong, although they didn't get the numbers. But they had seen which way the truck turned onto Ting Kok Road.

The report of a murder and an escape in a vehicle with cross-border plates created a stir at the local headquarters of the Hong Kong Police Force. The HKPF sergeant who got the report brought it to his captain. The captain gave orders to alert all police stations, with emphasis on those that could provide quick coverage of escape routes to the north between Tai Po and the border. Eurocopter AS332 Super Puma L2 helicopters were dispatched to cover the road the truck had taken out of Tai Po heading north.

British Aerospace Jetstream J-41 fixed-wing aircraft, which maintain regular offshore patrols for drug trafficking, illegal immigration, smuggling, and environmental pollution, were also put on alert. The pilots were ordered to concentrate their operations around Starling Inlet and Mirs Bay. The HKPF Marine Police was directed to focus its patrols in those waters as well, and to increase its normal complement of harbor patrol launches and inflatable boats with as many additional craft as could be mustered.

The captain in charge of the hunt also called the Commissioner of Police, who alerted the head of Public Service, the section of the government that controls the police force. The Public Service Director, reached at his home, put in an immediate call to the office of the leader of Hong Kong, Chief Executive Chan Liwei, to request an urgent meeting.

Thirty minutes later, the chief executive was talking with the public service director in the study of his spacious home on Victoria's Peak. He sat on a richly upholstered chair in a room lavishly appointed with Chinese blackwood furniture, jade cabinets, and silver and porcelain objets d'art.

In his early sixties, Chan Liwei was a gray-haired man with an aristocratic bearing—a DIY veneer that hid a youth spent hawking jade and hustling tourists for rides on junks. He caught—made—a break when a Hong Kong developer shopping for jewelry for his wife was impressed with his savvy and brought him into his property business. He worked as a courier at first, speeding documents around the island. He eventually got into the office, began making his own deals, and moved to the top of the organization.

After the joint declaration by China and Britain on December 19, 1984, announcing an agreement for the 1997 Chinese takeover of Hong Kong, Chan took advantage of ancestral ties to an official in the Communist Party leadership to develop close ties with the mainland. He deepened those links in the years that followed until the present time, when he became China's choice to be Hong Kong's chief executive.

Outside, looking through the bay window, Chan saw wave after wave of heat lightning quietly illumine the darkened sky. Birds chirped at a nearby waterfall in the near-wilderness beauty of bamboo, vine, fern, and Chinese pine that grow on the peak.

Chan was under pressure from Beijing to get more control over prodemocracy forces in the Hong Kong "Special Administrative Region." The Hong Kong SAR had been promised special status—"one country, two systems"—for fifty years following the 1997 transfer of power from the British to the Chinese.

After a brief honeymoon, China's intrusion into Hong Kong's affairs had made everyone's fears come true. China issued "interpretations" to clauses in the Basic Law—Hong Kong's Constitution—that limited universal suffrage and gave it more power to direct the ex-British colony's political future. It had sailed guided-missile destroyers, frigates, and submarines through Victoria Harbor in a show of force to commemorate an anniversary of the Chinese navy. It marched the PLA through the streets of Hong Kong in a national holiday parade.

Chan had just backed down from passing new security laws to clamp down on freedom of expression; he hoped the concession would appease the protesters. Instead, it emboldened them, and more demonstrations followed. The mainland made it clear that Hong Kong needed a strong reminder of who was in charge.

Chan saw this as his chance to show he could command, and get back in China's good graces. He picked up the telephone and called the Commander of PLA Forces Hong Kong, telling him to treat the incident as a matter of national security and directing him to work with the HKPF in whatever fashion he deemed necessary.

China had stationed a PLA garrison in Hong Kong when it resumed sovereignty. The garrison consists of army, navy, and air force units, deployed at fourteen military sites under the direction of the Central Military Commission of the People's Republic of China. These PLA Forces Hong Kong are expressly forbidden to interfere in local affairs.

The PLA garrison commander called the police captain in Tai Po. The two men mapped out a strategy to coordinate the hunt. In addition to the HKPF forces already on the scene, they would dispatch pursuit craft and patrol boats from Tolo Harbor; four Chinese-made Zhi-9 helicopters—rehashed versions of the Eurocopter AS365N, itself formerly the Aerospatiale Dauphin 2—from the PLA Air Force stationed at Shek Kong; and a squadron of PLA Special Forces stationed not far from Tai Po in Fan Ling.

The Special Forces soldiers headed up the highway from Fan Ling toward Sha Tau Kok to reinforce the border area. The patrol boats and pursuit craft left the harbor and sped out Tolo Channel for Mirs Bay. The Z-9 choppers took off from Shek Kong and headed for the area between Plover Cove and Starling Inlet. The HKPF Super Pumas were already crisscrossing the road from the reservoir south to Tai Po.

On their way west from Tai Po on the road to Yuen Long and the far coast, the men in the small pickup truck reeking of fish and carrying John Shay heard the sound of the whirlybirds taking off as they passed alongside the barbed-wire-protected grounds of the Shek Kong garrison.

Once they passed the garrison, the pickup was only ten miles from Hong Kong's western coast. It had to slow down as Tolo Highway gave way to a narrower, older road near Kam Tin, site of a small village built in the 1600s and fortified with eighteen-foot-thick walls for protection against bandits, invaders, and tigers. Today it only has four hundred residents, all with the surname Tang, one of the so-called Five Great Clans that settled Hong Kong's New Territories—and a daily influx of tourists who come to be photographed with a Tang.

Just past Kam Tin was Yuen Long, another old market town transformed by development as Hong Kong's dense-pack flowed outward from the gorged center. The pickup moved slowly through the town. The mood in back tensed whenever the truck stopped. Each time, Shay watched Hu and his men slide their hands toward the guns wedged in their trouser waistbands.

Shay again asked Hu who he was. Hu wouldn't tell him. Shay figured it was a rival gang in a power gambit. He wondered if he was in better or worse shape.

The truck settled into a steadier pace after it left Yuen Long. Shay figured they were on a country road—there were more bumps, and they were no longer stopping for what he guessed had been traffic lights. The pain from his beating had settled in at a level he could endure—not indefinitely, but he didn't think this ride would take much longer. Hong Kong wasn't a big place. Wherever they were going, they couldn't be far from it. If the truck hadn't stunk of fish, he would already be smelling the sea.

The pickup slowed to a crawl. Hu and his men clutched their weapons. The truck came to a full stop and then inched forward. It swung an arc to the right and then back left before resuming its normal speed.

One of the men pushed his face to the canvas backing and squinted out a hole. He turned back to Hu and said something. As Hu grunted and relaxed, the man made another comment. All three Chinese laughed. Shay looked at Hu, who smiled.

"A car break down. He say, 'Made in Japan.'"

forty-one

On the other side of Hong Kong, a PLA Z-9 chopper was the first to spot the decoy truck. It had gotten beyond Tai Mei Tuk and the edge of Plover Cove Reservoir and was making its way along the water's edge toward Bride's Pool. Roaring overhead and keeping pace with the vehicle, the Z-9 radioed position to the other two helicopters and told the pilot to contact central command. Then it dove, coming in at a steep angle a hundred yards in front of the truck and thirty feet off the ground.

The truck rumbled on, straining in second gear up the ascending terrain along the ridge of the reservoir. The Z-9 went to its loudspeaker. It ordered the truck to stop, staying even with it and above as the vehicle climbed the hill.

The second Z-9 relayed the coordinates to the command post. Three police cars were sent to intercept. Two headed south from Bride's Pool, and another raced north from the harbor area. The southbound cars set up a roadblock two miles from the truck's last sighted position, stretching their cars lengthwise across the narrow road.

Three HKPF policemen set up flares and fluorescent markers a hundred feet in front of their cars. A fourth policeman did the same behind the roadblock and waited there to halt traffic. The other PLA Z-9s and HKPF Super Pumas raced to the scene. The PLA Special Forces squadron headed south as well.

Hong Kong reporters followed the hunt on the police radio. They were hounding the information offices of the government, HKPF, and PLA Hong Kong Forces for information. The chief executive's office issued a terse communiqué.

"At approximately ten o'clock this evening, five men were killed in a factory on Dai Wang Street in the Tai Po Industrial Estate. Four or five men were seen leaving the site in a medium-size Isuzu truck with the dual license plates of Hong Kong and Guangdong Province. The men are being sought by a joint force of Hong Kong Police and PLA Hong Kong Forces. They are, by virtue of their actions on Dai Wang Street, assumed armed and dangerous."

Television, radio, and Internet broadcast the story immediately. More riveting than the crime and chase was the involvement of the PLA Hong Kong garrison in what appeared to be a criminal matter. After it entered Hong Kong, the PLA Hong Kong Forces had abided strictly by the Basic Law and Garrison Law—to fulfill their defense role within a legal framework that mandated strict separation of duties between Hong Kong police and the soldiers.

This was the first instance of PLA involvement in a Hong Kong internal matter. Condemnation was swift, even from organizations that previously held back from criticizing the mainland. As the story leaked, leaders around the world called upon China to honor her promises regarding noninterference in Hong Kong's internal affairs.

The Chinese government justified the use of the PLA garrison forces by saying this was a matter of national defense. China ordered detachments of its Forty-Second Army forces in the bordering province of Guangdong to a state of alert.

The driver clutched the steering wheel tightly as he climbed the hill overlooking the reservoir. On both sides of the road, ferns and treetops blew wildly from the disturbance created by the whirring helicopter blades. As he rounded a bend, the driver saw the flares, and behind them the police cars.

He slowed the truck. The two men in back checked their weapons as he shifted into first gear. He stopped the vehicle, turning its wheels to the side and pulling the emergency brake.

One of the policemen manning the blockade went back to his car and radioed headquarters that the suspect truck had been stopped.

Another cop challenged the vehicle.

"Throw out your weapons and come out," he yelled into a bullhorn.

Nobody stirred.

"I repeat, throw your weapons to the ground and leave the vehicle."

The truck driver and police could see each other through the truck windshield. The driver slid his right hand across the seat and picked up his gun. He pulled it across his lap while staring ahead at the police; then he raised his hand in the air and threw the gun out the window. The cop next to the one with the bullhorn shone a light when he heard the noise. After a few seconds, he saw the gun.

"Now get out of the truck," the first cop said.

The driver did as he was told. But when the policeman ordered him to come forward, he shook his head.

"I am returning to my truck," he said. "I have thrown away my weapon and exited the truck to speak with you. Myself and my compatriots are citizens of 'New China.' We wish to avoid bloodshed at all costs. But the men in the back of the truck are armed and have been instructed to return fire. We wish to speak to a representative of our government." He paused. "Our sovereign government, in Guangdong Province."

The cop listened in astonishment as Colonel Hu Weimin's top lieutenant spoke to him in a calm, commanding voice. The policemen moved toward him.

"I shouldn't have to remind the HKPF of the delicacy of relations between Hong Kong and China at this moment," the driver said. "Bring a representative of our Guangdong government here immediately."

He reached for the door of the truck and got back in. The policemen looked at one another. After a few words, the lead officer returned to his vehicle. He radioed the demand back to the command post in Tai

Po, where a sergeant brought it to the captain in charge. The captain called the Hong Kong Police Chief, who in turn contacted the chief executive. The captain told him the demand.

The leader of Hong Kong shot to his feet behind his desk.

"He wants what?!"

Chan Liwei wanted to end the standoff quickly; the last thing the Hong Kong chief executive needed was to appear weak or incompetent again in China's eyes. He contacted the Guangdong government, where the premier and party secretary felt the same urgency to sweep the matter under the rug, as a one-time aberration perpetrated by psychologically unstable misfits.

Guangdong choppered in a go-between to negotiate with the men. The emissary promised them a fair hearing, and more effectively threatened their families—going backward three generations, even if he had to dig up their graves, and forward unto eternity—with an unimaginable world of hurt.

The men surrendered three hours after the stalemate began.

forty-two

"Your call to the Chinese president has gone through, Mr. President," the aide said.

Rodgers picked up the phone. "Mr. President, how are you?" he asked the Chinese leader.

"I am well," Zhao Guozhi's translator said, after his answer in Mandarin. "And yourself, Mr. President?"

"I am fine, thank you. And your family?"

"Also well. And yours?"

"They are doing well. Thank you for asking."

Rodgers paused. "It's good of you to speak with me today."

"My line is always open to you, Mr. President," Zhao said.

"That's good. Our countries have more in common as the years go by. We need to emphasize and build upon these things, and resolve the differences between us that challenge the relationship."

"That is well said, Mr. President. It is my hope as well."

"Good," Rodgers said.

Rodgers looked at the officials in the room—the vice president, secretaries of state and defense, national security adviser, deputy undersecretary of defense for Asian and Pacific affairs, director of national intelligence. Also in attendance were the heads of homeland security, the CIA and FBI, and the chairman of the joint chiefs of staff.

"Mr. President, it has come to my attention that your government may have in its custody a US citizen by the name of John Shay."

It was DHS who had given the president the information about Shay. This was a matter that would normally be handled initially by lower-ranking officials from State. But after piecing together the story, it appeared that something much bigger might be at stake.

There was a pause on the other end. "It is more accurate to say, we are seeking Mr. Shay."

"Is he free to leave China when you find him?"

"He is part of an investigation we are conducting."

"May I ask what that investigation involves?"

"It is an internal matter."

"I see," Rodgers said. "I have no desire to interfere in your country's affairs. At the same time, I am responsible for the safety of all US citizens. I trust, once the investigation is complete, Mr. Shay will be allowed to return home."

"If he has committed no crime, he will be freed," Zhao said.

Rodgers looked around the room. "How long will the investigation take? We would like to think Mr. Shay would be given the benefit of a quick process."

"Certainly, Mr. President. We will complete this as quickly as possible."

"Good. It's kind of you to give me your assurances. Please give my regards to your wife."

"And mine to yours," the Chinese president said.

Rodgers put down the receiver and tapped his fingers on the table. He had held off protesting the use of the PLA garrison in Hong Kong—that could be handled at the embassy level. He didn't want to get China's dander up and complicate retrieving Shay.

"He's not giving us much," he said. He looked at Pete Cloninger, the head of the CIA. "You think they have him?"

Cloninger was six foot six. The trunk of his body was ungainly, tilted to the side. He was in his early sixties. "Yes, Mr. President," he said.

"Options?"

"China's holding a trillion dollars of our debt," Cloninger said. "We could threaten to welsh if they don't give up Shay."

Everyone laughed.

"No grab and snatch," the secretary of defense jumped in, throwing a reproving glance at Cloninger. "We can't get in there, not even a small force. But we can reposition units, in case the opportunity presents itself."

"Let's keep this at the level of dialogue," the secretary of state said, as if scolding a child. She was an attractive woman, sixty, auburn hair still lustrous, face a little puffy owing to time, circumstance, and habit. She had a big smile that drew you in, although she used it just as often as an all-knowing put-down. She was dressed smartly, in a custom-tailored suit fitted and stitched on a recent diplomatic trip.

She took off her glasses. "We've got an open line to China's leadership. They are as interested as we are in resolving this peacefully. The last thing we need is another military situation. We're stretched thin around the globe."

"All the more reason to reposition units," the national security advisor said. He was a liberal professor turned hard-ass; it had become a tiresome arc inside the beltway. "The Chinese are thinking the same thing—we'll never consider a military option, we can't handle it right now. But if we can't, we have to show them we can. We have to demonstrate that we have reserve combat capability."

"Pete, why don't you recap," Rodgers said.

Cloninger picked through the sheets of paper in front of him—notes from conversations with Nora Young in Hong Kong, Bill Lewis at the Machinists, federal agents Moss and Waite of ICE, agents on the ground in Hong Kong and China, contacts within the Chinese army, and analysts' attempts to piece it all together.

"We believe John Shay uncovered an operation that is skimming automotive parts from a US company's manufacturing facility in Shenzhen, in Guangdong Province," Cloninger said. "According to our sources, the parts were fenced by a distribution ring controlled by a trading company within China's Forty-Second Group Army, in the Guangzhou Military Region. The ring was selling them to a Chinese automotive company in the north—also with Chinese army ownership connections, this time to the Nanjing Military Region, which is responsible for defending northeast China and includes the Shanghai garrison.

"The wrinkle is, one of the army guys in the trading company stealing the parts is connected to a Triad gang in Hong Kong. Triad hoods counterfeit goods to make money—something our friends in al-Qaeda like to do. We know al-Qaeda's cash is drying up as we squeeze their financing. It's gotten into things like narcotics trafficking and cigarette smuggling to make up the difference."

Cloninger looked around the room. "Counterfeiting goods is another moneymaking opportunity for the terrorists. Knockoffs are estimated to be up to 7 percent of world trade, and cost global companies $600 billion in sales each year. American industry alone foots a $250 billion bill. The business is especially lucrative on the sales and distribution side. If you're not doing actual production, entry costs are low and profit margins are high. Terrorists have been distributing counterfeit versions of consumer items like Nike sneakers, Gucci handbags, Duracell batteries, Calvin Klein jeans." He smiled. "And Calloway's Big Bertha, for those of you who pretend to golf."

Several officials smiled.

"We think the terrorists may be branching into industrial items, with higher price tags," Cloninger said. "Six months ago an al-Qaeda operative was tracked to Hong Kong. We believe he hooked up with someone in the Guangdong military and also Triad hoods. Our intelligence also indicates he met with a German named Hans Tanner. This guy has been in Asia for years. He started as a representative for a German carmaker, one of the first automakers to enter China. He left after a few years to freelance deals throughout Asia. True to his expertise, he specializes in auto parts."

"But do we know for sure that terrorists have anything to do with this particular situation?" the president asked.

Cloninger shook his head. "No, sir."

Rodgers stood up. Everyone did the same.

"All right, let's follow up the al-Qaeda lead. And keep the ambassador buzzing around his Beijing colleagues—I want John

Shay back. First of all, because he's ours—I'm sick and tired of Americans getting snatched in faraway places. Hell, I *met* this guy, I know him. Second, if this gets out, who knows what it will do to the strike. We've got picket lines and demonstrations at car dealerships across the nation. The longshoremen just authorized a sympathy action up and down the Atlantic and Pacific coasts. The unions are calling for a rally in Washington. This is a mess that could get a lot worse."

forty-three

The pickup slowed as it entered Lau Fau Shan, a fishing village on the coast of Deep Bay. The truck pulled into an unpaved lot across from an alleyway. The driver rapped twice on the partition between the cab and bed.

Hu's men got out first. Shay followed, sliding along the bench and stepping out of the truck. He winced at the pain in his ribs as his feet touched the ground and bore the weight of his body. Hu followed him, holding the fish baskets and straw hats. He gave a basket and hat to Shay and to each of his men.

Shay put on the hat and looked around as the truck pulled away. The sky was overcast; there were few streetlights. Tucked in among thick foliage, he could see lights in the windows of houses. He could make out little else, save the alleyway, which was covered with a corrugated roof. And the smell of sea, raw with salt and wind.

"Move quickly through passage," Hu told him as they entered the alley. "Do not look to side."

The path was only three feet wide, with raised steps on either side leading to a larger work area. Shay saw drain grates in the pavement below their feet as they moved along the narrow center aisle. He heard loud conversation and glanced sideways, saw women cleaning fish on wooden cutting boards, large metal tubs at their feet. A mom-and-pop op with three small tables and orange plastic chairs served workers on break.

Several times during the walk, Shay and the men had to step up from the center aisle to let pallet trucks with tubs of fish pass through. The young men pushing them were impatient, jiggling and maneuvering them through an aisle that wasn't more than two inches wider than the width of the pallet bed. They looked on the verge of coming to blows as they bumped and jostled each other in the close quarters. As he waited above the aisle for the men to pass, Shay looked at the piles of fish on the cutting boards. The women preparing the fish chatted and smiled. No one paid him any mind.

At the end of the passageway was an open-air market. The noise was deafening, men shouting and pushing for position near tubs where the fish splashed and cupped gray scales where they were weighed. As they made their way through the market, Shay saw a wooden pier, and open water beyond it. On the opposite shore were high-rises and hills; to the left, he saw a bridge spanning the water. He thought back to the maps he looked at during the flight. None of Hong Kong's two hundred-plus outlying islands seemed that close. Macau wasn't that near either.

They were going to China.

Shay stopped as they stepped onto the pier.

Hu squeezed his arm, pressed the gun in his side. "Keep walking."

Shay grabbed Hu's wrist and twisted it behind his back, taking his gun. Before his men could react, Shay had his arm around their leader's throat and the gun pressed into his cheek.

"Drop your guns," he said. He reached down, pulled Hu's knife from the sheath.

"Don't be stupid, Mr. Shay," Hu said. "We are here to help."

"Who are you?"

"It is no matter. Remain with us and you will be safe."

"Not good enough," Shay said. "Tell them to drop their guns."

Hu nodded to his men, who dropped their weapons on the ground.

"Now kick them in the water."

The men looked at him; Hu nodded. They did what Shay ordered.

"Let's get out of here," Shay said.

He turned Hu around. Facing him were fishermen with knives and gaff hooks.

"It is useless, Mr. Shay," Hu said. "Even if you could get past these men, you wouldn't be safe. The authorities would arrest us for the shooting in Tai Po." He nodded at the weapon Shay was holding. "Especially with your fingerprints on my gun. It would be your word against ours."

"What's in it for me in China?"

"Your freedom."

The fishermen were moving closer. Shay figured he had to risk it.

"Let's go," he said. "Your men first."

Hu nodded to his men, and they walked out onto the pier. On the beach below the rickety structure, piles of empty oyster shells stretched from the sand to the shallows. Boats were docked for the night, pulled onto the shell-caked shore with their outboard motors cocked at forty-five-degree angles. Other boats were out in the bay.

A sampan was docked just shy of the pier's end. The wooden boat was about twenty-five feet long and had four large square boxes set in the middle. Standing on the prow was an old woman, who couldn't have been five feet tall. She was wearing a round, wide-brimmed straw hat and dressed in a black, loose-fitting tunic blouse. Her black pants were rolled up above her knees; her feet were bare. She held a large bamboo pole that rested on the shallow seafloor and stretched another five feet above her head into the air.

At the back of the boat was a younger girl, wearing glasses and sipping from a can of Coke. She was also barefoot, also wore loose-fitting black pants rolled above her knees, and wore a sweatshirt with the legend **S.O.A.P.** Unlike the old woman who never changed expression, the teenager looked worried. She put down the can of soda.

"This boat," Hu said.

Shay motioned for Hu's men to climb in first. Hu followed, and Shay got in last. Hu pointed to the boxes. "We must get inside, so the patrols won't see us."

"You first," Shay said.

Hu and his men got into the boxes. Shay secured the tops with rope and then lay down flat on the bottom of the boat and motioned for the old woman to cast off. The woman said something to the teenager, who reached over the side and undid the rope tied to the pier. The older woman tightened her grip on the pole, her left hand raised high and right hand below. She pushed off the silt bottom. The vessel moved away from the pier.

When they were out of the shallows, the old woman pulled her pole out of the water and sat down on the bench at the prow. The teenager started the outboard motor. She used her right arm to work a piece of metal tubing that controlled the rudder.

The boat picked up speed as it moved from shore. Farther out into the bay, more junks came into view. Some were anchored, with weathered strands of rope extending into the water to hold traps and lines. Shay heard soft chattering on the vessels.

The breaks in the clouds were more frequent now, and the wind had picked up. Sky and stars lighted the surface of the water. The moon began to shine, first indirectly, its light bending around the cloud cover or escaping through an opening. Then the clouds disintegrated into brushstroke lines, and the moon shone more brightly through the moving strands. Finally, cleared of all encumbrance, it basked in clear black space, like the brilliance it was.

The sampan had passed the halfway point across the bay when the old woman saw him. The inflatable boat was drifting noiselessly on the current. He lay flat in the small, tube-shaped boat, his forearms resting on the inflated bulge. His hand was cupped around a pair of night-vision binoculars as he moved his head slowly back and forth.

He was one of several Marine Police officers who patrolled this area of Han Hoi Wan—Deep Bay—where the swim from the tip of land that juts out from China across the bay to Lau Fau Shan is only two miles.

Scanning the surface of the bay's waters, the marine cop took in the old woman's sampan. She had been crossing at night for years, each return trip taking place the same time every evening. He still stopped her occasionally, checking the four crates that were invariably empty upon return and filled with the crabs she had caught in China's waters on the outgoing trip.

Her boat puttered along a hundred feet from him when it crossed his path. He was looking beyond it, to the left, at two teenage girls waving to him from the back of another boat. The sampan carrying Shay and Hu and his men passed by and out of view, its waterline lower than it should have been with the weight of the men.

But the patrolman didn't notice. He kept gazing into his binoculars, distractedly moving them in an arc in front of him, listening through an earphone to the police channel, where reports on the standoff with the decoy truck at Mirs Bay and the use of PLA forces in Hong Kong had the entire island on edge.

forty-four

The teenager cut the engine as they approached shore. Shay raised his head and saw a light flash twice. He smacked Hu's basket. "How many are meeting you?"

"Too many for you to deal with," Hu said through the thick weave.

Shay scanned the beach as the old woman pushed off with the pole to move the sampan through the shallows. The girl tilted the motor out of the water and adjusted the rudder to straighten the boat's glide.

When the boat hit sand, five soldiers ran out from the cover of nearby woods. Two grabbed the prow and began to pull; the others came around the side to push. Shay stood up and waved Hu's gun.

"Get back," he said, jumping into the water.

The soldiers looked back and forth between Shay and the baskets.

"Back on the beach," Shay said, pointing the pistol in that direction.

Hu called out from the basket. The soldiers moved away from the boat. Shay used Hu's knife to cut the ropes that held the baskets shut. Hu and his men stood up.

"Get out of the boat," Shay said.

Hu nodded to the men. Shay followed them onto the beach, his arm around Hu's throat. A dozen soldiers came out of the woods. They trained their weapons on Shay.

"Give me back my gun," Hu said.

Shay put the gun to his head.

"Tell them to drop their weapons."

"Impossible," Hu said. He called out to one of the men. Gunshots peppered the sand by their feet. "They will kill me if I give that order. Stop wasting time."

Gunfire broke out in the woods behind the soldiers. They returned the shots, backing up toward the water. Shay dropped to the ground, pulling Hu with him. He glanced back when he heard the motor start up. The boat was pulling away from shore.

"What's going on?" Shay asked.

One of Hu's men flung an automatic rifle to his side. Hu reached for it. Shay pinned his hand to the sand.

"Let go, Mr. Shay," Hu said. "We're in a fight for our lives."

The soldiers were spread-eagled on the beach, taking cover behind overturned boats and pieces of driftwood. Shay looked at Hu, their eyes meeting. He let go of his hand. Hu grabbed the rifle. "Over there," Hu said, getting up and running.

Shay followed him. They took cover behind a boat.

Hu began shooting. He smiled at Shay. "Why don't you join me?" He nodded at the pistol Shay had taken from him on the pier.

"Who am I shooting at?" Shay asked. "The people rescuing me?"

Hu dropped lower during a barrage of gunfire. When it eased, he popped up and got off several rounds. "Hardly, Mr. Shay," he said.

"Who are they?"

"Probably PLA. Elite unit, recon and strike force. Commanded by Beijing or Shanghai Military Region."

"Who are you?"

"Also People's Liberation Army," Hu said. "Guangzhou Military Region, Forty-Second Group Army, Special Forces Dadui."

"You're fighting each other? Chinese against Chinese?"

Hu nodded. "A little skirmish." He paused. "At least, that's what I think."

One of Hu's men dove behind the boat where Shay and Hu had taken cover. He pulled a radio off his belt and handed it to his commander; Hu patted him on the shoulder. Hu spoke with someone on the other end, listened for a few seconds, spoke again. He clipped the radio to his belt.

Hu and the soldier raised themselves to resume shooting. The soldier fell down dead. Hu twisted sideways and fell as a bullet tore into his shoulder. One of the attacking forces made his way to cover at the edge of shore, where he had a better line of fire at Shay and Hu. He began shooting.

Shay grabbed Hu and ran him to cover behind another boat. They drew heavy fire on the way. Hu caught his breath as he looked at Shay and was about to say something. Shay changed clips and raised himself to get off another round.

The gunmen from the woods had killed most of Hu's men and were moving closer to the boat where Shay and Hu had taken cover. Shay heard a new, larger burst of gunfire from deeper in the woods; the shooting stopped in their vicinity. Hu's remaining men got up from their positions and started moving toward the woods. The attacking troops were caught in a crossfire.

Hu smiled. "The 'cavary,'" he said.

forty-five

Guangzhou

Shay was standing at the window of his room in the Garden Hotel, looking across the street at the concrete buildings. The windows of the apartments looked like voids in the sunless day, a lifeless honeycomb. He heard loud rumbling as a column of tanks came into view, making its way up Huanshi Dong Lu. There had been military activity all day.

He felt stronger after two days' rest, one of them in a hospital where he was treated in a room next to Colonel Hu Weimin, who led the rescue attempt. After they fought off the opposing troops, they were brought to Guangzhou. He was still under guard.

The telephone rang. "Yes?"

"Mr. Shay. It's Gao Liang. How are you this afternoon?"

"Good."

"Would you like to join me for a drink downstairs?"

"Okay."

Shay passed through the arcade of tourist shops on the ground floor. Gao greeted him in a far corner of the lobby. The Guangzhou official had looked in on him several times in the hospital. Now he was "hosting" him at the hotel.

"Mr. Shay, looking better and better. And feeling that way, I hope."

"I'm fine," Shay said.

They climbed two steps to a raised lounge area covered with red carpet and area rugs. Blue porcelain flowerpots sprouting thin ferns decorated the periphery; chairs were grouped around low tables to form the seating areas.

Two guards took up position as they sat down.

Shay rested his arms on the ornamental arms of the chair. They were deep auburn wood, heavily polished; the arms rose and fell like an undulate body in motion. They ended at Shay's fingertips in the head of a dragon, its mouth and eyes open wide, ravenous.

Gao ordered two Tsing Taos. The waitress returned with the beers.

"Are you satisfied with the doctor?" he asked, glancing at the gauze on the back of Shay's head as the waitress poured the drinks.

"He's good," Shay said. "Any word yet?"

"That's why I came," Gao said.

Shay took a drink. He felt the foam tingle his lips as the liquid passed through the froth and into his mouth.

"You cannot leave," Gao said. "The Chinese government has forbidden it. It seems you have uncovered too much knowledge about what is going on in the Chinese plant of the company your union is striking in the United States. Your government is negotiating with Beijing as we speak."

Shay turned as more soldiers came through the lobby door.

"Let me call my family," he said.

Gao shook his head. He had refused several times. The phone had been removed from Shay's room. "It is not wise to contact anyone at this point."

"Why a hotel then? In the open?"

"It makes it appear we are not defying Beijing, but simply investigating the matter ourselves," Gao said. He smiled. "I think your government in the United States would also not look kindly on you being in jail." Gao looked around at the foreign business officials and tourists in the lobby. "Beijing would be reluctant to stage a police or military action in such a public place, where many non-Chinese stay."

"How far is this going?" Shay asked. "Within China itself?"

Hu Weimin had told Shay about the tensions between the south and central regions, and his vision of a breakaway country.

"It has already gone far," Gao said.

"What will happen?"

"I do not know. It will be hard for the government to save face." He paused. "But it will not launch an operation against our province. This is simply impossible."

They were seated near a bronze statue Shay figured must have been twelve feet tall. The male figure, holding a scepter, looked like a combination sage and warlord. A gold ball rested on the top of his black staff; black strands of hair hung down from his mustache and chin. His lips were painted red. He was wearing a four-sided gold crown.

Gao took a sip of beer. "At least, I think."

forty-six

Nora put down the phone after another conversation in Chinese and looked at Hannah.

"John is in Guangzhou."

"A prisoner?"

"Yes and no. He is under the control—and protection—of a government and army faction in the province."

"Who are they? Who are they protecting him from?"

"They represent the best-case scenario for China," Nora said. "I've been dealing with these individuals around software piracy. They're committed to bringing law and order to the Chinese Wild West—getting the army out of moneymaking, cleaning up political corruption, complying with the norms of global business. They're protecting John from the opposite."

"What's that?"

"Other Guangzhou political and army elements, allied with state-owned dinosaur companies that can't compete without favoritism and corruption; Beijing and Shanghai interests, battling Guangzhou for regional supremacy around economic development and political control; Triad gangs, in Guangzhou and Hong Kong. The people I'm talking to turned a gang member. That's how they found out where John was held in Hong Kong."

"How will it play out?"

"The United States is trying to negotiate John's release. The Chinese deny having him. Which is correct—he is being held by province officials, not the central government."

Nora paused. "I'll be honest with you. Beijing does not look kindly on interference in its internal affairs. I know several foreigners who have been detained in China. The Chinese imprison anyone they want, for whatever reason they want, and however long they want. Prison conditions are primitive. Abuse is common."

"Will your friends in Guangzhou protect him?"

"As long as it serves their purpose. My contact is a high-ranking Communist Party official in the Economic Ministry. He is with John now." She paused. "John is an important, but lesser, piece on the board. His sacrifice could be part of the game."

Hannah didn't have to think much before she defaulted to her MO of choice in tough situations—escalation. Make everyone understand there was a price to be paid for their actions, and that you were not going away.

She picked up the phone, called Mei Wang, and asked her to come to the Shangri-La right away.

Mei arrived within the hour. She told Hannah she had gotten a call from the police. They had identified Lin Xueqin's body.

"I'm so sorry," Hannah said, putting her arms around her.

Mei nodded through her tears. She looked up.

"Your Mr. Shay? He dead too?"

"He's alive, but in danger. I need your help."

Mei pulled away from Hannah's embrace. She reached into her pocket, took out a tissue, and wiped her eyes. "Xueqin would want that. Mr. Shay promised help us. Xueqin would want repay kindness."

Hannah told her what she was thinking.

Mei nodded and took out her mobile. "We have people in place, in Hong Kong and China."

Mei dialed a number and spoke, nodding for emphasis as she made each point. The conversation lasted less than a minute. She tapped out a text message and sent it to her contact list. She put down the cell phone and took out a laptop from her knapsack. She set it on the desk.

"Room have Internet?"

Mei looked under the desk and found the connector, answering her own question. She plugged in and logged on, wiping another tear. She sent an instant message and received an updated list of available proxies. She got to a site and began typing.

"What are you doing?" Hannah asked.

"Going around 'Great Firewall of China,'" Mei said. "Web is monitored, censored by fifty thousand Internet police—'mud crabs,' we call them. Government closes news and discussion groups, bulletin boards, blogs. Requires you register, put spies in Internet cafés. We move chat rooms and wikis to proxy servers outside mainland; more difficult for government to follow computer traffic. Democracy friends around world have software that let us use their computers to route messages. Also use aliases, encryption … hide text in image files … mix fonts … avoid or misspell keywords, trick search filters."

Five minutes later, she snapped down the top. She put the laptop and phone back in her knapsack.

"I must go."

"How long will it take?" Hannah asked.

Mei stood up and walked to the door. She looked back, softness in her expression.

"I launch social mobilization app, developed by Xueqin and friends at Tsinghua University," she said. Her face hardened. "Tomorrow, people assemble across harbor, in Central District. Soon, actions begin in China. I call in morning with information."

"Thank you," Hannah said.

Mei eked out a smile. "Let us hope for great success."

Hannah looked at Nora after Mei left the room.

"I hope you're not thinking of using that phone."

Nora shook her head. "This is your show, honey." She got up and walked to the door.

"Good luck," she said, turning to Hannah as she left.

Lewis was pacing, awaiting news from Hannah, when Dolores patched her through.

"He's in Guangzhou, in southern China," Hannah said. "He was being held in Hong Kong, like they said. A Chinese army group freed him and took him across the border. The trick is getting him out."

"This is a government matter," Lewis said. "I talked to someone in the president's office. They're in discussions with the Chinese leadership as we speak."

"And have been for two days," Hannah said. "I think I've got a better way."

Lewis realized going against the government would mean hell to pay. Still—you wouldn't be American unless you thought you could do things better than it could.

"What do you need?"

"I want you to call every major trade union. Tell them what happened, tell them what we want them to do."

"What's that?"

"Sympathy strikes. Walk out, right away. A bunt won't get us off the island."

Lewis smiled at Hannah's baseball lingo—courtesy of Shay, no doubt. It was what the ballplayers from the DR said when asked why they swung for the fences.

"It's got to spread fast," Hannah said. "It will pressure the government—both of them, Chinese and American. Tell the unions a Machinists official was taken prisoner by the Chinese while visiting a Lambal plant that's outsourcing jobs to China. Tell them he met with banned trade-union organizers in China. Say we need this action to free John. That it will help the union movement in China, be a big win for labor. And it's not just human rights—it will increase the cost of goods produced there, make relocation less tempting. It's the perfect bottom line—morally just, with a financial payoff."

"I'm beginning to see why John wanted you in this union."

"One more thing," Hannah said.

"What's that?"

"Give me the number of Klaus Henders."

"Something going on he should know about?"

"Oh yeah," Hannah said. She told him what she was thinking.

As he listened, Lewis couldn't believe he had tried to drum her and Shay out of the union. He realized he should have worried less about succeeding for his race and more about doing the right thing. He had been on eggshells since he had been put in charge, leery of every step, not wanting to give the naysayers anything they could use against him. He felt like he had two thoughts for everything. One came directly—what he wanted to do. The other hovered, immediately afterward—think about what it would look like.

He remembered what he tried to drill into the kids on the Boys and Girls Club team—sports is about doing the right thing, fast. Life is too, he thought. You can't be of two minds.

Screw it, he thought. The world was going to hell in a handbasket. Might as well shut it down, for its own good.

Then thinking, it's lose-lose—lose my job, lose the union.

Hell—win-win is overrated.

"I'll flip the switch."

Hannah called Henders and told him what was happening.

"We would like you to join us," she said. "The metalworkers in Germany, and other unions throughout Europe."

"We will help in any way we can to free Mr. Shay," Henders said. "We also support the workers of China. Let me put it to the council. I believe they will agree."

"Will you contact the other unions? You know them better than we do."

"Of course," Henders said.

Hannah knew there were several union federations based in Europe. One was European, had seventy-five-plus unions, represented sixty million members. An international confederation headquartered there had more than two hundred organizations in 152 countries and a membership of a hundred and fifty million. There were also twelve global groups that linked national unions from trades or industries—

like metalworking, transport, public service—at the international level. Let him sort it out.

"Mr. Henders, time is critical. Everything must happen quickly."

"I understand."

When Hannah hung up, she collapsed on the bed. She was exhausted; the long flight had worn down her last bit of energy. She felt used up, from all the travel for the strike and her anxiety about PD. After a few minutes, she managed to sit up, take her clothes off, and toss them onto the chair. She pulled the covers over her and hit the pillow.

forty-seven

The Machinists struck across North America. The union, five hundred thousand strong, shut down production wherever members worked, from aircraft plants on the West Coast, to lawnmower and snowblower factories in the Midwest, to a motorcycle factory in Pennsylvania. The strikers were joined on the lines by spouses and children, who marched with them along the fences in front of the plants. Some supporters brought grills and coolers; kids set up lemonade stands and sold drinks to passersby and motorists who stopped. Cars honked and waved.

Other unions met in emergency sessions to vote on whether to join in. The industrial unions especially, bitter after years of watching jobs go to China, were furious that China now held captive one of their own. At the meetings, workers stood up and addressed the leadership, not only angry about what had happened to Shay, but venting frustration at the economy in general—the layoffs, the rollbacks, the bitter atmosphere and ceaseless anxiety in the constant drive to cut costs. Union leadership was pounded by a groundswell of resolutions to stand alongside the Machinists.

The chemical workers walked out next. Tom Hardin, the guy John Shay visited after the accident in Houston, leaped at the chance to repay the favor. Hardin was in Philadelphia when Lewis called. He convened an emergency session of the executive council of the Philly local. Workers streamed out of a nearby refinery and manned lines outside the office and production complexes. Locals across the country joined in.

Jack Cafferty had worked closely with New York hospital workers during their early struggles for union recognition. When Lewis called and asked for their support, union members led a march up the East Side to the Chinese Embassy, carrying posters that read "Free John Shay" and "Labor Rights for Chinese Workers."

The hospital workers' umbrella union issued a call for selective job actions by its 1.6 million members—mobilizing nurses, doctors, social service workers, building cleaners, police and corrections officers, librarians, Head Start employees, maintenance workers, lab technicians, and nurse assistants across the country.

New York City's labor council met in emergency session. The council includes four hundred local unions representing more than a million workers in the public and private sectors of the city economy—teachers, truck drivers, sewing machine operators, train operators, dockworkers, doctors, nurses, orderlies, construction workers, cooks, janitors, and jazz musicians. Council officials had attended the service for Cafferty at St. Patrick's; its members lined the procession route to pay their respects.

As the executive board sat in session, its workers began to walk out across the city's five boroughs. Members of the carpenters union dropped their tools and walked off a construction site on the Upper East Side. At a repair facility in the Bronx, telecom workers took a show of hands and left the building. The actors union shut down film production at New York City locations. Dockworkers from the Atlantic District extended their action beyond the imported car boycott, and refused to do any work on city and Jersey docks.

The labor council, already angered at the tough stand New York's mayor was taking in contract talks, fanned the brushfire of its locals' spontaneous walkouts and called for more strikes. Asbestos, bakery, electrical, and elevator workers, operating engineers, and hotel and restaurant employees all took actions. The subway workers voted to join in. Its members operate the subways, maintain the trains and tracks, staff the token booths, clean the platforms and cars, and service and repair mechanical equipment. People began pouring into the streets of New York as the A and D lines shut down.

The archbishop addressed the American faithful, calling on them to press their elected leaders to help free John Shay. He republished the encyclical letter of Pope Leo XIII, first issued in 1891. In it, Leo criticized the concentration of wealth and power, spoke out against the abuses that workers faced, and demanded that workers be granted more rights. The nineteenth-century pontiff also upheld the right of voluntary association, specifically commending labor unions.

Shay's father got involved. He called his old firehouses—ladder companies in Manhattan and Brooklyn, a truck company in Rockaway Beach, engine companies in Astoria and Harlem. At each firehouse, he spoke directly with the captain or lieutenant. The ranking officers passed his message to officials at the New York City's locals of the fire officers and firefighters.

Off-duty officers and firefighters began to assemble. One group rallied at City Hall; others gathered outside the Chinese Embassy shouting for Shay's release. Word went to national headquarters in Washington and from there to the organization's affiliates representing firefighters and paramedics in communities in the United States and Canada.

Firefighters will do anything for their own. Across the country and Canada, they began to rally in support of the retired captain's son from New York.

The auto union was angry about the boycott of car dealerships, but led by Bogdanich, it jumped on board to help free Shay. The actions began at an assembly plant in Fairfax, Kansas, where local members, fed up with givebacks in their own contract, dropped their tools and shut a sedan production line. At a plant in Lansing, Michigan, they halted production of SUVs. The action spread to Chicago, where the local walked off the lines that produced light trucks.

Ohio workers in the steel industry acted next. Battered by consolidations and layoffs, the steelworkers began wildcat strikes nationwide, from Columbus to Albuquerque. On the West Coast, dockworkers extended their job action against foreign automobile shipments by refusing to unload container ships queued outside the

Long Beach and Los Angeles ports that were carrying Chinese goods. The union called work-to-rule slowdowns—where employees refuse to lift a finger beyond the minimum specified by their contract, and follow safety and other regulations to the letter—in the Great Lakes and Gulf Coast Districts.

In San Francisco, traffic backed up on both sides of the bay as union workers voted a work-to-rule action by the maintenance crew on the Golden Gate Bridge. Truckers struck transport companies, calling back drivers from their delivery routes to the terminals. Mine workers, furious a major mine company had just gone Chapter 11 and canceled pension benefits so it could be sold to a nonunion competitor, voted to shut down selected coal mines, beginning in West Virginia.

Mine worker retirees joined active workers on the lines. As news reports showed the elderly men walking slowly outside the mines, retirees from steel, auto, and other industries began to show up outside their old plants. The media coverage zeroed in on the plight of retired workers, whose benefits had been stripped as companies turned over every rock they could to reduce costs.

Lewis leafed through a bulletin—his communications staff was updating him hourly. The telecom workers union, responding to the action of the local at the Bronx repair depot, began job actions across New York, initiating varying levels of work stoppages at major employers in media, including the big networks and newspapers.

Lewis turned the page and read that bakery workers were staging slowdowns at food-processing plants. A construction union voted to slow late-stage work on projects throughout the nation, issuing a call to its painters, drywall finishers, wall coverers, glaziers, glassworkers, and floor-covering installers.

Child care workers had marched to City Hall and the Chinese Embassy in support of Shay. Textile workers had struck clothing manufacturers. Hospitality worker locals were mobilizing room attendants, cooks, waiters, bartenders, and desk clerks across the country. The action was disrupting hotels, motels, restaurants, cafeterias, hospitals, schools, bars, airports, bus terminals, and stadium concessions. Vegas was scrambling to keep running, hit by walkouts at the casinos and hotels.

Lewis scanned through the international pages of the update. In Germany, Klaus Henders had made the case to his union board. The metalworkers struck car assembly plants in Bremen, Dusseldorf, Rastatt, and Sindelfingen. Already irate at the threatened loss of ten thousand jobs, its workers hit another carmaker at Bocchum, Russelsheim, and Kaiserlautern. They slowed down assembly operations in Berlin, Dingolfing, Landshut, Munich, Regensburg, and Wackersdorf.

Henders had egged on trade-union leaders throughout Europe. The English and Irish trade unions called out workers. The Italians disrupted planes, trains, and municipal transit across Italy. In Spain, sympathy actions were spearheaded by its two trade-union confederations. Another national confederation led the walkouts in Portugal.

In France, the trade unions were quick to live up to their reputation for militancy, led by autoworkers in Sochaux, who walked off the job and pressed for a general strike. Swedish trade unions called for their two million members and sixteen member unions to launch actions in support of Shay and the rights of Chinese workers. The Czechs threw the weight of their member unions into protests. In Belgium, the national union federation mobilized its 1.2 million members.

The strongest European support for Shay and China's free-trade-union movement came from NSZZ Solidarnosc, in Poland. Solidarity was born in the 1980 strikes at the Lenin Shipyards in Gdansk, where workers organized to establish a union based on international labor standards and independence from the state. The union staggered walkouts throughout Poland and organized mass demonstrations in Warsaw, Krakow, Katowice, Wroclaw, Poznan, Radom, Czestochowa, and Lodz. It also sent representatives across Central and Eastern Europe and the Baltics to enlist support for the action.

Lewis put down the printout. He was never a "workers of the world, unite" type of guy; he focused on people and events in front of his nose. But he couldn't help but be moved by the outpouring of support for Shay. He began to see what Cafferty had always talked about: that the same idea that gave birth to the Machinists—you don't have to struggle alone in this world—could be extended further, to all the unions themselves.

forty-eight

The next morning, after receiving Mei's call, Hannah left the hotel and walked to the terminal. She stood at the railing as the Star Ferry chugged across the water from Kowloon to Central. Sunlight sparkled and danced on the waves in glittering, blinding patterns, drawn and reshaped so quickly you could never fix the form.

She thought about Jack—their time together, his leadership of the union. She wished he could see what was unfolding, the global strikes. He talked about it often, the great labor actions of the past. He might have been the only one in the union besides her who believed it would happen again, she thought, wiping her eyes.

He always said that somewhere, sometime, it was going to be needed. That no matter how weak labor had become, no matter how ineffective it appeared, when that time came, only labor could pull it together. Only labor could bring the numbers to bear. Only labor had the guts to do what needed to be done. There's no replacement for displacement, was his saying—linking the car maxim about cylinder volume and horsepower to labor's heft and power.

She felt something in her hand and clenched the railing, bracing for a tremor. She remembered her father steadied himself against a chair, a wall, anything fixed.

The ferry downshifted with a roar and slowed as it approached shore. It settled in with a couple of big bumps against the dock. Hannah got off and heard the noise as she began walking into Central. She saw police running in small teams, setting up positions on street corners and at the entrances to buildings. Then she saw the human surge—people turning a corner, shoulder to shoulder, twenty to a row, the entire width of the street, row upon row behind them.

They were chanting. Many held signs, a number in English: "Democracy in Hong Kong," "PLA Forces Out of Hong Kong," "End One-Party Rule," and "Justice for Lin Xueqin." She also saw signs that said "Free United Machinists' John Shay."

She made her way to the corner and looked down the street. It was flooded with people as far as she could see. She walked on the sidewalk, keeping pace with the marchers. The demonstrators remained orderly as they passed office buildings and luxury shops.

This wasn't antiglobalization freaks and anarchists, smashing windows while they mixed a good time with half-baked ideas, she thought. It was the real thing—a mass movement, challenging for power.

This is what I signed on for.

Hannah met Mei Wang at the rendezvous point.

"I can't believe it," she said. "How could you organize this so quickly?"

"There are demonstrations recently," Mei said. "We are practiced."

They looked out at the crowd.

"Intervention of PLA Hong Kong Garrison in criminal matter that does not need national defense make people very angry," Mei said. "They see Beijing promise of 'special status' empty." She took a breath. "Many also angry about killing Lin Xueqin."

Hannah put her hand on Mei's shoulder. "I'm so sorry."

Mei nodded and gave her a thankful smile. She motioned for Hannah to move—a squad of police were trotting down the sidewalk toward them.

"What will the authorities do?" Hannah asked.

"No violence in past. Maybe different this time when demonstrations start in China."

"Have you heard anything? I haven't seen any reports." Hannah had ducked into a hotel lobby to catch the TV news while waiting for Mei.

"You will not see news," Mei said. "Chinese authorities will not speak of situation. They not let press get close."

They looked into the street as a noisy group of demonstrators streamed past.

"Our activists have camera phones, video recorders," Mei said. "We record actions in China, send files to Internet."

They walked to an open area where a podium had been erected. A speaker was shouting into a megaphone, exhorting the crowd. Hannah saw HKPF converging from several directions.

"This worry me," Mei said. "We not have advance permits. I usually not see so many police."

A man came over and spoke to Mei, gesturing at Hannah. Mei shook her head.

"What is it?" Hannah asked.

"He wants you to speak. It would not be good idea."

"These people are here for John Shay, as well as for their own cause. I want to say something."

Mei shook her head. "Police not like it."

Hannah smiled at her as she climbed up the steps onto the stage and stood next to the current speaker. Mei climbed up after her and asked the man for the megaphone.

Mei looked out at the crowd and spoke in Chinese, extending her arm toward Hannah. The crowd cheered. She handed Hannah the plastic horn.

Hannah held the pistol-grip handle with a slight tremble and looked out at the crowd. She worried about her voice, if the symptoms would rear their head there.

"My name is Hannah Stein, and I am a representative of the United Machinists Union of America," she said.

A number of people cheered. Mei translated through a second megaphone. The rest of the demonstrators joined in.

"I want to thank you for your support for John Shay, who is being held captive in China." Mei translated to more applause.

"I also want to offer you, on behalf of my union, on behalf of all of labor in the United States, our full support in your struggle for democracy and worker rights in Hong Kong and China. And our support for noninterference by China and respect for the freedoms it has promised the Hong Kong Special Administrative Region."

Mei translated, and the crowd roared.

"It is unfortunate we have to take to the streets to win these freedoms," Hannah said. "But this is necessary when political leadership will not listen to the people. It has happened before, many times in history. Today it is happening again. If the authorities want us to leave, they must acknowledge our demands. When they do this, we will be happy to return to our jobs and our homes, which is where we want to be."

As Mei continued to translate, the demonstrators chanted loudly, punching their fists into the air. A scuffle broke out below the stage; police and demonstrators began to fight. A group of demonstrators pushed a police line deeper onto the sidewalk; a policeman fell through the window of a store. The police began to beat the demonstrators, driving them back into the street. People were falling, trampling one another, screaming. Organizers shouted for everyone to leave. Leaders activated the megaphones' built-in sirens, the signal the crowd should begin to disperse along predetermined retreat routes.

Hannah's eyes darted downward to the front of the crowd as a man pushed his way through the first row and raised a gun. She heard the popping sounds and tried to duck and move. As the man was overcome by the screaming throng, she heard herself say, "Oh," then clutched her stomach and looked down—there was blood on her T-shirt. She dropped to her knees—surprised and then queasy and faint—and crumpled to the ground.

Someone ran to get the ambulance that the rally organizers had arranged to be on standby in case of need. Mei kneeled on the stage over Hannah, who was moaning and holding her hands over the wound. Mei looked at the spreading blood.

"You will be all right," she said. "You will be all right."

The ambulance pulled up to the front of the stage. Two paramedics jumped out and bounded up the wide steps carrying a stretcher that had a satchel with portable resuscitation equipment attached to the gurney. The EMTs coaxed Hannah to lie flat and examined her, gently palpating for evidence of injury. They asked her who she was, what had happened, and where the pain was. Hannah told them her name and said she had been shot. She said her stomach was sore and she was feeling badly.

Her response was strained but audible, indicating to the emergency responders that her airway was intact; one checked with a stethoscope and confirmed bilateral breath sounds. She was cool and clammy over her extremities. They saw the bloodstained shirt and pants. A quick examination of the abdomen revealed a single, reddish-brown hole in the right lower quadrant; dark blood trickled from the wound. A quick glance and palpation of the back, chest, and flanks failed to reveal an exit wound.

As the men worked on Hannah, Mei fished through her purse. Kai Chan had told her the union leader was a man named Bill Lewis. She found his card; it had his home number. She called him on her mobile and told him what had happened.

"Oh God," Lewis said. "How is she?"

"She going to hospital," Mei said. "I call soon as can." She hung up.

The paramedics placed the stretcher beneath Hannah and carefully logrolled her onto the hard-plastic spine board. They covered her with blankets and secured the straps. They carried her down the steps and then released the wheels and pushed her up the ramp into the back of the ambulance—waving Mei off when she tried to get in. At that moment, two men grabbed Mei and dragged her screaming to a car. One of the EMTs watched her being taken away as he retracted the ramp and shut the doors. The ambulance sped off.

En route the EMTs started an IV in her right arm and hooked her up to normal saline. They placed a mask that had an attached reservoir connected to an oxygen tank over her nose and mouth, securing it with an elastic band around her head. They put a monitor on her fingernail bed to measure her capillary flow and oxygen saturation. One EMT applied a dry gauze four-by-four-inch dressing with manual pressure to staunch the wound, while the other checked vitals and assigned numbers to the Glasgow Coma Scale for her eye, verbal, and motor responses. Her pulse was thready—in and out, weakening. She was getting colder as her peripheral blood vessels started to clamp down—the body, realizing it was running out of blood, redirected flow to the main organs.

One of the paramedics called it in. "This is Hong Kong EMS Unit 52. We have a twenty- to thirty-year-old female with a GSW to the belly. Heart rate 110, BP 80 over 60, satting 92 percent non-room air. She's got a GCS of 14. We've established a large-bore, 16-gauge IV access in the right antecubital fossa. We're two minutes away, awaiting instruction."

"Bring her in," was all the emergency room doc said.

Lewis called his admin Dolores at home.

"Hannah's been shot in Hong Kong. Get me the White House. I don't care how you do it; get someone on the line."

Lewis lived in Harlem, twenty blocks from Hannah's parents on Manhattan's Upper West Side. He spoke softly with his wife as he dressed. He kissed her, checked the cell charge, and left the apartment. The streets were empty. Walking east, he saw the first softening of dawn through the narrow canyon of his side street. He took a call from Dolores, who patched him in to a White House aide. Lewis briefed him on what had happened. He demanded the government take action to bring home Hannah and Shay.

Lewis waited a minute on Broadway before a taxi screeched to a stop and sped him to the home of Charles and Esther Stein. The Steins were slow to answer the intercom. Esther Stein buzzed him in. Upstairs, she opened the door. Lewis saw from the look on her face that he had already told her all she needed to know.

"It's Hannah, oh my God," she said.

Charles Stein approached slowly, dragging his foot. He put his arm around her. Lewis enveloped both of them with his huge arms and frame.

"I don't have all the details," he said. "She was shot in Hong Kong during a prodemocracy rally. My last contact was with the person taking her to the hospital."

Charles Stein broke from Lewis's grasp. He took small, halting steps as he shuffled to the phone. He took out his wallet and the top-of-the-line credit card he paid a small-fortune membership fee for every year. He held the phone shaking, and dialed. His fingers trembled over each number as he keyed through the prompts to a person.

"My name is Charles Stein, and my daughter, Hannah Rachel Stein, has a life emergency in Hong Kong," he said; he grabbed at his stomach in a rush of nausea. "Please do not mistake my monotone voice for a lack of urgency; I have PD, Parkinson's disease. I need you to find out what hospital she's in and contact me with the details. If necessary, I need you to arrange for a medevac to the closest appropriate hospital and country, if you determine one is better-equipped to handle her condition. I need a charter flight for two, departing from New York immediately."

As he listened to the person on the other end, his hand shook.

"That's correct," he said, when satisfied with the agent's response.

Stein hung up and went to his wife. She was sitting on the couch. Lewis had gone into the kitchen to get her a drink of water. Charles stroked her hair and then kissed her cheek.

"Our little girl," she said. "Our little girl."

He drew her close.

forty-nine

Lewis watched BBC news as he waited for word about Hannah. The international confederations had carried the mass strike to the emerging world. In Latin America, Brazilian and Chilean workers had already been protesting against becoming "a marketplace for cheap labor and inhuman working conditions," as one declaration put it.

The Brazilians struck first, stopping auto and truck production at plants in São Paulo, the country's industrial heartland. The Chileans quickly followed suit. Mexican workers led walkouts across the country, including a demonstration that filled the Zocalo, Mexico City's great square. Agitators also convinced workers to take job actions at nonunionized maquiladora factories, on the border and in the interior.

In Central America, coffee workers demonstrated in Tegucigalpa, Honduras, where they were dispersed by police using rubber bullets and tear gas. Port workers struck in Acajutla, in El Salvador. Workers in Central American EPZs—Export Processing Zones, enclaves where the government offers economic incentives to lure foreign investment—walked out of offshore outsourcing factories in Belize, Costa Rica, Guatemala, Nicaragua, and Panama.

The South African trade-union movement, thankful for Bill Lewis's long friendship and service to the liberation struggle, struck after Lewis placed a call to its leadership in Johannesburg. The unions were fresh off a two-day general strike, demanding public works programs to soften a 25 percent unemployment rate; the organization and logistics for a countrywide walkout were intact.

The leadership council authorized a two-day action in support of the Machinists. They had laughed approvingly when they heard that Shay rocked out to township music.

The job actions propelled strikes across the continent, as the twin causes of Shay and Chinese workers—and Chinese companies' treatment of African workers—ignited already strained labor relations. Workers struck an airline in the Ivory Coast. In the Congo, they shut down a sugar company. The railways were disrupted by Angolan workers. Civil servants and teachers conducted work stoppages across Kenya, Niger, and Togo. Demonstrations erupted in Libya, and across Gabon, Swaziland, and Lesotho.

The newscast reported that Australian trade unions had launched a wave of sympathy strikes. In the Philippines, the trade-union confederation was already conducting an antisweatshop campaign, pressuring multinational companies to disclose who supplied them and what the working conditions were like in the plants. The unions were sending monitors to the factories, to encourage workers to report on compliance with agreed-upon codes of conduct, and lobbying the government to strengthen inspections and pass legislation to improve working conditions.

The Philippine strikes were centered in the export processing zones. Workers struck a clothing producer in Bataan. In Cavite, they shut down an electronics plant. Another group of workers, fed up with forced overtime, reduced benefits, and the firing of union officers, blocked supplier deliveries to a consumer electronics company in the Subic Bay Freeport Zone.

Lewis clicked off the TV. This had gone so far beyond their intent—to get leverage to help free Shay.

He couldn't decide if he was in the saddle, or bareback on a wild horse.

The White House

"Strikes across the United States, Canada, South and Central America," President Rodgers said. "Throughout Europe, Africa, and Asia. To free John Shay, and in support of the right to organize unions in China." He paused. "People demonstrating in Hong Kong."

He smiled. "You've got to love the pressure on the Chinese."

The others in the room made a show of amusement.

"Unfortunately, on us as well," the president said.

The mineworker job actions were already wreaking havoc on energy supplies, cutting coal deliveries to power plants. Hospitals were shorthanded; the ports were tied up in knots. Companies hired replacement workers, and there were clashes on the lines; strikers had been injured. Community and church groups were pressuring local and state officials and members of the House and Senate, who were pushing it back onto the president.

"The economy could nosedive in a heartbeat," Rodgers said, recalling stats from a morning meeting. He looked down the table at Saul Bernstein, deputy undersecretary of defense for Asian and Pacific affairs. Bernstein was his top China hand.

"Saul, where is this headed with China?"

Bernstein hunched forward and cupped his hands on the table. A rack suit and antsy manner telegraphed his academic past.

"There is little the Chinese won't do when they feel something is in their national interest, regardless of the train wreck that may follow," he said. "However, I don't think we have reached that point. They have seen Hong Kong demonstrations before and absorbed them with minor adjustments in policy. John Shay is a unique matter. I think it is likely they will put him in jail. Although I don't think they will throw away the key. Probably a couple of months. Long enough to show that you can't pressure them without paying a little price."

"A couple of months of Shay in jail? With strikes spreading across the United States and the world?" The president shook his head. "That's a big price tag."

"A lot depends on internal politics—what the new leader, Zhao Guozhi, thinks he needs to do to strengthen his grip on power and placate opponents within the ruling structure," Bernstein said. "This generation of Chinese leadership is confident. The country is making great gains, and they want to sustain that momentum. They understand China has a lot to lose by antagonizing the world. But they also feel that China offers the world so much opportunity, it can get away with just about anything."

Bernstein looked around the room. "Especially with us. International capital markets are in tatters; China is one of the few countries with cash. It has been using it to cement commercial and political relationships with Europe, Japan, Russia … even Canada and Latin America, on our doorstep. The Chinese have created de facto trading blocs of countries in Asia, Africa, and South America that depend upon its growth and appetite for raw materials to drive their economies. They have used bilateral agreements to build relationships naturally, as outgrowths of its surging economic development, as well as deliberately, as political counterweights to the United States.

"I believe President Zhao feels, already, that China has enough of these in place to make us think twice about the economic and political consequences of any action we might contemplate. These counterbalancing relationships are designed to keep other countries on the sidelines. To ensure that any action we take, we will have to take alone."

"We should move carefully," the secretary of state said. "The Chinese play hard/soft—fly off the handle, determine the resolve of their antagonist, and then make the best deal they can."

"Except when they don't," the national security advisor said. "If someone reacts too weakly, they push too far. If someone reacts too strongly, they can also push too far. Our response has to be calibrated perfectly."

"Let's not get all 'mysterious East' about this," the president said. "I think we all react in many of the same ways. My question is, will they give up John Shay?"

"In return for what?" the secretary of state asked. "We assure them we won't interfere in their affairs—no encouragement for the Hong Kong demonstrators, beyond a statement of support for the democratic process and a diplomatic protest against the PLA garrison action. Commercially, we assemble a package to dial down the trade disputes. Remove a couple of their companies we listed on the *Federal Register* for stuff they sold Iran."

She looked around the room. "We all know preventing these companies from doing business with the US government, and denying them the opportunity to buy controlled technologies from US companies, only contributes to the trade gap and hurts our economy."

She had another reason not to come down hard. She had just opened a back channel to China's foreign ministry, horse-trading US support for Chinese participation in G7 deliberations for limits on arms and technology sales to Iran. China was a member of the secondary G20 countries; it wanted to crack the inner circle of the G7. The secretary didn't want to sacrifice the inroads she had made with her contacts.

"Same old, same old," Rodgers said.

The secretary of state stared at him.

"Same old bad behavior, same old concessions, to get the unruly child to stop trashing the room. Can't we do something more forceful? To move them toward accountability? Toward responsible participation in the global structure?"

The national security advisor nodded. "I think they're ready for that. The new leadership wants change, but feels it has to be cautious. Maybe it's time to give them a push, to help them along."

An aide came into the room and handed the president a piece of paper. Rodgers read silently and then looked up.

"The Chinese fired three live missiles across the Taiwan Strait. It seems the Taiwanese have taken to the streets as well, in solidarity with the people of Hong Kong."

He looked around the room. "The Taiwan demonstrators are carrying placards calling for independence from China."

fifty

The scoop-and-run terminated at the hospital in a wail of sirens and flashing lights. Hannah was rolled through the sliding glass doors of the emergency department into the trauma bay, one of two designated rooms to the left of the entrance. The large, well-lit space had cream-colored walls and a stretcher in the middle of the room. There was a mobile cart stocked with intubation equipment, drugs, and surgical instruments; cabinets with glass windows—filled with tools and medications—ringed the periphery. A technician delivered a cooler with blood from the blood bank; another tech wheeled in an IV pole with a rapid blood transfuser, which squeezes the bag to pump faster than a gravity drip.

The trauma team had been assembled and alerted as to what to expect. Team members were dressed in medium-green scrubs with caps, masks, and goggles for eye protection and positioned around the bed. The paramedics unstrapped Hannah and moved her to the bed with the aid of the caregivers. The EMTs related the facts to the trauma team captain while Hannah was being transferred onto the bed.

Goran Krasnic was the team lead, an emergency department physician from a Boston teaching hospital who was working in Hong Kong with his colleague, Howard Yates, a trauma surgeon. The hospitals had swapped ED and trauma doc pairs for a six-week rotation, to observe and exchange best practices from each institution.

The urgency in the trauma bay was replaced by controlled chaos as Krasnic—tall and lean, an easygoing ex-navy guy from a family of Bosnian refugees—stepped through the advanced trauma life support—ATLS—protocol and the severity of Hannah's injuries quickly became apparent. More blood had accumulated around her clothing and the bedding. Her mental status was in and out, with incoherent moaning and random extremity movement.

Krasnic figured she had lost at least a liter and a half of blood and was in shock.

"Hannah, can you hear me?" he asked, leaning over the bed.

China's "test" of surface-to-surface missiles had been conducted near the Taiwanese port cities of Keelung and Kaohsiung. Two missiles landed near Keelung, twenty-three miles from the country's north coast and thirty miles from the capital, Taipei. The third missile landed near Kaohsiung, thirty-five miles off the southern coast. The two cities handle more than 70 percent of the commercial shipping that enters Taiwan. The proximity of the tests to the ports, and China's warning for ships and aircraft to avoid the target zones, brought international shipping and air traffic to Taiwan to a halt.

"It's a carbon copy of March '96," the secretary of defense said.

"Summarize our response then," the president said.

The secretary was squat and well-built. He had an arrogant frown he would parlay into a Cheshire smile if he saw an opportunity to showboat his brain.

"Our Seventh Fleet monitored Chinese live-fire exercises off the coast of Taiwan in March and April 1996," he said. "The forward-deployed *Independence* carrier battle group, with embarked Carrier Air Wing Five, sailed into the strait and took up position off the eastern coast of Taiwan. USS *Bunker Hill* operated south of Taiwan, using SPY-1 Aegis radar to observe the tests. Also with the *Independence* CVGB were USS *Hewitt*, USS *O'Brien*, and USS *McClusky.* A second carrier battle group, led by the *Nimitz*, left the Persian Gulf and arrived in the South China Sea within days. Accompanying *Nimitz* and embarked Carrier Air Wing Nine were USS *Port Royal*,

USS *Callaghan*, USS *Oldendorf*, USS *Ford*, USS *Willamette*, USS *Shasta*, and USS *Portsmouth*."

"How effective was that?" Rodgers asked.

The secretary of state shook her head disapprovingly.

"Madam Secretary?" the secretary of defense said, annoyed at the interruption.

"It was too strong a response," she said. "We humiliated the Chinese. We shoved it in their face, for all the world to see, that they were powerless to confront us in their own seas."

"I disagree," the national security advisor said. "It was humiliate them or embolden them. And what happened next? Tensions in the strait diminished, and relations between the United States and China improved. We saw increased high-level exchanges, and progress on bilateral issues like human rights, nuclear nonproliferation, and trade."

"The Chinese said they would never let us do that again without military repercussions," the secretary of state said.

Thomas Quinn, the chairman of the joint chiefs, nodded. Eyes turned on him. Quinn was an admiral, the first navy guy in years to oversee the services. He was a tall, fit man, with a quiet demeanor that revealed little of the ferocity with which he waged war. The Serbs found that out in 1999, when he commanded the carrier USS *Theodore Roosevelt* in the Adriatic.

Quinn looked around the room. "They said they would launch naval cruise missiles and sink one of our carriers. With their Russian-built Sovremenny-class destroyers, Sunburn antiship missiles, and Kilo-class submarines, they can now do it."

Rodgers turned to the CIA chief. "Pete?"

"The 1996 crisis erupted after a chain of events over several years," Cloninger said. "In October 1994, the aircraft carrier USS *Kitty Hawk* got tangled in a three-day running encounter with a Chinese Han-class nuclear attack sub in the Yellow Sea. The following year, Taiwan president Lee Teng-hui spoke at his alma mater, Cornell University, where he repeatedly used the terminology 'Republic of China on Taiwan,' challenging Beijing's 'One China' formulation. China denounced Lee's visit and initiated tests of short-

and intermediate-range nuclear-capable missiles. The Chinese also mobilized PLA forces in Fujian Province—directly across the strait from Taiwan—and moved aircraft to the coast."

He paused. "Today, relations between the United States and China are reasonably good, our trade tensions notwithstanding. Both sides have more at stake in maintaining these relations than ever before. Yet, in my estimation, the present situation is the most serious we have ever faced. The Kuomintang Nationalists who fled the mainland in 1949 after losing the civil war have been replaced by native-born Taiwanese with little interest in joining China. They'll build factories in China and do business there, but they don't want to become part of it. But the Chinese won't allow them to go their separate way. China reunification is the cornerstone issue for the regime. The Chinese also believe an independent Taiwan would set off separatists in Tibet and in Xinjiang province. The Xinjiang separatists—radical Uighur Muslims—are being trained by the East Turkestan Islamic Movement based in Pakistan and Afghanistan. Xinjiang is one-sixth the land mass of China. The province is chock-full of oil and other natural resources; the Chinese have nuclear test sites there.

"The Uighurs are tough nuts to crack. They lived hardscrabble all their lives along the old caravan routes in central Asia. Converted to Islam in the fifteenth century, had a brief life as the East Turkestan Republic before Mao. There's nine million of them in Xinjiang. They don't like being ruled by China's Han leaders, or being overrun by the Han settlers Beijing is throwing at them. We've all been briefed on the violence between the Uighurs and Hans. ETIM leaders had contact with bin Laden in the Afghan camps before 9/11. China has called ETIM its biggest terrorist threat. They don't want global jihad opening an outlet store in their western lands."

"The dudes we sent to Bermuda," someone said—referring to the four Uighur prisoners at Guantanamo, spirited from solitary to sun and fun. Everyone laughed.

The CIA chief smiled. "China feels this may be the best window it has to get Taiwan back. The Taiwanese independence movement could grow stronger in the future. The Chinese know we're spread thin around the world. They're also counting on the fact that we need them—for business, to restrain North Korea, in the fight against terror. And to stop selling missile technology and weaponry to rogue states like Iran."

"How would they attack?" the president asked.

The chairman of the joint chiefs looked at the secretary of defense, who nodded to take the ball.

"We believe a frontal amphibious assault, supported by air attack, is unlikely," Quinn said. "China doesn't have the sealift capability. The Taiwanese coast is basically mudflats—from shoreline to anywhere between two to five miles out to sea—and would bog them down. Taiwan also has a qualitative advantage over the PLA's numbers edge—in fighter aircraft, surface warships, air defenses, even ground force capabilities."

The secretary of defense chimed in. "A failed invasion of this magnitude would weaken the armed forces, delegitimize the Communist Party, probably topple the government. It would wreck the PRC economy and irrevocably alienate the people of Taiwan from the mainland." He paused. "An attack on this scale would also force the United States to respond."

"So what do they do?" the president asked.

"The logical military course is an overwhelming first strike, using the fifteen hundred short-range ballistic missiles China has placed on the Fujian coast," Quinn said. "This attack, combined with electronic warfare and computer viruses to blind antimissile defenses, would take out Taiwan's air defenses and early warning systems, level the airfields, and devastate the command, control, and communications centers—the intelligence and command facilities on Yangming Mountain, the Combat Air Command and Control Center in downtown Taipei, the Combined Operations Center at Yuangshuan, and the Communications Center at Longtan. By inflicting such a rapid defeat on the Taiwan military before we could bring our forces to bear in the region, China is calculating we would not risk retaliating against them, escalating a conflict that was essentially over."

"But we don't think China will do that either," the secretary of defense said. "Not in response to this level of provocation—a band of Taiwanese marching in the street, shouting themselves hoarse for democracy. We think they have something else in mind. If China is intent upon taking back Taiwan now, we believe it will commence hostilities with sea denial—a naval blockade, to disrupt shipping and the economy—which they've partially accomplished already through the live-fire missile 'exercise.' China will then use subs and surface vessels to lay minefields, threatening to sink any commercial vessel that crosses a line they draw. It will follow with information warfare against economic targets like Taiwan's banking system, stock market, and IT grid. PLA information warfare units will tweak US info systems, to tie down our resources and make us nervous. Maybe aim a laser at one of our positioning satellites, remind us they can mess up our eyes in the sky."

He shook his head. "And put another hundred years' worth of debris in space, like they did when they shot down their own satellite in a test firing."

He cleared his throat. "PLA sleeper agents, already in place in Taiwan, will conduct attacks on critical military and civilian infrastructure—the electrical grid, the transportation network, and so forth. Beijing will use these actions to 'cascade' the crisis over a tightly defined period of time. Each action will take place separately, so the Chinese can assess the effect and the response from Taiwan, the United States, and the rest of the world. Yet the time period will be compressed enough to move deliberately toward the end goal. The Chinese believe a single, massive move would leave us no choice but to retaliate. They feel that if they can conduct a series of actions—each one below the threshold that would trigger our response—they will gain the upper hand in the conflict, while handcuffing us at each turn. They also think they can break the will of the Taiwanese this way."

"Is that true?" the president asked.

"It's not clear," the national security advisor said. "In fact, the opposite may be the case. The Taiwanese also feel they have a small window of opportunity this decade to assert themselves. Their qualitative military advantage will soon be gone, as China rapidly modernizes its armed forces. If there was ever a time to move decisively toward independence, this may be it."

"I agree with that, except the final conclusion," the secretary of state said. "In the end, the Taiwanese will put personal safety and business relationships above any notions of liberty. These aren't Concord minutemen we're talking about—" feeling a pinch of pride in her New England roots. "One and a half million of their twenty-three million people live on the mainland and do business there. When push comes to shove, money will talk more loudly than some ideologue on a soapbox."

Rodgers cut short the give-and-take and asked everyone to leave the room. He leaned back in his chair and swiveled toward the window. The fall sky was clear, bright blue, as if there was not a care in the world. Lately he had been focused on political calculations with his advisors around his reelection campaign. This was so far beyond that scheming; the continued existence of the United States was at stake.

He couldn't help but wonder if he should just let Taiwan go. Does that make me weak? A relentless mass had been building over the years, pointing in that direction. The growing strength of China, and its deepening stranglehold over Taiwan through pervasive—*invasive* worked better for him—economic ties. The rise of China's armed forces. The sheer distance from the United States, and its already overextended armed might. The deep exhaustion of Americans, maybe even the military, after the long Iraq and Afghanistan campaigns.

He remembered the Taiwan Strait used to be called the "Black Ditch." He had a sudden image of driving his Silverado, back home in Indiana, off the road into a gulley.

How much—for others' sake—is enough? he thought. America had a world of problems of its own. How much of the world's troubles could it shoulder beyond that?

How far down can we reach?

fifty-one

Hannah didn't respond to the doctor but kept moaning. The trauma team moved through its choreographed assessment, each member with a preestablished position and behavior at the bedside. Krasnic at first stood at her head to evaluate her airway. He then moved about Hannah, doing his ABCDEs—airway, breathing, circulation, disability, and exposure—to identify all injuries. He spoke clearly to the recording nurse on her left side, who wrote the information in the chart.

He repeated his dictum to the team: "If it's dark, you have to shine a light in it. If there's a surface, you've got to press on it." As he conducted his primary survey, team members reported continually to him on their secondary surveys—checking from head to toe for other wounds or injuries—and he acknowledged and acted when needed.

Hannah began to thrash about violently. Krasnic was worried that her mental status was so altered that she was going to cough up the contents from her stomach into her lungs, risking aspiration pneumonia. He instructed the nurse to administer twenty milligrams of etomidate and 120 milligrams of succinylcholine. She did it and said, "I've given twenty of IV etomidate, I've given 120 of succinylcholine." Krasnic had been stressing closed-loop communication to the ED team—if he asked the nurse to do something, the nurse repeated the orders after executing them.

After sedation, Krasnic supervised the resident physician as she performed an intubation to raise Hannah's oxygen level and protect her airway. The resident used a laryngoscope to see into Hannah's trachea and then put the plastic endotracheal tube between the vocal chords. She pulled out the stylet—the wire that holds the tube in place—and bagged her for oxygen.

Krasnic examined Hannah's chest, noting diminished breath sounds on the left. He told the resident on that side to place a large bore #36 French chest tube into the left chest. There was a rush of air with the creation of the two-centimeter opening. The combination of blood and air when the tube was placed indicated the bullet had gained access to the left chest from entry in the right lower quadrant of her abdomen.

Krasnic watched as way more of Hannah's blood than he had hoped to see began to empty through the chest tube into the collection system.

At the White House, Rodgers reconvened the team and pressed for more information.

"What about Hong Kong?" he asked.

"I don't think the Chinese worry much about them," the secretary of defense said. "They perceive them as soft and decadent, incapable of rising against the regime. They believe the existing police force, supplemented by the PLA garrisons stationed there, can control the situation."

"Guangzhou. What's going on there?"

"One of our senior commanders serves as our liaison with the Chinese military," the director of national intelligence said. "He has spoken with officers in the Forty-First and Forty-Second Armies, which constitute the Guangzhou Military Region. These armies operate very successful commercial trading companies, having taken advantage of the southern province's first experiments with capitalism during the Deng Xiaoping reign. Beijing wants a bigger slice of the economic pie for itself, Shanghai, and other regions. This has set these regions—and the armies and trading companies associated with them—on a collision course. Zhao and the central government have been making it hard for the armies of the south to conduct business as usual. They've been turning down loan applications, prosecuting corruption, steering investment away from the province.

"The operation John Shay uncovered is part of that dynamic. We have now confirmed that it was a Shanghai automotive company, focused on the luxury end of the market, that was receiving the Lambal parts. The company is launching its own brand and can't ramp up production fast enough to fill orders. Its quality also didn't pass muster with the buyers of high-end models. Lambal Interior builds the best seating and car interiors in the world. It was running only one shift because Beijing wouldn't let it sell outside the province; the central government is leaning on both domestic and foreign automakers to source their components from regional suppliers. The second, contraband shift at the factory was a way to bypass these restrictions and sell parts made in Guangdong to a final assembly plant in Shanghai. This, by the way, was the key issue in the original strike here in the United States—Lambal needed to build another plant in China, in a location acceptable to Beijing, to sell to automobile companies in other parts of China. The union is battling them tooth and nail to prevent that."

"And shutting down the country on the side," the president said.

The DNI nodded. "John Shay was tipped off to the theft by a worker in Lambal's Mexican plant, who traveled to China to help set up the Shenzhen facility. Shay was given corroborating information by a member of China's underground trade-union movement. He was kidnapped in Hong Kong by Triad hoods operating an off-the-books distribution ring with elements of the Forty-Second Army trading company. A ransom demand was made to the United Machinists in the United States. Shay was freed by a Forty-Second Army special operations team that brought him to the province's capital city of Guangzhou.

"Beijing and Guangzhou are now in a standoff over who should have him in custody. Beijing wants Shay for leverage in its dealings with us and to reassert its supremacy over the province. Guangzhou wants assurances from Beijing that it will be free to conduct business as usual, without interference from the central government. The wild card is separatist elements in the provincial government and southern army."

"Someone else wants to break away from China?" Rodgers asked.

Everyone laughed.

"It's contagious," the national intelligence chief said. "The separatists are not much interested in a deal—they want the crisis to deepen. Beijing may give them what they wish for. The worse things get, the more pretext the Chinese government will have to justify a crackdown, in the name of national unity."

"Al-Qaeda," the president said. "I haven't heard anyone speak about them again. Do we now feel there's no connection?"

"We're not sure," the DNI said. "There has been at least one meeting between an al-Qaeda operative and an officer from the Forty-Second Army. This army, or renegade elements within it, may feel it's losing the struggle with Beijing for control over its business operations. It might be looking to al-Qaeda for a new distributor to move goods. For all we know, an al-Qaeda/China connection may even have central government blessing—one more screw Beijing can turn on us, for political and economic leverage. Bottom line, we don't know."

The president took a drink of water and looked around the room. "Just when we get counterinsurgency down pat, we have to face the PLA." He paused. "Send a single carrier strike force to the Taiwan Strait."

"Mr. President," Quinn said, "with all due respect, a diplomatic show of force means a different thing to diplomats than it does to the military. I understand your reasoning, and what you want to accomplish, but in the military we have to plan for all contingencies. And the worst contingency here is, we saunter in there for a show of force and lose an aircraft carrier. Maybe the Chinese have sixty more Su-30MKKs than we know about—they've done a lot better job than the Russians of concealing their military capability. Maybe some Sukhois somehow get through and get off a couple of missiles. Next thing you know, we've got a carrier listing at thirty degrees in the Pacific. Then the Chinese figure what the hell and they send a sub they know they're going to lose, but it's worth it to get off a torpedo and sink the whole damn boat. It's only a show of force, nobody expects anything to happen, but there's going to be hell to pay if there's an aircraft carrier sunk and everybody starts screaming war."

The secretary of state shot him a look. The armed services head glared back.

"Madam Secretary, do you understand what it would mean to lose an aircraft carrier?" he asked. "It would be abject defeat. It would be like one of our cities getting bombed."

Quinn paused. "What if there's a mistake? You've got human beings out there looking at radar screens, peering down from cockpits at the water. They're absolutely paranoid, paralyzed, at the thought of losing that aircraft carrier. The premier thought in everybody's mind is, we're going to go where the president told us to but we're so frightened we're going to get killed that we're going to kill anything and everything that moves, because we are not going to let this aircraft carrier sink.

"Maybe a hotshot Chinese pilot—an aggressive guy who's already had a bunch of close calls—pushes the envelope one time too many with one of our guys. Maybe it's a language problem. Suppose a Chinese and an American fighter plane have an unexpected meeting engagement? Their pilots are supposed to be good English speakers. Maybe this kid is the grandson of a Politburo member—it's a plum career, he got in through nepotism, he's not the highest card in the deck. They meet somewhere in the Pacific, alarms start honking in their cockpits, the pilots are screaming at each other, 'This is the United States naval attack force and you need to clear this area, this is the Chinese attack force and you'd better clear this area,' but they're not sure what the other is saying and boom … somebody shoots somebody down.

"It could be a target acquisition error. We're great at acquiring targets, but you have to analyze a server farm of information to pick the right one; maybe we choose wrong. Or the Chinese throw us a curveball—we expect them to go into a defensive shell, but they make a bold move. They invade islands in the Batanes and Ryukyu chains, commandeer a civilian airfield for their fighters and fuel tankers. China has already conducted military exercises of these mock landings. Planes and patrol boats are always buzzing around those islands, because of disputed natural gas rights."

He walked up to the screen and pointed, in turn, to two sets of dots. "The Ryukyus run down from Japan all the way to Taiwan. The Batanes are in the Luzon Strait, where the Pacific merges with the China Sea, part of a sea lane between the Philippines and China. Mavudis, or Yami, the northernmost islet in the Batanes, is only thirty miles from the strait. The Senkaku islands, part of Japan's Ryukyu chain—claimed by both China and Taiwan, who call them the Diaoyus—are just as close.

"These would be acts of war against the Philippines and Japan, but it would pinch off the sea lanes to the strait and put our strike group in a box. It would give the Chinese the tactical equivalent of two aircraft carriers—squadrons of SU-30s, on unsinkable rocks in the Pacific. The Chinese couldn't defend them; they're too far from China. But they could appeal to the world, say we didn't mean any harm to the Japanese or Filipinos, we were acting in self-defense. It turns what was a pretty clean US demonstration of force and support for Taiwan into a mess. It's a military step they could take to seek a diplomatic victory, forcing our fleet to slow down. We would either have to slaughter them—with all the diplomatic fuss that would cause—or halt our transit to the strait."

"Diplomatic *fus*s!" The word exploded from the secretary of state.

Quinn smiled at her. "My point is, we have to plan worst case. We have to be ready to shut down their communications, kill their antiaircraft, and disrupt their airfields, with the objective of achieving air supremacy. If anything is going to happen, it's going to be an air war."

"What do you recommend, Thomas?" the president asked.

"Three strike groups," the JCS chairman said.

"Are you mad?" the secretary of state said. "The Chinese would go berserk."

"In light of recent history, I would think politicians would recognize that in military matters, the military knows best," Quinn said. "That when you make a military decision based on a political calculation, you end up with a protracted mess. Or even worse, defeat."

"We'll announce one, preposition the others," Rodgers said. "Move them as close as we can without giving much away. Thomas, brushstroke your planning for us."

The admiral nodded. "We've already backward planned, from the achievement of the objective. In this case, there are two goals. The first is to make sure that, if we move a carrier strike group forward and things don't go well, we're going to have backup groups ready to come into the fray. We've been conducting exercises to surge air force, navy, and marine aircraft into bases in Japan; although this is primarily in case of conflict on the Korean peninsula, such a deployment could also provide support to Taiwan. We can also forward deploy aircraft to the Philippines, and even Vietnam—we've strengthened military relations with these countries, in response to China's growing naval threat and its claims on undersea oil blocks in disputed waters—to provide additional coverage.

"The second aim is the defense of Taiwan. We do that by achieving air supremacy over the strait. Our view is, nothing happens to Taiwan unless China achieves air superiority. DESOP—that's the Deputy Chief of Staff for Operations"—he looked at the secretary of state when he unfurled the acronym, infuriating her; she knew what it meant—"has already cranked this thing up."

The chairman of the joint chiefs looked around the room.

"We're going to give the Chinese evidence that something's coming and bad things are about to happen if they continue on their aggressive course."

fifty-two

The nursing staff sent off the blood draw for blood typing and blood-gas analysis. The nurses took a blood-pressure assessment by palpation of the radial and carotid pulse. Hannah's blood pressure was no more than 70 mmHg—she was in shock. The team began giving her packed red blood cells—O negative blood for a woman of childbearing age, the universal donor for young females—and the exam continued.

Krasnic saw that the abdomen was distended—"most likely with blood," he dictated aloud. "There are no exit wounds. The bullet is not palpable beneath the skin. There is blood running from the hole in the right lower abdomen to the flank and collecting in a pool along the side of the patient. It is not voluminous but persistent—most of the bleeding is internal."

The team rolled Hannah to the side, and Krasnic examined her back to rule out other wounds; none were found. He noted that her skin was cold, clammy, and pasty in color, without the usual pink tone of normal skin. He called for a supine portable chest X-ray—it confirmed that the bullet was in the lower left chest. He then ordered a focused abdominal sonography for trauma—FAST—to identify if there was blood in the belly or in the chest around the heart. He started the FAST in the right upper quadrant, the most gravity-dependent area in the body. This recess is not filled with fluid under normal circumstances and is the first place blood would accumulate.

"FAST is positive. I've got free fluid in Morrison's pouch."

That was enough for him. He was worried the bullet had gone through one of the major blood vessels in the belly and could cause an exsanguinating hemorrhage—bleed out. They had to quickly clamp down those blood vessels and tie them off. Death begins in radiology, was his saying—don't dally with tests in a life-threatening situation.

The trauma surgeon had entered the room and was reading the nurse's notes as he listened to Krasnic, whom he had trained in Boston. Yates's expression twinned jovial and taut in a single look—a perfect pairing for his work and a workable demeanor for life.

He took the baton. "Patient shows minimal blood-pressure response to packed red cells," Yates said. "She needs to go to the operating room for immediate control of bleeding. Book me a room for a GSW to the belly that's hypotensive and tachycardic."

Guam, US territory, Marianas

Vice Admiral Robert T. Laughton, commander of the US Seventh Fleet, allowed himself a second of disbelief after reading the orders from the commander, US Pacific Fleet. The Seventh Fleet had port call in Shanghai earlier this year. He remembered the sailors raving about a machine that separated silkworm cocoons—they saw it during tour of a factory, where they watched the entire silk-making process, from silk to cloth. They played basketball against Chinese sailors. The fleet's brass quintet staged a concert at the Shanghai Children's Home.

The Seventh Fleet is the largest of the navy's forward-deployed fleets, consisting at any one time of sixty to seventy ships, two to three hundred aircraft, and forty thousand navy and marine corps personnel. Its forces operate from bases in Japan and Guam and are rotationally deployed from Hawaii and the West Coast of the United States.

The fleet directly supports the three principal elements of US national security strategy—deterrence, forward defense, and alliance solidarity. Its area of responsibility encompasses more than fifty-two million square miles of the Pacific and Indian Oceans—a geography stretching from the international date line to the east coast of Africa, and from the Kuril Islands in the north to the Antarctic in the south—more than fourteen times the size of the continental United States.

Vice Admiral Laughton embarked on the USS *Blue Ridge*, the Seventh Fleet's command ship. His flagship and a part of the strike force, including the USS *George Washington*, Surface Combatant Force Seventh Fleet, and Destroyer Squadron 15, were docked on Guam in preparation for an exercise.

When the orders came, the vice admiral was inspecting the hull of the USS *Patriot*, a mine countermeasures ship. The ship's hull is constructed of oak, Douglas fir, and Alaskan cedar, along with a thin coating of fiberglass, to take advantage of wood's low magnetic signature during mine countermeasures operations.

Laughton returned to the *Blue Ridge* and delivered the orders to Rear Admiral Janice Stanger, the first woman to command a carrier strike force. Strike Force Commander Stanger commanded the USS *George Washington* (CVN 73). Commissioned on July 4, 1992, the one-thousand-foot-long Nimitz-class supercarrier spearheads Carrier Strike Group Five. With the motto "Spirit of Freedom"—taken from a letter General Washington wrote during the American Revolution—CSG-5 is the navy's only permanently forward-deployed carrier strike force, operating out of Yokosuka, Japan, at the entrance to Tokyo Bay.

When Stanger received the orders, she got the same charged feeling she had the morning of 9/11, when the *George Washington* was operating off the coast of Virginia conducting routine tests. She was part of the officer team that day when the ship was diverted north with its air wing and spent three days providing airspace defense for New York City and the surrounding area in coordination with North American Aerospace Defense Command (NORAD).

Stanger scanned her lineup card. Sailing with the *George Washington* would be the Aegis guided-missile cruisers USS *Cowpens* (CG 63) and USS *Shiloh* (CG 67) and the destroyers of DESRON 15—the USS *Curtis Wilbur* (DDG 54), USS *John S. McCain* (DDG 56), USS *Fitzgerald* (DDG 62), USS *Stetham* (DDG 63), USS *Lassen* (DDG 82), USS *McCampbell* (DDG 85), and USS

Mustin (DDG 89). Two Los Angeles–class attack submarines home ported in Guam—the USS *Buffalo* (SSN 715) and USS *Oklahoma City* (SSN 723)—would pull ahead to throw the downfield blocks. The USNS *Impeccable* (T-AGOS 23) ocean surveillance ship—not directly assigned to the carrier strike force but always at sea—had the Surveillance Towed Array Sensor System (SURTASS) to gather underwater acoustical data to track submarine contacts at long range. A couple of logistics combat ships had been assigned to the strike force—the USNS *Richard E. Byrd* (T-AKE 4), with its six thousand long tons of dry cargo capacity for ammunition, provisions, stores, spare parts, and potable water, and the USNS *Walter S. Diehl* (T-AO 193), a fleet replenishment oiler that could cart 180,000 barrels of fuel oil and aviation fuel.

Stanger gave instructions to her strike group staff. She was a commanding five foot eleven, her face lined by time, family, and career, but as lean today as she was thirty years ago as a local Troy, New York, kid and freestyle distance swimmer churning out seven thousand yards a day at practice for the hometown Rensselaer Polytechnic Institute team—in between NROTC training and drills, and earning dual degrees in electrical and nuclear engineering at RPI.

As she issued orders, she was thinking this wasn't going to be a cakewalk like'96—she had studied the tactics and maneuvers in that crisis. Last year a Chinese diesel sub surfaced near the *George Washington* in the Philippine Sea southeast of Okinawa—undetected until that point. China had also improved its long-range air-strike force of planes and missiles. Between sea, air, and electronic weaponry—and its ability to carry out asymmetric mischief—it packed more punch than at any previous time in history.

Carrier Air Wing FIVE is known as "the nation's only 911 air wing." The strike force of seventy-five planes, a critical combat strike element of Battle Force Seventh Fleet, is the only forward-deployed carrier air wing in the US Navy. CVW-5's arsenal includes Strike Fighter Squadrons VFA-27, VFA-102, VFA-115, and VFA-195, flying

F/A-18E and F/A-18F Superhornets, and Tactical Electronics Warfare Squadron VAQ-141, flying the EA-18G Growler. Other assets are Airborne Early Warning Squadron VAW-115 flying the Hawkeye 2000, VRC-30 Detachment 5 flying the C-2 Greyhound, and HS-14 flying the HH-60F/H Seahawk.

CVW-5's home base when not embarked on the *GW* is the Naval Air Facility in Atsugi, Japan, a city of two hundred thousand on the Sagami River in the Kanagawa Prefecture on the main Japanese island of Honshu. Several squadrons were at the base—twenty miles from downtown Tokyo—when the orders came, including VFA-27, the Royal Maces.

The Royal Maces conduct carrier-based air-strike and strike-force escort missions, antiship operations, battle-group antiair operations, and surveillance and intelligence collection. The unit operated off the coast of Somalia in support of Operation Restore Hope and deployed to the Arabian Gulf in Operation Southern Watch, the multinational mission to monitor Iraqi compliance with the no-fly zone. The squadron participated in coalition strikes against Iraq in 1993 and flew against al-Qaeda and Taliban forces during Operation Enduring Freedom. It provided close air support and strike sorties against Iraqi forces in Operation Iraqi Freedom.

The F/A-18E Superhornets of VFA-27 were the first to take off from Atsugi, streaking out over Tokyo Bay en route to Guam and the *George Washington* as other CVW-5 aircraft prepped on the field.

fifty-three

Hannah was wheeled from the ED to the operating room through brightly lit corridors and swinging doors. She was placed on the OR table in a supine position as the surgical team cleaned up at scrub sinks in an adjoining room. A nurse painted her abdomen, chest, neck, and bilateral groins with a brown-yellow iodine solution. The residents and nurses applied drapes around the expansive sterile field from chin to knees.

The surgical team was dressed in gowns, hats, and masks and wore light cream-colored gloves. The first assistant pulled on Hannah's skin from the other side of the table, putting it under tension as Yates made a generous midline abdominal incision—from the base of the chest to right above the pubic bone—with a #10 blade. As he instructed the nurse to remove the sharp knife from the table, he noted there was not much bleeding from the incision, reflecting Hannah's low blood pressure.

He was hanging tough with that, convinced that permissive hypotension—leaving the blood pressure intentionally lower—gave the patient more opportunity to form clot. The conventional response was to pour in fluids to maintain a normal blood pressure. But the body has its own ability to lower the pressure and form clot. If you give cold fluid and raise the pressure, it makes the patient more likely to pop off the protective clot and rebleed. That's the last thing he wanted to do until he was in a position to clamp and control where the bleeding was occurring. Seeing this approach in action was a big reason why the hospital had brought the Beantown docs to Hong Kong, as part of their information gathering for a series of new trauma centers they were building in China.

Yates opened Hannah's muscle fascia and entered the abdominal cavity; there was a gush of dark blood. The trauma team quickly inserted multiple white laparotomy packs into the opening to tamponade the bleeding. The anesthesia team now began to catch up with blood loss, giving Hannah packed red cells, fresh frozen plasma, and platelets.

When the bleeding slowed, the packs were removed in a sequential fashion, beginning with the quadrants in which there was no active bleeding. This allowed Yates to narrow down the field to those areas that needed to be addressed first—beginning with the bleeding, followed by bilious contamination of the abdomen. He temporarily controlled the bleeding with direct compression in the region of the infrarenal aorta.

He saw that the small bowel had been divided by the bullet. He controlled the bleeding in the mesentery—the double layer of membrane that connects the middle and lower sections of the bowel—then litigated the ends of the bowel with a stapler device to control ongoing contamination.

But the forceful arterial bleeding resumed.

On the secure line at the White House, the American and Chinese leaders exchanged niceties before Rodgers took the ball.

"Mr. President, in response to your live-fire missile exercise near the Taiwanese port cities of Kaohsiung and Keelung, I have dispatched a US carrier strike group, with an embarked air wing, to the Taiwan Strait," he said. "The group will take position outside the strait but not enter at this time. Its deployment is a restatement of our commitment to stability in the region, as articulated by the Taiwan Relations Act."

The Taiwan Relations Act was ratified by Congress in 1979. It declared that any effort to determine the future of Taiwan by other than peaceful means, including boycotts or embargoes, would be considered a threat to the peace and security of the Western Pacific area and of grave concern to the United States.

"The United States is not unsympathetic to China's aspirations in the global community," the president continued. "We are mindful of the enormous crises your country has experienced during its long march to greatness. We understand you have territorial issues, remnants of colonialism and civil war, that are of great importance to your country and people; we struggled with similar issues ourselves in centuries past. We further understand you have many economic and political issues to reconcile as you transition from a developing country into a global power.

"But with that global power also comes heightened responsibility. The world community depends upon the leading powers to peacefully resolve crises—those that involve them directly as matters of national interest, and others that concern them indirectly as areas of global concern. We seek to find just such a peaceful resolution to the current situation."

While listening to Rodgers, Zhao was skimming a briefing packet an aide handed him. Several additional US carrier strike groups appeared to have changed itineraries. US nuclear attack and ballistic missile submarines had disappeared from their ports, and were assumed to be in deep water. The United States was flying fighter aircraft and antiaircraft missile batteries into Taiwan, and moving air squadrons and wings to Okinawa and the Philippines. Chinese commercial ships had been buzzed by aircraft in international waters; one reported sighting a periscope. C-17 and C-5 cargo aircraft flying into Andersen Air Force Base on Guam were backing up on the runways. The Chinese military reported difficulty communicating with its satellites; some of their computers were down. It fingered either the National Security Agency or US Cyber Command as the culprit—whichever was currently ascendant in their endless turf war.

The Chinese president put down the papers. "Mr. President, we share your desire for a peaceful world, and agree that much of the responsibility for that peace rests on the shoulders of the great nations. But the United States has demonstrated, by its actions in Iraq, that it also believes in the right of a state to take unilateral, preemptive, and lethal action when national interests so dictate."

"You are correct, Mr. President," Rodgers said. "In response to a direct attack upon our homeland, and after assessing the potential of further attacks, we did invade and overturn a sovereign state."

"Why then, through your current diplomatic and military maneuvering, would you discourage China from doing so much less?" Zhao asked. "In Taiwan, we would only be exercising our rights over a Chinese province, whose instability may threaten our country and region, and perhaps the entire world."

"We both know it is not as simple as that, Mr. President," Rodgers said. "I mentioned your history and territorial issues for a reason. No country can control the circumstances that are thrust upon it in the world. In the course of your history as a nation, in the aftermath of civil war and the exile of the losing side to Taiwan, you have been burdened with a difficult situation.

"I understand the enormity of the choices you face. For many years, we have tried to resolve this situation. And we have not been successful, in many ways. But we have been successful in one way—it has never led to military conflict. I believe this must be our first and foremost goal—to lessen the chances that miscalculation or overreaction, on either side, lead to a graver situation. Our second goal must be equally clear—to continue to work together to peacefully resolve your issue with Taiwan. As intractable as it may seem, we must continue to try to find a solution."

He paused. "Maybe we will not find one, Mr. President. Perhaps, through our efforts, we will only sustain the momentum, and it will be left to another generation to find the way. But let us leave that generation this legacy. One of peaceful dialogue and sincere effort, not brinkmanship. And possibly, a disastrous result."

"Mr. President, I share your concerns," Zhao said. "But this is a matter for China to decide, not the United States. Taiwan is many thousands of miles from your shores. This is an issue of direct national interest to us. To you, it is geopolitical maneuvering, to maintain your power and influence in Asia."

"Every great nation, yours and mine alike, acts on the world stage," Rodgers said. "I don't need to remind you in this conversation of your many interests and activities around the globe, in countries and regions far beyond your own borders." He didn't want to complicate the discussion but had no choice. "In addition to the peaceful resolution of this matter, we also seek the return of John Shay and Hannah Stein."

"These citizens of yours have broken capital laws, and contributed to a destabilizing situation in Hong Kong, Taiwan, and Guangdong Province."

"For this unrest to erupt, it would seem you have many dissatisfied citizens and internal issues you need to deal with. These things have little to do with two Americans."

A silence followed.

"Mr. President, my first responsibility is to ensure the safety of every American," Rodgers said. "This exchange between us began over the matter of John Shay and because we had reason to believe an illegal operation in your country might in some way benefit terrorists. We are not certain of this terrorist connection, but we will continue—with your assistance, we hope—to pursue it. We will be providing your Ministry of Public Security liaison agents in Washington with facts in the case shortly.

"Our focus now is on defusing the crisis over Taiwan and Hong Kong and securing the release of John Shay and Hannah Stein. I need Mr. Shay to be delivered to the American authorities in Guangzhou or Beijing. I need you to allow Ms. Stein, who is hospitalized in Hong Kong, to be placed under direct US protection at that facility. And as soon as practical, to be allowed to leave the country."

Rodgers looked around the room. Everyone sat quietly, returning his gaze.

"Mr. President, there is much to be gained for both our countries in resolving this matter to our mutual satisfaction," Zhao said. "However, Mr. Shay entered China illegally and refuses to turn himself in to Chinese federal authorities, even though we have insisted he do so. Miss Stein, as regrettable as her situation is, was participating in an illegal assembly in Hong Kong. I cannot accede to your request."

"I'm very sorry to hear that, Mr. President," Rodgers said.

fifty-four

The trauma team replaced the packs. They applied direct manual pressure to control the bleeding sufficiently so Yates could quickly expose and then clamp the supraceliac aorta, located above the stomach but deep in the retroperitoneum—the back of the stomach cavity. Hannah's blood pressure began to drop. But the clamp slowed the bleeding enough to let him sharply dissect the retroperitoneal tissues and begin to expose the infrarenal aorta.

Yates had to move the abdominal contents out of the way. He elevated the transverse colon in the direction of the ceiling, pulling the colon up out of the wound and laying it, with the mesentery, onto Hannah's abdominal wall. The left colon was packed away with laparotomy packs, pushing it to her left side to facilitate exposure of the retroperitoneal structures and the overlying hematoma.

Further dissection of the left side of the aorta showed him that the left renal artery and vein had been divided by the bullet and were actively bleeding—bright red arterial blood and deeper blue venous blood were welling up into the depths of the wound. The artery and vein were surrounded by hematoma—blood accumulating outside the vessels—that had flooded the surrounding tissue.

Yates tried to spread the hematoma apart so he could identify the tissue planes and see the source of the bleeding. It was beginning to feel like a JV maneuver to him—his rule was to get control of the bleeding first, before entering the hematoma. But you can't always get perfect control. When there's a large collection of blood, you don't see the anatomy well until you get in there and get the area evacuated; only then can you better control the bleeding. You can't fix what you can't see.

There was another rush of blood; Hannah's pressure dropped again. Yates caught a glimpse of indicting eyes from the nurse who called it out—seconded, he thought, by a glance from the anesthesiologist. He didn't know what the Hong Kong-based trauma team was thinking, but he could guess because he was starting to think it himself—pour in fluids and raise her pressure. It was a tough call, with a life at stake—ride out the low pressure so the blood could coagulate and the flow lessen so he could expose the injury, or raise it and increase the bleeding, making it more difficult to get at the source.

He kept to himself that this "modern" technique—over the past four to five years, hospitals had begun the practice of delaying aggressive fluid resuscitation until you gain surgical control of bleeding—was outlined as early as 1918.

Sixty seconds more, he told himself, checking her BP on the monitor.

I'll give it one more minute.

People's Republic of China

At China's largest oil field in Daqing, in Heilongjiang, the northeasternmost province of the country, the state-owned oil company had been reducing production to conserve the field's dwindling reserves. As oil output decreased, the laid-off workers had been demonstrating to protest severance terms.

They were preparing for another rally when the network of activists set in motion by Mei Wang before her abduction contacted them. A flash mob blocked the entrance to management offices; others sat on railroad tracks and disrupted train service. The workers declared the formation of their own union and elected representatives.

Workers from oil fields in the northeastern province of Liaoning staged a solidarity demonstration when they heard about the Daqing protests. Local authorities sent paramilitary police and deployed a PLA tank regiment to suppress the gathering. Angered by the police and army intervention, more than six thousand miners staged protests in two additional cities in Liaoning, blockading the railway lines.

At a textile factory in Suizhou, in Hubei Province in central China, workers had been staging protests to recover unpaid benefits since the plant declared bankruptcy. After meeting with the underground union organizers, the textile workers occupied the factory grounds and gathered outside key municipal buildings.

Police from Suizhou and neighboring towns dispersed them, and blocked the arrival of hundreds more heading to the scene. Large numbers of demonstrators were injured in the confrontation, along with twenty police officers.

Workers at a machinery company in Henan Province barricaded the factory entrance, protesting decreased benefits from a corporate restructuring; other workers blocked roads leading to the factory. Retired workers from a steel company in the southwestern province of Guizhou blockaded the highway in front of their factory. The protesters, most of them between sixty and seventy years old, were receiving a small monthly stipend, less than the minimum wage. They demanded that their pensions be transferred from the factory to the public social security network.

In the capital city of Nanjing, in Jiangsu Province on China's eastern coast, thousands of workers surrounded the offices of a state-owned petrochemical enterprise after an action meeting with organizers from Mei Wang and Lin Xueqin's group.

The workers blocked roads leading to the factory in the Jianye District. When authorities sealed off the district, crowds gathered at both ends of the shutoff area. Another group massed at the Nanjing Massacre Memorial to discuss their strategy.

The first labor actions took place at the SOEs—state-owned enterprises that the Chinese government was restructuring, closing, or privatizing, where workers had protested previously to demand back wages and compensation for bankruptcies and layoffs.

Encouraged by the union organizers, the unrest began to spread to China's private companies. Faced with saturated demand and competitors' price cuts, a consumer electronics firm in Mianyang City in Sichuan Province was pushing workers to reduce operating costs by 50 percent. Cuts of that magnitude were impossible to achieve through productivity—the firm began to lower wages and cut benefits. In response, workers slowed down and sabotaged the lines. They dropped their tools and walked out altogether at the urging of organizers working among them who belonged to the movement.

At an aluminum producer in China's eastern Anhui Province, workers had been simmering about production speedup as management drove them hard to strengthen financial results. The job action began in the rolling mill that produced train wheels, led by an organizer from the underground group who had gotten himself hired at the plant. When the train-wheel workers walked out, the action quickly spread to the wire-rod, steel-plate, and steel sections.

At a joint-venture auto company in Hubei Province, plant capacity was initially set too low for the market demand, and frontline supervisors' harangues to accelerate the line to meet the upwardly revised targets had brought tensions to a head.

The banned trade-union movement group found a willing workforce at an evening meeting at an autoworker's home. The workers began to slow production the next day. Then, after a heated confrontation on the paint line, workers walked off the job, followed by their coworkers in welding, assembly, and final inspection.

Bai Cuifen was a slight twenty-two-year-old woman who had left her family home and the small plot where they cultivated rice in Jiangxi Province for the economic opportunity and city life of Guangzhou. She worked at a textile factory on the outskirts of the city, where the employees were migrant workers like herself from China's rural provinces who worked twelve- to fourteen-hour shifts, seven days a week. After protesting the killing schedule for months, the workers walked out during the second shift.

Cuifen and her girlfriends were talking, laughing, and texting as they strolled back and forth on the line in front of the factory gates. It felt like a day off. The company's security guards were watching them and even flirting with them, asking for their phone and dorm room numbers; one of her friends obliged.

Suddenly the guards were withdrawn, and another group—province riot police—came running at them, attacking them with steel pipes. Cuifen's friends and the other strikers began screaming and trying to get away. Cuifen backed up, but raised her camera phone above her head to record the scene. After she filmed a few seconds, she uploaded the footage onto the Internet, showing the strikers being beaten.

Cuifen moved farther back from the violence, logged into her live video-streaming feed app, and raised the phone again. Viewers now saw the strikers fighting back, in real time. A couple of worker groups broke off and began smashing factory windows. They set a company car on fire at the plant entrance.

Two police, seeing Cuifen recording the scene, came running at her. She began yelling and pointing at them with her free hand while she held the phone above her head. Viewers saw a blur of batons, shields, helmets, and visors as the video went dead—the last images a close-up of asphalt. They heard the sound of Cuifen's screams as the police knocked her and the phone to the ground.

Which the world also saw, in a wildly bouncing image—one of Cuifen's girlfriends had come back looking for her, and she raised her own camera and captured the video as she ran toward her friend, hollering at the police to stop.

Across the country, Chinese paramilitary forces from the People's Armed Police, reinforced by regular army units, repressed the strikers and protesters fiercely with beatings and arrests, especially in the outlying provinces. They were joined in their violence against the workers by private security forces—like the ones hired by American companies to battle labor in the organizing drives of the 1930s.

China shut down ISPs, portals, and Internet cafés. It jammed cell phone lines—even entire mobile networks in the affected regions—and began interfering with social-networking sites to prevent the news from spreading. *Weibo*—microblogging sites—turned off their comment functions; they deleted selected user accounts and turned their names over to the authorities. Mei Wang and Lin Xueqin's network developed workarounds with proxy servers, moblogs, and tweets, to keep the information and images flowing.

As the demonstrations increased and word spread across China, military and security forces began to hesitate and back off—especially in Sichuan, where soldiers who helped in the rescue operation after the earthquake had formed strong bonds with the local people. The military was also reluctant to intervene when confronted by ex-soldiers among the demonstrators who had been demobilized—and were unable to find work at state-owned factories, as was the tradition in the past.

Some troops even joined the demonstrators, who were now taking over factories and government buildings with little opposition, and expanding their actions to protest the growing inequality in Chinese society. Farmers gathered in rural provinces to protest land seizures, political corruption, the pollution in their fields. In one town, villagers threw stones at trucks delivering coal to a lead smelting plant—hundreds of children had become ill from its operations. In another, a corrupt official who took farmland for development was brutally murdered.

Members of the clandestine group, ordinary workers, and citizens watching the events unfold uploaded videos of the demonstrations to sharing sites. The images were picked up by news outlets and beamed around the world, followed by footage of breathless, ten-second interviews with protesting workers that were conducted live by the underground trade unionists during the street battles.

fifty-five

Shay saw the story about Hannah's shooting on the TV in his room. He opened the door and told the guard in the hallway he needed to see Gao.

They met downstairs in the lobby.

"A beer?" Gao asked, raising his hand for the waitress.

"I'm turning myself in," Shay said.

"That would be unwise."

Shay stood up. Gao nodded to the guards, who came forward.

"You will be put into prison," Gao said. "You may be killed there. At the least, they will attempt to break your physical body, and your mind."

"China won't let Hannah Stein leave Hong Kong without something in return," Shay said. "Hong Kong demonstrators are carrying placards demanding my freedom, so China will be blaming me. If I'm in their custody, they might let her go. My life for hers."

"A sacrifice bunt," Gao said, thinking of his nephew on the Guangdong Leopards executing the play. "To move your teammate one base closer to home."

Shay almost laughed—these guys play ball? He remembered what Nora said—first they seem so different and then you begin to see yourself in them.

"If you give me up, it will also lower tensions between Beijing and Guangdong."

Gao took a drag on his cigarette. He felt, in giving Shay up, he would lose an advantage in his dealings with Beijing. But the country was on the verge of great violence. He could surrender a valuable asset to the central authorities at a critical moment for the country. He was going to need all the goodwill he could get. Hu Weimin's stunt with the decoy rescue truck—having his lieutenant proclaim a "New China," then demand to speak with a representative of Guangdong Province as if it were a separate entity from China—was going to be difficult to explain.

Gao had exploited Hu's extremism to get the army officer to undertake the mission. While he shared the same belief—that Guangdong, Hong Kong, and Taiwan together, separate from Beijing and the rest of China, could form a powerful, progressive state—he would never make such a daring declaration of independence from the central government. Not at this time.

"I will call the necessary people," he said.

Gao handed over John Shay at Guangzhou's Baiyun Airport. The handoff positioned him where he wanted to be. He had rescued Shay from corrupt army and business elements that were jeopardizing China's position in the global economic order with their operation at Lambal's Shenzhen plant. Now he was turning him over to Beijing central authorities to lessen strains between Guangdong and Beijing, and between Beijing and Washington.

Gao gave a sealed pouch to the ranking official on the plane. It contained the names of a Chinese military officer and an al-Qaeda operative—the two people Nora met in the Hong Kong restaurant. Gao got the army man's name from Nora—that's what she traded for his information on Shay. Guangzhou Triads had extracted the terrorist's identity from a member of a competing gang in Hong Kong.

Gao knew that this was valuable information to Beijing. It wouldn't mind the counterfeiting ring stealing from the Lambal factory in Guangzhou; it handled the military dipping into the pot with kid gloves. Al-Qaeda was another matter—China didn't want Xingjian turning into Chechnya.

As part of the deal with Gao, Beijing agreed to transfer the men who drove the decoy truck on the Hong Kong raid that freed Shay from a jail in Hong Kong to Guangzhou. Gao promised to prosecute them vigorously; he was already planning how to rig the proceedings. If he lost the backing of the regional armies—whose special forces commandos had commandeered Shay's rescue—it wouldn't matter how much Beijing supported him.

The prisoner transfer was a major concession from Beijing, one he hadn't expected. It followed on the heels of recent central government legislation allowing nine southeastern provinces—including Guangdong—and two administrative regions to coordinate regional economic policy more closely. There had also been a series of agreements between Hong Kong and Shenzhen to link their economies more closely.

The center wasn't holding as strongly as before; it was ceding more power to the edges, Gao thought. That was how he expected to achieve the eventual separation. Not with the single, wrenching struggle that Hu Weimin favored, but through a series of small movements toward that goal, gaining strength with each success.

It was just a matter of time, he thought, as he watched the plane with John Shay take off for Beijing. China was simply too big, the differences between the Communist functionary North and the entrepreneurial go-getter South too great.

The separatists in Xinjiang and Tibet were just a taste of the great schism to come, he thought, as the plane disappeared quickly into the low gray sky.

As soon as he had word that Shay was on the plane, China's president ordered the commander of the Nanjing Military Region to redeploy PLA forces from other parts of the country and to reposition aircraft to the coastal areas facing Taiwan, as part of final preparations for the joint sea-air military operation.

The Nanjing Military Region, based in Nanjing, encompasses the Jiangsu, Zhejiang, Anhui, Fujian, and Jiangxi provinces. Comprised of the First, Twelfth, and Thirty-First Group Armies, the Nanjing MR's southern section faces Taiwan and is home to a number of China's medium-range missiles—including the two that were launched across the Taiwan Strait.

The Nanjing MR is the frontline launching point for an air-sea assault on Taiwan. During a major military campaign against Taiwan, the Nanjing Military Region becomes part of the "Nanjing War Zone," which includes the three group armies, elements from group armies based in the adjacent military regions of Guangzhou and Jinan, and Chinese airborne and marine forces.

Major-General Huang Yungfu, an expert in amphibious warfare, commanded the Nanjing Military Region and the PLA's First Group Army. When he received the order, the major-general was reviewing two reports—one on a group army sea crossing and landing exercise, the other detailing a special operations exercise using high-speed boats in combat drills to seize beach objectives.

Huang dispatched orders to the commanders of the Twelfth and Thirty-First Group Armies and the group armies in Guangzhou and Jinan. He confirmed that air assets in the Nanjing MR were in place, that supporting aircraft were in transit from other parts of China, and that navy ships from China's East, South, and North Sea Fleets had set sail for the rendezvous points.

Taiwan is ninety miles from the Chinese coast. Huang ordered final combat checks of the Nanjing Military Region's Dongfeng 11 and Dongfeng 15 SRBMs—short-range ballistic missiles, with operational ranges of up to almost four hundred miles.

China's military went into lose-no-assets mode, dispersing large weapons platforms like ships, artillery, tanks, and aircraft. US reconnaissance satellite photography showed the Chinese leaving their bases. Armored tank divisions mounted up and rolled into fields throughout the countryside and then dug in. Ships left port, and submarines disappeared. The Chinese began moving ammunition to airfields. US intelligence saw a decrease in commercial aviation; all the Avgas was going to the PLA Air Force.

As the United States flew aircraft into airfields in Taiwan, the Chinese flew planes into their airfields opposite Taiwan. They began building new airfields, reinforcing and bunkering them, sandbagging the aircraft closest to Taiwan. One airfield opposite Taiwan typically had a dozen permanent revetments and twenty-four aircraft. Suddenly US reconnaissance saw fifty aircraft and new roofs on the revetments.

The Chinese sicced a botnet on US defense computers, carpet bombing them with traffic. Hackers attacked sites at Treasury, Transportation, the Secret Service, the Federal Trade Commission, even the Department of Homeland Security. China also jammed a communications satellite. And it initiated first mechanisms for antisatellite weapons—the United States had observed China's first ASAT test when it shot down one of its own broken satellites, and knew what to look for when they were getting ready to shoot.

NORAD and US Northern Command (USNORTHCOM) are both headquartered at Peterson Air Force Base in Colorado under the direction of a dual-hatted commander. The commands serve as a central collection and coordination facility for a worldwide system of sensors—aboard satellites, ground-based, and airborne radar and fighters—designed to provide an accurate picture of any aerospace threat.

The president received a tactical warning from the commander at Peterson—the base from which the Chinese had fired a previous antisatellite weapon was getting active. Missiles were showing up in their silos.

fifty-six

Finally, direct compression near the source of the bleeding and manual pressure over the infrarenal aorta were sufficient to slow the bleeding. It was enough to allow Yates to better visualize the injury. He carefully dissected the left renal artery and vein and then clamped and sewed the vessels shut with 4-0 polypropylene sutures.

With the bleeding now controlled, the team removed the packs in the left gutter. Yates used Metzenbaum scissors to sharply separate the tissue planes that attach the left colon to the inside of the abdomen. He moved the colon back toward the midline to expose the areas of injury behind it; this revealed the left kidney, with the surrounding hematoma.

He had already done a quick eval of the right kidney—via ultrasound with a Doppler probe—and got a strong pulse, satisfying himself that it was healthy and would be adequate to maintain renal function in the absence of the left kidney.

With a combination of sharp and blunt dissection, Yates removed the residual renal attachments of fibrous tissue in the retroperitoneum.

He began to remove the kidney.

Circuit breakers are the thresholds at which stock trading is halted market-wide based on single-day declines in the Dow Jones Industrial Average. The points are adjusted quarterly. At their current setting, a twelve hundred-point drop in the DJIA before two o'clock would halt trading for one hour; a 2,400-point drop before one o'clock would stop it for two hours. A 3,650-point plunge shuts the market for the remainder of the day, regardless of when the decline occurred.

The circuit breakers were invoked twice, and then trading was suspended in New York and on all remaining exchanges worldwide after the Dow collapsed below the 3,650-point trigger at 2:17 p.m. The Hong Kong, Shenzhen, Taiwan, Shanghai, Singapore, and South Korean exchanges had already closed. The dollar fell as China's central bank began an unscheduled selloff of US currency from its foreign reserves.

The White House was deluged with calls, letters, and e-mails from union members and citizens, demanding it bring John Shay and Hannah Stein home. Congress was in an uproar. Its members made speech after speech on the Senate and House floors to express their outrage and demand Shay's release, calling for trade measures against China.

In New York, firefighters broke off their demonstrations at the Chinese Embassy and marched to a downtown building after hearing on talk radio that a Chinese firm had acquired it for its US corporate office. Chinese executives looked out their windows on the fifth floor as the firefighters marched back and forth in front of the building.

Radio, television, and print reporters converged on the scene, transmitting images and interviews across the country and around the world. Radio and television commentators called for a boycott of Chinese products. "That would be every damn thing under $19.95," one radio talk show host said. "I don't care anymore if I can buy a can opener for sixty-nine cents. I'd rather spend $3.49 and know that it means a factory is humming in Indiana, paying good wages to the people who make them—two shifts worth of production a day, dammit. And more factories like it, making things all over the United States. Stuff that won't kill you or your kids, because it's not poison or defective."

His outburst got traction, putting the big box stores in the crosshairs. Antiglobalists swung into action, setting up protest lines outside All-Goods, the biggest of the big boxes and their all-purpose bogeyman. Which in this case was on the money—shipments to All-Goods alone accounted for 10 percent of the US deficit with China.

The Chinese matched in kind. A TV commentator in Shanghai said China should throw out US companies and purchase goods from suppliers in countries that did not meddle in her affairs. Pro-boycott messages flooded instant messaging networks like QQ. Chinese bloggers campaigned for China's central bank to stop propping up US trade and budget deficits by buying its government bonds, calling for a new global reserve currency to replace the dollar. A radio personality in Shanghai urged consumers and businesses to forego US software for open-source or Chinese solutions. Protesters in Beijing trashed US-based fast-food stores.

The president was handed the note about the market shutdown after he hung up the telephone with the Japanese prime minister. During the call, he had requested that Japan's Self-Defense Forces provide the same fueling and logistics support in this crisis that they had offered in the Indian Ocean during the invasion of Afghanistan.

Japan leaned toward yes. It was already in the process of repositioning its defenses from Russia and toward China and North Korea. It was worried about China's ongoing military buildup and increasing aggressiveness in blue-water encounters with its vessels as they squabbled over islands and gas exploration rights in disputed waters in the East China Sea. It was angry about the violent anti-Japanese protests and economic boycott that had broken out across China over the disputed islands. The Japanese political establishment was also being challenged by a new generation of leaders, not brought up to be as sensitive to China's wishes based on guilt from the Second World War.

But the last thing Japan wanted was to choose between China and the United States. Much of Japan's recovery from a decade of stagnation had been achieved through trade with the Chinese. China had replaced the United States as its largest trading partner, providing Japan with an inexpensive outsource workforce and export market. The two countries were the second- and third-largest economies in the world. Thousands of Japanese companies had operations on the mainland.

But China was flexing too much muscle. It was American power in the region that kept China in check and let Japan concentrate on its economy. If China overran Taiwan, naval and air bases on the island would allow it to project military strength eastward into the Pacific, threatening sea lanes vital to the Japanese economy.

Demonstrators had taken to the streets of Tokyo and Osaka as the government debated the US request for logistical support. The protesters called for the reconstitution of the Japanese armed forces and an immediate program to develop nuclear weapons.

The United Nations called an emergency session of the Security Council. The Pope issued a plea for peace.

Rodgers scanned his latest briefing. He again had half a mind to let Taiwan go. The Japanese would rearm, and we could pull out our military; let China and Japan puff their chests and duke it out, deal with places like North Korea without us. But the instability would country-hop one place to the next and inevitably reach our shores.

The things you could do if you could ignore the consequences, he thought. Or if you could act like other countries—and refuse to act.

Not that that was always bad. He knew from experience that America had a tendency to barge in, to move too soon. The rest of the world had the opposite inclination—to hesitate, to wait too long. He had come to understand that you need both—one to prod, the other to curb. And that either way, you would have to come together to clean up the mess.

He had spoken with a number of world leaders. All wanted peace, and all wanted to be left out of this. No one wanted to antagonize China, especially Germany and France. The European leaders didn't want to risk commercial access to a country that they believed, in the not-too-distant future, might equal or supplant the United States as the premier market in the world. The European Union had already become China's largest trading partner. Germany's prime minister had visited China several times, bringing an entourage of cabinet ministers and corporate executives; France welcomed China's leader with pomp and circumstance, and bathed the Eiffel Tower in red for a state visit. The French navy even undertook joint maneuvers with the Chinese in the South China Sea.

The Europeans were also cowed by Russia, which voiced support for China in a communiqué citing the two countries' "eternal friendship." Russia dusted off its broken record about cutting gas supplies to Europe and spun it on the turntable. It scheduled "routine" bomber sorties close to Alaska, announced a squadron from its North Sea Fleet would head to the Caribbean for naval exercises, and sent the nuclear battle cruiser *Peter the Great* to Latin America for another exercise. A Russian nuclear attack sub showed up two hundred miles from Georgia on the US East Coast; another surfaced off Greenland.

Rodgers called the Taiwanese president. Taiwan's leader thought his cat-and-mouse game—resisting China's "One China" dictum and pushing toward independence, backing off when China blustered—could go on indefinitely.

But China had never gone this far. There had never been such a buildup of battle-ready forces on both sides. The Taiwanese president wanted to back down but didn't know how. The people of Taiwan were taking to the streets in defiance of Beijing. They reprised an earlier demonstration, where they linked one million hands up and down the length of the island. Taiwan's president was doing what he had to do to prepare to defend the country, but he was counting on America to resolve the crisis.

After he got off the phone, Rodgers leafed through a document summarizing Taiwan's response to Beijing's moves. The Taiwanese air force had almost five hundred fixed-wing aircraft, including fighters (F-5E/F, F-16A/B, and Mirage 2000-5D/E) and fighter/ground attack aircraft (F-CK-1A/B, Taiwan's indigenous defense fighter). With limited airspace over the strait, Taiwan had only scrambled a portion of the aircraft, concealing the other planes in hardened mountain bunkers near Hualian and Jianyi. Taiwan had moved the rest of its arsenal to high readiness—E-2T airborne warning and command (AWACS) aircraft, army units, armor and artillery, SAM batteries, a Patriot air defense system, and naval frigates and guided-missile destroyers. It began to call up its Civil Defense Corps.

"What a mess," he said, looking around the room. "Something else we don't want, but have to deal with. Alone, as usual."

He had no problem sharing power with the rest of the world. But what about sharing responsibility? he thought. Did the world really think we wanted to be the Lone Ranger? Americans wanted nothing more than to be left alone, to their own pursuits, their families, their lives. We butt in because nobody else steps up.

"What are we, the designated driver for the world?"

Everyone laughed.

The president tapped his fingers on the desk. He was in the Oval Office, just a few advisors around him.

"Maybe the Chinese feel the same way," Bernstein said. "They can't possibly want this either."

"What does that matter?" the national security advisor asked. "We have to deal with what they are doing. Not what they 'want.'"

"But what they want is key," Bernstein said. "And I believe what they want is what we want—for this to go away. I don't think they're preparing to attack Taiwan. Not that they wouldn't—at another time, under different circumstances. But this is a dress rehearsal, a scripted exercise, conducted at an unplanned time for political effect. One aim is to rally the country around the leadership, put a damper on the strikes and protests. Another is to intimidate Taiwan and Hong Kong. The third is to show us how important Taiwan is—what they're willing to risk, what the cost would be for us to respond. Each time they do something like this, regardless of our response, they believe it will further weaken our resolve, until one day they just walk in and take the province back."

"Thank you for your input, Saul," Rodgers said. "Would you leave us now?"

Bernstein got up and left the room.

fifty-seven

Shay had been blindfolded and handcuffed on the plane. When it landed, he was led down the steps onto the tarmac and pushed into a car. He listened to the labored breathing of the person sitting next to him for the first part of the ride. Then his seatmate lit a cigarette and began to chat in Chinese with the others, who were in front.

Shay figured he had been in transit maybe half an hour when the car stopped. The door on his side opened. Someone reached in, grabbed him, and pulled him out. He felt gravel underneath his footsteps as they walked. When they passed through a door, he was walking on concrete, indoors. They stopped twice as what sounded like metal doors opened and then shut behind them. At one point, they waited an extra few seconds for the door to open. The person holding onto Shay's arm pushed him forward.

Shay heard the door lock behind him as the momentum from the shove carried him forward. When he steadied himself, he listened carefully but didn't hear any sounds. He advanced gingerly in the direction he was facing, taking small shuffle steps until the tip of his right foot touched a surface. He moved the edge of his shoe back and forth along the wall and back outward a few feet, establishing in his mind a cleared seating area. His hands still tied behind his back, he turned to the side and leaned his shoulder forward, touching what he figured was a wall. He turned his back to it and slid down into a sitting position.

He guessed he had been sitting for an hour when he was startled by the metal clang of the door opening. Someone came over and undid his blindfold. His eyes blinked at the harsh overhead bulb and then focused on the man standing in front of him. He realized he was in a cell as he looked up at a man dressed in a uniform. Shay didn't know whether he was police, PLA, state security, or what.

"I want to know everything you learned from the splittist Gao Liang, your host in Guangzhou, and his henchman Hu Weimin, who rescued you from the Hong Kong industrial estate," the man said. "These two, and their band of separatists, will bring great ruin to China if their plot is not uncovered and stopped."

The man was Chinese, maybe five foot eight, overweight in that common way of men in their fifties. He spoke softly, with a trace of English accent—probably from some tony UK school his plugged-in parents sent him to, Shay thought.

"My name is John Shay," Shay said. "I am an American citizen. I want to speak to someone from the American Embassy."

The man lit a cigarette. "Tell me what you know about Lin Xueqin and Mei Wang. Tell me about their illegal union activities."

Shay flashed back to Lin, lying dead on the floor in the room where they had been held in Hong Kong. He didn't know who Mei Wang was. He remembered what Lin said about Chinese prisons. But he was done talking to these people. It wasn't going to change his outcome, just get others in trouble.

He just hoped they stuck to the deal—him for Hannah.

He repeated what he had just said.

The man smiled, revealing a couple of crooked, darkened teeth.

"Mr. Shay, China is in turmoil. Strikes are taking place across the entire country; separatists are plotting to break up the nation. Soon, the world will learn the awful lesson of what happens when our country is in chaos—it spills over violently into their affairs."

He shook his head. "I would think your country would have learned the perils of overthrowing strong rulers. In Iraq, you had one powerful government facing off against another, Iran, on its border. The two states cancelled each other out, with their hatred of the other and wars against each other. When you removed one strong ruler, you only freed another to wreak havoc on the world."

Not your business, Shay blurted to himself. Don't even talk about a place where American soldiers shed their blood.

The man flicked his cigarette ashes on the floor.

"China is no different," he said. "Every country has its own distinct nature, and knows what leadership and social order best serve its population. You may think Lin Xueqin and Mei Wang represent a great hope for the Chinese worker, but by their subversion, they will only bring calamity on the working class. I need you to tell me what you know of their organization, so we can put a stop to this before it gets any worse."

Shay continued to bite his tongue. He didn't know the first thing about resisting interrogation, but one thing seemed clear—don't take any bait. Don't give them a way into your head.

"My name is John Shay. I am an American citizen. I want to speak to someone from the American Embassy."

The man shrugged. "They all say something like that at first, Mr. Shay. Then, after a day or two—or maybe just a few minutes, or an hour, depending on who I send in—they beg me to tell them if there are any more secrets they can share with me."

Hold out, Shay said to himself. Lewis—or even Rodgers—was coming for him. He could feel it—or made himself feel it. It didn't really matter which.

"My name is John Shay. I am an American citizen. I want to speak to someone from the American Embassy."

Westchester County, outside New York City

Anne brought out another pot of coffee for her mother and sisters. They had come to stay with her. Her sisters brought their kids—partly because they didn't trust their husbands to take care of them, but mostly to keep Michael's spirits up; it's hard to be upset if you're a nine-year-old with half a dozen cartwheeling cousins in the house.

It wasn't only family that lent support. When the news of Shay's captivity broke, neighbors who had appeared standoffish came by daily, with homemade lasagna and fresh-baked pies and scones. Members of her teachers' union checked in on her, and were organizing a job action. A lawyer on the block helped keep the press out in front of the house at bay, through his connections in the publishing world. Michael and his cousins also worked over the news crews with water pistols and high-powered soakers.

Earlier in the day, Anne, her mom, and her sisters and the kids had taken the train into the city and then cabs to the base of the Brooklyn Bridge on the Manhattan side. They walked across the bridge, to the delight of the children, who yelled to get their parents' attention when they looked to the right and caught sight of the Statue of Liberty on Liberty Island in New York Harbor. The kids had fashioned signs and jutted them into the air at a news helicopter above as they crossed the span. Michael carried "Free My Dad"; his cousins hoisted "Free My Uncle John." Anne's read "Free My Husband, John."

On the Brooklyn side, they walked to the Ladder 118 fire station on Middaugh Street; Shay's father was already there, standing out front talking with the current LT. He had been lieutenant at the station for twelve years. The family walked back and forth in front of the firehouse with their signs, Michael holding his grandfather's hand to guide him. At one point, a firefighter came out and asked them to move—they had a call. A moment later, the big red doors opened and the trucks came barreling out, sirens and horns blasting. Normally the firefighters didn't turn them on until they got a few blocks away, a courtesy to neighbors. But they made an exception for Michael and his cousins.

At home that evening, after putting the kids to bed, the sisters sat up late reminiscing about old times. They recalled hours playing hide-and-seek in their large walk-in closets, hiding under or behind the hanging clothes, often bringing down the entire clothes rack and then running and hiding somewhere else because they knew they were in trouble. They laughed at memories of the antics of their three brothers—especially the time the boys went down to the basement, climbed onto their father's workbench, opened the door to the fuse box, and proceeded to unscrew every fuse, as the house went dark one section after another.

They laughed themselves silly remembering how they played school in the playhouse, an old chicken coop. Her sisters reminded Anne how she would round up the neighborhood kids and teach science lessons, about the earth spinning on its axis, naming the equator, lines of latitude, longitude, and so forth. She dressed like one of the nuns, using an old black dress and a black scarf and white band cut from construction paper for the habit. She would use a stern voice with the younger kids, send the bad boys to the "principal's" office—a corner of the coop. They laughed uncontrollably when one of them remembered that a neighborhood mom actually asked if they were going to have "summer school," her kids had learned so much.

"Remember the berry patch?" one of Anne's sisters asked, pouring out more coffee, and everyone began laughing again.

They had a large raspberry patch on the farm. Anne's mother would sell the raspberries to a local retailer; the money she made during the short season paid for their tuition at St. Agnes Catholic School. But for the kids, it felt like those three weeks went on forever. They had to pick berries in the early morning before it got too hot. They wore old coffee cans—Hills Brothers, Folgers—around their waists to hold the berries. The cans were held in place by worn neckties attached to pieces of clothes-hanger wire, which had been looped into small holes their father punctured in the cans.

Anne's mom had them in stitches when she reminded them how, every morning without fail, one of them would say they had to go the bathroom. After five minutes, she would tell one of them to stop picking and go see where the other was. Then, after five more minutes, she would send another of the children to get the first two. She repeated the drill until eventually she was all alone in the berry patch, bending way down to snatch every last hidden raspberry from the thick bushes before their Uncle George made the daily pickup. Her kids then reminded her how, every morning, when they would come down for breakfast before heading out to the patch, a heaping bowl of fresh raspberries would await them at the kitchen table. "Oh, raspberries again?" they'd all moan as they poured cereal and milk in their bowls and topped it off with a scoop of the fruit.

"Someday you're going to really appreciate them," their mom would say—repeating it tonight, to howls of laughter—followed by, "I'll see you in the berry house shortly."

At bedtime, Anne shared her bed with one of her sisters, as she had done in childhood. The ache, hurt, and fear was hers alone. But she was never left alone with it.

All the girls had been busy bees growing up, and their constant buzzing had become the sound of the house.

fifty-eight

The White House

Rodgers had moved everyone to an operations room. An aide came in and handed him a note. He read it and then looked up. "Chinese students from Beijing University are marching toward Tiananmen Square; students from other universities have joined them along the route. They're chanting their call from 1989—'Dialogue, Dialogue.' PLA troops and armor have ringed the square. Army helicopters are circling above the students, dropping leaflets telling them to disperse."

Another aide entered the room and gave him another printout. The president scanned it. "The Chinese have locked down Lhasa. The Tibetans are back in the streets, calling for independence and the return of the Dalai Lama. Several high-ranking religious figures set themselves on fire. The demonstrations and crackdowns have spread to Tibetan minority enclaves in the neighboring provinces of Sichuan, Qinghai, Gansu, and Yunnan."

Rodgers glanced back down at the paper. "The Uighurs in Xinjiang are at it too. They marched in the capital Urumqi, burned cars and buses, overturned police cars and set them on fire. The Chinese killed dozens, rounded up young men in the Xiangyang Po quarter. Uighurs also took to the streets in Yining, Aksu, Kuqa, Kashgar, and the southern city of Khotan—with banners calling for

Muslims to join their independence movement and create an Islamic state. The police shot another bunch of people."

"Where's Falun Gong?" the CIA head asked, referring to the banned spiritual group. "Didn't they get the party invitation?"

"Let's help them," the director of national intelligence said. "The Tibetans."

Everybody looked at him.

"We can stir that pot. Amp up our Tibetan-language broadcasts on Radio Free Asia." The DNI glanced around the room. "RFA broadcasts shortwave from the Northern Marianas and a number of secret locations. Tibetan activists call in via telephone or encrypted Internet programs like Skype. As we pick up the details of the demonstrations, we can broadcast them, let the others know what's going on. It will make the Chinese divert troops, give them one more fire to put out. Then we can offer our good graces to help settle it down." He looked around. "In exchange for Shay."

The secretary of state glared at him. "Give the Chinese another reason to machine-gun monks? I don't think so."

"Can you find him?" the president asked. "Have the satellites come up with anything?"

"We lost him coming out of the Garden Hotel," the CIA chief said. "Half a dozen SUVs exited underground parking at the same time. Each one took a separate route to different airstrips outside the city." He paused. "China has a lot of prisons. But we think we've narrowed it down to three. We think it's one of the 'black jails'—extralegal detention centers where they stash people who make a stink about local corruption and land grabs but who haven't actually committed any crimes."

"Can we get in there?" the president asked.

"We can now," the CIA head said.

The secretary of state looked at Cloninger.

"When the *George Washington* port called in Shanghai, we 'left' a few sailors behind," he said. "Not sailors, exactly—a platoon from one of our SEAL teams. We dispersed them across the major cities—Beijing, Shanghai, Guangzhou. They took various jobs. A couple of them teach English. Several work at US/China joint ventures, courtesy of an executive who's ex-military. Another guy entered a foreign exchange program as a student."

He shook his head. "One of them is even an underground cage fighter."

The secretary of state looked crazed at this point.

Cloninger continued. "We've assembled them all in a safe house in Beijing. Gotten them weapons and equipment. They're awaiting our word."

"You know how the Chinese would react to this?" the secretary of state said.

"No more pandas for our zoos?"

Rodgers wiped the smile off his face as he turned to the secretary of defense.

"It's fifteen hundred miles from Guam to Taiwan. Where's Commander Sanger?"

The secretary of defense pointed at the image on the screen. "Seventh Fleet."

On the water, the carrier strike group moved across the ocean like a huge, space-age transparent dome, two hundred and fifty miles in diameter, sixty thousand feet high at the apex. Fighter aircraft flew combat air patrol overhead. Airborne Early Warning aircraft flew at their full range, projecting radar into the distance for danger. Destroyers sailed along the margins to form screens, and up front on antisubmarine patrol. The USS *Buffalo* and USS *Oklahoma City* attack subs surged ahead to delouse the area. Nothing—not friendly shipping, not fishing fleets, nothing—would be allowed inside the dome.

Operations on the carrier's four-and-a-half-acre flight deck focused on launching and recovering aircraft to maintain the screen. Crewmen maneuvered planes on the flight deck and shuttled them on four elevators between the flight deck and hangar bay. Everybody concentrated on his or her tasks; there was all kinds of room for mishaps. Aircraft have to take off at night with live ordnance. People see things they don't actually see. Ships detect submarines that aren't there, or fail to detect submarines that are. Civilian aircraft get tangled in the sphere.

The Taiwanese had sent a planeload of liaison officers to join the strike group. The incoming aircraft checked in via the antiair screen set by the CGs and DDGs. They were authenticated via Identification, Friend or Foe (IFF) systems and tracked in on 3-D air search radar. Sailors and commanders double- and triple-checked the radar and communications as the aircraft passed through the outer perimeter and the strike group parted each successive curtain of the screen.

Another aide burst into the room; she handed the secretary of defense a note. He read it and then looked at the president. "China has retargeted its longer-range missile batteries on the coast toward our bases on Okinawa and Guam. It has raised the alert level for its arsenal of land- and sea-based nuclear-tipped missiles that can reach the United States."

"Mr. President, the majority of Chinese ICBMs are solid propellant DF-31/A's, but a number of their intercontinental ballistic missiles are still liquid fueled," the chairman of the joint chiefs said. "You can't keep a liquid-fueled rocket juiced all the time because the fluids are corrosive. I understand the Chinese have a no first-use policy, but fueling their rockets would be the upper limit in terms of their preparations. If the Chinese begin to fuel ICBMs, there are ten generals outside this door who are going to barge in and start dancing on your desk. I might climb up with them."

"Send the second carrier strike group directly to the strait—to back up CSG-5 and to be closer to the Korean Peninsula, in case the North Koreans try to take advantage of the situation," Rodgers said. "Step up force readiness in Okinawa and Japan."

He looked around the room. "We walked this through last night. I would say this is the last straw. Agreed?"

He held the gaze of each official. Each nodded.

"Place USSTRATCOM on DEFCON 3," the president said.

The officials walked quickly out of the room to go to their stations. The president shook hands and shared a quick word with each as they left. He put his arm around the chairman of the joint chiefs at the door.

"They still keep that pizza box in the Minuteman silo, with the slogan on it?"

"Anywhere in the world in thirty minutes or less, or your next one is free."

Both men smiled and then didn't.

fifty-nine

Hannah's parents had called from the plane, but the hospital, unable to validate their identity, would not release any information about their daughter. They were watching satellite TV during the charter jet flight when the feed switched to the Oval Office. The president was at his desk, looking directly into the camera.

"My fellow Americans. You have all been watching the news unfold these past hours and days. At every turn of events, the United States has responded, in a measured way, to the challenges it faced. Tonight, we have learned that China has retargeted long-range missile batteries on its coast toward our bases on Okinawa and Guam, where forty-five thousand brave armed forces members serve our country. China also raised the alert level for its arsenal of land- and sea-based nuclear-tipped missiles, which have the capability to reach the United States. In response, I have ordered the United States Strategic Command to raise our defense readiness condition to DEFCON 3."

USSTRATCOM is headquartered at Offutt Air Force Base in Nebraska. Its mission is to provide the nation with global deterrence capabilities and synchronized actions to combat adversary weapons of mass destruction. It brings to bear integrated intelligence, surveillance, reconnaissance, space and global strike operations, information operations, missile defense, and command and control to dissuade or defeat aggressors.

DEFCONs are defense readiness conditions—progressive alert postures in response to situations of varying military severity, for use by the joint chiefs of staff and the commanders of unified commands to increase combat readiness of US forces. DEFCON 5 is normal peacetime readiness, DEFCON 1 maximum force readiness. DEFCON 3 is an increase in force readiness above normal readiness.

"The United States has been at DEFCON 3 three times before in its history," Rodgers said. "In 1962, in response to the presence of Soviet missiles in Cuba, we went to that heightened status and ordered our B-52s on airborne alert. We did it again in 1973, when Egyptian and Syrian forces launched a surprise attack on Israel. On September 11, 2001, during the attack of the Islamist terrorists, we also went to DEFCON 3.

"On only one of these occasions, during the Cuban missile crisis, did we increase our alert level to DEFCON 2—a heightened state of alert, ready to strike at targets within the Soviet Union. On all three occasions, we were able to lower the alert level shortly thereafter. It is my sincerest hope and prayer the same will happen again. Through our continued negotiations with the Chinese, and the mutual desire on both our parts to resolve this crisis peacefully, God willing, this trying time will pass.

"But our adversary must not confuse hope with steadfast will. The United States has been challenged many times in its history. It has always responded to those challenges, with whatever level of diplomacy—and sometimes, regrettably, force—was required. We will do so again this time.

"This evening, as you sit in your homes with family, loved ones, and friends, I ask you all to say a prayer for the United States of America. For the hope that we will quickly defuse this crisis, and continue to move forward on our long, inspired journey as the oldest continuous democracy in the history of the world, dedicated to the freedom of all who live upon our shores. May God bless you, and may God bless America."

Esther Stein began to cry; Charles tightened his arm around her. He remembered Hannah as a little girl, how she said she was going to change the world—really, Daddy, I'm going to, she insisted. She would come with them into the radish fields in California, pulling her little wagon behind her with bottled water for the migrant workers. She spent days in homeless shelters, teaching kids to read and write. He saw her on the floor of their apartment with her friends, writing slogans on placards, stapling them to sticks for their marches. He welled up when he saw her as just a little girl in his arms.

He couldn't be prouder. And it couldn't hurt more.

He blamed himself for pushing her into that life. I ran roughshod over her; force-fed her, made sure she believed everything I did. Pushed her away from her love of science and poetry. Belittled her choices, told her they were not as important as social justice. Got her all worried about this stupid world; had her think about every damn problem in it, feel she had to fix everything.

Fucking sixties.

Then he thought, it wasn't the sixties, it was me. As he'd gotten older, weaker from the disease, he'd begun to take stock of his life. He realized he was the same with everything, not just politics. He found fault everywhere—people, the apartment, the city, a sloppy supermarket shelf … everything.

Even my daughter.

It wasn't a critique of the world, or people. It was my own screwed-up personality, foisted on everyone and everything. What on earth was perfect, anyway?

Her.

He took his arm off his wife and tried to take a breath. His body was rocking, dipping forward, diving. His arms began to flail. He tried to fold them, but they broke away. He got his hands underneath his butt, pressing down with his weight to hold them against the chair seat. Esther stroked his hair and tried to calm him.

God, you've taken so much from me, he thought.

Please don't take her.

sixty

The Taiwan Strait

Kinmen is a small group of islands off China's southeastern coast. Taiwan administers the archipelago; China claims it as part of Fujian Province. The shortest distance from the main island—also called Kinmen—to Chinese territory is two and a half thousand yards.

Kinmen occupies a key position in the Taiwan Strait. Known to the Taiwanese as Quemoy—"Golden Door," in the Min language—it blocks the mouth of China's Amoy Bay. The island became a flashpoint during the Cold War when Chiang Kai-Chek fortified its defenses and stationed troops there for the reconquest of China, after leading his one million followers across the strait following their defeat in the civil war.

The US Seventh Fleet sailed into the strait in 1950 to prevent Mao from attacking Chiang and Chiang from storming the mainland. After President Eisenhower lifted the naval blockade, Mao shelled Kinmen from August 1954 to May 1955. Mao turned his artillery on Kinmen again in July and August 1958.

Directly across the Taiwan Strait from Kinmen is the Chinese port city of Xiamen, in Fujian Province. Xiamen attracts substantial Taiwanese business investment through its proximity to Taiwan, its status as a Special Economic Zone, and the fact that the local dialect, *minnanyu*, is nearly identical to the dialect spoken in Taiwan.

An Xiamen Air flight filled with Taiwanese factory managers and their families—along with three computer executives from the United States, who worked at their company's Xiamen manufacturing site—had just taken off when the tower radioed the pilot that China had closed the airspace over Fujian. The pilot was ordered to return immediately, stranding the Taiwanese and the American corporate officers on the mainland as China and Taiwan ramped up their military mobilizations.

At the same time, a group of teachers and students from a junior high school on Kinmen was sailing across the Taiwan Strait on an excursion to Xiamen. A Chinese surface vessel headed out to intercept the boat, ordering it to return to Kinmen. When Taiwan overheard the radio conversation, it sent its own ship from Kinmen.

The children began screaming and crying as the two ships faced off on either side of their boat. The teachers moved through them, trying to calm them. A group of boys were running back and forth from one side of the ship to the other, to see the vessels of both China and Taiwan. One of them climbed onto the railing to get a better look.

The Chinese vessel began circling the sailboat aggressively, rocking it with its wake. The Taiwanese craft dispatched to the scene was unable to radio the Chinese to tell them to stop due to an unrepaired receiver on the Chinese boat. A Taiwanese sailor drew a pistol and fired it into the air. The shot startled the boy and came just as the sailboat shifted suddenly, throwing him into the sea.

A crewman in the sailboat tossed a tire overboard, but the boy was unable to grab it. The sailboat captain sent out an emergency call that was picked up by the Chinese and Taiwanese. Both launched motorized inflatable boats to make the rescue. The Chinese got there first. The boy was flailing in the water, trying to keep his head above the waves.

One of the Chinese crewmen dived into the ocean and swam to the boy as the other sailor nudged the rescue craft closer. The boy disappeared beneath the water. The sailor dove under, came up a few seconds later alone. He spit out water, took a breath, and dove again. The students and teachers on the sailboat became quiet. A few held each other, sobbing. The sailor surfaced again, alone. Someone on the sailboat let out a wailing cry. A second later, the sailor pulled the boy's head above the water.

When they saw the boy spitting up water and moving around, the students and teachers on the sailboat began to yell and then clap and cheer. The sailor swam back to the boat, the boy in tow. The second sailor reached over and pulled him to safety.

The students and teachers continued to call out and clap. Tears were streaming down their faces as they waved and shouted to the mainland Chinese sailors, who were navigating their craft toward the sailboat. The boy was brought onboard.

The PLA Navy sailors cried themselves as they chatted briefly with the Taiwanese in their shared minnanyu dialect. The teachers and children waved ceaselessly at the sailors as they returned to their vessel and headed back to China's shore. The Taiwanese boat escorted the sailboat back to Kinmen.

One of the students captured the drama with a cell phone. When he got home, he uploaded the video to his personal page on WangYou, and it spread quickly to other video-sharing sites in China. His parents took him to the local television station. The station manager ran the footage and transmitted it to the parent media company on Taiwan. It was shown immediately on Taiwanese television, interrupting national emergency broadcasts on the call-up of Taiwan's military and civilian defense forces.

The video—titled "Golden Door" by news organizations, after the Min-language name for the island—was picked up by international outlets and run throughout the world. A state-owned broadcaster in Guangdong showed it in China. Youku and Tudou registered 33 million hits in the first six hours it was up.

Protesters demonstrating around the world to secure John Shay's release and freedom for Chinese workers to organize added new signs to their sticks—"Peace between China and Taiwan" and "Take the 'Golden Door' to Peace."

sixty-one

Beijing

An aide clicked off the monitor after the news clip of the rescue. Zhao turned away from the screen and looked around the room, trying to gauge the reaction of others. He was concerned about the strikes and protests inside China, but more so about calls in the United States for a boycott of Chinese goods. He could put down internal unrest with the back of his hand, but China's economy was weakening amid the worldwide slowdown, and depended on US consumers for growth, employment, and the stability of the regime.

The majority of China's 1.3 billion people were peasants. The party had been bringing them on a steady march into cities and factory jobs and out of their poverty. The party counted on that for its legitimacy. The global slowdown in trade had already punched one hole in that strategy. Zhao didn't know if he could afford another.

But you couldn't let anyone in the world tell you what to do. Not if you wanted to stay in power, he thought, looking around the conference table at the other six members of the Politburo Standing Committee of the Chinese Communist Party, the highest decision-making body in the party. None showed a trace of emotion. He wondered if anyone had been touched by the child's rescue.

In the room, in addition to China's president, were the premier, the executive vice premier, the head of National People's Congress, the leader of the Chinese People's Consultative Conference, the chairman of the Ideology and Propaganda Leading Small Group, and the secretary of the Central Commission for Discipline Inspection.

Also in attendance was the previous leader of China. Unlike in the past, when China's outgoing kingpin would retain his role as chairman of the Central Military Commission and head of the Chinese military for a couple of years, he had relinquished the position in deference to party unity. Zhao asked him to attend as a courtesy—and because he knew his own victory in a behind-the-scenes fight to consolidate power was not so clear-cut.

Zhao wondered if the ex-president had been in contact with any generals. He himself had cultivated the military heavily, to win its allegiance and build his own base. He ramped up military spending, promoted generals to senior positions, and adopted a hawkish stance in diplomacy and territorial claims. He agreed to their long-term objective of force projection, not just homeland defense.

Zhao looked again at China's ex-leader, who took a tough line toward Taiwan and the United States. The previous president held his eyes for a second and then reached forward and adjusted the folder in front of him, straightening it slightly.

Zhao thought, you can be soft in one place—as long as you are hard in others.

sixty-two

An aide entered the room and handed the secretary of defense a note. The secretary read it out loud. "Chinese fighters—Russian-made Su-30MKKs—feinted at Squadron VFA-27, the Royal Maces. Four F/A-18 Hornets broke from the pack and drove them off."

Another aide came in. "Mr. President, the Chinese leader is on the line," she said.

The operation isn't over until you talk to the family, Yates said to himself, remembering the counsel of a mentor; he still found it one of the hardest things to do. He was walking down a brightly lit hallway. He had been at home, but came in when he was informed that Charles and Esther Stein had landed in Hong Kong and had come to the hospital.

He retraced the last steps of Hannah's surgery as he pushed through a set of swinging doors. After he removed the kidney, the bleeding had stopped, the colon was allowed to fall back into its normal position, and he reapproximated the position of the ends of the small bowel with a stapling device to reestablish continuity. He closed the abdominal incision with a suture to the fascia and stapled the skin. He had allowed himself a moment of relaxation after the strain, while he watched the nurse apply a dry sterile dressing to the wound.

He had decided the bullet could stay where it was. It had entered Hannah's right lower quadrant, injured the small bowel, left renal artery, and vein, and then entered the lower left chest. He repaired the two-centimeter defect it left behind in the posterior diaphragm with a simple suture closure. But the slug was buried deep within the muscles and tissues of the chest wall—he would do more damage if he chased it down. Hannah's body would wall it off with a foreign body reaction and form a capsule of scar around it.

She was lucky it was a lower-velocity civilian projectile, he thought. The small-caliber bullets he saw in Boston—he was guessing 9mm here—tend to enter the body, create some havoc, and then lose their kinetic energy and end up just beneath the skin—or in this case, buried within the muscles of the left chest wall. The damage is mostly confined to a narrow tract—the blast effect rarely exceeds two to three centimeters beyond the bullet tunnel. Still, that was plenty to tear the small bowel in half and eat up the kidney.

Yates slowed his gait when he saw two guards outside Hannah's room. One of them grabbed the ID hanging off his neck, looked at it, and made a call on a mobile. Yates wondered if Hannah was in custody and if she would be allowed to leave Hong Kong. As the guard held onto the ID card while he spoke on the phone, Yates wondered what the hell his hospital in Boston was doing, doing business with these people.

The guard released the laminated identification card and let him pass.

The Steins rose from their chairs at Hannah's bedside when Yates entered the room. Charles got up slowly. His left arm was shaking, and he was exhibiting a "pill rolling" tremor in his right hand—rhythmic, back and forth movement of the thumb and forefinger. Yates saw the movements, observed his shuffle and masked face. He made a note to have him seen by a Parkinson's specialist before he left the hospital.

The trauma surgeon cued them with a smile and short, affirmative nods.

Hannah's parents sobbed as Yates wrapped his arms around them.

"She's going to be fine," he said; he had a daughter himself. "Your little girl is going to be fine."

Yates explained her injuries and the surgery. They flinched when he told them he had to remove her left kidney, but he reassured them it was okay. He told them he left the bullet inside—explaining why, and telling them the damage had been done by the projectile moving through the tissue and that it would stay put and do no further harm.

"She will have residual metal in the body," he said—instantly chiding himself for the stiff, clinical language; it was something his wife was always reminding him about.

"She'll be getting to know the TSA," Charles Stein said.

Yates smiled. "Probably exchange holiday cards."

The doc told them Hannah would remain intubated in the ICU until she warmed to normal body temperature of 37 degrees Celsius and woke up sufficiently to breathe on her own. This would probably occur in about six hours, at which point the endotracheal tube would be removed. She would require intravenous pain medication to manage the incisional pain. He said she would favor sleep, but would be arousable and responsive. Her oral intake would start on postoperative day two and consist of sips of water. She should be able to resume a regular diet in four to five days and be discharged.

"I expect slow improvement, with good days and bad days, marked by less than optimal sleeping and eating habits," Yates said. "In six weeks, she should be back to a normal routine, with minimal to no pain and resumption of typical activities."

Charles Stein vowed he would never bad-mouth a doctor again.

Looking at Hannah, he silently spoke the Hebrew meaning of her name.

He has favored me.

President Rodgers lifted the receiver. The two leaders exchanged greetings.

Zhao spoke first. "Mr. President, I am happy to inform you that Mr. Shay is now under the protection of our government. It was with great difficulty that we were able to rescue him from renegade political elements in our southern province of Guangdong."

"That's good news," the president said. "How is he?"

"He is in good health. There had been some fighting, but his injuries were treated. We have been informed he will heal quickly."

"When can he be returned to US custody?"

"I have two requests."

"And they are?"

"We are experiencing unprecedented disturbances throughout China. Mr. Shay and his union have assisted outlaw elements posing as trade unions in our country. I would like your assurance this aid will cease."

Rodgers saw that as a loser, not only in principle. The strikes across the United States were shutting down the economy. Turning his back on Shay and Hannah would be spark for the tinder.

"The freedom to organize, bargain collectively, and strike are guaranteed American rights," the president said. "These freedoms are also guaranteed by the United Nations' International Labor Organization, through ILO Conventions 87 and 98. American trade unions have long-standing affiliations with other organizations throughout the world. I cannot tell them how to conduct those relationships."

There was a pause on the other end.

"Like yourself, I am sure, I have been deeply moved by the rescue of the child by our PLA sailors in the Taiwan Strait, and by the world's call for peace between China and Taiwan," Zhao said. "In that spirit of peace, my other request is that your carrier group reverse the course it is taking toward the Strait of Taiwan."

"Glad to have it back," Rodgers said. "Once I have your assurance that you will discontinue live-firing exercises across the strait and stand down the missile batteries you have pointed toward Taiwan"—he looked around the room—"and elsewhere. I have also been informed that Chinese land and air forces are deployed in an aggressive manner on your coastline. And we are monitoring naval movements in the direction of the Taiwan Strait from your fleets in the East, South, and North China Seas."

The president paused. "I need a restatement of your commitment to a peaceful resolution of the Taiwan issue. I need that restatement now."

"That has always been our intention," Zhao said.

Rodgers looked at Bernstein and then at his secretary of defense and national security advisor. "I will give an order to freeze deployment of the carrier strike force at its current position," he said. "You will pull back your forces from Fujian, lower alert levels at all missile installations, and turn around your fleets. I look forward to confirmation of such from our intelligence services and military commanders. If I receive this confirmation, I will lower our alert level. If I do not receive it in two hours, I will conclude this is not a military exercise and will reraise our military's readiness level. I will also recommit the carrier force. This time it will sail directly into the strait, along with a second carrier-based strike force and other additional forces as recommended by my military advisors.

"I will instruct our embassy in Beijing to contact your office to make arrangements to free John Shay. I assume embassy officials can also work out the details to allow Ms. Stein to leave Hong Kong when she is able."

"Just one more thing," China's leader said.

"Yes?"

"This episode has created a complicating element in Chinese/US relations. We are committed to a strong trade relationship with your country, and many American companies rely on China to produce the goods they sell in the United States. We have smashed the counterfeiting ring operating in Guangdong Province as part of our ongoing commitment to the defense of intellectual property. I would not want to think that the lawless activities of a single factory, and the problems that have arisen from that, would jeopardize our mutually beneficial relationship in any way."

"Mr. President, I am a servant of my country, its people and political institutions," Rodgers said. "As such, I must await the will of the people, as expressed through their opinions and the Congress, for any final determination in this matter."

Take that, you SOB, he thought.

"Very well, Mr. President," Zhao said. "I thank you for your expression of good intent. And I look forward, hopefully, to both our countries continuing their present course of strengthening our relationship. It is through these good relations that we are able to welcome American companies that come to China to improve their competitiveness and participate in our market." He paused. "This relationship is also necessary to justify our purchase of American goods and services."

He paused again. "Mr. President, may I speak frankly? We are your largest creditor. A good relationship is necessary in order for us to continue investing our foreign exchange reserves in your country, through the purchase of the Treasury notes, corporate bonds, and mortgage securities that fund your deficit account and capital markets. It is a strong foundation for our cooperation in global political matters—like the situation in North Korea, proliferation of weapons of mass destruction, and the fight against terrorism. With all your country's responsibilities and commitments in the world, any disruption in this relationship would surely result in significant economic and political setbacks for the United States."

Take that, you SOB, right back at me, Rodgers thought.

"Thank you again for your cooperation in this matter," Rodgers said.

The leaders said good-bye. Rodgers put down the phone.

"The son of a bitch blinked."

He smiled. "And spit at the same time."

sixty-three

The National Mall in Washington overflowed with more than a million people. Union members and supporters had come from across the country and overseas. People nearest the stage began to clap and cheer as Shay moved toward the microphone. Applause rippled back through the crowd. The noise was deafening by the time he took the mike.

"Brothers and sisters," he began, using the traditional union greeting he had always avoided, thinking it overblown, "I want to begin by thanking you personally—on behalf of myself, my wife, and my son—for your efforts to secure my freedom."

He took a breath, catching his emotions. "I can't tell you how much it has meant to me, and to my family, to know you left the security of your jobs to strike for my life."

The crowd responded with a roar. A Secret Service agent on stage pressed a finger against his earpiece and said something into a lapel mike. Metro DC cops and officers from the Special Operations Force of the US Park Police's National Capital Region were also on the podium. The stage was erected at Third Street, facing west, in front of the Capitol Reflecting Pool and the steps of the Capitol. The three protective services had positioned their forces among the crowd on the lawn and up and down Madison and Jefferson Drives, alternating visible presence with plainclothes mingling.

"I also want to offer my thanks to our friends in Mexico and Latin America," Shay said. "In Europe, Hong Kong, across Asia. In Africa,

Australia, the Philippines. And to the Chinese, who have suffered such grave losses in their effort to establish a democratic trade-union movement in their country."

Shay thought of Lin Xueqin as he held up his hands to quell the chanting crowd.

"This is a historic day," he said. "We have seen something not witnessed for many decades, if ever—people around the globe striking and demonstrating, in unison, on behalf of a common cause." He paused. "Jack Cafferty would have been a proud man today. *Is* a proud man. Today, with us still."

He drew another breath as the mass of people clapped.

"None of us on the podium here—," Shay said, turning and extending his arm to the three rows of speakers seated behind him. Front and center was Bill Lewis. The presidents of all the major industrial unions were there. Also on the stand were Klaus Henders; representatives from the global union confederations; and banned trade-union organizers from the emerging world.

"None of us can know where this will lead," Shay said, turning back to the throng. "But it won't be back to the same way of doing business. Even though none of us fully understand what a new way of doing business will look like."

He scanned the scene. American flags flapped in the cool fall wind—held up amid the signs and placards, fixed on flagpoles that lined the lawn, ringing the war memorials. The people stretched in front of him to the Washington Monument and beyond. They spilled over the sides of the Mall and across Madison and Jefferson, filled the spaces between the national museums, to the edges of Independence and Constitution Avenues.

"But I do know this," Shay said. "We started something that can change the way companies and employees do business with one another. We have to hold the ground we fought so hard to gain."

He jabbed his finger into the air. "You are not going to fix this economy by waging war on the hardworking people of America. There will be no more, they get bailed out, we get bowled over."

The crowd erupted in a roar; Shay held up his hands.

"We can't push too far, because it takes both sides, labor and management, to make a company, an economy, a country prosper. They can't suck us dry—but we can't lock them down tight. They have to roll up their sleeves and pitch in—we have to button down our collars and face facts. We have to work *together*, in a new balance of power, a new equilibrium of responsibility, to take us where we want to go.

"We have to remember—we are in this together. It's us … as Americans. In the world, sure—but against that world too. Competing with it."

He paused. "What we mostly have is each other. We have to make this work."

He stopped, to thunderous applause. He was awed by the show of power in front of him, by the force labor had wielded during the global strike. It didn't change his belief that individuals bore responsibility for their fate, but everyone needed a hand. It renewed his commitment to unions, to his work at the Machinists. Trade-union members had saved his life. He owed them a debt of gratitude he was glad to repay.

He realized, at that moment, that he was never completely at home in, or away from, the working class. That made him a bridge between it and the rest of America. He had become the face of labor, of those who toiled behind the scenes without a face. He was going to get them a better deal. Or one hell of a sendoff trying.

He raised his hands several times, until the cheering ebbed.

"Big words, I know," Shay said. "Maybe too big, and we can't live up to them. But we must try. We must, both sides, try to find a way, in the chaos of this process, to move forward. To order relations between labor and management in such a way that, as the global economy grows … it brings us with it."

The multitude before him were cheering, clapping, striking their fists into the air.

"Because as we have said at the bargaining table—you *will* bring us with you."

Shay stood there for several minutes, unable to silence the crowd. At one point, he was swept with doubt. He wondered if he was filling them with empty words, unrealizable dreams. Life would do what it was going to do, no matter what. For all our efforts, we were always just trying to catch up. Like the kids at his soccer practices doing dopey drills—chasing the ball where it was, with no idea where it was headed.

They finally quieted, to hear what he had to say next.

"Now I want to introduce someone whose effort, and sacrifice, are probably the single most important reason why I am standing before you today," he said.

He turned as Charles Stein shuffled forward, wheeling his daughter slowly to the front of the stage.

Hannah smiled at Shay. He bent down and kissed her on the cheek.

He gave her the mike as the crowd exploded in a roar.

sixty-four

The downstairs bell rang. Hannah wheeled herself to the door—having a bad day, using the wheelchair. She reached up and pressed the intercom button. "Yes?"

"Me."

She buzzed open the door to her building and returned to her desk. She looked over the list of people and organizations, wondered if she was missing someone who could help. Mei Wang was still in custody. China's leader was making amends to his people after the unrest, but her crime was too much to let go. She had been swept up, along with dozens in her group, for fomenting the strikes and demonstrations. Only an international uproar had prevented her from being transferred from jail in Hong Kong to China, where she would have been swallowed up into God knows where.

That, and the fact that she was pregnant with Lin Xueqin's child.

Hannah glanced at the clock—it was 9:30 p.m., 10:30 a.m. tomorrow morning in Asia. She'd start calling at ten, spend a couple of hours on it.

Then she had to prep for the poetry slam. It was coming up in two weeks. She felt like she would be able to do it physically. But she was having trouble with the script. The words were flowing, but they didn't have much to do with politics or financial crisis. After her brush with mortality, most of what she was writing was personal.

After years of pushing it aside, focusing on things outside myself, she thought. She was always thinking about what drove society, not the forces inside her. She thought that stuff was indulgent; she frowned at others who talked nonstop about themselves, their relationships. She disowned personal discovery after listening to everyone drone on about it.

Lying in the hospital in Hong Kong, she realized she had flipped things too, reversed their importance; put things on top that should have been below, and vice versa. She wondered now if it was all filler—politics, the union—to take up space inside. Displace what was there, to not deal with it.

She thought about how she would pour over the *New York Times*, the *Wall Street Journal*, the *Economist*, and lap up the minutest details about everything.

Still important, she thought; I won't stop learning about the world, or ignore its tears. But right now she wanted to learn about the new man in her life, about herself, about the way the two of them were together.

She had also rediscovered her love of science. She first got interested as a teen, studying her father's condition. She resubscribed to the journals: *Science*, *Nature*, *Cell*.

She had just read a paper on RNA. A researcher claimed to discover how nucleotides, the building blocks of RNA, originally assembled themselves. When he worked through the possible combinations, he realized an intermediate had gone back and recombined with the original, producing the RNA.

You don't take Route 1—a direct line from A to B—to your destination, she thought. You can't ever really figure out how to combine things to get what you want. Instead, you end up in some intermediate state—which, over time, finds its way back to couple with the original, to bring you where you were headed all along.

She wondered how that worked. Either things had a logic that wasn't clear—or it was wild, indefatigable energy, trying everything until it comes up with something. She thought of all the mishaps, the unlikely steps, the intermediate stages … they get you to a place that can't be reached by methodical assembly, one deliberate step after another. They get you there by returning—with a wrinkle—to your beginnings.

It was suddenly there, in front of her. She realized she had been getting back at the powerlessness she felt around her father by dominating older men. That was her twisted helix—a mix of resentment and pleasure in letting him control her; later, lashing out to reclaim the power, with that same concoction of resentment and pleasure.

She remembered the three-card monte game on the street. Sleight of hand here too, she thought—go back to the thing that hurt, change it into something with sexual pleasure; relive it, but with a kicker. Straight-up Freud. Like a Midleton shot—it wallops you, but with an inviting finish.

She took a sip of Coke, thinking, first you're the puppet, jerked by strings. Then you become the puppet master, yanking on another. But it's still the same show.

Simple when you see it, she thought. As if you stepped out of the play, and into the audience.

The doorbell rang. Hannah wheeled herself to the door and unlocked it.

Steve Lerner came in and plopped the takeout bag on her lap. He closed the door and locked it, grabbing the wheelchair handles.

"Prawns with broccoli in garlic sauce," he said. "The indigenous food of the Upper West Side." He pushed her to the table, singing the Chinese menu line from "Werewolves of London."

Lerner was a research scientist who lived in her building. He was from Minneapolis and worked in the department of biomedical engineering at Columbia—cell signaling, microfluidics, cell/matrix interactions for tissue repair and grafting. He was tall, lean, and bony, dark hair moussed up in a couple of directions. He sang in a band called Endocrine Disruptors.

He called her every day when she was in the hospital in Hong Kong, and every day after her return. She had invited him over a week ago. He'd been coming every night since. He was thirty. And he wasn't slaphappy. She tested him.

He turned the wheelchair—a little too quickly—so she could face the desk.

Hannah felt a twinge in her abdomen. She was still healing from the wound.

She turned to him. "You realize this is the last time—*ever*—I'm going to let you push me around."

She hoped to God it would be true. The PD tests were scheduled for next week, a boatload—neurologic exam, blood work, X-rays, CAT and MRI imaging. Even then the diagnosis might not be definitive, the neurologist had told her. Multiple neurologic movement disorders had similar symptoms. More than likely, the tests would show a diagnosis other than Parkinson's, or be inconclusive.

Lerner stroked her hair. She smiled at him.

Inconclusive worked, she thought.

After her brush with death, anything but was gold.

Two weeks later, Hannah stood with the other performers in the back of the room. Her legs felt wobbly; it was her third day out of the wheelchair. She felt the usual jitters—the urge to run away, have a drink. She topped it off with worry that the tremors might appear on stage. She went over her notes and nodded indifferently to a guy hitting on her—although his line was stupid enough to be funny: "Didn't I see you in Hong Kong?"

The first poet finished his slam. Hannah shook her head—his riff was off the wall. She remembered why she could only pop in and out of the arts, never make her life there. Then she thought, I should talk. The person you make fun of is probably the person you are.

She was introduced and got a big hand as she walked along the wall to the mike in front. She turned to face the audience. She was wearing a Team Fox tee, from the Michael J. Fox Foundation for Parkinson's research. She didn't know if she had PD, but her dad and others did, and it was time to get involved. She leaned into the mike.

"Shoot 'em up in Hong Kong, bang bang, I fall down, it hurt bad"—she held her stomach—"but I get better, slowly. Gut feeling ... it means something new to me now. But a man called while I in hospital, he called every day, and I come home and he call every night, and now he come to me every night, and I think I love him. Gut feel."

She looked at Steve Lerner. He was sitting in the second row at a table with Shay and Anne. She hadn't told him. She smiled when she saw him smile.

"Before I didn't know love, I didn't plug in that socket, stayed away from it, with unavailable men—who it turns out are very available, you know what I mean?"

A few women laughed.

"But they were good men, don't mistake me. I did not choose just anybody, I picked real people, we had real times, shared real thoughts. But you know, when things get bad, they get good, but then when they get good, they get bad again, because maybe I'm sick now. This guy, he published a paper in 1817, 'Essay on the Shaking Palsy.' His name was James Parkinson, and maybe I have this. Testing will tell, no, time will tell, whether the neurons degenerate and the brain can't generate body movements and you shake and get stiff and walk and talk funny, but we all shake and get stiff and walk and talk funny."

A few people laughed or clapped.

"But I will face this, because I'm done running away"—she turned, took two quick steps away from the mike, returned; the audience laughed—"just as our country will face itself and not run away. It will find its new way, and I will find a way to stay with that, stay with the union, because union is what we need, union to rope in business, union with another, union with ourselves, with all parts of ourselves."

She took a breath. "Because you battle life, and you battle yourself, and in the tent, on the plains at night, after a long day of skirmishing, there is only union with another, and with yourself. You make your own union hall, marble and mud, hiccup your dreams through a relentless world until, in time, a stockinged face with a gun stands ready to rob the vault, the safe, the only safe we have, the one we build when the basement and the attic swap places … when below becomes above, and above becomes below … when both become us, when we become our selves.

"But I digress. Like a river I rush around things and dislodge others, and I pray for my parents, and I pray for myself, and I pray for you, I pray for this world, and I prance for all time, and oh, here comes a tremor"—her fingers really did tremble—"shake with me, we all can shake together"—she exaggerated the shaking; some in the audience joined in—"shaken and stirred, take your elixir neat or take it mixed, but take it down you will, one gulp after another, until drunk with days you roll on the rails to your self, and even if you hurtle headlong, maglev, bullet train, TGV"—said it like the French, tay-jay-vay—"you still find yourself like a turtle, years, and tears, after the fact, but what does this have to do with financial crisis, tonight's theme? Everything. Because when you're thinking things like this, you're not fucking somebody over."

She walked into the crowd toward Steve's table as they began to cheer.

She stopped after a few steps.

"Free Mei Wang! Free Mei Wang! Free Mei Wang!" she shouted, her fist in the air. The audience joined in; some stood, and then everyone did, and chanted with her.

The judges voted her through to the second round.

sixty-five

"Cool?" Shay asked.

"Way cool," Michael said. He moved his finger along the glass cover, tracing the shapes of the Chinese characters underneath. Gao Liang had taken the watch off his wrist and given it to Shay when Shay joked he didn't get the present his son asked for.

Anne came into Michael's room and sat down on the bed. She looked at the watch and then at Shay. "Isn't that what this was all about? To keep this stuff out of America?"

"Oh yeah," Shay said.

"I can keep it, right?" Michael asked, looking back and forth between them.

"Sure," Shay said. He got up. "Night night, big guy, I love you."

"Night night, Daddy, I love you too."

Anne stayed upstairs to help Michael pick out a book. Shay went downstairs and grabbed a beer. He opened it with his lucky Green Bay Packer can opener and took a slug en route to the living room.

He sat down and put the bottle on the end table, thought about Nora Young. He enjoyed the memory, but in a compartment labeled *Dangerous Goods*. He laughed, remembering what her brother said about being Russian. He had figured out her tattoo. It was the flag of the Oglala Sioux—eight white teepees in a *hocoka*, or camp circle.

He reached for the remote and winced, his ribs still sore from the beating he took from the gang member in Hong Kong. There was no second beating when he was detained in China. After the initial threats from the interrogator and a few more questions, he just sat in the Chinese jail hungry and cold for two days until his release.

Shay clicked to a ball game. It was barely watchable, a massive brand assault. The grating digital rip of the network logo coming at you like a launched droid. Promos popping up incessantly; the TV looked like a twitchy Web page. Every facet of the game for sale: the weather conditions, the starting lineup, the defensive nine, the scouting report … brought to you by …

Why not sell every pitch? He rang up a few branded balls and strikes as he settled into the game. Out of the blue, he remembered Joe Woods. His grandfather had told him the story years ago. He was a kid from his grandfather's old neighborhood, near the Queensboro Bridge in Long Island City, where he lived during the Depression.

Woods had scarlet fever. His grandfather said he was a great pitcher but tired easily. After the game he would sit for hours resting on the bench, before he was helped home by the kids. When he couldn't pitch anymore, he moved to left field.

Shay's grandfather had been recruited to the elite team to play first base. The second baseman told him that, on a one-hop single to left, Woods had such a great arm that he would try to throw out the batter at first. His grandfather looked at him like, right. But then someone singled hard to left. He saw the batter running like crazy to first and then turned to see the throw whistling toward him from left field like it was shot from a rocket as he felt frantically with his foot for the bag.

His grandfather attended the funeral. Joe Woods died at the age of sixteen.

Johnny Damon came up. He swung at the first pitch, shattered his bat hitting a weak grounder to second. After he was called out, he rounded the bag and jogged back down the first-base line. He picked up the broken shard and looked around with a grin.

No one in baseball had a personality like him, Shay thought. He always looked so happy to be there. The way I feel now. *God bless*—remembering what the bum said after he gave him money outside the parking garage.

He thought about Joe Woods. Not as fortunate.

Shay watched the game as the events circulated through his mind. The Machinists had settled with Lambal. They gave him a pass for stepping up to the plate with the ransom money. They also acknowledged that the automotive market in China was too big to ignore, and that if Lambal didn't invest in China, it would lose the business to competitors from Europe, Japan, and other Asian countries.

But they added conditions, to get more work for their members in the United States. Lambal had to send union teams to China, at premium above scale, to train production crews there. Union members in the United States would build the advanced tooling for the Chinese plants. That not only meant more work for the Machinists—it helped Lambal safeguard his intellectual property. Another contract clause made sure Lambal kept the focus on expansion, not dirt-low wages. It prohibited him from exporting China-produced components or finished goods back to the United States, or to any markets outside Asia, without consulting with the union. Shay thinking, it was an agreement neither side liked, so it might work. The only way to satisfy everyone was to please no one.

Lambal's bodyguard confessed that he was hired by Bodewig to make the arrangements to kill Cafferty; he cleared Lambal of any role in the counterfeiting operation, Cafferty's death, or the attempt on Shay's life. Meinrich, the race driver, was picked up in Monaco by Interpol and confessed to running Cafferty off the road. He fingered the man who contracted for the hit; the description matched one Hans Tanner, a.k.a. Karl Bodewig. Interpol issued an alert for Tanner, along with Ma Yongrui.

Meeting Nora Young in Hong Kong hadn't been an accident. The ICE agents in El Paso had notified Homeland Security after Calderon's conversation with Shay. DHS put that information together with Nora's tip about the hookup in Hong Kong between the Guangzhou military officer and the Middle Eastern guy. The deputy secretary himself asked her to bump into Shay, keep tabs on what he found out.

DHS was still checking the lead about the connection between the counterfeiters and al-Qaeda.

Beijing arrested the Guangzhou military officer who ran the trading company, along with three officers from the Shanghai garrison. They were charged with conspiring to supply Islamist radicals with counterfeit goods from Chinese factories for distribution around the world. The Chinese put a bullet in the back of each one's head. They would have done the same to the al-Qaeda op, but he was long gone. Gao Liang, the provincial official, had also been arrested, along with Hu Weimin and his soldiers from the beach.

President Zhao was visiting cities, towns, and farms where the strikes and protests had occurred, trying to paper over the grievances. He increased benefits for workers displaced by failing state-owned enterprises. He strengthened government oversight of minimum wages, the length of the workday, and health and safety conditions. He retargeted economic investment—shipping terminals, railways, highways—to the affected regions, to close income gaps.

But the worker uprisings still had China on edge. Shay and the Machinists were pushing for a congressional resolution, backed by money, to aid the free-trade-union movement there. The Machinists and other unions were training people in the underground trade-union movement, both inside the country and abroad.

Interest in unions had also surged in the United States. People saw them—again, after so many years—as a defense against raw market law. A poll said fifty million workers in America would join a union if they had a chance. A lot of those people were coming forward now. The unions were hiring and training organizers as fast as they could, to keep up with calls from unorganized workers across the country for reps to visit their facilities and begin the registration and voting process. The requests were coming from manual, service, and professional occupations—everyone from low-wage manufacturing and service workers and immigrant laborers to librarians, engineers, dental hygienists, systems analysts, pharmacists, even judges and lawyers.

A number of US unions, led by Lewis and the Machinists, ratcheted up merger talks, to strengthen their bargaining positions with employers and to end their battles with one another to sign up new members or poach existing ones. They began talks to organize across entire industries and borders, versus just individual companies. They demanded permanent seats on company boards. They contracted with independent inspection companies to review products across America—stressing how unions could play a role in monitoring and guaranteeing healthy and safe goods. They launched training and apprenticeship programs to draw in more workers and give companies more reasons to partner with them, to get access to those skills. They vowed cooperation on drives—like truckers refusing to deliver to buildings where janitors were organizing.

Shay took a sip of beer. He wondered if the unions could rise to the task, take advantage of the opportunity. If they could remodel themselves for the new world—from flat-out them-versus-us antagonists, to shrewd, albeit contentious, partners, focused on mutual success. That depended on the companies too—if they could moderate their drive for efficiency, stop trying to squeeze blood from a stone.

But the reality was, all the king's horses and all the king's men couldn't put things back together again while there were still low-wage choices to drive down the standards of competition. As long as the emerging world remained underdeveloped, capital would seek it out. Raise those wages—by organizing labor—and there would be no place else to go. Goods would cost more. But if the tradeoff was better pay and working conditions and safer products, how hard would that be to swallow?

The US, European, and other regional unions were pushing for international agreements, negotiated at a global level, to establish global rules of conduct and wage standards. It was the first collaborative action the worldwide union movement had managed to get off the ground. The first time they had acted with the same coordination as the multinational corporations, taken a global stance against global capital.

Shay wondered if it would all backfire. It took outsize drive to start, build, and grow a company—business might not take the risk without the chance for outsize reward. Absent that big payday, there might be less investment. It was a wild, untamed wash of money that bankrolled globalization, powered the climb from poverty in the emerging world. How do you wring out a balance between excess and just enough?

He remembered a show he watched with Michael on the Discovery channel, about the Vikings plundering Europe. Slipping into the harbors, stealing silently inland up the rivers in their long war boats, they looted the place and left a wake of devastation.

But their forays opened up trade and travel routes, connected communities, peoples, and markets, laid the groundwork for development.

Outsourcing, with its predatory motives, yet accompanied by the transfer of technology and know-how, had turned out to be a similar, unwitting agent for the integration of poorer countries into the global economy.

He wasn't getting misty-eyed about the prospects. Globalization held the promise of interdependence, and a shared, vested interest in peace. But with more competition for resources, markets, and jobs, somebody was going to rub someone the wrong way, threatening an already strained world order. One day your sailors are learning about silk making and playing basketball with Chinese seamen on a Shanghai court—the next day, they're steaming locked-and-loaded toward the Taiwan Strait. He had met Vice Admiral Laughton in Washington, heard the story.

The whole thing seemed like a blessing and a mess, at the same time. Globalization was like the universe, he thought, recalling a Hannah science tidbit—expanding but flying out of control, with a dark energy that was pushing galaxies apart.

That would take billions, trillions of years to play out.

Globalization was coming to a head much sooner.

Anne came downstairs after checking on Michael. She sat on the sofa and patted the cushion next to her. Shay got up from his chair and sat down beside her. He thought about telling her about what happened—and didn't happen—with Nora Young. He realized he had jeopardized his own source, her and Michael—from which, for him, all things flow and rise—when he had been tempted to outsource, to go somewhere else, where things were cheaper. No disrespect to Nora—in this personalized definition, cheaper meant quicker satisfaction, less responsibility, not needing to deal with the tough stretches in a marriage.

He put his arm around Anne, remembering the day they got married. In the weeks beforehand, it crossed his mind he might freeze up and have to face a choice of going through with it or not. But that morning he woke up calm; everything felt right. He remembered feeling so relieved. As the years went by, even with the ups and downs, there were only a few times he thought of leaving, and the thought disappeared overnight.

All those years he had felt—or came back to feeling, whenever he doubted it—that it was right between them, fated. But now he embraced it—chose this life, which always seemed before as if it had been chosen for him.

He looked out into the family room, at the toys, books, playing cards, socks, chess pieces scattered on the floor. Like globalization, he thought. This blessed mess.

Anne nestled into his shoulder.

"Feel like another night out in the city?" he asked.

"Sure. Got something in mind?"

"This bar, in SoHo. I think you might like it."

He knew she would. She had great style, he thought, conjuring an image of the place where he had met the German trade unionist. He imagined her getting ready, running her mirror gauntlet—first the one in the bedroom, getting dressed; then the downstairs hallway mirror, a second check; finally making her way to the last station, a mirror in the mudroom, where she kept a roll of shipping tape to pat off lint.

He was in that mood where you love the little things; they mean everything to you. This life felt right just the way it was, with all its imperfection—the love and warmth, mixed with the hassle and commotion, the worry and exhaustion—in some crazy, beguiling blend of restless dissatisfaction and calming embrace.

He wanted to take her back to Ottawa, walk her out onto the Alexandra Bridge, and ask her to marry him all over again.

"There's a hotel upstairs," he said. "We could stay the night."

"That sounds like fun," Anne said. She paused. "It's been a while."

Shay looked at her. Her mouth was her most beautiful feature. Her lips were full, yet fine, clearly drawn. The top lines of the upper folds rose from a sharply defined center V and took loft, arcing like sketched wingspan, the grace of a bird in flight. He was seeing her fresh, in light washed by rain. He wanted to tell her he always loved her, and had only begun.

"Michael's sleeping?" he asked.

"Like a baby."

He squeezed her tight. "Like our baby."

"Mmm," she said, curling her arm around the small of his back and laying her cheek on his heart.

acknowledgments

I need to thank a number of people for their assistance in the writing of this book.

In military matters, I tapped the experience of Piers L. Wood, LTC (Retired) USA, and relied on the diligence of Joseph Trevithick, a research associate at globalsecurity.org and historical consultant for Ambush Alley Games.

For medical expertise, I drew upon Eric Goralnick for his ER savvy; Eric is the assistant clinical director in the department of emergency medicine at Brigham and Women's Hospital and an instructor of medicine at Harvard Medical School. For his trauma and OR knowledge, I thank Jonathan Gates, a vascular surgeon and trauma surgeon director for the BWH Trauma Center. When our conversations began, Jonathan was an information source; he became a true collaborator.

Special thanks to my college roomate, Stu Mushlin—master clinician in internal medicine at BWH and assistant profesor of medicine at HMS—for the referrals.

Thanks to the iUniverse editors, proofers, and London team for their assistance.